LADY OF PASSION

A Selection of Recent Titles by Freda Lightfoot

The French Historical Series

HOSTAGE QUEEN *
RELUCTANT QUEEN *
THE QUEEN AND THE COURTESAN *

The Lakeland Sagas

THE GIRL FROM POOR HOUSE LANE
THE WOMAN FROM HEARTBREAK HOUSE

The Manchester Sagas

DANCING ON DEANSGATE
WATCH FOR THE TALLEYMAN

The Champion Street Market Sagas

WHO'S SORRY NOW?
LONELY TEARDROPS

Novels

TRAPPED
HOUSE OF ANGELS

Historical

THE DUCHESS OF DRURY LANE *
A LADY OF PASSION *

* *available from Severn House*

LADY OF PASSION

The story of Mary Robinson

Freda Lightfoot

This first world edition published 2013
in Great Britain and the USA by
SEVERN HOUSE PUBLISHERS LTD of
19 Cedar Road, Sutton, Surrey, England, SM2 5DA.
Trade paperback edition first published
in Great Britain and the USA 2013 by
SEVERN HOUSE PUBLISHERS LTD

British Library Cataloguing in Publication Data

Lightfoot, Freda, 1942-
  Lady of passion.
  1. Robinson, Mary, 1758-1800–Fiction. 2. Great Britain–
  History–George III, 1760-1820–Fiction. 3. Biographical
  fiction.
  I. Title
  823.9'14-dc23

ISBN-13: 978-0-7278-8287-5 (cased)
ISBN-13: 978-1-84751-487-5 (trade paper)

All Severn House titles are printed on acid-free paper.

Severn House Publishers support The Forest Stewardship Council [FSC],
the leading international forest certification organisation. All our titles that
are printed on Greenpeace-approved FSC-certified paper carry the FSC logo.

Typeset by Palimpsest Book Production Ltd.,
Falkirk, Stirlingshire, Scotland.
Printed and bound in Great Britain by
TJ International Ltd, Padstow, Cornwall

Prologue

Woman of Letters

My portrait you desire! and why?
To keep a shade on mem'ry's eye,
What bliss can reason prove,
To gaze upon a senseless frame!
On looks eternally the same,
And lips that never move.
But what are features? What is form?
To combat life's tempestuous storm.

Mary Darby Robinson
'Stanzas for a Friend' who desired
to have my portrait

1800

'So you were once the beautiful Mrs Robinson?'

I stare up at the man, this ruffian who has burst unannounced into my bedroom, shocked by his sudden invasion upon my privacy. Maria, my beloved daughter, is flapping about him like a startled pigeon, while my first thought is to protest that I still am beautiful. But I say nothing, as I know this to be untrue.

My health has improved recently, and on the rare occasions I've visited London I have ventured out in my carriage to take the air. But I cannot claim that driving about Hyde Park excites the interest it once did. I am no longer a leader of fashion, the doyenne of Drury Lane, or the adored mistress of a royal prince, powdered, patched and painted to the utmost power of rouge and white lead. Fashion is a sylph of fantastic appearance, the illegitimate offspring of caprice – decked with flowers, feathers, tinsel, jewels, beads, and all the garish profusion of degenerated fancy.

No artist now begs to paint my portrait. My auburn hair is turning to a dull grey, the blue of my eyes look quite washed out, and the delicacy of my features are now somewhat drawn. No lady of fashion would trouble to copy my style of hat or gown, no gentleman pause for a glimpse of my ankle, knowing I will not be stepping down from my carriage, nor parading along the walkways. In truth my beauty has indeed faded, assuming one subscribes to the theory that it is but skin deep.

My looks and health may not be what they were, but my spirit remains strong and resilient. I have spent the last several months working long hours, as always, writing essays for the *Morning Post*, commenting on society as I so like to do. I still write and edit poems for them, but as my debts continue to mount I must push myself ever harder.

My dear friend Coleridge came to London last November, also to take up a position on the *Post* and supply them with political comment. He enjoyed a Christmas Eve supper with Maria and me, which was most delightful. Godwin too was also present, as were many of our friends. I enjoy life as best I can despite the difficulties I must contend with. Coleridge has even inveigled upon his friend Southey to include a poem of mine, 'The Haunted Beach', in the latest *Annual Anthology* that he edits. It is not the first request of this kind, but Coleridge admires the 'fascinating metre', as he describes it, vowing it inspired his famous poem 'The Rhyme of the Ancient Mariner' which he included in his *Lyrical Ballads* published a year or two ago. I am deeply flattered. The theme is about how haunted I am by isolation, as much as the landscape the poem describes, and entirely suits my melancholic mood.

Yet however famous my poems and novels, only my erstwhile lover and my publisher seem to have profited from them.

Today I have been confined to my bed, as is so often the case, and am only too aware of my own fragility, that violent convulsions could result from the slightest disturbance to my peace and tranquillity. Yet I am determined to remain calm, even as I face what I have long dreaded. The shabby little bailiff thrusts a subpoena into my hand and his callous words rattle my startled brain.

'You are under arrest, Mrs Robinson, for debt.' Turning to my daughter, who is quite beside herself with anxiety, he orders Maria to assist me to dress. 'I am instructed to take your mother to the sheriff's office where she will temporarily reside while she settles with her creditors. If she fails to do so within the next few days, then she'll be transferred to the Fleet.'

I feel the blood drain from my face at this horrifying prospect. Being only too familiar with that establishment, I have no wish to enter its portals ever again. Maria and I look at each other in terror. My head is spinning, my heart pounding in my breast. Could this really be happening to me again? Have I not suffered enough?

'How foolish of me to imagine that I might find sanctuary here at Englefield Cottage,' I say, unable to keep the bitterness from my tone. In recent years I have become something of a recluse, not even able to afford to visit family in my old home city of Bristol, which I would so love to do.

Maria rushes to my side. 'You mustn't let them take you, Mama. We will fight this.'

Gathering my courage, I smile and pat her cheek, noting its paleness. 'Fetch my warmest gown and wrap, dearest, and perhaps two petticoats. Prison cells are cold places.'

I surrender myself to the inevitable and allow my daughter to dress me, then my manservant to assist me to the bailiff's carriage where I am conveyed to dubious quarters in the sheriff's office. The room does not even have the benefit of a window for me to look out at the sun. To be fair, that good gentleman is kindness itself, perhaps out of pity, for which I am truly grateful even as I smilingly grit my teeth in frustration.

In the miserable days that follow I write to the Prince, hoping for a response, and to my dear friend, William Godwin, with resolute good humour. 'I assure you that my feelings are not wounded, neither is my spirit dejected . . . I have had various proposals from many friends to settle the business – but I am too proud to borrow while the arrears now due on my annuity from the Prince of Wales would doubly pay the sum for which I am arrested.'

For this reason I do not rush to write to my old friend, Sheridan, feeling that I have troubled him enough in recent years. Besides, like my lover, he is even deeper in debt than myself. And Godwin knows well enough that I would never call upon

my husband to relieve my difficulties, despite being legally entitled
to do so. How could I, a woman of pride and follower of my
dear friend and William's own much lamented wife, the late Mary
Wollstonecraft, so demean myself? Do I not still greatly revere
her feminist doctrine? Perhaps I have always felt this need for
equality, this inner pride in myself, even when I was a foolish,
spoiled young miss taking her first faulty steps into the world.

The Prince's predictable response is that 'there is no money at
Carlton House!' He is very sorry for my situation, but his own
is equally distressing.

'You will smile at such paltry excuses, as I do,' I write to
Godwin, 'but I am determined to persist in my demand. Half a
year's annuity being nearly due, which is two hundred and fifty
pounds. And I am in custody for sixty three pounds only!'

My dear friends do come to my aid, perhaps prompted by
Godwin, and within a few days of humiliating captivity, the paltry
sum is paid. I am a free woman again, much to my beloved
daughter's relief.

Oh, but how did I come to this pretty pass? How can it be
that a woman who possessed both beauty and talent in her youth,
who was courted by the highest echelons of society, finds herself
so poorly placed, so desperately vulnerable?

Could it be because men always betray me? If so, then why?
Is it the consequence of my own foolishness or simply the curse
of being beautiful? As a young girl I knew little of the world's
deceptions, as if though I had been educated in the deserts of
Siberia. But then even my own father let me down. What sort
of a start in life is that for a much-adored daughter?

One

A Most Sensitive Child

Who has not waked to list the busy sounds
Of summer's morning, in the sultry smoke
Of noisy London? . . .
The din of hackney-coaches, waggons, carts;
While tinmen's shops, and noisy trunk-makers,
Knife-grinders, coopers, squeaking cork-cutters,
Fruit barrows, and the hunger-giving cries
Of vegetable vendors, fill the air.

Mary Darby Robinson
'London's Summer Morning'

1767

I shall ever remember the day we arrived in London, the wonder
of it, the grandeur of the people in their fine carriages, the
excitement that burned in my breast at just ten years of age. But
having sold our home and all our possessions I knew that my
mother felt bewildered and cast adrift, overawed by the noise,
the sights and smells of this great city. Summoned to Papa's
lodgings in fashionable Spring Gardens, and ordered to bring my
brother George and me with her, she had donned her best gown,
pinched some colour into her cheeks, and set out with hope in
her heart that the loneliness of the last few years might be over
at last.

My father's cold reception destroyed all of that.

'Is this the best you can manage?' he demanded. 'This measly
sum cannot be all the money you've raised!'

'I did the very best I could, Nicholas.'

'It is nowhere near enough,' he snapped.

My father was a man of some spirit and did not suffer fools

gladly, but, much as I adored him, I was alarmed and deeply troubled to see him treat Mama so callously, when they had once been the most devoted of couples.

'What more could I have done?' Her plea was heart-rending. 'I sold our precious home, all the furniture, every item we possess save for the modest box of clothes we've brought with us, exactly as you instructed. Shamed and humiliated before our friends and neighbours, I have lost everything.'

She had indeed, including her youngest son, my beloved brother, William, who died of smallpox last year, aged only six. He was the second child Mama had lost to that disease, my sister having perished at just eighteen months some years ago. In view of this grief, the trauma of being abandoned by her husband, and then to be made homeless, had been almost too much to bear.

My mother was no great beauty, but she was slender and vivacious, and as Hester Vanacott, born of a well-to-do family, had in her youth attracted many suitors. Her parents had not approved of her attraction to a young man in trade. Seeing how badly her husband's betrayal had hurt her, I wondered if she had since regretted having chosen Nicholas Darby.

As a prosperous Bristol merchant, Papa had initially provided well for his family: a large house, elegantly furnished in the most expensive and sumptuous style. Wine and fine food had graced our table where he liked to entertain his many guests. My brothers and I enjoyed the best schooling, and every indulgence. Even the bed I slept in bore covers of the richest crimson damask, my dresses of the finest cambric. And during the summer months we would move to Clifton Hill to benefit from the purer air.

Perhaps it was because he was an American that my father possessed such a bold and reckless nature. But to our great misfortune his streak of restlessness and craving for adventure could not be quenched. How I ached for him to find happiness and contentment at home with his family, but innocent and gauche as I then was, I knew it was not to be.

My privileged childhood had ended the day Papa set sail for his native land and embarked upon a wild and perilous adventure to establish a whale fishery on the coast of Labrador, and attempt to civilise the Esquimaux Indians. Mama had been devastated by his departure, refusing to risk her life upon a stormy ocean, or abandon her children. My father thought her cowardly and obstinate but, loving her as I did and not wishing to lose her, I had been secretly relieved. Life without either parent would have been bleak indeed. I believed she showed great bravery by staying at home and attempting to provide a stable life for us under the most difficult circumstances. Money and letters did not always arrive on time, or at all for months on end, as Mama stubbornly reminded him in the argument which was growing louder by the minute.

'In the three years since you left us, Nicholas, I have done my best to hold the family together, even in the face of learning of your infidelity with . . . with that woman.'

'Her name is Elinor,' he coldly responded.

I glanced anxiously up at Mama, hoping she wouldn't disgrace herself by weeping. Being quite old enough to appreciate the pain she felt in her husband's betrayal, I rested a comforting hand upon her arm so that she was aware of my support. My disappointment in my father was keen. Had I not adored and worshipped him my entire life? But Papa had found himself a woman willing to live with him in the frozen wastes of America. Rumour had it that this Elinor was one of the Indians he had gone out to help, that there might even be a child, but Mama valiantly stiffened her spine and made no mention of these suspicions. As always, she focused entirely upon us, her adored children, and kindly patted my hand, acknowledging our closeness.

'Mary has continued to attend the school run by the Misses More, and is already proficient in French as well as reading, writing, arithmetic, and needlework of course, essential for any young lady. George too is doing well, and John settled into his apprenticeship. I dislike this interruption to the children's lives and education.'

'Miss Hannah is most complimentary of my ability to recite poems,' I excitedly put in, longing to make Papa proud of me. 'I knew Pope's "Elegy On The Death of an Unfortunate Lady" before I was eight. And the sisters took the entire school to see *King Lear* at the Theatre Royal, Bristol's new theatre. It was most thrilling, and not at all sad. In this version Cordelia was saved and Lear survived. Oh, how I should love to be in such a production.'

He ignored my chatter as if I had never spoken, brushing off my childish enthusiasm with scant attention. 'The children will be educated here in London from now on, and you, Hester, will lodge

with a respectable clergyman's family. I shall return across the
Atlantic to launch a new venture.'

Mama stared at him aghast. 'You are going overseas again? But
that is sheer madness! Did the Indians not burn your settlement
last time, and murder many of your people? How can you be so
foolish as to risk your life again?'

'Do not exaggerate, Hester. Only three men died, although
unfortunately we did lose several thousands of pounds worth of
ships and equipment.'

I winced at this, hating the implication that it was almost worse
to lose boats than lives.

'And what of the financial disaster that followed?' Mama bravely
persisted. 'Are we not now facing ruin?'

'It was unfortunate that my patrons reneged on their promise
to offer protection against any losses, but I have every faith the
scheme will fare better next time. I shall employ experienced
Canadian fishermen.'

This news was a death knell to Mama's hopes, but even she
could see that her arguments were falling on stony ground, that
my father's thoughts were already far from the needs of his family.

I blamed his mistress, this Elinor who held Papa in such fatal
fascination. He was, I believed, the hapless slave of a young and
artful woman. Were men always so fickle? My own pain was as
deeply felt as Mama's, and from that moment I believe every
event of my life has more or less been marked by the progressive
evils of a too acute sensibility.

And so our new life in London began. I attended a young ladies
seminary in Chelsea, where I was instructed by a Meribah
Lorrington. She was the most accomplished and extraordinary
woman I ever had the good fortune to meet, being conversant
in Latin, French and Italian, a brilliant arithmetician and know-
ledgeable on astronomy, if something of an eccentric. Unfortunately,
she had one sad failing. She was a martyr to drink, in spite of
her father being a stern Anabaptist.

When not intoxicated, Mrs Lorrington would delight in her
role of teacher, having only a small class of five or six pupils. It
soon became clear that I was a particular favourite.

'You are my little friend,' she would say. 'What would I do

without you when I am so lonely, having lost my beloved husband?'

'I shall always be your friend,' I told her, as I had grown quite fond of her, and would listen with avid attention to her every word.

A year went by under her care, in which I applied myself rigorously to my studies. I was a sensitive, rather dreamy child with a somewhat melancholic imagination. I put this down to the fact that I was born on a stormy night in November 1757, at Minster House in Bristol within the shadow of an Augustinian monastery, where once the prior had lived. My mother would often tell of how the wind had whistled round the dark pinnacles of the minster tower, the rain beating in torrents against the casements of her chamber on the night she gave birth. The tempest has dogged my footsteps ever since.

As the house even then was sinking into decay, we eventually moved to a far grander abode, but in those early years I loved to hear the melody of the bells, a rhythm that became very much a part of my soul. As was the music of the organ and choir. I would often creep down the winding stair, or crouch under the eagle lectern to listen.

'Why do you not play with your brothers on the green?' Mama would ask.

'I like the music better,' I would stubbornly declare, although my greatest love was poetry. I liked to read the epitaphs and inscriptions on the many tombs and monuments, which was what led me into the world of verse.

At the ladies seminary, Mrs Lorrington encouraged this passion, and my love of books, and would often read to me after school hours. It was she who first inspired me to put pen to paper. I would happily show her my early attempts at romantic verse, knowing she would applaud these juvenile efforts, where I might quail at showing them to Mama for fear of making her blush.

Every Sunday evening I would visit my mother at her lodgings, where we would take tea together, and I would tell her of my week's activities. She was often tearful, greatly missing my company, and filled with guilt over the way our family life had disintegrated. Sometimes other guests would be present. On one occasion a friend of my father's called to offer his compliments.

He was a captain in the British navy, and I could tell by the way he kept glancing my way, that he was quite taken with me.

'What a delightful daughter you have, Mrs Darby.'

'She is most talented,' my mother proudly agreed. 'Pass the captain another cake, dearest,' she instructed me.

I did so, struggling to suppress a shudder as I felt his fingers deliberately brush against mine.

'I am beginning to wish that I was not shortly off to sea, as I would very much like to become better acquainted with your beautiful daughter.'

Mama smiled, casting me a sideways glance of pleasure indicating I should be flattered by such compliments. At that time I was barely aware of my own burgeoning beauty. Tall and olive skinned, like my father, I thought of myself as swarthy, with curly, auburn hair, somewhat darker than my brothers. My eyes were blue, and rather too large for my small, delicate features. I was at that gawky, awkward age, neither woman nor child. The captain, however, clearly found something in my appearance to please him, for he went on to make the most astonishing proposition.

'Madam, perhaps when I return from my expedition I may call again, and if the young lady is still unattached at that time, you will permit me to declare myself.'

Mama was so startled she very nearly choked on her tea. 'Sir,' she spluttered. 'Have you any notion how old my daughter is?'

He considered me in all seriousness. 'Sixteen, seventeen?'

'She is not quite thirteen.'

His jaw dropped. 'You jest, madam.'

'I'm afraid not. She is admittedly quite mature for her age, but a child still. Tell him your birth date, Mary dear.'

When I politely obliged, now struggling to stifle my giggles, he almost dropped his cup and saucer in his eagerness to depart, and fled the room flushed with embarrassment. Sadly, a few months later we heard that his ship had foundered at sea, and this gallant officer perished.

For me the incident was significant in that it was my first taste of my burgeoning beauty, which was to chart my life's path. I began to notice how young men would gawp at me, or shyly blush if I returned their adoring gaze. Fortunately, my sheltered background and strictures set by a dominant father, albeit an absent one, maintained my innocence. I was, as Mama had said, still a child.

Two months later my life was again torn apart when Mrs Lorrington was obliged to close her school, partly from lack of funds to maintain it, and partly I suspect, because of her peculiar addictions. I was sent instead to a less outlandish establishment in Battersea. A boarding school run by the very sensible Mrs Leigh. I might have been happy here, were it not for my father's neglect. The money he had intermittently paid ceased altogether, and my mother was obliged to remove me. Fortunately, my brother George was allowed to remain under the care of the Reverend Gore, at Chelsea.

'What am I to do now?' I cried, mortified by the loss of my education, the access to the books and verse which were so essential to my soul.

'I am sure your papa will resolve the situation, given time,' my distressed mother insisted, with a faith I knew she did not entirely feel. I waited with growing impatience for the matter to be resolved, but weeks went by and no money came. The future looked grim.

Undeterred, and with a rod of steel in her character that I could only admire, Mama came to a decision. 'We can wait no longer. You have been properly and most tenderly brought up, well educated, yet you are without the advantage of fortune to which you had every reason to expect would be yours. In the circumstances, therefore, we have no choice but to provide our own.'

How I adored her. As cheerful as she was naïve, my mother was the most inoffensive of women with not a streak of ill temper in her. If she had a fault it was to spoil her children, whom she saw as fatherless and as bereft and lonely as herself. The loss of her security, and the way she had been abandoned by the man she had loved most dear, made the deepest impression upon me. My heart was filled with pity and love for her. Never, I thought, will I allow any man to treat me with such callousness.

This decision having been made, Mama rented a house in Little Chelsea, and managed to fit it out as a young ladies' boarding school at modest cost, then set about hiring assistants.

'You, Mary, shall assist by teaching English to the youngest girls.'

'But Mama,' I protested. 'I am but fourteen and have not yet finished my own education.'

'I am quite certain that you will do well at the task.'

In truth I found it exciting to be permitted to select passages for my young pupils to learn. I would often read my favourite verses to them, and suitably moral lessons on saints' days and Sunday evenings, recalling those I had memorised as a child. I thoroughly enjoyed sharing my passion for poetry with the little ones, and didn't mind in the least having to supervise them at their toilette, and see that they were properly dressed for their lessons or church.

One evening, with the children in bed and my mother visiting a friend, I was left in sole charge and sat reading by the light of the window. From time to time I would glance out and, quite by chance, saw a poor beggar-woman in the street. She was wandering recklessly about, her dress all torn and filthy, her face hidden beneath a tatty old bonnet so that it was difficult to judge her age. But she seemed to be in dire danger of being run over by passing carriages. Taking pity on her sorry state, I went out to see if I could be of assistance. I smelt the gin on her breath, but in pity slipped a few coins in her pocket, politely enquiring if I could be of any further help. She quickly grasped my hand and pressed it to her lips.

'Sweet girl, you are still the angel I ever knew!'

I recognised the voice instantly, and, tilting back her bonnet, looked into a pair of all-too-familiar dark eyes. 'Mrs Lorrington, can it truly be you?'

It was indeed my old teacher, and my heart went out to her to see such a proud, well-educated woman the worse for drink. I helped her into the house, supporting her as she half stumbled up the steps and offered her the facilities to bathe, gave her food and clothing. But the moment she had finished the meal, she insisted on leaving.

'There is really no need for you to go. We have a spare bed and you are most welcome to stay.'

'You are as ever, most generous, child, but I have no wish to be a burden upon your dear mother.'

'You would be no burden, Mrs Lorrington. This is a school,

and Mama would readily offer you employment, I am sure of it. You would have no need then to resort to the evils of the bottle ever again.'

She gazed upon me with a rare sadness in her eyes. 'Would that were true, but I fear I'd be of little use to her. I thank you for the supper, and bid you goodnight.' So saying she pulled open the door and stepped out into the night.

'You will call again, will you not, now that you know where we are, and perhaps meet Mama?'

'It would be my pleasure.'

Somehow I sensed her words to be insincere. 'At least tell me where I can find you?' I cried, but she hurried away without a backward glance, disappearing into the darkness. I never saw her again. I heard later that she ended her days in the workhouse. What a wretched conclusion for so accomplished a woman! Nothing of the sort, I vowed, would ever happen to me. I took this lesson to heart and I doubt I have touched a drop of alcohol from that day to this.

Papa arrived home not many weeks later, having run into fresh problems with his latest project. He was shocked to discover his wife had become entirely independent.

'How dare you embarrass me in this way?' he roared. 'Have I not enough to contend with, being robbed of thousand of pounds' worth of seal skins that were ready for market, and accused of illegally employing French fishermen, without my own wife turning against me?'

'If I am still your wife, it is in name only,' my mother valiantly responded. 'How did you expect us to survive once you stopped sending us money? Were we to be left to starve?'

'You do not know the meaning of the word,' he scorned.

'Perhaps not, but you should be grateful for my inventiveness, and your own daughter's skills, not castigate us for them.'

'You are nothing but a trial to me, woman, and I have trials enough. The military seized my equipment and I am now obliged to beg the Board of Trade for compensation. I certainly need no further humiliation from my own wife. You have wilfully tarnished my reputation by publicly revealing to the entire world your unprotected situation, as if you were an impoverished widow.'

'It is no fault of mine that I have no protection, and I might as well be a widow for all the use you are as a husband,' she sobbed, the tears rolling down her cheeks. But I could see she was wasting her breath. Within a very short time my father had closed our little school, and dismissed all the pupils.

Mama found us lodgings in Marylebone, while my father set up home with his mistress in Green Street, Grosvenor Square, a sorry state of affairs so far as I was concerned. He would call upon us from time to time, but the money he provided by way of support was scanty as he was already heavily involved in yet another new venture to the Labrador coast.

My mother endured this latest blow to her fortunes with the patience of conscious rectitude, while my own sense of loyalty was torn between the two of them. Much as I loathed the way Nicholas Darby had destroyed my mother's life, leaving her to largely fend for herself, he was still my father and I loved him. I took the opportunity to call upon him regularly, for I guessed he would not remain long in London. We would walk together in the fields near his home, and he freely confessed to me the great attraction he felt for Elinor.

'You complain that Mama has humiliated you, yet you daily destroy her dignity by openly living with your mistress. How can you justify such hypocrisy, Papa?'

'I cannot deny that I am besotted with her. Elinor is everything to me.'

'And what of us, your family? Do we mean nothing?' The hurt I felt inside, as a result of my father's callousness, cut deep into my sensitive heart.

'You will ever be dear to me, but we cannot choose whom we love. It is something that simply happens to us, often against our wishes.'

I was to remember these prophetic words many years later when yet another man betrayed me.

One morning we called upon the Earl of Northington. He was one of my father's patrons, residing in Berkeley Square. Papa presented me as the god-daughter of the late Lord Northington, consequently we were received with polite attention. I was fascinated by his lordship's handsome good looks, being quite the young rake, and, as a politician, a man of some influence. He invited my father to dine with him a few days later in order to further discuss their business. I was not included in the party as I was merely a young girl of fourteen, but he was most civil towards me, and flatteringly gallant. Thereafter I became a frequent visitor to the house, where I was ever certain of a welcome.

Shortly after that, Father again left for America, although not without first issuing a stern injunction to my mother. 'Take care that no dishonour falls upon my daughter. If she is not safe at my return I will annihilate you!'

I saw Mama tremble, even as she stoutly responded. 'As if I would allow such a thing to happen. I think you may rely upon my good sense to properly protect my own daughter.'

'Let us hope so, or you will live to rue the day you ever crossed me.'

Once he had gone, she breathed a sigh of relief and instantly began planning to move us all to Southampton Buildings in Chancery Lane.

'Must we move yet again, Mama?' I complained, in my overly dramatic way. What a spoiled child I still was.

'Yes, dearest, I am placing myself under the protection of a lawyer, Samuel Cox.'

I turned this over rather crossly in my mind. 'Why? Is he offering you legal help in some regard?'

'Indeed, if that should ever become necessary, he most certainly would. But a woman is much more secure with a man to look out for her,' Mama declared, blushing slightly.

I dared not enquire further into the nature of their relationship, being old enough to understand that a man offering protection to a woman often involved sexual favours. I certainly had no wish to consider such matters with regard to my own mother. She was happy at last, which was all that mattered. But I would never forgive my father for deserting us.

My education was to be finished at Oxford House, and it was here that my talents finally flourished. The governess, a Mrs Hervey, expressed great admiration over my facility for dramatic recitation. And as my dancing teacher, John Hussey, was at that time ballet master at Covent Garden Theatre, he generously offered to procure me an audition. I was bursting with excitement. The

dream of treading the boards had been growing in me ever since
the school visit to see *King Lear* with the Misses More. Now it
looked as if it might actually happen. All I needed was my
mother's consent, which even at my most optimistic I realised
would be hard to come by.

'We wondered if perhaps you would allow Mary to try for the
stage,' Mrs Hervey politely asked, having called at my home
specifically to make this request.

Mama started, shocked by the very idea. 'My daughter, upon
the stage?' she cried. 'Never!'

'It is true that actresses do not generally have a good reputation,' that good lady admitted. 'However, there are many examples
of respectable females who, even in that most perilous of professions, have preserved an unspotted fame. Would you at least permit
Mary the opportunity of an audition, to consult some master of
the art as to her capability?'

'Indeed not! Her father has left very firm instructions that our
daughter must be most carefully protected.'

Mrs Hervey used every persuasion she could think of, but
Mama was adamant that she would never permit such a thing.
Regretfully, my governess took her leave. I at once turned upon
Mama in a lather of childish temper.

'How can you be so selfish? You know full well that this latest
expedition of Papa's will thrive no better than the others. How
am I to make my way in the world without a fortune, and no
means of earning a living? Tell me that! Do you wish me to spend
my entire days as a governess, or companion to some doughty old
lady? There is money to be made in the theatre, and I believe I
may have a talent for acting.'

'And I have made my feelings on this matter very plain, Mary.
I dare not cross your father. This discussion is closed.'

But I did not allow it to be closed. In the coming days I
constantly returned to the subject: nagging, pleading, begging my
mother, even resorting to tears and tantrums as young girls are
apt to do. At last I wore down her arguments and managed to
touch her soft heart. An audition was duly arranged for me at
Covent Garden Theatre.

Sad to say it proved to be a disaster. I gave a rendition of one
of Jane Shore's speeches from the tragedy of that name by Nicholas

Rowe. But what did I, a girl of fourteen, understand about the emotions of a royal mistress? I was so devastated at the thought that I'd made a complete fool of myself, I cried for hours into my pillow.

'Why did I imagine I could ever act?' I sobbed.

'But you can do the most marvellous recitations, dearest,' Mama reminded me, heartsore at my bitter disappointment.

'They said I was too gushing, too insincere and shallow.' I howled with pain all the more at thought of the harsh criticism.

Unable to bear my misery, she poured out her heart to her new lawyer friend and it was Mama's protector, Samuel Cox, who brought the light back into my young life. By chance he knew Dr Samuel Johnson, who in turn was acquainted with David Garrick. It was therefore arranged that I should meet the great man himself.

I at once set about learning all I could about David Garrick. My ballet teacher was most helpful in this regard and informed me that he was not only a brilliant actor but had transformed Drury Lane. He had apparently banned the young bucks from sitting on the stage and harassing the actresses, greatly improved the sets, and installed better lighting by putting in oil lamps with reflectors that could be directed to a particular spot on stage, producing a more atmospheric effect. He was also adept at revising a play to better please his audience.

'Most importantly, he has a naturalistic style,' John Hussey told me. 'And do remember to speak up and not drop your voice when you do the audition.' There was much more advice of this nature, but I was so riddled with nerves I could barely take in a word of it.

Mama accompanied me to Mr Garrick's grand house in Adelphi Terrace. My knees almost gave way as I entered through the pillared hall to be shown into an imposing drawing room, the like of which I had never seen in my life before. The elaborate ceiling was a veritable work of art, with a circular panel of Venus surrounded by the Graces depicted in a series of medallions that were quite beautiful.

I felt completely overawed, but I must say Mr Garrick was charm itself, and his wife, a delightfully pretty woman, being the former dancer Eva Maria Veigel, even more so.

'Welcome to our home,' she said, ushering Mama to a comfortable sofa and calling for tea and scones to be served.

I took no more than a sip of tea, and was far too nervous to eat.

'Come and sit by me, child, and tell me all about yourself,' Mr Garrick urged, patting the chair beside him. I glanced across at Mama who gently inclined her head, so I accepted the invitation, sitting up very straight with my hands folded neatly in my lap, as she had taught me.

'I believe you wish to be a famous actress, now why is that?'

He seemed such a nice, jolly old man that I readily answered. 'Because I think I have the talent to do it well.'

He put back his head and roared with laughter. 'A good enough answer indeed. Then why don't you show me some of that talent.' And he gently silenced his wife's polite chit-chat by pressing a finger to his lips.

I stood before him, my knees all atremble, and began to perform my prepared speech from the play *Jane Shore*, which at least my ballet teacher's friend, Thomas Hull, had approved of, even if the managers of Covent Garden had been less than impressed. I'd said no more than a few lines when Mr Garrick held up one hand to stop me.

'Why are you declaiming so loudly? Am I so old that you think me deaf?'

'Indeed no, sir. I was instructed to speak up and project my voice.' I experienced again that sinking sensation of dreaded failure.

'I want you to put yourself inside the head of Jane Shore. How does she feel about losing her royal lover? Is she afraid of what might happen to her? I wish to hear sincerity in your voice. Direct your speech to me as if you and I were simply engaged in a private conversation. But give it *feeling*, child. Can you do that?'

I nodded and, taking a breath, continued, this time concentrating entirely upon what I was saying, feeling it, living the emotion. '"The scene of beauty and delight is chang'd. No roses bloom upon my fading cheek . . ."'

He heard me out without further interruption. When I was done he sat back in his seat with a soft sigh and quietly applauded, making my cheeks flame bright crimson. Then turning to his wife he smiled. 'I believe we have found ourselves a little treasure here, my dear.'

'I believe we have.'

'Do you not think her voice very like Susannah Cibber? Now there was an actress, and she had a fine singing voice too. Do you sing, dear?'

I shook my head. 'I can sing in tune, but have never considered myself to be a singer,' I confessed.

'No matter, I believe we can make an actress of you.'

My heart swelled, almost bursting with happiness. 'Oh, Mr Garrick, I don't know how to thank you.'

He rolled back in his seat on that cheerful laugh of his. 'With hard work, dear girl, with hard work. Now we must plan a suitable debut for you, one that will fill the theatre and bring in the critics. I shall train you for the role of Cordelia, and dash it, I may play Lear myself. I shall expect you first thing on Monday morning to begin rehearsals.'

I walked home in a daze of glory, floating high over the wet London pavement upon which we trudged. And so great was her pride in my success that my mother was almost in tears. But as we sat together over supper that night, while I in my vanity contemplated a thousand triumphs, Mama's thoughts returned to reality and her greatest fear.

'It would be so much safer if we found you a good husband.'

'No, Mama. I have set my heart upon the stage.'

'Oh, my dear! What your father will say when he hears, I dare not begin to contemplate.'

Rehearsals progressed well and I enjoyed myself immensely. The hours I passed in Mr Garrick's society were utterly enchanting and engrossing. Although *King Lear* was a tragedy, in Garrick's version Cordelia marries Edgar instead of being hanged, which was a great relief to me. I drank in every word of advice the great man gave me, all too aware of his generosity in taking such a risk with an unknown actress. Would anyone even come to see the play? I worried. But my tutor appeared quite sanguine in his expectations of my success, and every rehearsal seemed to strengthen his flattering opinion of me.

If my performance was good, he would laugh and proceed

to dance a minuet with me by way of celebration. Or after a particularly long and taxing rehearsal, he might say, 'Sing for me, child,'
and I would happily sing one of the favourite ballads of the day.

'You have a beautiful tone of voice, so very like Cibber.'

But I did not always please him. At times he would seem restless and peevish, which upset me until his wife explained that he
suffered from gout which could make him rather crotchety. He
did have a somewhat fiery temper which I took care not to
inflame. Only when Mr Garrick was on stage could I be entirely
certain of how he might react. But I adored him, and he was
the most generous of tutors. He also had the most brilliant,
piercing dark eyes, and smiled and laughed a great deal.

'Now I wish you to frequent the theatre, Mary, and familiarize
yourself with its practices before your debut. You and your dear
mother may make full use of my box.'

Even Mama was in favour of taking advantage of such a treat,
and the word soon spread that I was Mr Garrick's new protégée.
Any sense of awkwardness I might feel in that role quickly passed
as the word buzzed about that I was the juvenile pupil of Garrick
– the promised Cordelia. My young heart throbbed with impatience for the hour of my trial.

Admirers flocked to my side, showering me with compliments
and attention. It was utterly thrilling to be the object of such
intense interest whenever I appeared at the theatre. I had turned
fifteen, a dangerous age, and was too easily flattered.

One evening, Mama and I were at the theatre with a small
party of her friends, when an officer in full dress uniform had
the effrontery to climb into our box. My mother was appalled.

'Young man, what are you about?'

'I wish to see for myself this great beauty everyone is talking
of,' he said, his eyes fixed upon me.

He was not unhandsome and, bemused as I was by this attention, I confess to being utterly fascinated by the fellow's daring.
I was also aware that half the audience were avidly watching the
little scene, eager to see what happened next. But then I'd already
discovered that observing who was present in the audience, and
what they were up to, was as fascinating as anything that might
be happening on stage.

This officer, however, had reckoned without my mother.

'You will desist this instant or I shall call the manager and have you removed,' she sternly ordered.

'Perhaps another time,' he said, and smilingly sketching a bow he obligingly retreated and climbed back out of the box.

A few nights later as we alighted at the theatre from our sedan chair, Mama said, 'I believe that young officer has followed us. How very vexing.'

As a young girl beginning to feel my power I was deeply flattered by such persistence, whoever he might be. Later, a letter was delivered to Mr Garrick's box, where we sat enjoying the performance, conveyed to me by a servant-woman.

'What does it say?' my mother asked.

I stifled a giggle as I read it. 'The writer declares his most ardent love for me. He avows himself to be the son of a notable family, and offers me marriage no less.'

Startled, but deeply curious, Mama snatched the letter from my hand to read the missive for herself. Then putting up her quizzing glass she searched the audience for a sight of its author. The gentleman concerned raised a polite hand by way of acknowledgment. 'How very forward of him, although I must say he appears most graceful and really quite handsome,' she commented, studying him most carefully. 'Perhaps we may allow him to be introduced to us, after all.'

I was shocked by her sudden turnabout. 'Pray do not start your matchmaking, Mama. I am entirely resolved to become an actress, and not at all inclined to favour the addresses of any captain.'

'But he sounds most suitable.'

'By which you mean of good family and blessed with a fortune.'

'It is what your father and I both want for you.'

I rolled my eyes in despair. 'Papa is thousands of miles away across the sea, and I intend to make up my own mind what I do with my life.'

'You are far too young to make such decisions. The injunction your father laid upon me keeps me awake night after night. I must take the greatest care of you, dearest, and make every effort to find a more appropriate solution to our difficulties.'

I understood perfectly that she was nervous of arousing my father's vengeance, but I firmed my lips and refused to discuss the matter further, my mind quite made up. All my young life I had been indulged, granted whatever my heart desired, and, spoiled child that I was, determined that such a state should continue.

Nevertheless, at my mother's instigation, an evening or two later a mutual acquaintance did present my suitor to us with all due ceremony. I paid no heed to his name, but made every effort to put the fellow off. 'Why would you wish to take an actress for a wife?' I challenged him. 'Is this some long-held dream of yours? Would it not damage your good standing in society to be connected to such a disreputable creature?'

He looked slightly discomfited by my questions. 'I rather assumed that any young lady who accepted my offer would readily relinquish such a daredevil plan.'

'Of course she would,' Mama quickly interjected. 'My daughter's future has not been firmly fixed at this stage.'

'Yes it has,' I stubbornly demurred.

'Mary, good manners, please.'

I turned my back on him and fixed my attention on the stage. 'I believe the play is about to begin.'

'Then I will return at a more convenient time,' he said with a bow, and thankfully, took his leave.

To my great relief, the friend who had presented the captain to us, perhaps alarmed for my safety by what he had witnessed, caught up with us as we were about to leave the theatre.

'I beg you not to take too seriously a single word he says, Mrs Darby. The fellow is an out and out rogue where women are concerned. I fear he has some scheme to dishonour your daughter, as he is already married, his wife young and most charming!'

'Oh, my goodness!' Mama put her hands to her cheeks in shock, her consternation all too evident. 'You see what danger you have put yourself in by becoming an actress,' she scolded me, in that way mothers have of turning their own mistakes upon their offspring.

The incident did not, however, dampen my pleasure in flirting with all the other young rakes who hovered about me like bees round a honey pot. I was a young beauty on the verge of a new adventure, so why should I not make the most of it? Thrilling as all this might be, the stage still seemed to me the very criterion of human happiness. But then my gaze fell upon one young man in particular, who quite captured my attention.

He was a solicitor's clerk and I saw him almost every day as he worked in the lawyer's offices of Vernon and Elderton in the buildings opposite our lodgings in Chancery Lane. He would sit in the window gazing adoringly across at me, casting flirtatious glances which I readily returned.

I thought him most handsome, his countenance overcast by a kind of languor, possibly as a result of sickness, which to my sensitive soul rendered him even more interesting. Sometimes, when I approached the window, he would bow before turning away in a show of emotion, as if he were dying for love of me.

'What is it you find so interesting at that window?' Mama wanted to know, and coming over spotted my admirer gazing upon me with open adoration. 'Goodness me, girl, are we to have would-be suitors invade our own drawing room?' And she quickly closed the shutters.

Of course, I opened them again when she wasn't looking, and often the young clerk would have me in fits of giggles even as our languishing glances continued unabated. I was not about to allow my mother's indignation, or the stern threats of an absent father, to prevent me from doing whatever I pleased. Mama fancied every man a seducer, and every hour one of accumulating peril! To me, but a young girl, it was but the mildest of flirtations, and enormous fun.

One Sunday, Mama was persuaded to accept an invitation to dinner at Greenwich, issued by a colleague of Mr Samuel Cox, her protector. I was also invited, and prepared for the event with some excitement, always delighted by any excuse to dress in my finest. It was then the fashion to wear silks, and I chose a gown of pale blue lustring, with a chip hat trimmed with ribands of the same colour. I was most pleased with the result, and, vain as I was, hoped to produce a stir of admiration.

As our carriage stopped at the Star and Garter at Greenwich, who should step forward to hand me from the carriage but that very same young clerk from the lawyer's office in the Southampton Buildings.

My mother swiftly expressed her indignation. 'Who is this young fellow?' she hissed in my ear.

I judged it best not to respond, blushing to the roots of my auburn curls, secretly relieved that I had tweaked them to perfection, and that in my new gown I presented a pleasing picture for any young man to admire.

'May I present Mr Thomas Robinson,' said Mr Cox's friend, a Mr Wayman, and the gentleman who had arranged the dinner. I offered the young clerk a simpering smile before lifting my chin and walking away to join the rest of the party. I certainly had no intention of allowing him to imagine that I favoured him.

Mr Wayman, however, sang Mr Robinson's praises at length for the entire evening, mentioning his future expectations from a rich old uncle, and of his likely advancement in the legal profession. 'He is, madam, most taken by your daughter.'

'He and a dozen others, all better men than he,' was Mama's chilling response.

Thomas Robinson himself said nothing. I would have enjoyed a little conversation with him, but he seemed content to sit and gaze adoringly upon me, which was immensely flattering yet at the same time somewhat disappointing.

Our party dined early, after which Mama insisted that we return to London without delay. The young clerk remained at Greenwich, apparently for the benefit of the air, having recently recovered from a bout of sickness, as I had suspected. But if *he* had taken the opportunity to gaze upon me, then *I* had most certainly reciprocated the compliment, finding him even more handsome and agreeable at close quarters than he'd appeared from across the street.

How vulnerable I was, my emotions easily stirred by a good looking young man and a few seductive glances.

Perhaps in a bid to put an end to what she perceived as a dangerous flirtation, Mama removed us to York Buildings in Villars Street. But only a few days later, proving he'd had no difficulty in finding us, Thomas Robinson paid my mother a visit. If her manner was at the outset frosty, he was in no way disheartened. The secret smiles I cast him may have helped to raise his confidence, but he wisely paid greater attention to winning over my mother.

'I see you are fond of books, madam,' he politely remarked, glancing at an array upon our shelves.

'If they are of a suitably moral and religious character,' she agreed in a most high-flown manner.

The next afternoon he brought her an elegantly bound edition of James Hervey's *Meditations Among the Tombs*. 'This is but a small token of my respect,' he told her.

'Oh, my goodness, how very generous.' Mama was startled, and secretly touched by the gesture.

Mr Robinson brought more books of a similar nature, of which my mother was indeed fond, winning her round with these attentions so that she began to look forward to his visits.

'There is a good deal to be said in favour of this young man,' she admitted, casting me a sly glance to judge my reaction to this generosity.

Whether I was quite so fascinated by him is open to doubt as my head was filled with my debut, the date of which was rapidly approaching. And then came a most devastating blow: my brother George fell ill with smallpox.

It was a most agonising time. How my mother coped I shall never know. Having already lost two children to this dreaded disease, she now had to face the possibility of losing another. I quickly postponed my debut in order to help her care for poor darling George. To my surprise, Mr Robinson continued to call regularly, readily ran errands for us, brought food, even sat with my little brother to allow us the opportunity to rest. Day and night he devoted himself to the task of consoling my mother, and of attending to her darling boy. He was quite the kindest and best of mortals, indefatigable in his attentions.

'You would do well to seriously consider Mr Robinson as a husband,' Mama said, all sign of her former disapproval now dispelled. 'Few young men would take such a risk with their own health. He must care for you very deeply.'

I did not answer, finding it far too emotional a time to even consider my own future when my brother lay sick in his bed. Besides, my heart was still set on a career in the theatre, and I thought myself far too young even to be considering marriage.

Fortunately, the smallpox turned out to be a mild strain, but as George began to show signs of recovery, it was my turn then to fall sick. I was utterly devastated, terrified that the pox would scar and disfigure my beauty.

'My would-be suitor will soon flee now,' I mourned to my mother. 'As will every other.'

But he did not. Mr Robinson was most assiduous in his attentions, forever at my bedside as if resolved to prove the depth of his affection for me.

'He cares nothing for his own safety, wanting only to see you well again,' Mama assured me when I protested. 'He has made his feelings quite plain, and has asked for your hand in marriage no matter what the outcome of your illness, even if you are scarred. What more can he do to prove the strength of his ardour? And I confess I should adore him as a son-in-law. Will you accept?'

I stifled a sigh, my head aching far too much for me even to think clearly. 'I cannot deny that his devotion has made a deep impression upon me, Mama, but my affections for him are more that of a sister, rather than a wife. I have no wish even to flirt with him now.'

'But that is only because you are ill, dearest. Once you are quite yourself again, and I feel sure your beauty will be unimpaired as we are taking every care, I am quite certain your feelings for him will be stronger than ever.'

'Mama, please desist. I have no wish to think of marriage when I am about to embark upon a career in acting.'

'If you do take to the stage, then it will be quite against your father's wishes, and my own,' she sternly reminded me.

'Why do you blow so hot and cold, one minute weeping with pride at my success, the next doing everything in your power to prevent my debut happening?' I cried, rubbing my aching brow with tense fingers.

'Because, as your mother, I can see a better future for you in the care of a good husband than acting the trollop on stage. Think what your father will do to you, and to *me*, for allowing such a plan to go ahead. In his eyes you will be dishonoured.'

'I will *not* be dishonoured. I am merely to act in a play with Mr Garrick.'

'Can you name one honourable actress who has not had her

character besmirched by rumour and gossip, one who has gone on to marry a respectable husband?'

I thought hard, anxious to produce at least one name, but my silence spoke volumes. Actresses were indeed viewed in the light of the roles they played, as harlots and whores, as women of low morals who cheat upon their husbands, and very few gained respectability.

She kissed my cheek, as if my lack of response settled the matter. 'Then promise me that once you are fully recovered, you will accept this young man. Was he not prepared to make the ultimate sacrifice in order to win you?'

'Oh, Mama, you ask too much!'

'His uncle, a Mr Harris from Carmarthenshire, is extremely wealthy, and young Thomas the old gentleman's sole heir. I ask you, dearest, to exercise more common sense in making practical provision for your own future. And do not deny that you are fond of him. Did you not go against my wishes in the first place by opening the shutters to encourage him?'

I could not deny it. But was this how it felt to be in love? Excited, flattered and confused all at the same time? I supposed that it must be, and there were certain attractions in marrying a pleasant young man with expectations. Nor did I have any wish for my father to blame my dear mother for any failing on my part. The emotional blackmail she exerted upon me was enormous, and in view of the fact she had almost lost two more of her children, even if we were both on the road to recovery, how could I deny her some peace of mind at last? Having been abandoned by a husband, did she not deserve some tranquillity in her life? I was young and impressionable, and undoubtedly intrigued by Mr Robinson's ardent devotion, so that as the days passed and Mama continued to cajole and gently bully me, almost hourly reminding me of her vow to my father, my resistance began to crumble.

When Thomas Robinson came and asked for my hand, I was still in a most vulnerable state. 'I can bring you no dowry,' I asserted.

'I do not ask for one. I shall have plenty of money for us both, once I come of age.'

'I might have seriously considered your offer, Mr Robinson, but . . .'

'Call me Tommy, or Tom, if you prefer.'

Either name seemed far too familiar and I blushed, rather prettily judging by the way his gaze focused so intently upon my face. 'I am far too young to take on the duties of a wife. Perhaps in a year or two.'

'I can afford to employ servants, and provide you with every comfort. My expectations are good. In addition to my salary I have an allowance from my uncle of £500 a year.'

Mama and I had enjoyed few comforts in recent years. I tried another tack, one which was very much of concern to me. 'But what would happen to my mother? She has suffered enough in her life, I couldn't abandon her.'

'There would be no need. I'm very fond of Hester too, and perfectly agreeable to her coming to live with us when we are wed. She could perhaps oversee the domestic arrangements.'

I was deeply touched. Few young men would relish sharing their home with their mother-in-law, let alone making the offer voluntarily. I was convinced, in that moment, that he must genuinely be in love with me. He certainly had much to offer. Consequently, despite my misgivings I found myself casting him a shy smile. 'Very well, then I accept,' I said, surprising even myself.

The banns were called even as I lay on my sickbed, published on three successive Sundays at St Martin's Church, and the day for our marriage was arranged.

Two

Reluctant Bride

When the dull hours no joy could bring,
No bliss my weary fancy prove;
I mark'd thy leaden, pond'rous wing,
With tardy pace, unkindly move.

Mary Darby Robinson
'Stanzas to Time'

As I lay in bed fretting in my sickened state, others were busily making plans to turn my world upside down. Fortunately, both George and I made a full recovery, but by then all arrangements for the wedding had been made.

'I am delighted to say that the ceremony will take place within weeks,' Mr Robinson – as I still thought of him – informed me. 'Although I must ask you to keep our union secret for a little while.'

I was stunned by this request, doubts again bubbling to the surface. 'Goodness, you cannot expect me to embark upon an engagement, let alone a marriage, and tell no one. That would be quite untenable.'

'I know it is a great deal to ask, Mary, but it is only for a short time.'

'Why must it be kept a secret? Are you ashamed of me?'

'Far from it. The reason is that I still have three months to serve before my articles expire. Also, before I met you, there was a young lady forming an attachment to me who had every hope of a matrimonial union between us.'

'Then perhaps you should wed her instead,' I icily responded. 'I shall play second fiddle to no one.'

His face now a bright crimson, he hastened to reassure me. 'The affection was cherished only on the lady's part. Once I come of age I shall be free to control my own life and put an end to her hopes.'

This sounded reasonable enough, while at the same time warning bells were sounding in all this talk of secrecy and I quickly saw a way out of my dilemma. 'In light of this news, perhaps we should delay the date of our wedding until you do come of age. I still feel far too young for marriage, in any case. Moreover, I shrink from the idea of anything remotely clandestine. I can see no benefit in secrecy, quite the opposite, in fact.'

'I assure you, beloved, that I am filled with impatience for the ceremony to take place which will make you mine for ever.'

I fell into a fit of sulks, not much caring for the idea of being in the possession of any man. This was not at all what I had planned to do with my life. I was a woman of passion, for theatre and verse, and one of pride and independence. My father had provided me with an excellent education, in which I'd become something of a blue stocking always with my nose in a book, or happily composing my poetry. I thought how, throughout my childhood, I had only to say I desired something and my wish would be granted. Somehow, that facility had been lost in the misfortunes that had overwhelmed our little family in recent years.

I began to weep and, hearing my distress, Mama bustled in and began to scold me and mop up my tears. 'Think of the disapprobation which your father would not fail to evince if you should choose to adopt the theatrical life in preference to an honourable and prosperous alliance. Remember that it is a most demanding profession. Your health would suffer, I am sure of it.'

'My health is strong, Mama, pray do not fuss so.'

'You surely haven't taken a fancy to that libertine officer?' she said, ever watchful for my safety.

'Of course not!' I was appalled at the very idea, although he still persisted in writing to me, and as I began to get out and about again I discovered to my horror that the impertinent fellow continued to follow me, which was most alarming.

'You see what dangers you put yourself in by insisting on the stage as a career,' Mama warned.

The subject was returned to day after day, my mother rebutting every argument I put forward. 'But I feel so guilty towards Mr Garrick who gave so generously of his time, believing entirely in my talent. Let me at least postpone the wedding until after my debut.'

Mr Robinson took my hand and kissed it most tenderly. 'You must allow that your parents have every reason to fear for your good name and safety. Your beauty, your very youth, make you vulnerable to the unwelcome attentions of the lecherous rakes who frequent Drury Lane. Have you not experienced that already with this notorious officer? Your honour would be jeopardised the moment you set foot upon a public stage.'

Mama agreed. 'You might find yourself obliged to marry some man far less amiable and well-placed than Mr Robinson here, simply for protection. One who would not approve of my forming a part in your domestic establishment.'

The bond with my mother was strong, as was my sense of responsibility and pity for her, so I found this line of argument hard to refute. Yet I retained an instinctive repugnance at the prospect of a clandestine marriage.

It was no surprise when I received a letter from Garrick expressing his impatience, demanding that my mother allow me to fix the date of my debut.

'You must write and relinquish the project at once,' Mama insisted. 'You cannot keep him dangling any longer.'

'I will write soon,' I agreed, still shying away from burning this particular bridge. My passion for the theatre might have been born out of my love for verse and recitation, but it would undoubtedly have provided me with the independence for which I craved. Mr Robinson and my mother were, however, united in their opposition to my pursuing this dream. I spent my days in torment, and my nights tossing and turning over the decision I had made. Why had I permitted the banns to be published? Did I even love Mr Robinson?

But the arguments and pressure applied were too strong for me to resist, my desire to protect my mother paramount in my mind, and finally I gave in.

The wedding took place on the twelfth of April, 1773, with the venerable vicar of St Martin's, Dr Erasmus Saunders, officiating.

'Never have I performed this office for so young a bride,' he said at the conclusion of the ceremony.

I merely smiled, choosing not to mention I was but fifteen, as innocent as the simple Quaker-like gown I wore for the occasion. This was not at all how I had imagined my wedding would be. I had dreamed of a love match, of meeting my soul mate. Yet I knew not the sensation of any sentiment beyond that of esteem for Thomas Robinson, all flirtation quite gone between us. Love was still a stranger to my bosom. But no matter what my misgivings, I was now a married woman: no longer Miss Mary Darby but Mrs Robinson. The prospect alarmed me and I felt deeply thankful that, once the honeymoon was over, I would be able to continue living with Mama, while my new husband resided elsewhere. At least for the present until he came of age and our marriage could be made public.

The wedding breakfast took place at a friend's house where I changed into a dress of white muslin, and a chip hat adorned with white ribbons, a white sarsenet scarf cloak, and slippers of white satin embroidered with silver.

Mama, and Hanway Balack, a friend of Mr Robinson, were to accompany us on our wedding journey. I was relieved about this too as I was not yet ready to be alone with my new husband. That night we drove to an inn at Maidenhead Bridge, Mr Robinson and myself in a phaeton, my mother and Balack in a post-chaise behind.

'Goodness me, you look like a bride,' said the inn keeper the moment he saw me walk in, unaware of the secret ceremony that had just been performed.

I was startled, and in a panic began to wonder how I might escape, horrified to realise it was far too late. The deed was done. I might give every appearance of being a happy, beautiful bride dressed in the height of fashion, but in my heart I nursed a deep regret at the opportunity I had lost for an independent future.

Later that evening while my husband and Hanway amused themselves in cheerful good humour with ale and wine over a game of cards, I took a stroll with my mother in the gardens. I wept a little, unable to control the emotional turmoil churning inside me. 'Oh, Mama, I confess I am the most wretched of mortals!'

She looked at me askance. 'But why, dearest? You have nothing to fear. Have I not explained sufficient of what will be required of you on this, your wedding night? Tommy adores you, I am sure he will be most gentle.'

I brushed these trifles aside. 'That is not what I meant. I might respect Mr Robinson, but there is no powerful joining of our souls. In short, I do not love him.'

'I think you are simply confused and overwhelmed by events, dearest. In any case, love will come, once you stop pining after a lost dream.' And she briskly set about mopping up my tears.

Thankfully, my husband was too far gone in his cups to trouble me that night, for which I was vastly relieved, since I was both exhausted and melancholic. The next day we went on to Henley where we enjoyed, if that is the word, a ten-day honeymoon. Tommy, as I was obliged to call him from then on, proved to be affable enough, easy-going, likeable and good-natured. And when it came to losing my maidenhead, Mama had been quite right. He was indeed most gentle with me.

But where was the passion I had so longed for, the sensation of two bodies melding as one? Nothing of that sort occurred in our bed, not the first time intimacy took place, nor the nights following. I honestly wondered what all the fuss was about. In the romantic verses I had read, nowhere had I seen mentioned a bored indifference on the part of the bride. It wasn't that I found his kisses unpleasant, nor did I ever protest when he made love to me. But while he went about the business, I stifled a despondent sigh and stared at the ceiling, hoping it wouldn't take long.

On our return to London, Mama and I rented a house in Great Queen Street, Lincoln's Inn Fields. The property belonged to a friend of my mother, and while being handsomely furnished, with many valuable works of art, it was somewhat large and old-fashioned. In its favour, it was convenient to Chancery Lane where my new husband would continue to reside at the house of his employers, Vernon and Elderton, in Southampton Buildings.

My most painful task was to write to Mr Garrick to inform him that not only was I married, but would not now be taking up his offer of a career upon the stage. I felt I owed it to him to tell him the truth, despite my promise to keep our union secret. Tears spilled out on to the page as I wrote, and when, a few weeks later, I met Mr Garrick himself in the street, I hesitated to approach him. But on seeing me, he hurried over to congratulate me, expressing the warmest wishes for my future happiness.

'That is most kind of you, sir, and I beg your forgiveness for having let you down so badly after all your time and effort, not least for your faith in me.'

'I bear you no ill will, Mary. Love must come first, and the decision was yours entirely.'

'Indeed it was not. To my infinite sorrow I was compelled to put the needs of my family: my mother and younger brother, before my own. This way they have the security Mama craves.'

'Without the threatened loss of your reputation? I do understand. I was aware your mother never entirely approved of your becoming an actress.'

I felt myself blushing. 'If there were any way I could change her attitude, I would do so. I deeply regret the sacrifice I've been asked to make, and the loss of a career I would have loved.'

'The loss is entirely ours, that your beauty and charm will not, after all, grace our stage. But should you ever change your mind, then you know where to find me.'

His words rang in my head for days afterwards, and quite a few tears dribbled sorrowfully down my cheeks as I dwelled on this lost opportunity. The chances of it ever coming again seemed remote indeed.

With too much time on my hands I grew bored and restless, and took to visiting places of historic interest, such as Westminster Abbey, with a new female friend with whom I had recently become acquainted. The dim light of the Gothic windows, the hollow sound of my footsteps echoing in the lofty aisles, and the nostalgic memories that the scene inspired, offered a soothing sense of meditation. I needed these moments of solace as I was beginning to dread the prospect of an early pregnancy. The last thing I wanted was to appear to be a fallen woman when I was in truth respectably married. Three months had slipped by and my situation had not improved.

'When do you come of age exactly?' I asked my husband. 'I am naturally anxious to make our marriage known as soon as possible.'

'I will inform you when the time is right, until then you must say nothing,' he insisted, which was most unsatisfactory.

'This is no proper marriage,' I complained to my mother. 'Tommy still will not allow me to announce my new status. Why will he not treat me with proper respect? What if I should be with child?'

Mama looked shocked. 'Do you think you might be?'

'Not that I know of, but how can I be certain? For all we are living apart, my husband visits me regularly so I could fall at any time.'

'I agree it is odd that no date for Tommy's coming of age has ever been mentioned.' Frowning, she became increasingly thoughtful in the days following, and finally turned to her protector, Mr Cox, for advice.

'I will make some enquiries, dear lady,' he promised her.

Within days he returned with devastating news. 'It may surprise you to learn that Mr Thomas Robinson came of age some time ago. Nor is he in fact the nephew of this alleged "uncle", the Mr Harris who lives in South Wales, but his illegitimate son.'

'*Illegitimate?*' Mama cried in horror.

I thought for a moment she was about to faint as she collapsed on to a sofa. I hurried to burn a feather in case I should need to revive her. After all the care she had taken, to discover this unsavoury truth was devastating for her, and for me. I felt as if my sacrifice had been entirely in vain.

'And is this Mr Harris not even wealthy?' she asked, in tremulous tones.

'Oh, indeed yes, he is a man of some substance, although strangely reluctant to acknowledge his sons.'

'Sons?' I queried, in some surprise.

'There is an elder brother, a Commodore William Robinson, at present in India under the patronage of Lord Clive. Both boys are apparently the result of a liaison with a laundry maid.'

Mama groaned as I sank on to the seat beside her, equally stunned. With an elder brother, whom Tommy had conveniently failed to mention, his financial prospects would be bleak, even without taking into account his illegitimacy. And I was fully aware that he had already borrowed money to pay for the wedding and the honeymoon.

'I have made a terrible mistake,' my mother sobbed. 'I should never have promoted the union, never have insisted upon this marriage.'

'It was not your fault, Mama, it was his. He lied to us, which is unforgivable.'

As Mama wailed all the more into her handkerchief, I was the first to rally. 'Mr Cox, would you be so good as to ask my husband to call upon us this evening, when we might discuss this matter with him?'

Tommy came that evening, as requested, if subdued, having been warned by Mr Cox of what he might expect.

Quite her old self again, Mama was bristling with anger and wasted no time in coming to the point. 'We have heard the most alarming news that not only have you already come of age, but that you are *illegitimate*! Can this be true?'

Tommy stared at her aghast. It was clear that the possibility of our discovering the full extent of his secret had never crossed his mind. 'Not at all. It is entirely false,' he babbled, falling over his words in his eagerness to convince us. 'Who told you such nonsense? Whoever it was has maligned my honour,' he protested, with precious little conviction in his tone.

'How we came upon these facts is immaterial. Nor is it *your* honour that concerns me, but my *daughter's*. What *matters*, young man, is that you have practised upon us a gross deception.'

'I swear I am not illegitimate. Mr Harris is indeed my uncle and nothing more.'

'Whatever the truth of your birth, you are giving the impression that my daughter is a kept woman, when she is no such thing. If you truly love her and wish to continue seeing her, then you must forthwith publicly declare her status as your legally married wife.'

Knowing how she inwardly raged, I marvelled at my mother's composure, and keeping my own emotions carefully in check, I chipped in with a comment of my own. 'Either you agree to introduce me to your family as your wife, or I shall accept Mr Garrick's offer and go on the stage after all.' Perhaps a part of me still longed for the latter solution, but I was again disappointed.

Tommy was instantly contrite. 'I confess I am nervous of

offending my uncle. I need to be cautious as he could well cut me out of his will altogether should I marry without his consent.'

My husband looked so devastated, so anxious, that I couldn't help but feel some sympathy for him. Yet I pressed on. 'Since the deed is done, that is a risk you've already taken. Therefore, I insist upon my position being made plain. Would you prefer your "uncle" to discover that you had put me in the family way without the benefit of the church's blessing?'

All colour drained from his cheeks. 'You are not . . .?'

'It is difficult to be certain about such matters,' I said, gently putting one hand to my flat stomach to deliberately imply that I might be. Why should I be the only one to worry? He did not know that my courses had come as normal this month.

Mama again intervened, her expression stern and unyielding. 'I will not stand by in silence and see my daughter's reputation irrevocably damaged. This marriage must be made public at once, or we will take the matter into our own hands and you will not like the repercussions. It will be *your* honour in ribbons then.'

Tommy swallowed, then grasped my hands in his. 'We will leave at once for Bristol. Once you are settled there I will go on alone to South Wales, to herald your arrival and prepare the way, as it were. I will return for you when I am sure you will be given a cordial welcome.'

This wasn't quite what I'd hoped to hear. 'And how long might that take, pray? How am I expected to cope alone, in Bristol?' I had no wish for my relatives to see how I'd allowed myself to be duped by this man's lies.

'I shall see that you have a few guineas for your keep, and the name of a friend you can apply to for more, if necessary.' Turning to Mama, he added, 'Then I will happily present Mary, as my bride, to my uncle.'

'Splendid!' Mama said. 'And I shall accompany the pair of you as far as Bristol, so that my daughter will not be left alone.'

'There really is no need, I will take good care of her,' Tommy protested.

Mama gave him a chilling smile. 'There is every need, if you are to leave her unattended. While her father is absent it is my responsibility to ensure that my daughter's honour is properly protected, at least until her new status is publicly acknowledged.'

Seeing that my mother would not be moved on this point, Tommy had little choice but to concede defeat, and hire a carriage large enough for three.

Tommy made something of a tour of our journey to Bristol, stopping off at Oxford to visit various colleges, and pausing to admire the palace at Blenheim. I believe he was attempting to pacify my aggrieved mother. Once we arrived in Bristol she took great satisfaction in meeting up with old friends and family again, and was determined to keep up appearances by presenting her new son-in-law as a young man of considerable expectations. For his part, Tommy wasted no time in leaving for Tregunter in Carmarthenshire, as promised.

After four months of marriage I was growing accustomed to my new husband, to his inherent weakness and impulsiveness, and although love did not form the basis of our relationship I did feel a certain sense of duty and honour towards him. He was not a difficult or an unpleasant man, if a rather foolish and devious one, and was ever kind to me.

As we waited impatiently for Tommy to return from his mission to have me accepted by his family, Mama and I could not resist visiting the minster house where I had been born. Walking those same paths upon which my infant feet had trod filled me with a sweet nostalgia. Had the place always looked so dark and gloomy, the paint peeling and the house so decrepit? I wondered.

'Look Mama, here is where I would climb upon that long stone bench, and here crawl beneath the brass eagle in the middle aisle, under which I would sit and childishly sing with the anthem, or chant the morning service.'

'You were ever a sensitive and dreamy child,' Mama agreed with a sigh, almost as if she had never quite understood my passion for the rhythm of words and verse, this other world I occupied inside my head. Even now, poems would emerge almost of their own volition which I would scribble in my notebook in some private moment. Tommy didn't understand my passion either, calling it an obsession.

One afternoon when we returned to our lodgings, I was handed a letter from my husband, announcing his safe arrival at Tregunter.

'At last we have news,' I said, ripping it open to quickly scan the contents. 'Tommy says his uncle is disposed to act handsomely. He did not at first dare admit to the fact we were already wed, implying we were merely affianced, fearful of abruptly announcing that he had been already some months a husband.'

Mama clicked her tongue in annoyance. 'The man is a coward as well as a liar!'

I read on. 'He did admit the truth in the end, to which Mr Harris responded: "If the thing is done, it cannot be undone." His uncle also expresses a hope that the object of his nephew's choice is not too young, "as a young wife cannot mend a man's fortune!" Oh dear, I fear he is to be disappointed in that regard too, although Tommy has told him that I am nearly seventeen!'

'Yet another lie. You are but fifteen and a few months.'

'Mama, please, what does a small fib about age matter? Mr Harris hopes that I am not handsome as he says "beauty without money is but a dangerous sort of portion".'

I couldn't help but smile even as my mother very nearly exploded with fury. 'Is he accusing you of using your beauty to advantage in some dishonourable manner?'

'As you well know, Mama, I am a woman of pride as well as passion, and well able to speak up for myself.'

'Indeed you are. And passion for poetry, rather than the less salubrious sort. Has Mr Harris agreed to see you?'

'He says if it is true that I am a gentlewoman, then he can have no reason to refuse.'

'I am relieved to hear it,' Mama drily remarked.

'Tommy concludes by saying that he will return shortly to fetch me.'

This news seemed to cheer her, but what I did not mention was that my husband's letter also urged me to write to a Mr John King, or 'Jew King' as he was more often addressed, a money broker who resided in Goodman's Fields. I was already acquainted with the gentleman as he had frequently called upon Mr Robinson during the first months of our marriage. When I'd enquired as to why he called so often, I'd been instructed to treat him with all due deference. It was made clear to me that he had lent my husband a considerable sum of money in lieu of his expectations. The fellow had even accompanied us for the first part of the journey as far as Oxford. Now Tommy wished me to request yet another small loan to pay for my travel arrangements to Wales. I felt rather dubious about this. I hated to be in debt to anyone, and he was not a man I particularly liked. But I did as my husband bid me without question, as a wife must.

The letters between Mr King and myself grew quite friendly over the following days, even a little flirtatious. While I might privately have wished to discourage him, I dare not, for the sake of the money my husband owed him, and the fact we needed more.

'. . . you express so much friendship, that the hardest task I ever undertook in my whole life, is how to return thanks suitable to the favours I have received from you . . .' I wrote, doing my utmost to sound polite.

He would flatter me with talk of the theatre and poetry, whereas Tommy cared little for such things. His letters could become quite amorous and I would remind him of my marital state. But should he imagine himself in love with me, then let the delusion stand for now, so long as he sent the money we craved.

When I thought I'd flattered him sufficiently, I tactfully explained how we were in need of his assistance. 'I shall depend on your promise this week for I am really distressed.'

His letters reminded me so much of London, and made me long for our return, but I was greatly relieved when my husband at last arrived to collect me.

The journey to Tregunter proved to be a nightmare. Crossing the River Severn to Chepstow in an open boat as it pitched and tossed against a strong tide was extremely perilous. We were drenched in equal parts by the rain and the water that washed over the sides of the vessel, the wind blowing up a terrible storm. It seemed as if every part of my life must be marked by a tempest.

'I pray you not to judge my uncle too harshly,' Tommy warned, holding my head as I voided the contents of my stomach yet again. In my misery I thought enviously of my mother safely left behind with friends in Bristol. 'He is an eccentric, living life as he chooses, with only my sister Betsy, and a housekeeper for company.'

I looked at him askance. 'You have a sister?'

He flushed crimson. 'I do.'

'How much more is there to discover about you, I wonder?'
The next day as we drove through the majestic panoply of the
Black Mountains, their summits swirled in wisps of white cloud,
Tommy urged me to conceal my true age. 'I have told my uncle
you are almost seventeen, let us fix upon that, shall we?'

I readily consented as I had no wish to appear a child.

Later, as we drove through the enchanting Wye Valley, I thought
I had never seen a more romantic, beautiful setting in all my life,
and was happily engrossed devising a poem in my head when
the post-boy drew the carriage to a halt outside Tregunter. It was
not at all what I had expected as a new mansion was in the
process of being built, meanwhile the family resided in one of
the estate cottages. But the estate itself appeared large and wooded,
so I quickly stepped down from the carriage, eager to meet my
new family.

My first sight of Mr Harris was of an old man dressed in a
brown fustian coat, a scarlet waistcoat bordered with gold braid,
and a pair of woollen spatter dashes. These were a form of leggings
that encased his lower legs from knee to shoe, rather than the
silk stockings one might expect a gentleman to wear. This rustic
image was topped off with a curly-brimmed tricorne hat trimmed
with gold lace. An eccentric indeed. But he embraced me most
cordially, offering a surprisingly warm welcome.

'How delightful to meet you at last,' he said, as if he had been
eagerly awaiting my arrival.

I dipped a polite curtsy. 'And I you, good sir. I have heard so
much about you from your nephew.' I rewarded him with my
most winning smile, and noted with some satisfaction how the
effect of my charms caused him to seemingly melt before my eyes.
Beauty was not then such a disadvantage, I thought, hiding a smile.

My sister-in-law, however, was another matter altogether.

'Allow me to introduce Miss Elizabeth Robinson, your
husband's sister,' Mr Harris said, indicating the frumpy young
woman who had come to stand at his side.

If I thought it odd that he referred to her as such, and not as
any relation to himself, I didn't have long to reflect upon the
puzzle. Small of stature with ruddy cheeks and a snub nose that
turned sharply up at the point, she barely grasped the tips of my
fingers longer than a second, her plain face rigid with disapproval.

Her gown was of chintz, the gaudiest imaginable, and her cap a veritable profusion of coloured ribbons, making her look far older than her twenty years.

I, of course, was more modestly and stylishly attired in a dark claret riding habit, with a white beaver hat and feathers.

'Good afternoon,' she managed, mouth curling with distaste as her gaze flicked over me with great condescension. 'Goodness, Tom, I'm surprised a lawyer's wife finds it necessary to dress like a duchess.' And tossing back her head with haughty disdain, she spun on her heel and led me into the house, her spine as stiff as if a steel rod held it in place.

'Do not rise to her cattiness,' Tommy whispered in my ear, as he followed me inside. 'It will only make matters worse.'

I would not demean myself, I thought.

There was yet another person for me to meet, as the house was run under the strict jurisdiction of a crabby old housekeeper, a Mary Edwards, or Mrs Molly as I dubbed her. She seemed to be ever present, sat next to Mr Harris at table, and even joined us in the parlour of an evening. A more overbearing, vindictive spirit never inhabited the heart of mortal than that which pervaded the soul of the ill-natured Mrs Molly. If she made any effort to make my stay comfortable, I was not aware of it. No warming pan was put in our bed, no breakfast brought to our chamber, my clothes were not laid out or put away for me, nor even brushed.

'She has much to do,' Tommy said, when I complained. 'And I can keep you warm at night.'

I turned from him with an irritated sigh. This visit was not turning out well.

Fortunately, I soon became quite a favourite with his 'uncle', or the squire as he liked to be called. Not that I saw much of him as he was seldom in the house, save for meal times. He would be out from sunrise to dusk, riding his small Welsh pony about his large estate as he conducted business with the tenants. Squire Harris was indefatigable in his duties, and as justice of the peace and a strong Methodist, he would entertain us with tales of how he frequently fined the locals for bad language, despite his own oaths peppering every third sentence.

But he was never anything but the perfect gentleman towards

me, and most friendly, while the hearts of Miss Betsy and Mrs Molly were cold as stone. They saw me as an interloper, nothing more than a gold-digger who had married Tommy for his money. Always supposing there was to be any inheritance, of course. Both ladies clearly nursed the fervent wish that I'd never set foot in their house, which filled me with sadness and a silent fury.

If anyone, either a neighbour paying a call, or worse, the squire himself, offered anything approaching a compliment on my good looks or choice of gown, they would glance at each other with eyes burning with envy, as if I were a threat of some sort.

I freely confess that I probably did flirt a little with gentlemen guests, but then I was most dreadfully bored. There was little in the way of entertainment at Tregunter, save to drink ale with the squire in the evenings, and attend the Methodist chapel with him on Sundays. Most days I would ride out with Miss Betsy, although I confess I had great difficulty in stifling my mirth over her choice of costume. She would drape a coarse garment made from goat's hair, which she called a camlet, about her shoulders, and wear a high crowned bonnet.

'I see no necessity for a fancy beaver hat, or fashionable riding habit,' she coolly chided me, as I artlessly queried this rigout.

I was delighted to discover the cottage housed a harpsichord, and a fine selection of books in the library. But any hope I had of enjoying either, was soon quashed.

'A good housewife has no occasion for either music or books,' Miss Betsy tartly informed me. 'It is all very well to appear accomplished, but you have no money to support such fancy ways.'

I endured her caustic comments with as much patience as I could muster, but I viewed both these two ladies with pity in my heart. What care I how they judged me? Did I not have beauty, charm, elegance and style, all of which attributes they were sadly lacking?

But then one day Squire Harris kissed my hand and said, 'I would take you for wife myself, were you not already married to Tom.' For all he was old enough to be my grandfather, I was filled with trepidation that he appeared to be declaring himself in love with me.

'I think, Tommy, it is time we took our leave.'

My husband agreed, but on the morning of our departure Squire Harris announced he would accompany us to Bristol. Miss Betsy hastily attempted to intervene.

'I'm sure that will not be necessary, Squire. Tom and his wife will survive the journey perfectly well without your assistance.'

'The weather is most inclement for the crossing,' Mrs Molly hastily put in. 'You had far better remain safely at home.'

'Nonsense, I shall see the dear girl safely across the channel, and look forward to meeting your mama, Mary.'

Squire Harris quite took to my mother, and Mama reciprocated by introducing him to her many friends, all highly respectable. The four of us became quite the social gadabouts, and were invited to several dinner parties, while I continued to be something of an idol in his eyes. He would take any opportunity to dance with me, and after a glass or two of ale or wine, would sing to me, declaring that I was the most delightful of beings. He even sought my advice on new refurbishments for Tregunter House, and I helped him to pick out new marble chimney pieces.

'Choose them as you like, Mrs Robinson, for they are all for you and Tom when I am no more.'

So far as my husband was concerned, it was a comforting prospect that ultimately his 'uncle' intended Tregunter House and estate to pass to him.

Three

Young Lady About Town

The busy world, the sylvan plain,
Alike confess thy potent reign.
Queen of the motley garb – at thy command
Fashion waves her flow'ry wand;

Mary Darby Robinson
'Ode to Vanity'

The moment Squire Harris tired of Bristol and left for South
Wales, Tommy and I set out at once for London. I felt a deep
sense of relief, coupled with excitement, as I had greatly missed
being in town.

'Now that our future is secure and my prospects confirmed by
the kindness of my uncle, we can make ourselves more comfortable,'
Tommy announced, and the moment we arrived he immediately
set about finding us new quarters.

As we could now live together openly as man and wife, we
rented a newly built house at Number 13, Hatton Garden, a
district popular with the newly prosperous, whether they be
merchants or moneylenders. We then commenced to furnish it
with particular elegance. Tommy hired servants, purchased new
clothes for us both, and bought a phaeton and a pair of greys,
plus a saddle horse for his own use.

'Are you quite certain we can afford all of this?' I would ask
when my husband agreed to the purchase of silk wallpaper, or a
beautiful Persian carpet.

'I do assure you that in every respect I am perfectly competent
of arranging our finances.' He always grew irritable when I ques-
tioned him about money, implying I knew nothing. This was
probably true since as a child I'd never needed to consider the
cost of anything, not until Papa left.

And now I was to enter society – a thrilling prospect.

'If the stage has been denied me, then at least I shall step out and make my debut in the broad hemisphere of fashionable folly,' I announced with dramatic vehemence.

'You will dazzle all with your beauty, my love,' Tommy agreed, thrilling me to the core. 'We shall begin with the pleasure gardens of Ranelagh this very evening.'

'Oh, but I have nothing suitable to wear,' I cried, in a typically feminine fluster.

He cupped my face between his hands and kissed me most sweetly. 'Whatever you choose to wear, you will be the most beautiful woman present.' He then presented me with a most expensive watch, beautifully enamelled with musical trophies. I was moved by his generosity, my heart warming to his compliments and kindness.

I decided that as all the fashionable ladies would be wearing elaborate gowns of satin or silk, no doubt much beruffled and flounced, I would present the very opposite picture.

I wore my simple Quaker gown which ensured that I stood out. It was of light brown lustring with close round cuffs. I left my auburn curls unpowdered, upon which I pinned a plain round cap and white chip hat, without any ornament whatsoever. And indeed on this, our first visit, it proved to be a most satisfying evening. All eyes were upon me as we strolled among the groves.

I had been launched upon society in complete triumph.

Tommy and I soon became regulars both at Ranelagh and Vauxhall. I enjoyed the former for its classier style, the concerts at the Rotunda, the pretty Chinese pavilion and the exciting allure of knowing I might meet a lord on the turn of a path. Riff-raff were deterred from attending by the half-crown entrance fee. The latter I loved for its music and artworks. Vauxhall's wooded wilderness of elm, lime and sycamore were a delight, as was strolling down the romantic Druids Walk for a candlelight supper of cold meats, salad and cheese, custards and tarts.

We also enjoyed attending balls, concerts and masques at the newly opened Pantheon in Oxford Street, which was rapidly becoming the most fashionable place for the wealthy to assemble or listen to music.

The very first time we attended the Pantheon I spent hours

at my toilette in order to make the best of myself, not an easy task as I was by then with child, and my increasing figure required some artful disguise. Deciding, as always, to be my own woman, I again declined to wear the fashionable hoop the court ladies wore, which I thought clumsy and unflattering. Instead I chose a simple gown of pale pink satin trimmed with broad sable, enriched with some delicate point lace which my dear mother had presented to me.

The moment we entered through the colonnades, I sighed with pleasure, entranced by the magic of the scene. 'Goodness, how very splendid it all is. And just look at this magnificent dome, so typically Roman with its ornate plasterwork, classical statuary in niches, and the double tier of elegant boxes.'

'The most splendid box is the one in the centre, which belongs to the royal family,' Tommy informed me.

I looked at him, eyes shining. 'Are you saying that we might meet a royal prince?'

My husband laughed at my childish excitement. 'We might indeed.'

The gilded company, in particular the beauty of the ladies, far excelled even the amazing architecture, certainly to my naïvely innocent gaze. These included Lady Almeria Carpenter, who was lady-in-waiting to the Duchess of Gloucester; the famous actress, Mrs Baddeley; the Countess of Tyrconnel; and the celebrated beauty the Marchioness Townshend.

I settled myself upon a sofa to observe the rich and famous promenade in their courtly hoops and towering hair styles, all powdered, perfumed, and lavishly decorated with high-flown feathers, flowers and extravagant bows. The buzz of the room was utterly thrilling, but I soon became aware that while I drank in the glories of the fashionable scene, others were watching me with equal attention.

Two dandies, who appeared to be flirting with the marchioness, glanced towards me, and one loudly enquired of the other, 'Who is she?'

The caustic impertinence in his tone startled me, and I was on my feet in an instant, taking my husband's arm. 'I fear I am turning into a curiosity. Perhaps we should take a stroll, or return home for supper.'

Tommy chuckled. 'As you wish, my dear, although it is not to be wondered at that you are the centre of attention.' The whispered questions grew louder as we promenaded, occasionally pausing to talk to friends, and I became increasingly shy and ill at ease.

'Who is that young lady in the pink dress trimmed with sable?'

'Who can she be?'

'Can she be a courtesan?'

'Surely not, although she has a pretty face.'

'I have not seen her about town before.'

'Nay, I think I spotted her at Vauxhall, but I know not her name.'

Their brazen impudence unnerved me, but then one gentleman, who looked vaguely familiar, said, 'I believe I do know her. It is Miss Darby, or am I mistaken?' And he bowed to me with a marked civility.

It was the Earl of Northington, my father's patron who had been so welcoming to me as a young girl. I was most relieved to see a familiar face.

'You are quite correct, my lord, or at least I was Miss Darby. My name now is Mrs Robinson.' I indicated my husband, upon whose arm I rested one trembling hand.

'Then I hope I may be permitted to pay my respects and join you.' Much to my surprise and delight, Lord Northington proceeded to walk round the Pantheon with us.

'How is your father?' he politely enquired. 'Still on his expedition I expect, which will hopefully be more successful than the last.'

'Indeed, sir.'

'May I also compliment you on the improvement in your own person, Mrs Robinson. You have grown into quite a charming young lady.'

'Thank you.' I could feel my cheeks start to burn, very likely caused by the heat of the rotunda, or else my condition, and I suddenly came over all faint.

Seeing my distress, Tommy quickly led me to the tea room where sadly there was not a single seat to be had. Fortunately he found a sofa close to the door where there was at least a breath of fresh air, and sat stroking my hand while Lord Northington hurried off in search of refreshment for me.

Two gentlemen approached, whom Tommy cheerfully welcomed. 'Ah, here are two of my good friends,' he said, and proceeded to present Lord Lyttelton and Captain Ayscough.

Minutes later, Lord Northington returned with a dish of tea, which I accepted with heartfelt gratitude, quietly sipping it while the men talked and joked together. Knowing that I was anxious to depart, my husband went in search of the carriage while I hovered in the vestibule.

'You would be welcome to use my carriage,' Lord Lyttelton offered.

'There's really no need.' I had never met the fellow until that evening, but found the intensity of his gaze upon me somewhat disturbing, as if he were stripping away the gauze of my gown to view the naked flesh beneath. I was greatly relieved when Tommy returned to say that the carriage was ready.

We swiftly departed, but this introduction marked the start of a difficult period in my life, one in which I soon discovered that beauty could be a curse as well as a bounty.

The following morning I received three callers: Lord Northington, Lord Lyttelton, and Colonel Ayscough. Naïve as I was, I made no protest as they insisted I receive them, despite my husband not being present. I may have been a wife in legal terms, but at heart I was still little more than a child, albeit one soon to become a mother. I was dressed somewhat déshabillé, nor was I wearing any powder or paint, which no doubt enhanced my youthful appearance. Lord Lyttelton instantly commented upon it.

'I had not realised how very young you are,' he coyly remarked. 'In my opinion no woman under thirty years of age is worth admiring, even the antiquity of forty is preferable to the insipidity of sixteen.'

That he should say such a thing to me, on so short an acquaintance was appalling. I felt myself grow hot with embarrassment. The man was loathsome, his manners utterly abhorrent. 'Are you implying, sir, that I am too young to be attractive, or even to be married?

He feigned an expression of distress. 'Oh dear, have I made the pretty child angry?'

I knew in that instant this man would be a thorn in my

side. And so it proved. Lord Lyttelton led my husband away from
the domestic felicity we had happily built together, and, much
to Tommy's detriment, into a riotous life of gambling and drinking
with his aristocratic friends. Lyttelton continued to taunt me over
my absent spouse.

'Dear me, has the child been deserted,' he would say on finding
me alone yet again, caustically using this description in order to
belittle me. 'How sad to be a neglected wife.'

His supercilious attitude made me detest him all the more, and
I resolved not to respond. Instead, I buried myself in my writing,
applying myself to my poetry, which he would also ridicule.

'Amusing yourself by feigning a talent, I see. I seem to recall
Robinson mentioning that previous to your marriage you were
about to appear on stage in the role of Cordelia. How very daring!
Presumably, having failed at becoming an actress you have now
set your heart upon becoming a poet? A nobler ambition, perhaps,
if, as you say, one requiring a particular skill.'

I gritted my teeth and made no reply.

'I shall dub you Poetess Corry, in honour of the role you
never played.' At which jibe he roared with laughter, as if amused
by his own wit. But he was not done with me yet. 'I dare say
even bad poetry is some compensation against the neglect of a
husband who prefers the society of libertine men and abandoned
women.'

This from a man who was so sunk in dissipation that he had
recently abandoned his own wife of less than a year to run off
to Paris with a barmaid, whom he had no doubt also deserted.
His reputation was such that even being in the same room with
him could easily ruin my own, and possibly already had. Our
unwelcome alliance had recently featured in the gossip sheets,
Lyttelton being anonymously described as a 'Libertine Maceroni
who was laying siege upon a Mrs R-'.

I shuddered at the horror of it. 'God can bear witness to the
purity of my soul,' I wrote to Mama, anxious that she hear these
attacks upon my good character from my own hand.

Lyttelton was, I decided, overbearing and insolent, slovenly of
person, and the most accomplished libertine that any age or
country has ever produced. How I loathed his vulgar pride. Yet
my husband was flattered by this aristocratic friendship, and would

readily go off with him each morning about some mischief I'd rather not be aware. Gambling away more money we did not have, no doubt.

When next Lord Lyttelton called at Hatton Garden, I instructed my maid to inform him that I was not at home. She did so, only to return seconds later with the message that he wished to speak with me most urgently on a matter of grave importance. There seemed no alternative but to admit him, and at first sight I could see he was in some distress.

'I have a most confidential matter to impart to you, dear child, one of considerable moment to your interest and happiness.'

I started. 'Nothing, I trust in heaven, has befallen my husband!'

Lord Lyttelton regarded me with sadness in his gaze. 'How little does that husband deserve the solicitude of such a wife! I fear that I have in some degree aided in alienating his conjugal affections.'

Irritated by this fabricated sympathy, my response was brusque. 'Speak briefly, my lord.'

Fixing his gaze upon mine, he said. 'Very well, I must inform you that your husband is the most false and undeserving of that name! He has formed a connection with a woman of abandoned character, and lavishes on her those means of subsistence which you will shortly stand in need of yourself.'

I was horrified. 'I do not believe it!'

'Then I must attempt to convince you that I speak true. Remember that if you admit it was I who revealed his secret, I shall be obliged to fight Robinson in a duel, for he never will forgive me.'

A hollow sickness opened up inside. I had felt little in the way of love towards my husband at the start of our marriage, yet an affection had grown between us, and I'd believed utterly in his devotion and loyalty towards me. 'It cannot be true,' I weakly protested. 'You have been misinformed.'

'By whom pray, the woman who usurps your place in the affections of your husband? For it was from she that I received this information.'

'What is the name of this woman?' Even as I asked the question I had no wish to hear the answer.

'A Harriet Wilmot. She resides in Soho where your husband

visits her daily. You waste your affections on such a man, dear child. Leave him! Robinson is ruined, his debts such that nothing but destruction awaits you.'

I half expected to faint, or at least burst into tears, on hearing such devastating news in my delicate condition. Instead, I felt a deep and burning anger at Tommy's betrayal, although even more so at this man whom I blamed entirely for my husband's fall from grace. 'If that is true, then it is because *you* have sunk him by luring him into the foul habits of gambling and womanising.'

Lyttelton softly chuckled at my vehemence. 'I assure you, he needed no lessons from me upon either subject. But if you do not believe me, go and see for yourself. If you are truly the woman of spirit you make yourself out to be, then be revenged. My fortune is at your disposal. You have only to command my powers and I will gladly serve you.'

'Do you take me for a simpleton?' This rapacious rake was no doubt skilled in the art of disposing of the husband so that he might all the easier seduce the wife. In my case, he would fail utterly in this most nefarious mission.

I at once took a hackney coach and proceeded to the address of my rival, which Lord Lyttelton had given me.

By the time I arrived at the lodgings of Miss Harriet Wilmot, I felt sick with misery and waited impatiently while the coachman rattled the door knocker. A grubby looking servant girl opened the door.

'The mistress is not at home,' she stated, with very little conviction in her bored tone.

Stepping down from the coach, I adopted my haughtiest air and strode past her into the hall. All of a fluster, the maid fled, promising to inform her mistress that she had a visitor.

Walking straight into the drawing room I couldn't resist doing a little exploring while I waited. Opening the chamber door I saw a new white lustring sacque and petticoat lying on the bed. I was examining it with open curiosity, wondering if my own husband had provided these garments for her, when suddenly the woman herself appeared before me.

She was tall and rather handsome, if some years older than me, dressed in a gown of printed Irish muslin with a black gauze cloak thrown about her shoulders. On her head she wore a chip hat trimmed with pale lilac ribbons. On seeing me she appeared confused, almost fearful, and turned pale to the lips.

'No need to be alarmed. I came only to enquire whether or not you are acquainted with a Mr Robinson?' I smiled at her, wishing for an honest answer rather than revenge.

'I am, he visits me frequently.' Drawing off a glove, Miss Wilmot rubbed a hand over her cheek in a pensive fashion, as if fearful of what I might ask next.

I instantly recognised the ring she was wearing as belonging to my husband, and my heart contracted with pain. Seeing my interest she quickly covered it with her other hand, her gaze flicking over me, taking in the betraying swell of my belly. My condition was thinly disguised beneath a morning déshabillé gown of India muslin, which I wore with a simple bonnet of straw. Draped about my shoulders was a white lawn cloak bordered with lace.

'You are Mr Robinson's wife, are you not?' she asked, a tremor in her voice. 'If this ring was yours, pray take it.' Tugging it from her finger she thrust it at me.

I ignored the gesture. 'No, thank you.'

'Had I known that Mr Robinson was the husband of such a woman, in such a condition . . .'

I turned to leave, not troubling to answer, or respond to her pleas of guilt. My cheeks might burn with humiliation but I walked to the door, chin held high.

'I never will see him more, I swear,' she cried, hurrying after me. 'He is a most unworthy man. I never again will receive him.'

I paused to politely incline my head before calmly departing with every shred of my dignity intact.

It was not until the following morning that I mentioned to my husband that I had met Miss Wilmot. He stared at me aghast, but made no attempt to deny that he knew her.

'*I* did not seek her out,' he protested. 'It was no fault of mine. Lord Lyttelton suggested I call upon her. I did not intend to betray you, my love.'

I gazed upon him with cold indifference. 'Yet you did.'

'How did you discover her? Who was it that informed you of my conduct?'

'That is of no matter.'

He guessed, of course, that the person responsible for revealing his secret was the very same who had mired him in this tangle of infidelity in the first place, that he had himself been betrayed. Sadly, my weak husband was too proud to accuse Lyttelton of such treachery, or to eschew this dangerous friendship. Poor, foolish Tommy was convinced that Lord Lyttelton's influence at court would shortly gain him some honourable and lucrative position which would be to his benefit.

I was by now quite well known, with many female friends, and often attended card parties at the house of Mrs Parry, a woman of considerable talents, and the author of the novel *Eden Vale*. It was here that I met the actress, Mrs Abbington. I thought her a most lively and bewitching woman, and my mind turned with regret to my own hopes for a theatrical career. But it was liberating to talk with intelligent women, as sadly too much of my time was spent in the company introduced to us by Lord Lyttelton.

Among them was a George Robert Fitzgerald, the dangerous Irish duellist known as Fighting Fitzgerald. Despite his reputation, oddly enough I felt more comfortable with him than I did with Lyttelton. His manner was quite charming, or so I at first thought. 'Jew' King was also a regular visitor.

'Why does that fellow call so frequently?' I asked Tommy, irritated at finding the money lender constantly in my home.

'Do not meddle in matters that don't concern you.'

I guessed that these visits were connected with the large debt my husband had accumulated previous to our marriage, which, far from being paid off, was growing daily. But since any comments I made on the subject were dismissed, I said no more.

One evening, at Mr Fitzgerald's suggestion, a party of us visited Vauxhall. As it was a warm, balmy night, the gardens were crowded. We supped by the statue of Handel, and did not leave until the early hours. By then there was only my husband, Mr Fitzgerald and myself left. There was a disturbance, no doubt some drink-fuelled quarrel or threatened duel, there were many such, and the two men ran off to investigate. I almost followed them, but then thought it more prudent to remain in our box, considering my condition. Moments later, Fitzgerald returned.

'Where is my husband?' I asked, instantly concerned.

'We thought you had gone, so he went to look for you by the entrance. Allow me to conduct you to the door, where I'm sure we'll find him.'

'Thank you. He will be most concerned for me.' Taking his arm, we hurried towards the entrance on Vauxhall Road. Tommy was not there.

'Where can he be?' I was beginning to feel rather alarmed.

'No need to fret,' Fitzgerald said, attempting to soothe me. 'He has no doubt gone to fetch the carriage.'

'I cannot recall where we left it, but I know it was some distance away.'

'I could always transport you home myself. My chaise is around here somewhere,' he said, glancing about.

'There is really no need. I shall wait by the entrance for Tommy. If I am not here when he returns, he will be worried.'

'Where can the fellow have gone? I left him here not five minutes ago,' Fitzgerald grumbled. These words were barely out of his mouth when he stopped abruptly as a servant, holding open the door of a vehicle, appeared in front of us. 'Ah, here is my chaise. Allow me to be of service.'

I looked at it in surprise, instantly suspicious. 'Goodness, there are four horses harnessed to it, rather a large number for so small a vehicle, do you not think?'

He smiled at me. 'I like to be well prepared for any eventuality.'

'Such as finding a lady without transport?'

'Indeed!' He grinned, and I felt his arm come about my waist as he half lifted me on to the step of the chaise, the servant now keeping his distance.

To my horror, by the light of a lamp I caught the glint of a pistol in the pocket of the open door. What was going on? Surely the fellow did not mean to abduct me? Such tricks were almost common place in certain quarters and I began to resist, panic rising in my breast.

'Sir, what mean you by such conduct? Release me this instant or I shall scream.'

He paused only a moment to whisper in my ear, 'Robinson can but fight me, and I have not lost a duel yet.'

I can scarcely describe the extent of my fear at that moment, but somehow I found the strength to force him to loose his hold. I had half-turned to run when I saw Tommy striding towards me, calling out my name.

'Ah, there you are, Robinson!' Fitzgerald remarked with an easy nonchalance.

I flung myself into my husband's arms. 'We have been looking everywhere for you, Tommy.'

'And very nearly made the mistake of taking the wrong carriage,' Fitzgerald airily remarked. 'Mrs Robinson is alarmed beyond expression.'

I could say nothing to this, but was thankful to have my husband help me into our own carriage and drive home. Tommy appeared to have noticed nothing untoward, no doubt putting my distress down to my delicate condition, and the very reasonable explanation given by his friend. Alarming as the situation was, I consoled myself that it could have been far worse, had Tommy not appeared when he did. But since I could not prove what Fitzgerald's true intentions had been, and had no wish to risk my husband's life in a duel, I said no more on the subject. I simply avoided being alone with this dangerous Irishman in future. He continued to call upon me but eventually, when I was never 'at home', he gave up, no doubt turning his unwelcome attentions upon some other naïve female.

The poor state of our finances meant that we could no longer afford to stay at Hatton Garden and we removed to a house at Finchley, lent to us by a friend. I hoped to remain here at least until my child was safely born, and happily filled my days sewing pretty little muslin dresses, delicately trimmed with lace or ribbon.

'Only a few short years ago I was making silly little frocks for my dolls,' I said to Mama, smiling at the memory. 'Now I am soon to become a mother myself.'

'And a fine one you will make, dearest,' she assured me, fetching a stool upon which to rest my feet. 'But no more gallivanting. See that you take plenty of rest.'

'I assure you, Mama, I have no wish to go anywhere. I do not pine for public attention, and it is a great solace to have your company again, after your long stay in Bristol.'

'Mr Robinson's social life, however, appears to continue unabated.'

I heard the slight note of censure in her tone, but did not respond to it. 'I am content to amuse myself with the poetry I love.' Anxious as I was about the approaching birth, and my husband's debts, my writing was the one thing that kept me sane. Even as we talked I was scribbling down lines.

'Perhaps you should curtail your visits into town,' I suggested later to Tommy. 'In view of our straitened circumstances.'

'I have already explained that the matter is in hand,' he snapped, and continued his daily outings, sometimes accompanied by my young brother, George, who was visiting us at the time. The boy loved any excuse to ride his pony.

After returning from one of these trips, my brother chanced to mention that the pair of them had been to Marylebone, and that he had waited and held Mr Robinson's horse while my husband made a morning visit.

'But we have no acquaintance residing in Marylebone, that I can think of,' I said, rather puzzled. 'Where, in Marylebone, exactly, did you go?'

He carelessly shrugged, as boys do. 'I don't know, but he was some time inside. I grew tired of waiting.'

I was instantly alert. 'Ask to wait inside next time, and take more notice. Then report to me what you see.'

A few days later my brother came to me again with a tale. 'You mustn't let Mr Robinson know that I told you this, Mary, or he'll never take me anywhere again. He agreed to allow me inside only if I didn't say a word to you, and I did pay more attention, as you asked. He was visiting a lady, and she must be a very good friend of his.'

I felt an all-too-familiar sinking sense of betrayal. 'What makes you say so?'

He gave that little shrug again, more sheepish this time. 'By the way they talked to each other, and how he looked at her. She's quite pretty.'

Even a youth scarcely in his teens could draw conclusions of no favourable nature, and a deep sadness enfolded my heart.

My brother continued. 'I noticed a watch lying on the mantelshelf, Mary, very like the one that Mr Robinson once gave you. It was all enamelled and with musical trophies on a steel chain.'

Now my heart almost stopped beating as I had supposed this gift to have been sold off in the general loss of our property when my husband had been settling some of his debts. I wasted no time in challenging him on the subject.

'Do not blame my brother for this, but I know about your latest mistress, and that you presented her with a gift that was once mine.'

A flush of shame crept into his cheeks, although he made no attempt to deny my claim, rather the opposite as he immediately admitted his infidelity. 'I had no money to give her.'

'So you paid her with my watch.'

'I shall retrieve it for you.'

I gave him the benefit of my most scathing glance. 'I would not touch it ever again. She is welcome to it, and to you.'

He put his arms about me then, softly kissing my cheek. 'You know you don't mean that, Mary, my love. I am truly sorry. It is but the anxiety over our financial difficulties, and your current condition, that took me from the comfort of your arms. We must, I fear, move again before our creditors press us further. We shall leave for Tregunter first thing in the morning.'

I was horrified. 'Oh, please, no. I cannot leave my beloved mother when I am so close to my time. I need her!'

'I am sorry, my love, but you will be well taken care of by my family.'

'I very much doubt it.' Knowing that I would be obliged to once again tolerate the scorn of Miss Betsy and Mrs Molly filled me with trepidation. 'Why cannot she come with us so that she may attend me?' I already knew the answer from the sadness in his eyes.

'We cannot impose yet another uninvited guest upon my uncle.'

I felt I had no choice but to go along with the plan, albeit in a fit of sulks. We set out once more on the arduous journey to South Wales, despite my being only a few short weeks from giving birth.

The welcome we received on our arrival was even worse than I'd feared. Clearly they had been forewarned of our precarious financial state as Miss Betsy scarcely spoke a word to me, and

Mrs Molly was even more difficult than before. Squire Harris was from home, but even he, when he returned shortly after our arrival, greeted us with cold contempt.

'So you have escaped prison. Have you come here to do penance for your follies? You had much better have married a good tradesman's daughter, Tom, than the child of a ruined merchant incapable of earning a living.'

Leaving my husband to answer that charge, I fled to our old chamber where I wept tears of bitter misery.

The squire did not soften his stance towards Tommy, or me, in any way. One evening there was a large party invited to dinner, including two members of Parliament and their wives, and an old clergyman of the name of Jones. This latter gentleman elicited from me that I was but two weeks from my confinement.

'How wonderful that you are here in time to give Tregunter a new little stranger,' he said, and turning to Mr Harris, added, 'And fortunate that you were able to finish your house in time for a nursery.'

'Not at all,' replied Mr Harris with a caustic laugh. 'They came here because prison doors were open to receive them.'

I felt my cheeks burn with humiliation as an awkward silence fell upon the gathered guests. My husband was silently seething with fury, barely able to contain himself, yet somehow managed to hold his tongue out of duty.

In fact the manor house was not yet completed, and a few days later Squire Harris called me to his study. 'I'm afraid there is no nursery, and I have no accommodation for your approaching confinement.'

'Then where am I supposed to go?'

'You cannot simply turn her out,' Tommy protested. 'This is no fault of hers. And she *is* my wife!'

After lengthy family argument in which I took no part, it was decided that I should remove to Trevecca House, a place about a mile and a half distant.

'At least we will be together,' I softly reminded my husband who was beside himself with fury.

He gave me a bleak look. 'I cannot stay with you, dearest, much as I would like to. I must find some way to settle our debts and stave off our creditors.'

It seemed I was to be all alone, save for a servant woman, in the wilds of South Wales, when I presented this miserable world with my firstborn child.

I was not, after all, to be entirely solitary as Trevecca House also housed the Huntingdon Methodist Seminary. It was set at the foot of a mountain, one I dubbed the Sugarloaf because of its shape. The building was large, and a part of it had also been converted into a flannel manufactory.

Yet despite being surrounded by activity on all sides, I found it a great relief no longer to be subjected to the tyranny of Miss Betsy and Mrs Molly. They never called, neither did Squire Harris, even if I was no more than a mile and a half from Tregunter, an easy ride. Nor did my husband visit, though what he was doing to resolve our difficulties I had no idea. It seemed I had formed a union with a family who treated me as the most abject of beings, and I was obliged to endure their ignorance and haughty manner, as well as my husband's neglect.

Fortunately my spirit was able to rise above their powers to wound, much as the mountain towered over the white battlements of my habitation. At least I could wander at will and marvel at the soft wisps of cloud that misted their blue peaks. I would stroll along wooded paths, the trees, wintry branches spangled with the frosty dew of morning! Or I would sit at my parlour window and watch the pale moonbeams dart amidst the old yew trees that shaded our little garden.

'Oh, God of Nature! Sovereign of the universe of wonders! How fervently do I adore thee!'

The poet in me came to life once again as I happily scribbled my thoughts down on paper. I saw it as a gift that I could appreciate the true wonders of creation, and was content to enjoy this period of tranquillity. The scene brought balm to my troubled soul, and I little regretted those of fashionable folly we had left behind.

It was with great joy that I shortly afterwards gave birth to my darling child – my Maria Elizabeth, born 18 October, 1774. I cannot describe the moment when I first held her to my breast, when I kissed her tiny hands, her soft cheeks. In that moment of miracle when I cradled my infant to my heart, I was overwhelmed with love. She was the most beautiful of babies, and I the happiest of mothers. Her very existence brought light and joy to my dreary existence.

My nurse, Mrs Jones, a most excellent woman who had cared for me with every attention, came to me a couple of days later with a request from the workers in the factory.

'They ask if they might see the young squire's baby, the little heiress to Tregunter.'

'Oh, but it is far too cold to take her out so soon.'

'Ah, no need to fear, madam. We will wrap her up warm. Infants in these parts are very often taken out on the very day of their birth. And we don't wish to cause offence by having you appear too *proud*, now do we?'

I quickly assured her that I did not. So wrapping Maria Elizabeth in a length of warm flannel from their own factory, I presented my daughter to them. What a joyous day that was! How they cheered me, the ladies all wanting to cuddle the baby, while the men heaped blessings on the little 'heiress of Tregunter', which was how they insisted on addressing her.

'They say she is the very image of her father,' Mrs Jones told me, and I felt the kind of sweet gratitude that any new mother feels on hearing their beloved offspring praised.

That same evening Squire Harris called at last. 'I trust you are well,' he said, somewhat dismissively.

'I am most healthy, thank you.'

Seating himself by my bed, without showing the slightest delicacy over the presence of Mrs Jones, he proceeded to interrogate me. 'So now you have her, what do you mean to do with the child?'

I was at a loss how to answer this, and as I remained silent he continued with his unwanted advice.

'I will tell you. Tie it to your back and work for it. Remember, prison still beckons, and Tom could easily die in a gaol, so what then would become of *you*?'

I shivered with horror but again made no response. Where was the point in arguing? He had made up his mind that his son, or nephew as he insisted on viewing him, was feckless, and I some heartless trollop who had married Tommy for his alleged inheritance.

Miss Betsy came next, her plump hands as tightly folded as

her prim lips. She glanced nonchalantly at my child, so innocently asleep in her crib. 'Poor little wretch! It would be a mercy if it pleased God to take it!'

Such callous words served only to harden my heart against them.

My precious child was blessed by God in the little church on the hillside above Talgarth when she was but a week old. But my sanctuary was soon breached as letters began to arrive at Tregunter for Tommy, who had by now returned, scarcely allowing any time for him to enjoy our new daughter, my husband became obsessed with only one thought. 'We must flee. King and my other creditors have discovered our hiding place. We must leave at once.'

'Why do we forever seem to be on the run?'

'Because I dare not risk arrest. It would be the utter ruin of all my hopes of inheritance. We can expect no assistance from my uncle until this problem is resolved. Perhaps we could visit your grandmother?'

Mrs Jones was appalled by the very thought. 'You are far too weak to face the perils of such a journey, madam. Delay it for a little while longer, I beg you.'

I could not disagree with her, neither about the dangers nor my fragile condition. Yet my husband's liberty was at stake and the prospect of remaining without him at Trevecca, with only the ladies of Tregunter to call upon me, was even more terrible to contemplate.

'I shall make ready to leave with all speed,' I assured him.

No one from Tregunter came to bid us farewell as we left the very next day. We proceeded by post-chaise to my grandmother's house in Monmouth. Mrs Jones travelled with us as far as Abergavenny, cradling the baby on a pillow in her lap, from where we continued alone to our destination.

A beauty in her youth, at near seventy years of age my grandmother was still a pleasing woman, simply attired in a gown of black silk. She was somewhat pious, and mild in nature, but asked no questions about our situation and warmly welcomed us into her home, gushing over her new great-grandchild.

'I am a little concerned,' I confessed. 'As I know nothing of domestic matters, or how to take care of babies. I am still young at only seventeen, and Mama is not here to assist.'

She smiled at me with an easy confidence. 'Trust your maternal instincts, my dear, and all will be well.'

'But Mrs Jones has returned home, and I do not even have a wet nurse.'

'Then feed the babe yourself,' she suggested, with her usual good sense. 'It may not be the done thing in fashionable quarters, but quite commonplace in other parts.'

What a joy she was. I began at once to relax and revel in the homely comforts my grandmother offered. Her fireside was in complete contrast to that of Tregunter. And once I felt sufficiently recovered, I enjoyed walking by the River Wye, or exploring the ruins of Monmouth Castle which backed on to the garden of my grandmother's house. I would accompany her to church, take tea with her friends, and during the month of our stay, on one occasion even attended a ball.

'I believe my spirits and strength have been restored by the change of scenery,' I laughed, and my new friends flattered me by saying that I danced like a sylph.

As I was breastfeeding my child, I had taken her with me to the dance and slipped into an antechamber during the evening to feed her. But on our return home I was horrified when she fell into convulsions.

'The fault is all mine,' I cried. 'I should not have fed her so soon after dancing. I must have been agitated by the violence of exercise and the heat of the ballroom. Oh, what am I to do?'

I was frantic with fear. All night I sat cradling her in my arms, and although I tried many times to feed her, she would take nothing more from me. A doctor was brought but the convulsions continued. Neither my husband nor the doctor blamed me, but I could see by the expressions on their faces that they feared the worst as her condition was desperate.

By morning I'd had not a moment's rest, and friends who had heard of my trials called to make inquiries, and offer their heartfelt good wishes. Among them was the vicar who had preached to us so recently at my grandmother's church.

'May I take her for a moment,' he tentatively asked.

For twelve long hours I had allowed no one to move her as

she continued to fit. I knew the end must be near, that she deserved the last blessing this man of God may be about to offer. Yet I could not bring myself to relinquish my child to him.

'I have children of my own,' he explained, 'and have seen one suffer very like this. Will you allow me to conduct a small experiment?'

I realised that I had little to lose. Maria had no hope of survival if she went on like this for much longer. 'However desperate the remedy, I beg you to try.'

He proceeded to mix a tablespoonful of spirit of aniseed with a small quantity of spermacetti oil, and fed it to my child. To my utter joy and amazement, within what seemed only minutes the convulsive spasms abated, and in less than an hour she had sunk into a sweet and peaceful sleep. I cannot describe the relief I felt at her recovery. Never, as long as I live, could I ever thank this dear man enough.

My husband no longer felt safe at Monmouth, so yet again we prepared to flee. But on the day of our departure a writ was brought forbidding Tommy to travel. Some unknown creditor had issued it, no doubt thinking that since we were so close to his 'uncle's' house, payment for the debt could easily be found. We, of course, knew it could not. My alarm was infinite, the sum demanded far too large for us to have any hope of fulfilling it, and I refused, absolutely, to borrow money from my grandmother. Rather the reverse as I had no wish for her even to know of our distress. Fortunately the sheriff for the county was a friend of the family, a gentleman, and kindly disposed towards me.

'To avoid any unpleasantness, Mrs Robinson, I will happily accompany you and your husband to London, where perhaps his current difficulties may be resolved.'

We set out that very evening, not even stopping at an inn to sleep till we arrived in the metropolis, and hurried at once to my mother. By then she was living in Buckingham Street, York Buildings, and her joy at seeing me was boundless. She kissed me a thousand times. She kissed her beautiful new granddaughter, while Tommy went off to spend the day attempting to alleviate our difficulties.

He found lodgings for us near Berners Street, whither we

repaired that same evening. Once we were settled, I retreated once more into my own private world, turning my attention to my beloved poetry and a small collection I had gathered together for publication. I decided the moment had come to have them printed. They were somewhat immature, mere trifles, and I blush at my youthful arrogance in believing them fit to present to the paying public. But money was in short supply and it seemed worth the gamble.

While I was thus engaged over the coming days, friends began to call upon us.

'We are so pleased to have you back in town,' declared my old friends Lady Yea and Mrs Parry, but when they suggested I accompany them to Ranelagh, I politely declined.

'My husband has no wish to socialise at present, so pray excuse me if I prefer to remain a stay-at-home new mother gushing over my baby.'

'I am sure your dear mama will happily mind Maria Elizabeth for a little while. Do come with us, you cannot go on rusticating in this fashion. It is quite unacceptable for the woman of the world you have become.'

I preened myself a little at these words, for after two years of marriage I had grown taller, and had lost my girlish naïvety. I was also vain enough to know that I had matured into quite a beauty, and loved nothing better than to show it off. 'You are right. I have rusticated enough in the beautiful Welsh mountains. Perhaps it is time to step out a little.'

For my return to society I wore a simple gown of pale lilac lustring, in accordance with my style, my hair piled high and wreathed with white flowers. No jewels, flounces or ruffles in sight. The entire party complimented me on my looks, and with some trepidation at leaving the solace of the nursery and my beloved child, I accompanied the party to Ranelagh.

To my complete dismay the first person I saw on entering the rotunda was George Robert Fitzgerald. He looked equally startled, but instantly excused himself from his friends and came over to present himself.

'What a pleasure to see you once more out and about in the world, Mrs Robinson, and without your husband.'

'I am with friends,' I coldly informed him, as I had no wish to give the fellow the slightest encouragement. Why was it that if a man saw a beautiful woman, he felt the need to possess her?

Fitzgerald politely bowed and withdrew to rejoin his companions. Yet I was aware of this despicable Irishman watching me for the entire evening. Even when we quitted the rotunda early and were waiting for our carriage, I observed him in the antechamber.

Could it, I wondered, have been George Fitzgerald who had reported my husband for debt as revenge for my refusing his attentions? Or was it the moneylender, Mr King?

The following noon I was correcting the proof sheets of my volume of poetry, my foot rocking the basket crib in which Maria Elizabeth peacefully slept, when a flustered servant abruptly announced Mr Fitzgerald, and seconds later in he marched!

I was appalled. The fellow had no business calling when he must guess that my husband was from home. My table was spread with papers, and everything around me a muddle. Even my vanity suffered a stab of mortification as my morning dress, appropriate as it might be for nursing a child, was not quite up to snuff for receiving visitors. But there was no opportunity to prepare myself as he already stood before me, with that all too familiar wicked smile on his face.

I received him with a cold and icy mien, and could see that this discomforted him somewhat.

'What a pretty child,' he said, peeping into Maria's basket. 'But then you could produce nothing less.'

I thawed a little at this flattery of my adored child. I was a most diligent parent, a devoted mother. I fed, dressed, changed and cared for little Maria entirely myself, and she slept in my bed at night. In my view she was indeed one of the prettiest little mortals that ever the sun shone upon. I smile now when I recollect how far the effrontery of flattery has power to belie the judgment, but I did at least think to ask him how he had discovered where we were living.

'I followed you home from Ranelagh last evening,' he casually remarked, as if this were of no account.

He came again the following evening to take tea with my husband, and Tommy gave him a warmer welcome. Were we never to be rid of this man? In his wake came more invitations to Ranelagh and Vauxhall, so that in no time Tommy again met up with his old friends: Lord Northington, Lord Lyttelton, Captain O'Bryan, Captain Ayscough, Mr Andrews, and others.

'Ah, good to see you at Ranelagh again, Robinson. Shall we start up those card parties at your new abode, eh?' Lyttelton asked, as obnoxious as ever.

'I'm afraid the house is not big enough to accommodate such a large party,' Tommy demurred.

'We are staying with friends at present,' I hastily added, alarmed by the suggestion as we certainly couldn't afford such gatherings.

'Let us simply enjoy Ranelagh,' Tommy laughed. But if my husband imagined himself safe, he was soon disillusioned. Within days he was arrested on a debt of £1,200 and after three weeks in the sheriff's office, during which he was unable to raise the money, he was taken to the Fleet.

Four

Captive Wife

There's many a breast which Virtue only sways,
In sad Captivity hath pass'd its days . . .
Each new-born day each flatt'ring hope annoys,
For what is life, depriv'd of Freedom's joys?

Mary Darby Robinson
'Captivity: a poem'

1775

Poor, foolish Tommy! I could see no benefit in locking up my husband. How was he ever to repay the sum he owed if he were incarcerated? Yet such was the law. He was even obliged to pay for the privilege, as food and lodging were not provided free. The Fleet at Marshalsea, named after the malodorous river that ran beside it, housed as many as three hundred prisoners, many accompanied by their families. Those who were unable to pay would beg for aid through a grille installed in the prison wall on Farringdon Street specifically for that purpose. Utterly shaming! As I passed through the great stone-framed gateway into the prison to join him, I too felt a deep humiliation, even though I was not required to be there. Simply being in the presence of so many stinking, unwashed bodies was utterly demoralising.

We considered ourselves fortunate to be allotted two rooms high on the third floor, or gallery as it was more commonly known. Each gallery consisted of a dank, ill-lit passage that ran the length of the prison, with rooms on either side. Ours were each about fourteen feet by nine, with the rare benefit of a fire-place and an even more rare tiny barred window overlooking the racquet court. A tattered curtain, in lieu of a door, hung between the two rooms.

Here we enjoyed some degree of privacy, if not silence, as there was the constant banging of doors to jangle our nerves; the steady tread of feet shuffling along the passages, sobs and cries echoing in the dark of night beneath the vaulted roof.

I confess to being shocked at the first sight of our quarters. 'Are we expected to sleep in this filthy, flea-infested bed?' I asked my husband. The stink of urine and squalor of our surroundings made me retch, and I was thankful that I'd thought to bring our own bed linen, and basic crockery for our needs. 'Must we sit on these broken chairs each day gazing upon those vulgar words scrawled by previous occupants on the dirty walls?'

Tommy made no answer. My husband had sunk into a state of depression from the moment of his arrest, which was why I considered it my duty, as a faithful wife, to be with him in his hour of need.

'He is not worthy of such a sacrifice,' Mama had cried, outraged that I'd spent much of every day with him at the bailiff's office, let alone intended to incarcerate myself with him in the prison.

'He is my husband, and I have a duty as his wife!'

'Yet you say you have never loved him.'

'I feel great sympathy for him.'

'Many people die of fever in prison. Duty and pity will not save him.'

'Do not be too harsh, Mama. Poor Tommy surely deserves some comfort and affection?'

'Why should he, when he has let you down so badly?'

'Because it is not his fault that Squire Harris refuses to properly acknowledge him as his son, or that he is being difficult over Tommy having taken me for wife. And I did help spend some of the money, so should share the punishment. My only concern is for his health, and that of our child.'

'But how will you cope?' she asked, wringing her hands in anguish.

'I will cope because I must. Left to deal alone with the rakes pursuing me in town without my husband's protection does not greatly appeal either.'

Daily exercise proved to be essential in order to maintain health, and to keep up our spirits. My husband was reasonably fit and athletic, so I encouraged him to take part in the racquet games we could see from our window. Tommy became most skilled in the sport, finding the game a pleasant distraction. At other times he might play skittles, and the rumble of the wooden ball, the roars and cheers of the men would echo across the yard.

I naturally occupied myself with the care of my beloved daughter. I not only kept our rooms clean, but also scoured the stairs and passage close to our quarters. I considered holding back dirt and disease to be an important part of our survival. Finding the necessary funds for our keep was another. Squire Harris sent us one guinea a week which barely covered our lodgings, food and coals for the fire, plus the sums needed to pay our jailers a small garnish for supplying these necessities. I was therefore delighted when Tommy was offered work copying legal documents by his former employers.

'Oh, what a relief, and so generous of them. This will provide us with a much-needed income, from which we can set aside a few coins each week towards paying off our debts.'

Tommy only scowled. 'How can I work here, in this hellhole? It is too much to ask.'

'You could manage perfectly well. You have a table and chair, and we could send out for quill pens and ink. What more do you need?'

'My freedom.' And turning on his heel he returned to the racquet court, leaving me staring bleakly at the documents laid out on the table, a bitter disappointment in my husband that brought despair to my heart.

And then the answer came to me.

I was perfectly capable of carrying out this task myself, and did so. I spent hours copying the documents, while a young girl took care of little Maria for me. The legal firm were none the wiser, and the money was something of my own to keep for my child's needs.

Invitations and letters arrived for me by the score, mostly from Lords Northington and Lyttelton, Fitzgerald and others. Except for Lord Northington's they were all awash with sentiment and gallant proclamations of love, eagerly offering their protection and to release me from my degrading situation. I treated these rakes with all due contempt, only too aware of the price demanded for such a favour.

'When coxcombs tell me I'm divine, I plainly see the weak design, And mock a tale so common.' I made a note of these words for a poem I might write one day.

'As God can bear witness,' I told Mama, on one of her frequent visits, 'I have never entertained a thought of violating those vows which I made to my husband at the altar. I mean to keep my pride and virtue intact.'

'I should hope so, indeed. But how will you set about finding the money to gain your release?' she tactfully enquired, fear etched on her beloved face. 'Your little volume of poems is selling somewhat indifferently.' This news did nothing to raise my morale, but then we could offer each other little in the way of solace.

Sadly, not one of my women friends ever enquired after me. For all the cordial hospitality they had once enjoyed at my expense, they shunned me completely now that my fortunes had fallen. They refused to enter the dreary habitation I occupied, or even wrote a kind word to ease my lonely days. Their neglect, their envy, slander, and malevolence, hurt me badly, and from then on I felt no affection for my own sex.

The whole experience taught me never to depend upon a friendship.

Nine months passed by in this fashion, and not once in all that time did I cross the threshold to step out of that dreary place, save to walk in the racquet court of an evening with my husband for a breath of air, and to take a little exercise. My health was already impaired by the dire conditions, and I lived in constant dread of gaol fever, of a cough starting, or of my child falling sick.

It was during one of these walks that my little daughter spoke her very first words. What a delight that was! As her nursery maid jiggled my child in her arms, little Maria Elizabeth caught sight of the moon riding high in the night sky. She excitedly pointed with one small finger, then as a cloud passed over to obscure it, gave a soft sigh of regret, letting her little hand fall.

'All gone!'

The nursery maid and I both laughed out loud, for this was the expression the nursemaid often used when she'd fed Maria her last spoonful of porridge, or if she deemed it prudent to hide something from her.

These little moments of joy in an otherwise dull existence quite lightened all our hearts.

Next to the damp and disease, boredom was the killer in the Fleet. I regularly attended the chapel on a lower floor, and sometimes I would treat myself to a coffee and read the news-sheets in the coffee-room next door. Tommy was more likely to visit the taproom, although I did my utmost to discourage him, if only because we could ill afford to waste a penny on a tankard of ale, or tot of gin. Drunkenness was rife in the Fleet.

With too much time on my hands, as I did not have legal documents to copy every day, my thoughts centred upon my poetry. I naturally chose the theme of captivity for my next work, as that is what they called imprisonment for debt. I began composing a quarto poem of some length, my quill pen flying across the paper, albeit in crabbed, tiny handwriting as paper was a scarce commodity in prison. I reused the old envelopes and letters sent to me, since that was all I had. As I wrote, I sensed the style had improved upon my earlier attempts, if still with faults and laboured lines. But then I am never entirely satisfied with my own work, always hoping to produce better next time.

I wrote pastoral poems, odes, character sketches, and verse applauding life in town and country. How I ached to be back in the 'rural shade' of my sugarloaf mountain, marvelling at its mystical beauty. By contrast I would recall the hours I had once spent at my toilette when attending Vauxhall and Ranelagh, and how my beauty must rapidly be fading in this dark and dingy prison. I had no thought now of fashion and vanity, my dress as simple as my situation demanded. My pride lay in the pains I took to keep our clothes clean and neat.

Sometimes, of an evening, I would read what I had written to Tommy. 'Adieu, gay throng, luxurious vain parade, Sweet peace invites me to the rural shade.' But he showed little interest in my efforts, except to complain that my writing took up too much of my time.

'What else should I do to keep sane?' I retaliated. 'Besides, I hope to publish these poems, since one of us needs to earn some money.'

Irritated by my implied criticism of his own feeble efforts in that regard, he left me in peace. My mother, bless her, offered what consolation she could on her next visit, and an interesting suggestion.

'What you need, dearest, is a patron. I believe the Duchess of Devonshire is a great admirer and patroness of literature and poetry.'

'Is she indeed? Then I have an idea. Send young George round to her London house with a copy of my book of poems. Wait, I shall write a note to enclose with it, begging her to excuse its defects as it was my first effort when I was still but a child.'

My fourteen-year-old brother must have charmed the famous Georgiana, for the result of this inspired idea was an invitation to meet her in person. 'I can hardly believe it,' I said, excitedly showing Tommy the note. 'The Duchess of Devonshire apparently asked George for every particular about me, read my poems and expressed a wish to meet the author. I am to go to her residence in Piccadilly. What think you of that?'

He kissed me most tenderly on the cheek. 'I have always known that your cleverness would one day bring you notice.'

I smiled, knowing how difficult it was for him to admit he possessed a bluestocking for a wife. 'But would it be right for me to go? I have never set foot outside of the prison gate.'

'But you are perfectly at liberty to do so,' Tommy reminded me. 'And since you are so obsessed with poetry, talking about it with another woman might do you good.'

'That is not the object of my visit. I am hoping the duchess may be able to help get us out of this hellhole.'

I could see by his expression that he was sceptical. 'I very much doubt she can. Rumour has it she is beset with debts of her own, from her passion for gambling.'

I refused to believe this, determined to at least try. 'Oh, but what can I wear?'

Now he was laughing as he sauntered away, back to his friends and his games.

Fortunately, I had brought with me a plain brown satin gown, so when the day arrived, I washed myself thoroughly to take away any taint and stink of prison, and dressed with care. Then leaving my darling Maria in the care of her nursemaid, I set forth to visit the Duchess of Devonshire.

Stepping out into the open sunshine after so long a time living in semi-darkness, almost blinded me. The noise of the carriage wheels trundling by, the cries of the street vendors, were really quite nerve-racking. Yet it felt wonderful to hear the birds singing, to feel the cobbles beneath my feet, and breathe in fresh air that smelled of newly baked bread and fresh fish instead of rank decay.

The walk to Piccadilly was pure pleasure, the sense of freedom exhilarating, and the duchess's mansion when I reached it, left me speechless. A flunky in crimson uniform showed me into her presence, and as I nervously dipped a curtsy she smilingly indicated I should take a seat upon a blue and yellow striped sofa.

'Your brother has already told me a great deal about you, his pride in your skill as a poetess quite apparent. But I did not expect you to be so young.'

The duchess appeared equally young as I doubt there was more than a few months between us, although I dared not say as much. The copy of my poems that George had presented her now emerged from the folds of her silk gown.

'I particularly like this one,' she said, and began to read a few lines of my own work to me, while I sat blushing with pleasure and embarrassment.

She called for tea, and, encouraged to do so, I told her more about my life: of how my father had abandoned us, my mother's cry for independence by running a school, my own failed dream of becoming an actress, my unfaithful husband, and now being imprisoned for a debt we had not the means to repay. She listened enthralled, and I swear I saw a tear slide down her cheek.

'To have experienced such vicissitude of fortune was, I am

quite certain, entirely undeserved. I pray you will soon be free to begin life anew. Please accept every proof of my good wishes.'

She was the most charming lady, beautiful and cultivated. The best of women: sensitive, friendly, interested in my life, my poetry, and even my child. She wanted to hear all about Maria Elizabeth, and confided in me that having been married only eighteen months herself, she rather hoped she was already pregnant.

I was astonished and deeply touched when she took out a small purse and slipped a few coins into my hand. Despite my protest that I had not come begging for money, she insisted I take it.

'Use it for your precious child.'

As I rose to take my leave, thanking her most earnestly for her generosity, she said, 'And next time bring Maria Elizabeth with you. I do love children, and I'm quite certain she will be as charming as her mother.'

I could not find the words to express my feelings, and departed in something of a daze.

It was the first of many such visits. After that, I very often took Maria with me. My child would sit happily on the rug, or sometimes on the duchess's knee, being cuddled and caressed by my liberal and affectionate friend while we talked of poetry, or of marriage and children. I was, at all times, received with the warmest friendship. Then one afternoon, she made a most generous offer.

'When you publish your next anthology, you may use my name as patron.'

I was so thrilled I could hardly speak, but fortunately remembered my manners sufficiently to thank her. 'Oh, your grace, you are most kind. Every poem in it will be dedicated to you.'

Arriving back at the Fleet, and seeing no sign of my husband on the racquet court, I ran in a flurry of excitement to our rooms to tell him of this most momentous event.

'Tommy, where are you?' I called.

Hearing sounds coming from our bedroom I swept aside the tattered curtain and there he was: in bed with a woman.

He did not even have the grace to show any guilt, merely smiled rather sheepishly as if I'd caught him with his hand in a sweetmeat jar. I was devastated, filled with a burning rage, not so much from jealousy but more a deep sense of injustice and betrayal. While I, like a foolish devoted slave, had cleaned and scrubbed, worked and scribbled, and done my utmost to provide and care for my family, this reprobate of a husband had concerned himself only with his own debauched pleasures. He'd taken advantage of my absence to cavort with a woman of easy virtue little better than a whore.

Her name was Angelina Albanesi, the wife of our Italian neighbour, whom she visited regularly. We had come to know her husband, Signor Albanesi, well as he would often spend the evening sitting in our apartment talking about the world of gallantry, telling stories of intrigue and romantic chivalry. Although neither young nor good looking, I had always found him to be both entertaining and amusing. He could sing and play various musical instruments. But I was less enamoured of his wife. Whenever Angelina came, she never failed to intrude upon our privacy, and my husband made no attempt to stop her. Now I understood why.

She was, without doubt, a beauty, extravagantly gowned in richly embroidered silks and satins, trimmed with valuable point lace. Rumour had it she had formerly been the mistress of Prince de Courland, and afterwards of the Count de Belgeioso, the Imperial Ambassador.

It seemed she was now reduced to bedding my husband.

'Do not blame Tommy,' she said, as she leisurely pulled on her gown and began to calmly dress herself. 'A husband needs the care and attention of a loving wife, not one engaged elsewhere. Men do not value scrubbed floors or any of the other domestic chores you seem to imagine are so vital to your domestic bliss.'

I was seething with fury, hoping Tommy would intervene and dispute her claim. But, as ever when life grew difficult, he had quietly slipped away back to the racquet court. This was yet another battle I must fight alone. 'Cleanliness is vital if we are to maintain our health in this stinking hole.'

'Ah, but you waste your youth by incarcerating yourself here, and such sacrifice will not win his love. Fortunately, my own husband puts no such chains on me.'

'That is quite apparent. But you forget, I am only eighteen years of age and have plenty of my youth still to come,' I tartly reminded her, since the woman must have been well into her thirties, if not already turned forty.

She pulled back her long black tresses and I thought with some satisfaction how greasy they looked, with here and there a fleck of grey. 'If you would but acknowledge your own power, child, and break the fetters of matrimonial restriction, you could do so much better for yourself.'

'I am doing well enough, thank you.' I thought of my new book of poems for which the Duchess of Devonshire was willing to act as patron, once it was completed. If nothing else, that gave me hope. 'We will not remain here forever.'

Signora Albanesi laughed out loud as she tugged tight the laces on her gown, the fullness of her milk-white breasts spilling out above the neckline. 'A fond hope that will not be realised. Hundreds languish in the Fleet for years, and many sadly expire long before they are due for release. I did mention to the Earl of Pembroke that there was a young married lady in the most humiliating captivity with her husband. I told him that you were a person of some beauty, and he readily volunteered to offer his protection.'

'I thank his lordship for his generosity, but I assure you I have no shortage of similar offers. However, *I* respect myself too much to accept any of them.'

Collecting her wrap she strolled away, still laughing, as if I had said something highly amusing. I watched her go with a cold rage in my heart, resolving in future to avoid all conversation with the woman, although that would not be easy unless I could prevent her from visiting Tommy.

Later that evening I vented my wrath upon my straying husband.

'How diligently you courted me, how you persuaded and cajoled, and gently bullied me into marrying you, young as I then was and fearful of marriage. Yet from almost the moment the ring was on my finger, you have been dallying elsewhere. How dare you treat me so ill?'

'It was of no account. The woman means nothing to me.'

'Neither, it seems, do I. And her husband is our friend and neighbour!'

Tommy snorted. 'He cares not who beds his wife.'

'Evidently not!' A thought occurred to me of all those other times I had visited the duchess. 'Has he procured women for you in the past?'

'No one of any consequence, Mary. A man's needs must be satisfied.'

I was horrified. 'You mean only prostitutes, whores, any woman who'll lift her skirts for a penny. How dare you! Do you not appreciate the effort I have put into accepting the propriety of wedded life, and at so young an age? I have strived to do my duty as a wife with exemplary patience, my own chastity inviolate. And neither poverty nor obscurity, neither the taunting of the world nor your own neglect, has tempted me to make the smallest error in that regard. Yet you have not treated me with the same respect.'

He tenderly stroked my cheek, a guilty smile on his face as he pleaded for my forgiveness. 'It will not happen again, my sweet, I promise.'

'How can I believe you? I have borne too many humiliations with a cheerful uncomplaining spirit, have toiled honourably for your comfort, all my attentions exclusively dedicated to you and our child. Yet despite all that I have endured on your behalf, you treat me with utter contempt.'

'Sweetling, do not upset yourself. Let me stroke your head a little to calm you.' And leading me to the very same bed wherein he'd enjoyed his Italian strumpet, he proceeded to make love to me. How could I hate him yet still feel a duty to suffer his advances? And why did I still feel this fondness for him? What a fool I was!

How Tommy managed to pay off some of his debts I shall never know. I dare say a lucky night on the faro table operated in some dingy room of the prison was partly the reason. He also persuaded several of his creditors to cancel his debt with them, and gave fresh bonds and securities to others, so that on the 3 August, 1776, after fifteen months incarceration, he was finally discharged from the Fleet.

I immediately conveyed this intelligence to my dear friend, the Duchess of Devonshire, and she wrote me a letter of kind congratulation.

What utter bliss. We were free!

Five

Doyenne of Drury Lane

Was it some Spirit, SHERIDAN! that breath'd
His *various* influences on thy natal hour?—
My Fancy bodies forth the Guardian Power
His temples with Hymettian flowrets wreath'd;

Samuel Taylor Coleridge to Sheridan,
published January 1795
Morning Chronicle.

The first moments of freedom were a heady joy to my senses, almost as if I had been reborn. I now set aside the melancholy gloom of prison life as a bright new beginning beckoned. Nevertheless, I remained cautious and insisted we take modest lodgings. Tommy found us a small apartment that was perfectly neat and clean over Lyne's confectioner's shop in Old Bond Street.

And in no time at all we were back in the social whirl.

We visited Vauxhall where, as the evening progressed, we were welcomed by all our old friends and acquaintances. I almost forgot that they had so unworthily neglected me in my pleasure at being back in the merry throng. How blissful to compare this sweetly scented place of music and laughter, dancing and gossip, with the dark galleries of prison we had so recently known. After so long a seclusion from society, the joy of this moment was indescribable.

'Have you noticed,' I murmured to my husband, 'how some people feign ignorance of our past embarrassments?'

Tommy chuckled. 'While others accept it with the ease of fashionable apathy.'

Among the latter was Lord Lyttelton, who insolently remarked, 'Notwithstanding all that has passed, I believe the child is handsomer than ever.'

I made no reply, making it clear by my expression of scornful disdain that I still loathed the man. I certainly had no intention of allowing his flattery to go to my head. I was no longer a foolish child, but a mature woman of almost nineteen.

'So how are we to subsist honourably and remain above reproach, now that we have obtained your liberty?' I asked my husband as we took a stroll one morning, arm in arm in St James's Park, admiring the vibrant autumn colours of the leaves as they turned. 'We cannot risk running up more debts.'

'I have written to my uncle a number of times, requesting his support until I can return to my profession.'

'And what was his response?'

Tommy heaved a sigh. 'To date, every letter has remained unanswered.'

I tried to quell the sick feeling growing within. 'What hope do you have of returning to your old profession?'

'It will be difficult, since I did not complete my articles of clerkship.'

I firmed my lips against further questions. Where was the point in quarrelling with him? It was beginning to look as if I'd married a wastrel with no prospects. Instead I turned my thoughts to my own literary endeavours, which I hoped might resolve our difficulties, and made a mental resolve to speak to a printer at the earliest opportunity.

'Can it be Mrs Robinson?' I glanced up in surprise as a young man approached us. 'Perhaps you have forgotten me, Brereton, an actor from Drury Lane.'

I smiled in delight. 'Of course, we met during my rehearsals with Garrick.'

'We did indeed, how delightful to meet you again after all these years. And this must be Mr Robinson. Sir, you have a veritable treasure in this wife of yours.'

Tommy laughed. 'She frequently informs me as much.'

I presented my husband, and the pair of them got along so well that Tommy invited Mr Brereton to dine with us that very evening.

'Would you not consider a change of heart?' he asked, as we sat chatting over the cheese and port. 'I was so looking forward to acting with you, Mary. It would be a crime for you not to explore this promising talent of yours. You should at least take a trial.'

I was startled by this suggestion, having long since given up on the idea. Now hope surged again.

'What do you think?' I asked my husband. 'Would you consent?'

'I would, my dear, if it is what you want.'

I kissed him on the cheek, realising he was now willing to set aside his earlier disapproval to my becoming an actress as it might prove a means of providing the income we so badly needed.

'Can it be arranged?' I asked Mr Brereton, quite unable to quench the tremor of excitement in my voice.

'Garrick sold his half share of Drury Lane back in June. I shall put in a request on your behalf to Mr Sheridan, the new proprietor, and mention that you would like a trial.'

This could change our luck, I thought, considering the heady possibility of fame and fortune. Unfortunately the timing was poor as I was once more in a delicate condition. But to my complete surprise, days later Mr Brereton paid us a second visit, this time bringing Mr Sheridan with him.

'Oh, my goodness, pray forgive me, gentlemen, for my state of déshabillé. I was not expecting any callers this morning.' Maria Elizabeth was happily playing on the rug and, as usual, there were papers strewn everywhere.

'Do not trouble on my account. You look quite delightful, dear lady.'

Not only was Richard Brinsley Sheridan charm personified, he was tall and good looking, though not in any way a dandy despite the bright red waistcoat he wore beneath a coat of blue. He declined tea and went straight to the purpose of his visit. 'Both Garrick and Brereton wax lyrical about you, will you not recite some passages from Shakespeare for me?'

I flushed with embarrassment, suddenly a-flutter with nerves.

Not only was this man the new proprietor of the Theatre Royal, Drury Lane, in conjunction with his father-in-law, Thomas Linley, and a Dr Ford; he was also the much celebrated author of *The Rivals* and *The Duenna*. I felt humbled that he should even be present in my tiny drawing room, let alone expressing an interest in any talent I might possess. But his gentle persuasion was slowly winning me over for he was a man of manners as well as intellect, both of which were strikingly and bewitchingly attractive.

'Where shall it be? I cannot do it here – now – not with my child present and dressed in this careless fashion.'

'A small taste of your talent will suffice.'

My fears dissipated by his charming smile I agreed to try, and read a short extract from a speech by Juliet, as Mr Garrick had taught me. He listened with careful attention, applauding with enthusiasm when I was done.

'You are right, Brereton, we should offer the dear lady a more public trial of her talents.'

An appointment was thus made for me in the Green Room at Drury Lane. Mr Garrick, Mr Sheridan, Mr Brereton, and my husband were all invited to be present to hear me. With Mr Brereton's assistance, I performed a short scene from *Romeo and Juliet*, and without hesitation, my debut in that part was arranged. Indeed, Mr Garrick himself kindly undertook to be my tutor once again, despite my having let him down four years earlier.

'I am delighted to note that you recall all I taught you about being natural, of using your hands and facial expression to reveal emotion. Acting is about far more than mimicry. You have to feel the character, believe in her utterly. You need to become Juliet in very truth.'

Mr Garrick was indefatigable in bringing me to the right standard, frequently reading Romeo himself until he was utterly exhausted. I'd forgotten what an old man he was, but so generous at sharing his passion.

As before I was utterly entranced by him, drinking in his every word, eager to learn and to improve my skills. Perhaps this opportunity would prove to be the turning point in our fortunes, providing me with the independence I craved.

It is impossible to describe the conflicting emotions of hope and fear that overcame me when the day of my debut arrived. I was filled with excited anticipation. I'd written to the Duchess of Devonshire at Chatsworth informing her of my coming trial, explaining that as a newcomer I was to be paid £2 a week, and received a kind letter of approval by return, wishing me every success.

To my terrified gaze the theatre looked huge with its high domed ceiling and rows of boxes on all sides, each festooned with plaster flowers and medallions. I was overawed by its splendour. It had only recently been redecorated and refurbished by the famous Adam brothers with slender columns inlaid with coloured plate glass, gilt statuettes, and much crimson drapery and gold fringing.

Normally, few people would venture out to see an unknown actress, yet to my dazed eyes the theatre appeared crowded with the rich and the fashionable, all chattering and laughing and viewing each other through their quizzing glasses. I had been advertised as Sheridan's new discovery, Garrick's protégée, and they had come out of curiosity to see if I was worth the puff I'd been given. More alarming still, the pit was packed with noisy young bucks, critics and Garrick among them, each having paid four shillings to see me make a fool of myself.

'How can I face them?' I cried, heart pulsating with fear as I stood waiting in the wings. The smell of the grease paint and oil from the lamps that illuminated the stage were so strong in my nostrils I could hardly breathe. 'Oh, I am sweating so much I feel certain my make-up must be melting.'

'No, you look quite lovely.' The actress playing Juliet's nurse gently squeezed my arm by way of reassurance. 'Take some deep breaths and remember that the audience will be plainly in sight, because of the excellent lighting at the Lane. They are never dimmed as the spectators like to see what is happening offstage, as well as on. So remember not to look at the audience, not even a glance, simply let your gaze fall into the middle distance, taking care not to catch anyone's eye.'

I nodded, desperately striving to take in every word of advice she offered. 'I am shaking in my shoes merely thinking of it,' I said, my voice cracking with fear.

I smoothed my skirts, having chosen to wear a pale pink satin gown, richly spangled with silver, my head ornamented with white feathers. Surely my appearance at least would make a good impression? Later in the play, for the funeral scene, I would change into plain white satin with a veil of transparent gauze that fell from the back of my head to my feet. I would wear a string of beads around my waist, to which was suspended a cross. But would I ever get that far, or would my resolution fail? I grasped the nurse's arm in case I should faint.

Mr Sheridan's voice spoke softly in my ear. 'I have every faith you can do this, Mary.' And at length, with trembling limbs and fearful apprehension, I went on stage to face the audience.

The applause that greeted me as I walked on reduced me to a state of paralysis, and for a moment I stood mute, frozen with terror. Again that gentle squeeze upon my arm from my colleague, Juliet's nurse, and somehow I found my voice and began to speak. I was acutely aware of all eyes fixed upon me, among them the keen, penetrating gaze of Mr Garrick himself. But, as instructed, during the whole of that first scene, I never once ventured a glance at the audience.

I made mistakes, of course, not speaking loud enough being the worst, my fears having palsied my voice as well as my action. And once I nearly tripped over the grooves in which the flats ran. But I did remember to curtsy at any applause, and sprang gracefully off-stage at each exit, not forgetting to glance briefly back at the pit as I did so.

Garrick had made some changes to the play, rewriting some of Shakespeare's lines which I very nearly forgot, but with Mr Brereton playing Romeo my confidence gradually increased as the evening progressed. By the time the final scene came I managed to die quite convincingly, even remembering to keep on the green carpet so that I did not dirty my white satin gown.

And on my return to the Green Room I was greeted with a ripple of applause from my comrades, and complimented on all sides. But the praise I most welcomed was that from Mr Sheridan himself, for it was he whom I most wished to please.

'You have more than fulfilled my belief in you, Mary,' he murmured, tenderly kissing my hand.

To hear one of the most fascinating and distinguished geniuses of the age honour me with such a compliment, caused me to melt with joy. And as his lips touched my hand, however chaste the intention, my heart skipped a beat. For the first time in my life I felt a temptation to break my marriage vows.

The audience was by then being entertained by dancing and singing before the after-piece, an extravaganza with music, went on. But for me, my first night was over and if I had not actually turned into a star performer, the critics in the papers the next day declared that my looks were deemed deserving of approbation. And I had apparently shown promise, if in need of some 'polishing'.

The Drury Lane became like a second home to me, a dearly familiar place. But finding my way about the labyrinth of stairs and dingy passages backstage was never easy, cluttered as they were with step ladders, props and flats, and buzzing with some activity or other. People might be busy painting scenery, stitching costumes, providing sound effects, or secreted in a corner rehearsing lines before they went on.

Dressing rooms were equally hectic with dressers rushing about perhaps searching for a pair of gloves, attempting to disguise a stain on a gown, lacing up an actress's corset, buttoning her boots, or simply emptying a chamber pot. As with every other actress, I was allocated my own dressing table, mirror and candle, within a confined space marked out in chalk on the floor. The room stank of greasepaint, powder, false hair glue, gin, perfume and stale sweat. Some actresses, I noticed, had a baby in a basket close by, or a small dog on their lap.

I too had a dresser who helped with my coiffure and costume, although I liked to do my own make-up, using a light mix of powder and beeswax with a touch of pigment on my face, refusing to use the more common white lead as I believed this to be bad for the skin. I plucked my eyebrows suitably thin, added a dab of rouge on my cheeks, ceruse on my lips, and lamp black on my eyelashes. I might wear a beauty patch if the part demanded it, and always powdered my décolletage to a milky whiteness. This was all I felt necessary to enhance my beauty and I would then sit back and relax while my dresser adjusted my wig or dressed my hair, whichever was appropriate for the role I was playing.

Once I was ready to go on I would wait in the Green Room, keeping well away from the small stove where people would gather to keep warm, fearful the heat might melt my make-up.

My first role of the season was Ophelia with John Henderson playing Hamlet. The critics were kind and the next week I played Lady Anne to his Richard III, playing the role several more times.

In February 1777, despite being six months pregnant I played Statira in *Alexander the Great*, looking a picture in a gown of white and blue in classic Persian style, if I do say so myself. On my feet were richly ornamented sandals, and though it was an unusual costume with neither hoop nor powder, I felt both attractive and in character.

My next role was that of Amanda in *A Trip to Scarborough*. The play had been adapted from Vanbrugh's *Relapse*. Unfortunately, the audience had expected it to be a new piece and felt duped, disapproving of Sheridan having taken out all the spicier bits.

As always when displeased, the ladies began to hiss behind their fans, and the bucks in the pit to loudly complain. Mrs Yates, the leading actress, obviously fearing they might rise up and commit some atrocity as has occurred in the past, at once quitted the stage, leaving me to face the tumult alone. I was vaguely aware of Mr Sheridan from the wings frantically urging me to stay put and not quit the boards. I could not have moved a muscle as I felt frozen to the spot.

Then to my very great astonishment, the Duke of Cumberland, seated in the royal box close by, spoke directly to me. 'It is not you, but the play, they hiss.'

Not knowing how else to respond, I cast him a shy smile and dipped a low curtsy, which seemed to delight the house for they cheered and applauded. Thus encouraged, I felt able to speak my lines. Mrs Yates returned, and the play was allowed to continue.

The play ran for ten nights. This was followed by my benefit when I performed the part of Fanny in *The Clandestine Marriage*, and for which I earned the enormous sum of £189 10s. It was well attended, the boxes filled with persons of the very highest rank and fashion. Filled with a new confidence I looked forward with delight both to celebrity and fortune.

Mr Sheridan too was delighted, and despite having several dozen other actors demanding of his time, was most attentive of me, constantly praising my talents and taking an interest in my domestic comforts. 'I would very much like you to perform in my new play, *The School for Scandal*,' he said.

'I can think of nothing I would like more. But, as you see, my increasing size makes that impossible.'

'Then I must reluctantly accept your apology.' He kissed my

hand, and a tremor of emotion rippled the length of my arm, quite taking my breath away.

'I am heartbroken to miss such an opportunity,' I confessed. 'It would have been quite a coup for my career.'

'There will be other opportunities for us to work together, I am sure,' he said, with that certain light in his eyes that revealed so much about how he was feeling.

I was aware there was already gossip about us, and sternly warned myself to keep a grip on my emotions. A letter had appeared in the *Morning Post* by someone calling themselves 'squib' who implied that I was being promoted by my manager in exchange for sexual favours. I was outraged by such a charge.

Sheridan was most certainly attractive, and I respected him deeply. Never yet had I properly known love, which was an adventure still awaiting me. But he was married to Elizabeth Linley, a most charming woman, and I too had a spouse, if a neglectful one. It was impossible to avoid his society, or to deny the fact that there was indeed an attraction growing between us. But despite my undoubted youth and emotional vulnerability, I was no longer quite so naïve or foolish as I'd once been. Sheridan and I were good friends, partly because we shared Irish blood, my great-grandfather having been originally named McDermott before changing it to Darby. We also shared a dry sense of humour, and held similar views on the need for a proper education for women. But nothing intimate ever took place between us, as I would not be the one to break the sanctity of marriage.

I wrote a strong denial to the paper. 'Mrs Robinson presents her compliments to Squib, and desires that the next time he chooses to exercise his wit, it may not be at her expense . . .'

The first night of Sheridan's new play took place shortly before I gave birth to my darling second child, Sophia, named after my old friend Mrs Baddeley. She was baptised on 24 May, but six weeks after her birth, died in my arms of convulsions. They had come upon her exactly as they had with Maria Elizabeth, and I'd carried out the very same remedy shown to me by the kind clergyman, sadly this time without success.

I was utterly distraught.

We were by this time living in Southampton Street, Covent

Garden, and it was here that Sheridan had chanced to call on the very night my baby died. He found me with her still lying on my lap, as I was quite unable to relinquish her. I had known this man but five months, yet had seen much evidence of his sensitivity. Now, as he looked upon my child it came again to the fore.

'Beautiful little creature!' he murmured, with a sympathy that touched my very soul. 'I too have children, and can understand your very great distress.'

He sat and wept with me, so that I was not alone in my shock and grief. Alas! I never received such solace from my husband. But then I was not as loved by Tommy as I had once believed. I do not condemn him for that, as I know we cannot command our affections, as my father had once told me.

If he was upset at the death of his daughter, he gave little evidence of it. Like any man fearful of showing emotion he'd fled the house to drown his sorrows, such as they were, with his friends at the Pantheon or at the faro table. Wherever he might be, he stayed away for days.

'You will have heard the rumours among our acquaintances that your husband is now keeping two women?' Mama whispered, which did little to ease my distress. 'A dancer and a prostitute, apparently, so for all we know he could be with them.'

'Why would I care?' I snapped, my patience short. I had long since decided not to investigate Tommy's personal life too closely. I was, in any case, too sunk in my own grief.

I regretted that he was not more discreet in his infidelities; and that while he satisfied his own needs, he chose not to consider how much he exposed me, his wife, to the most degrading mortifications. But not even the pain caused by an unfaithful husband came close to the suffering of losing a much loved child.

The death of Sophia was so painful that I felt quite unable to appear again that season. Mr Sheridan suggested I visit Bath, to allow me time alone to grieve. From there I went on to Bristol – and it was in the place closest to my heart that I slowly began to recover. I returned to London in the autumn in time for the publication of my volume of poetry dedicated to the Duchess of Devonshire. It was well received with 'Captivity' and 'Celadon and Lydia' proving to be the favourites.

I made no effort to contact my husband, as we were by then living largely separate lives, he with two women in one house in Maiden Lane, while I took lodgings in Leicester Square.

Sheridan wasted no time in calling to welcome me back, and this time he was also keen for me to play comedy, which I did, playing Araminta in Congreve's restoration comedy *The Old Bachelor*, Emily in *The Runaway*, Fanny in *Joseph Andrews*, which was an adaptation of Fielding's novel of that name, and many more.

In April of 1778 I played Lady Macbeth for my next benefit, as well as writing a musical farce *The Lucky Escape* for the after-piece. I had never been so busy or so fulfilled. I felt as if I too had had a lucky escape, both from the Fleet and from my marriage. This success convinced me not to give up my hopes for a literary career alongside my acting one, so when Sheridan suggested I accept the offer of an engagement for that summer at Mr Colman's theatre in the Haymarket, I declined.

'I have no wish to tour,' I told him. 'I need the time between seasons to write, and have already refused several offers from provincial managers.'

'I most strongly recommend that you accept Mr Colman's offer. The Haymarket is hardly provincial, and it will be good for your reputation, Mary, to make an appearance there.'

I sighed, but agreed, for although my heart was with Drury Lane I needed the money to tide me over until the next season commenced. 'Very well, but on condition that I am allowed to approve the role.'

Mr Colman agreed to this proviso and the first part he offered me was that of Nancy Lovel in the comedy *The Suicide*. This was a breeches role which would give me an opportunity to show off my legs, which I've always thought quite shapely.

Having received the script, and impatiently waiting for rehearsals to start, I was astonished one morning while out and about to see a handbill announcing the production. Even more so when I noticed the actress Elizabeth Farren was to play the part that had been promised to me.

I wrote at once to Mr Colman. 'I demand an explanation for this.'

He replied, 'I'm afraid that I had already promised the part to

Miss Farren, as she has performed a season or more at the Haymarket, and dare not take the risk of offending her.'

I felt insulted and insisted that Mr Colman fulfil his promise according to our agreement, or release me from it entirely.

'I see no good reason to sign you off, as there are plenty of other roles you can play,' came his unfeeling response.

Now I was the one to turn obstinate, filled as I was with that familiar sense of betrayal. Why did everything always go wrong? The summer passed without my performing once, although I was vastly relieved to find that my salary continued to be paid weekly.

I reopened at Drury Lane on an improved salary of two guineas a week, by then residing at the Great Piazza on the corner of Russell Street, Covent Garden. Not the most salubrious neighbourhood but inexpensive and convenient enough to hear the call man who summoned actors to rehearsals. I certainly couldn't afford to risk a fine for missing one.

Tommy, so far as I was aware, remained in Maiden Lane, not too far away, although thankfully I rarely saw him, unless he needed to raid my purse for money.

Several more productions followed and I was happy to expand my repertoire, taking on nine new parts over the following months, including that of Jacintha in *The Suspicious Husband* in May 1779. It was witty, risqué, and my first breeches role, a part I adored. A week or two later I appeared at a masked ball at Covent Garden wearing Jacintha's scarlet costume, which shocked the fashionable ladies but amused and delighted all the gentlemen present.

'My only regret is that my dear friend Garrick did not live to see this latest success,' I said to Mama. 'Nor to see me at last play Cordelia in *King Lear* for my latest benefit in April, since he died in January. His passing marks the end of an era.'

I wrote an elegy to his memory. My mother was unimpressed.

'I dare say he was a most splendid, clever man, but I shall never reconcile myself to the fact he encouraged you to follow this foolish dream.'

'But I am doing well, Mama. Receipts from my benefit were £210, surely you consider that to be a good thing?'

She looked uncomfortable at my challenge. 'Of course, but

if you make so much money, why are you constantly crying poverty?'

'As you know, women have little control over their finances in marriage, particularly an unhappy one. Precious little money reaches my own purse as it is generally swallowed up by the gambling debts of my profligate husband. In addition, the bond creditors have become clamorous, and have appropriated the entire profits of my benefit.'

'Oh, I should never have prevailed upon you to marry that spendthrift.'

'Let us not think of it.' I quickly changed the subject, since my own predilection for spending did not bear too close an investigation. As an actress of note I felt I had an image to maintain, and my vanity was such that I had a weakness for showing off my beauty to its best advantage. 'At least the latest reviews are good. Even the *Morning Post* says "Mrs Robinson makes a prettier fellow than any of her female competitors."'

'Certainly prettier than Elizabeth Farren,' Mama agreed. 'She might have a sweet voice, but unflatteringly thick ankles. And so hard up she is often obliged to borrow clothes from other actresses.'

I laughed at this, feeling it some sort of revenge for her winning the Nancy Lovel role over me. 'She has an elegant figure and a natural grace, which makes her ideal to play the fine ladies of comedy. Fox certainly likes her well enough. They are said to have enjoyed a short affair.'

'Fox?'

'Charles James Fox, friend of the Duchess of Devonshire.'

'Ah, well I trust your own reputation remains unsullied, dear?'

'I do my utmost to protect myself from scandalous rumour, Mama, as you well know.' I smothered a sigh, feeling I had inadvertently stepped into dangerous territory, as this question never ceased to trouble her.

Actresses were seen as glamorous, romantic and exciting, yet it was perfectly true that the slightest glimpse of a shapely ankle, or décolletage on stage, labelled her a prostitute rather than an actress playing a role. Even Sheridan forbade his wife, Elizabeth Linley, a talented singer, from appearing. Prejudice against women in the profession remained strong.

'Nevertheless, I am constantly under attack from admirers who believe I must surely be available for purchase. Among them is the Duke of Rutland who offered me a settlement of six hundred pounds per annum if I would leave my husband and become his mistress.'

Mama gasped. 'How utterly shocking! What did you say?'

'What do you think I said? I politely declined, of course, explaining that I wished to maintain my good reputation in the eyes of the public, and be deserving of their patronage.'

She furiously fluttered her fan, as always when annoyed. 'I am relieved to hear it. It remains a painful regret to me that you chose to join this immoral profession. However, your dear brother, John, who is visiting from Italy, has agreed to see you perform.'

I clapped my hands in joy. 'Oh, Mama, that would be wonderful. I cannot wait to see him.'

I was excited at the prospect of seeing my dear brother again, and of enjoying some family approval. Sadly, the visit did not turn out to be quite as wonderful as I had hoped. The moment John saw me walk on stage he jumped up from his seat in the stage box, and instantly quitted the theatre. Clearly it was too much for a respectable merchant to witness such depraved behaviour on the part of a sister. I could only feel grateful that Papa was still out of the country.

Shortly after this, Tommy again persuaded me to make a visit to Tregunter. However repugnant it might be to my feelings, I agreed to accompany him only because I hoped to assist him gain the support he craved, and help bring about a reconciliation with his alleged 'uncle'.

Fortunately, on this occasion I was received with a greater degree of civility, almost warmly welcomed, which was astonishing.

'I dare say we must tolerate the immorality of your new profession, since it pays you such good money,' Miss Betsy said, with a sigh of feigned tolerance.

I did not trouble to respond.

The squire generously arranged several parties for my amusement, or else used my presence as an excuse to show off his new mansion, in which the three of them were now happily ensconced.

'You must tell us what to wear,' Miss Betsy simpered, quite at odds to her earlier comments on my style of dress. 'As you are now the very oracle of fashion.'

I was certainly viewed rather differently as Mrs Robinson, the promising young actress, to the person who previously came to beg asylum. I suffered their condescension as best I could, and Tommy and I rubbed along surprisingly well, being still friends if not lovers. Thankfully, we stayed only a fortnight in Wales as Squire Harris remained obdurate in his coolness towards his illegitimate son, and Tommy finally despaired of any reconciliation. I felt a great pity for him. Did I not know how devastating it was to be abandoned by a father?

We stopped at Bath on our way back to town, staying at the Three Tuns, one of the city's finest inns where by chance we met George Brereton, unrelated to the William Brereton who played Hamlet to my Ophelia. This fellow was a dangerous duellist Tommy had met at Newmarket races, and to whom he had foolishly given a promissory note in lieu of a debt.

'I am in no haste for payment,' he assured my husband, and I saw how Tommy almost sagged with relief. 'I most earnestly urge you to spend a few days in this most fashionable city.'

'We are in no hurry to return to London,' Tommy eagerly agreed, no doubt sensing an opportunity to win back some of his losses from this notorious gambler.

From then on, George Brereton became suffocatingly attentive towards me. Tommy need only leave the card table for a moment to order more food or ale, and he would grasp me in his arms, or declare his fervent love for me.

'If this is your true reason for encouraging my husband to remain in Bath, then you will be disappointed,' I coldly informed him. 'I am a faithful wife and honest woman, and have no intention of sullying my reputation with the likes of a reprobate like you.'

For some reason he seemed to find my refusal amusing.

I should, of course, have told my husband at once of these assaults upon my good name, but in view of this scoundrel's reputation, I decided the easiest way to resolve the problem was for us to disappear for a few days until he'd left. 'I have a fancy to visit my home town, since we are so near. Could we do that?'

Tommy was perfectly agreeable to this suggestion, and we took the post chaise to Bristol, finding accommodation in an inn in

Temple Street. The following day we were on our way to Clifton when a bailiff approached and my husband was again arrested for debt, for a sum quite beyond his power to pay.

The writ had been issued by none other than Mr George Brereton.

I was utterly mortified. 'How can this be happening to us all over again? Will you never learn? Why did you ever get yourself involved with such a villain?'

Tommy sank into that all-too familiar state of depressed resignation, not even begging the bailiff for time to pay, while a waiter quietly informed me that a lady wished to speak with me in an upstairs room.

'This may be some old acquaintance offering to help,' I told the bailiff, 'as we are well known in these parts. Pray do not take him yet, I beg of you.'

Eagerly I followed the waiter upstairs, but on entering the apartment found not an old friend as I had hoped, but George Brereton.

'Well, madam,' he said, with a caustic smile. 'You have involved your husband in a pretty embarrassment! Had you not been so cold towards me, not only this paltry debt would have been cancelled, but any sum that I could command would have been at his service. He must now either pay up, fight me, or go to prison, and all because you treat me with contempt.'

'You well know that he cannot pay you, but I beg you to reflect before you do anything you might regret.'

'I would have no regrets as I am completely under your spell. If you promise to return to Bath and behave more kindly towards me, then I will this moment discharge your husband.'

Understanding entirely what was expected from me, I burst into tears. 'I pray you show mercy. You cannot be so inhuman as to propose such terms!'

His eyes were devouring me even as he made to stroke away my tears. 'The inhumanity is all on your side. I should even now be with my wife who is dangerously ill,' he said, nuzzling into my neck.

'Then for heaven's sake release my husband!' I sobbed, pushing him away.

Mr Brereton only smiled as he rang the bell and ordered the

waiter to fetch his carriage. I was overcome with panic. If he left now, my poor foolish husband, and possibly me along with him, would be back in the Fleet within days.

'Very well!' I cried, making it clear by the severity in my voice that I was not to be trifled with. 'I will return to Bath.' But then something snapped inside and I lost all control. 'You are a dishonourable libertine who has no right to embroil me in your barbarous plans! I will inform that lovely wife of yours how treacherously you have behaved towards me. I shall proclaim to the world that you are a fornicator and a seducer.'

He visibly paled, realising I meant every word. 'I must insist that you be discreet.'

'I will do no such thing. Not while you insult me and hold my husband in your power. Your demands are outrageous, and I swear my honour and pride will not allow me to do anything improper.'

'How little does such a husband deserve you as wife! How can he prefer the very lowest and most degraded of your sex? Leave him, and fly with me. I am ready to make any sacrifice you demand. Shall I ask Mr Robinson to release you? Shall I offer him his liberty on condition that he allows you to separate yourself from him? By his ill conduct he proves that he does not love you, why then do you continue to support him?'

I was almost frantic with despair. How to refute such arguments? How could I explain that the arrangement suited me well? Having a husband, even a neglectful one, was a protection of sorts against rakes such as he. 'I have no wish to fly with any man. I am a respectably married woman.'

'Very well!' And snatching up a sheet of paper he scribbled furiously for a moment then flung it at me. 'Here, madam, is your husband's release. Now I rely upon your generosity.'

I was incapable of speaking, could do naught but take the paper from him with trembling fingers.

'Compose yourself, and conceal your distress. We want no awkward questions from the innkeeper. I will return to Bath where I shall expect to see you shortly, if you know what's good for you.'

Having issued this threat he stormed from the room, climbed into his chaise and drove away. Only then did I hurry downstairs to present the discharge to the bailiff, and with all charges dismissed we left the inn.

Tommy asked no questions, for which I was grateful, although I gave some garbled explanation of how I had persuaded the fellow to drop the charges, all the while worrying how I might disentangle myself from this mess. I had no wish to see Brereton engage my husband in a duel. Tommy may bluster, but he was no fighter, and whatever his faults and weaknesses, did not deserve to meet such a cruel end.

Of necessity we were obliged to return to Bath to collect the remainder of our possessions from the Three Tuns, and were also expecting letters in the post. But I had no intention of succumbing to George Brereton's demands.

'I want you to promise me never again to place your freedom in the hands of a gamester, or a libertine,' I sternly warned my husband.

He readily agreed, although he seemed oblivious of the peril attending either one.

Wishing to avoid Brereton, we collected our belongings and removed to the White Lion Inn. The next day, being a Sunday and with no post delivered, we were compelled to stay on, although we kept within doors out of sight. Then to my utter astonishment as I sat looking out the window, I saw George Brereton walking on the opposite side of the street with his beautiful wife and her equally lovely sister. So the story of her dangerous illness had been a lie!

Fortunately, he hadn't seen me, or so I thought. But then just as we sat down to dinner that afternoon, the waiter announced him. He coolly bowed to me, then turned to my husband. 'You may consider the promissory note paid off. I offer a thousand apologies that I harassed you for the money, and that I arrived too late to prevent your arrest.'

'It is of no matter,' Tommy said, the slightest note of scepticism in his tone.

'I hope I shall have the honour of seeing you both later this evening,' he said, and casting a meaningful glance across at me, bowed and took his leave.

We did not linger another hour. Immediately after dinner we set out at once for London.

* * *

I continued to be pursued by admirers including a royal duke, a lofty marquis, and a city merchant of considerable fortune. Every rake in town conveyed their esteem by showering me with gifts from milliners, mantua-makers and jewellers. The Duke of Rutland renewed his solicitations, and Sir John Lade, a pleasant young baronet, was a constant visitor backstage. He often came to the races as well as the theatre with Tommy and me. He was a good friend, no more than that, but I was in sore need of protection.

For this reason, and because relations between us had improved considerably, my husband and I again set up home together, renting a spacious and elegant house situated in the heart of Covent Garden. It was convenient in every respect, being close to Drury Lane, and our circle of friends increased almost hourly.

We would hold regular supper and card parties, the house thronged with visitors. My morning levees were so crowded I would happily while away the hours in gossip and chatter, when not required to learn a new part. In fact I was so enjoying myself I could scarcely find time for study. Mr Robinson played more deeply than was perhaps wise, but then for once in his life he enjoyed a huge win.

As a consequence of his good fortune we acquired horses, a new phaeton and I purchased several new gowns, my style followed with flattering avidity.

Mr Sheridan called one morning when I chanced to be alone. 'You know, Mary, that I am your most esteemed friend. I hold you in fond regard and with every respect, so I advise you now with all due courtesy, the dangers of running into debt. You are spending too freely, with such extravagance it could easily damage your reputation as an upcoming actress. Do not allow your new-found celebrity to lead you astray.'

'I am but enjoying the fruits of my success,' I responded, feeling slightly piqued by his criticism.

'And those of your husband's wins at the faro table, I understand. But you well know those will not last, and I lament that you are surrounded by too much temptation.'

His sensitivity was touching, every word he uttered beautifully sympathetic, making me blush with embarrassment. His warning seemed to indicate that he possessed some prescient knowledge, as if he knew that I was destined to be deceived yet again.

At that time I had been married more than four years, and Maria was nearly three years old. I'd been out in society from the age of fifteen, yet still there remained in me a vulnerable tendency to trust everyone around me. I believed every woman to be friendly, every man sincere, unless it was proved otherwise. Such faith in human nature was ever my downfall. But my life was about to change more than I could ever have envisaged.

Six

A Prince's Mistress

The prince gazed on the fair who caused his care,
And sigh'd and look'd, sigh'd and look'd and sigh'd again:
At length the vanquish'd victor sunk upon her breast.

Morning Chronicle
misquoting from John Dryden, 1780.

1779

The season was launched with me again playing Ophelia on 18
September, 1779. I followed this success with Viola, in *Twelfth
Night*; Nancy, in *The Camp*; Fidelia, in *The Plain Dealer*; Rosalind,
in *As You Like It*; Oriana, in *The Inconstant*; and several other
favourite parts. Then in November, Sheridan decided to stage
The Winter's Tale.

'The production will be in memory of our dear departed
friend, Garrick, and I would like you, Mary, to play Perdita.'

I was stunned and deeply flattered, if sensing envious vibes
from Elizabeth Farren. 'I would be honoured.'

This was to be Garrick's own version which told the story of
Perdita and Prince Florizel. By rights, I dare say that is what it
should have been called. Perdita has been brought up as a shep-
herd's daughter but is in truth a princess. In Shakespeare's version,
because of her rural upbringing, she is aware of the facts of life,
yet she is sweet and good, 'the queen of curds and cream'. In
Garrick's adaptation she has no knowledge of intimate love, which
he considered inappropriate for a young lady.

Some might find this dull, but to me it seemed the perfect
opportunity to show myself as a more serious and sensitive actress.
My gown was becomingly simple with a tightly-fitted jacket that
showed off my figure, my crook suitably ornamented with a

milkmaid's red ribbons. I sang a sheep-shearing song, and danced with the other shepherds and shepherdesses, and the reviews in the *Morning Post* hailed me a success, even if they expressed dislike of my costume.

On the second night, a week later, we had a full house and I was honoured by the presence of my patroness, the Duchess of Devonshire, who declared herself enchanted, as did the duke. Other notables included the Lords Melbourne, Spencer, Cranbourne and Onslow, each accompanied by their lady. I was deeply flattered.

Further accolades came my way when the *Morning Post* printed my poem 'Celadon and Lydia'. I could hardly contain my joy.

And then came the greatest surprise of all.

'You will be aware that King George and Queen Charlotte both love the theatre,' Sheridan announced a day or so later. 'However, their natural preference is for Covent Garden, particularly since I took over the Lane, as they disapprove of my political leanings. I am a Whig, as is their son the Prince of Wales, while the king himself favours the Tories . . .'

At which point he became engrossed in a convoluted explanation of how it had become a tradition among the Hanoverians for the son to pit himself against the father ever since George I. I listened with scant attention as I was not greatly interested in politics.

My friend and patron the Duchess of Devonshire was a highly regarded member of the Whig party, although I did wonder if perhaps this obsession acted as a distraction for her failure to produce an heir, the poor lady having suffered more than one miscarriage. Charles James Fox had apparently awakened this particular passion in her, which she saw as her life's calling. Why she thought so highly of the man I could not imagine, as he was known for his dissolute behaviour, marked particularly by drink and heavy gambling. Marshalling my straying thoughts, I made a valiant attempt to sound interested in Sheridan's rambling tale.

'I have certainly heard that the king does not care for Shakespeare.'

'Unless it be comedy,' Sheridan agreed. 'Which is why their majesties have commanded a performance of *The Winter's Tale* to take place on the third of December. They have no doubt heard of your success, Mary, and wish to see you for themselves.'

I put my hands to my flushed cheeks. 'Oh, my goodness!' Never had I imagined performing before the royal family, and was instantly filled with fear at the prospect. 'I am not worthy of such an honour,' I cried, but Sheridan only laughed.

'You are more than worthy. Have you not played Perdita many times already. You will do splendidly.'

As soon as my fellow actors heard the news they gathered about me in the Green Room, eager to offer their congratulations. All except for Elizabeth Farren, of course, who pouted rather childishly. She and I remained rivals for parts. 'Their majesties are not coming to see *you*, Mrs Robinson. It is the afterpiece, *The Critic*, the new satire Sheridan has written that they wish to see, not your milk-and-water rendition of Perdita.'

I paid her no heed, although when the night of the command performance arrived I was a bundle of nerves, almost too tangled in stage fright to go on. Even the scent of the grease paint, which I normally love, made me feel quite ill.

William 'Gentleman' Smith, who performed the part of Leontes, King of Sicilia, and one of the sweetest and kindest men I know, kissed my hand and smilingly exclaimed, 'By Jove, Mrs Robinson, you will make a conquest of the prince tonight, for you look handsomer than ever.'

'I hope only not to disgrace myself, sir.' I drew in a shaky breath, deeply touched by this uncalled-for compliment.

The royal boxes were adjacent to the stage, and could, in fact, be accessed by it. In one sat the king and queen, their attendants standing behind them, while directly opposite in full view of all that was going on backstage, was one occupied by the Prince of Wales and his brother Frederick. From where I stood in the wings, waiting to go on, I could see him quite clearly. He was seventeen, younger than myself by some five years, but apparently already skilled at fencing and boxing, also passionate about the arts and music, or so members of the Green Room had informed me. I thought he looked rather handsome, and didn't doubt he was a great favourite with the ladies.

I was wondering if perhaps his predilection for wine and women at so young an age was a reaction to the demands placed upon him by duty when Mr Richard Ford, the manager's son who was training to be a lawyer, suddenly appeared at my side.

'Allow me to introduce my friend George Capel, Lord Viscount Malden, to you, Mrs Robinson.'

'Good day to you, sir.' I dipped a curtsy, although meeting a stranger at the point of going on stage was a distraction I could have done without.

The gentleman appeared to be about my age and something of a dandy, as he was extravagantly attired in a suit of unlikely pink satin with silver trim, and matching pink heels. But he was pleasant enough and I talked to him for a few moments, privately wishing he would leave me in peace and take his seat in the theatre. I became aware, during our conversation, of the Prince of Wales observing us most intently from the royal box, which only served to unnerve me further.

It was almost a relief when finally the play began and I went on stage. Even then I was conscious of the prince's gaze fixed upon me, and of his making flattering remarks about me to his brother and equerries. My anxiety was such that I spoke rather too quickly and hurried through the first scene.

As the play proceeded I almost shivered as I spoke some of my lines, as if a goose had walked over my grave.

Oh, but sir, your resolution cannot hold, when 'tis
Opposed, as it must be, by the power of the king:

The prince's interest in me attracted attention from the audience, and from the king, but on the last curtsy the royal family condescended to return a bow to the performers. Then as the curtain came down, my eyes met those of the prince with a look that I never shall forget. He gently inclined his head and I blushed with delight and gratitude.

Whenever I was off-stage, Lord Malden had remained at my side throughout, was waiting for me even now as I made my way to the dressing rooms. 'Did you note how particular the prince applauded you?' he asked.

'I am delighted His Highness bestowed such kindness upon my performance.'

'It was at the suggestion of his uncle, the Duke of Cumberland, that he attended the play, and see for himself the new beauty who graces the stage of Drury Lane.'

I found it difficult to envisage royal princes talking about *me*, let alone admiring my beauty. 'I am flattered,' I said, unable to think of any more fitting remark.

'Prince George is a fine fellow, most amiable and cultured. His childhood was quite austere, you understand, yet he is charm personified, intelligent, elegant, cheerful and with a most affectionate disposition. Quite handsome too, do you not think?'

Lord Malden sounded very like a merchant expounding the virtues of his stock. But try as I might to escape, he kept me talking throughout the afterpiece until the evening's performance was over. By this time I was weary and anxious to get home to my darling Maria. I was hurrying to my chair, taking a short cut across the stage when I met the royal family coming from their box. Once again the Prince of Wales honoured me with a very low bow. Blushing with embarrassment, I quickly curtsied then fled.

I longed to be alone, to think on what had just occurred, to examine in my mind whether the prince had intended such marked attention. But as Mr Robinson had invited several guests to supper, and I was eager to relax and enjoy myself, I set the matter aside with a careless shrug. No doubt Prince George was as flattering with all the ladies. But the entire conversation that night was filled with talk about the accomplishments of the heir apparent.

Days later I was taken by surprise when Lord Malden paid me a morning visit. I received the gentleman with some degree of awkwardness as my husband was not at home, but then he seldom was. His lordship's embarrassment, however, seemed to far exceed my own. He started to speak – paused, hesitated, apologised, then started all over again.

'I hope you will pardon me, that I might rely upon your discretion not to repeat what I must communicate to you. My situation is a delicate one, and I beg you to act as you think proper.'

I could not begin to comprehend his meaning. 'Pray, sir, you must be more explicit.'

After several moments of hesitation and indecision, he drew a letter from his pocket. It was addressed to Perdita. I smiled somewhat wryly and opened what was clearly a *billet-doux*. It contained only a few words, but they were expressive of more than common civility. The letter was signed Florizel. So here was the reason he had monopolised me at the theatre the other night. Lord Malden was yet another admirer attempting to persuade me into his bed. 'Well, my lord, and what does this mean?' I sounded as annoyed as I felt.

'Can you not guess the writer?'

'Could it be yourself, my lord?' I drily remarked, already weary of this game and wishing the foolish man would leave me in peace.

'Upon my honour, no. I should not have dared to address you on so short an acquaintance.'

I did not believe him for a moment. Was I not hounded by arrogant men who thought they had but to wink an eye and I would fall into their arms? 'Then pray tell me from whom the letter comes?'

He again hesitated, seeming confused, as if regretting he had revealed himself in this fashion, or that he had undertaken to deliver the letter. 'I hope that I shall not forfeit your good opinion, but . . .'

'But what, my lord?'

'I could not refuse. The letter is from the Prince of Wales.'

I stared at him in open astonishment. What tale was this? Did he think me a complete fool? 'I find that hard to believe.'

'Then I beg you to read the missive again, for I swear it is so.' And to my great astonishment his lordship quietly took his leave.

If I read the letter once I read it a thousand times, yet still I could not bring myself to believe that it was written by the hand of our illustrious Prince George. Was this some trick by Lord Malden, meant to appeal to my vanity or test the propriety of my conduct? I tossed the missive aside, resolving not to think of it further.

But the following evening the viscount came again. My husband and I were holding a card party for half a dozen or so friends, so naturally Tommy invited Malden to join us. No doubt he saw the dandified lord as a means of winning back some of his previous losses. And as they played, yet again the Prince of Wales was the hot topic of conversation.

'His Royal Highness's manners are impeccable, his temper most engaging, and his mind replete with every amiable sentiment.'

Malden continued to sing the prince's praises with obstinate persistence, failing to concentrate on the game of faro even as my husband did indeed strip him of a fair sum. But the words resonated in my mind even as my heart beat with conscious pride. Could it be true that this paragon, this royal prince, wished to count himself among my admirers?

More letters followed in the ensuing days and I could no longer deny that they came from the prince. Lord Malden assured me His Royal Highness was concerned that I not feel offended by such intrusion upon my privacy.

I replied to each and every one of them, Lord Malden acting as messenger. But I was far too busy over the Christmas season to allow myself to consider the implications of such correspondence too deeply. I treated it as a mild flirtation, giving my full attention to playing Juliet and Viola in *Twelfth Night* over the New Year holiday, not to mention several cross-dressed roles. The prince was on occasion present, and I could not resist returning his languishing glances. Without doubt, an attraction, however light and flirtatious, was growing between us.

In February, Lord Malden persuaded me to attend an oratorio to be performed at the Lane, which I did, taking my seat in the balcony box. When the prince arrived with his brother, Prince Frederick, he saw me at once, and smiled. He held up a playbill, acknowledging me with small gestures, his gaze fixed upon me in that intense way he had. I knew not how to respond, not wishing my husband to notice the glances passing between us. But the prince continued to make signs, moving his hand across the edge of the box as if miming that he would write more letters. He whispered something to his brother, who also glanced across at me with particular attention. And when an equerry handed the Prince of Wales a glass of water, he raised it to his lips by way of salute.

So marked was His Royal Highness's conduct that many in the audience could not help but notice. A veritable buzz of curiosity seemed to be growing. Fortunately, my husband was too far gone in his cups to notice, but several of the bucks in the pit were highly entertained as they watched with avid attention the little scene playing out before them. To my acute embarrassment, their majesties likewise became curious as to what was going on, and when a note was delivered to my box asking me to withdraw, I was utterly mortified.

'What have we done to offend?' Tommy demanded to know, though whether he was truly ignorant of the situation that had led to this request, I dared not ask.

'It matters not. We must leave forthwith.' And with the utmost chagrin, we were obliged to quit the theatre.

'What am I to do?' I asked my mother. 'My female vanity might be flattered to know that the most admired and accomplished prince in Europe is claiming to be devotedly attached to me, yet I dare not risk accepting his offer to meet him.'

'He has asked to see you?' Mama asked, looking stunned, as well she might.

'Many times in the almost daily letters conveyed to me by Lord Malden. His Highness is most persistent, constantly declaiming his passion for me. He says that I have captured his heart and professes to be in love.'

'Oh, my goodness! But then he is a royal prince, accustomed to being granted all he desires, and already with a reputation where the ladies are concerned. He will say whatever he must to win you.'

These were the words one would expect a fond mother to make, yet I could not deny the power of his attraction. It was all so exciting, so thrilling and dangerously tempting. I had little experience of romance, having been obliged to endure a neglectful, unfaithful husband and many rapacious demands upon my person which were more lust than love. Nor did I have any knowledge of these other women the prince had apparently pursued. I knew only the feelings he expressed so lovingly towards me in his beautiful letters. I thought him the most amiable of men, but one admittedly subject to temptation.

'I have entreated him to recollect that he is but seventeen, and perhaps led on by the impetuosity of youthful passion.'

'You would be the one to suffer, dearest, if he should change in his sentiments towards you.'

'I am aware of that, Mama, and have begged him to be patient, to wait until he becomes his own master and knows more his own mind before he engages in a public attachment to me. Above all, to do nothing that might incur the displeasure of His Royal Highness's family.'

'Wise words, as many in the royal household would seek to undermine you in his affections. You would risk the public abuse which calumny and envy would undoubtedly heap upon you.'

'I most firmly believe that His Royal Highness means what he professes – indeed, his heart is too vulnerable to deceive or harbour even for a moment the idea of deliberate deception. There is a beautiful ingenuousness in his language, a warm and enthusiastic adoration expressed in every letter, which charms me. I find the poetic quality of his words particularly appealing.'

'Think on your reputation, Mary, and the dangers, were you to yield.'

She was speaking of a possible unwanted pregnancy, yet it was not unknown for a married woman to take a lover and for any resulting progeny to be accepted by her husband. Would Mr Robinson be so obliging? He was certainly in no position to criticise infidelity on my part, when he paid no heed to our wedding vows. Besides, there were ways and means of preventing such unwelcome events. I had heard tell of a shop in Covent Garden which sold cundums, made of sheep gut tied with ribbons which helped prevent such accidents. But I made no mention of this to my mother.

'I promise that I will do nothing in haste, Mama. As well as the loss of my reputation, I fear losing my independence, and the success I have achieved in my profession.'

'Then for once I must applaud the fact that you tread the boards.'

I knew in my heart that were I to quit my profession, and leave my husband, I should be thrown entirely on the prince's mercy. But for all my innate caution, my desire to be principled and sensible, the prospect of being the mistress of a royal prince was not without its attractions. I rather fancied being seen as a leader of the social scene, dressing in the latest fashions, bejewelled and riding in a fine carriage. I ached to be the best, to be noticed and loved. A foolish vanity, a flaw in my nature, perhaps because of my own father and even my husband, who had both betrayed and neglected me.

The prince's pursuit of me gathered momentum, his letters sometimes arriving twice daily, duly delivered by Lord Malden. On one occasion he wrote me a letter which I swear was written in his own blood, as he claimed that his heart bled for me. He sent a lock of his hair to my dressing room in an envelope marked 'To be redeemed'.

I was then stunned to receive, via Lord Malden, the prince's portrait in miniature, painted by the artist Jeremiah Meyer, beautifully set in diamonds. Within the case was a small heart cut in paper. On one side was written: '*Je ne change qu'en mourant*'. On the other: '*Unalterable to my Perdita through life*'. I swore never to part with this picture till the day I died.

Throughout the early months of 1780 the prince's correspondence continued, every day bringing new assurances of his affection and regard. Yet we never spoke a word to each other. I still declined to meet His Royal Highness for the reasons Mama and I had discussed. Then Lord Malden came to me one day and stunned me with his own declaration.

'I confess I regret ever having become embroiled in this business, for I now realise that I too have conceived a violent passion for you.'

I was momentarily at a loss for words. His lordship was a most pleasant young man and I liked him well enough. As Member of Parliament for Westminster he was also a person of some influence, and no doubt with excellent prospects. But I remained married to Thomas Robinson, and divorce was not only difficult but well-nigh impossible, even if I had loved him, which I did not. 'My lord – George – please do not add to the pressure already upon me.'

He didn't seem to hear my heartfelt plea.

'I offered to withdraw my services but the Duke of Cumberland paid me a visit early one morning at my house in Clarges Street, informing me that the prince is most wretched on your account. He implored me to continue to plead on his behalf, at least for a while longer. Yet I need you to be aware, Mary, that I would relinquish such duties for the prince in a moment, were you to give me the slightest indication that my own regard for you might be returned.'

Much as I might feel pity for Malden I knew I must dash his hopes, albeit as sweetly and tactfully as I could. 'You are a very dear friend, George, and always will be, but have I not gossip enough to contend with? Let us not encourage more.'

'Is there then no hope for me?'

I gently squeezed his hand. 'I am in sore need of loyal friends, and treasure you as such. Let us say no more on the subject.' After some persuasion he agreed, but despite every effort to prevent it, gossip about us was rife. It was generally mooted that I was not only mistress to a royal prince, but also to his 'royal pander'. I thought this an unpleasant description of my new friend, and most damaging to my own reputation. It was also wrong on both counts. But as vehemently as I might refute these rumours, I could do nothing to silence them.

'How long can we continue in this fashion?' I asked my husband, in some despair.

'By ignoring the gossip and going about our business as we choose.'

Wise advice, but then Tommy had the facility to be completely self-obsessed. I wished that I could emulate him as I worried far too much about how people might judge me.

So it was that we sparked yet more tittle-tattle in April 1780 when the three of us attended a masquerade together, poor Tommy being seen as my pimp. Attendance was so high that a one-way system for carriages had to be instigated, with horse's heads facing towards Hyde Park. The streets were jammed and we did not reach the doors until long after they had opened at half-past ten, and supper did not begin until one in the morning.

The *Morning Post* published a most disgruntled piece complaining about the usual collection of nuns, flower girls, milkmaids, shepherds and shepherdesses, friars, Turks and Persians. But they made a point of mentioning the three of us, describing Tommy as the 'pliant' husband, and Malden as the 'sulking hero'. They commented that I wore a pink jacket and coat-dress, with a loose gauze thrown over it, and that I appeared melancholy 'from the provoking inattention of the company'. If this were true, then why did I stay until well after dawn?

I did express my disappointment to Malden that the prince was not present.

'Prince George was certainly desirous of being here, but the king has forbidden him from attending masquerades as His Majesty considers them to be full of vice.'

I had to laugh at this. 'It is but fun, although I agree that the essence of a disguise does allow the freedom to act out a part one might not otherwise play.'

'Which the king deems to be quite inappropriate for a royal prince.'

'Because hiding behind a disguise is dangerous, rather as we actresses are viewed when playing a role?'

He grinned. 'Quite so.'

'Personally I have no objection to being recognised, but then I spend too much of my life in costume, pretending to be someone I am not. Besides, all is revealed at the designated hour when masks are removed, so where is the danger?'

Two weeks later the three of us attended a masked *ridotto* together at the Opera House, a venue I loved as the stage would be extended over the orchestra pit for dancing. It was perhaps foolishly reckless of me as I had a rehearsal to attend first thing the next morning, playing Imogen in *Cymbeline*. But I simply couldn't resist as the prince had promised to be there. Sadly, to my great disappointment, he did not appear, no doubt again barred from attending by the king.

He did, however, send me a pair of diamond earrings with a note from Florizel, by way of compensation for his absence. What a darling man! I had refused many gifts which His Royal Highness had wished to buy for me from Grey's, accepting only a few trifling ornaments whose value in total did not exceed one hundred guineas. I also made it clear that my acceptance of this latest gift did not in any way prove that I was for sale.

I enjoyed the evening, despite my disappointment, as a *ridotto* involves far more entertainment than a masquerade, and the three of us stayed until five in the morning. For this occasion I wore a domino and was transparently veiled, which showed off the diamond earrings to perfection. Malden was most admiring of my appearance.

'You look more beautiful than ever this evening, Mary, in your diamonds and rubies.'

For once the *Morning Post* too complimented me, saying that I shone with 'unusual lustre', speculating that Lord Malden himself must have given the gems to me.

Tommy and I spotted the piece as we sat browsing the news sheets in a coffee house together, since we could not afford to buy them all at threepence a time. We were partly amused and partly infuriated by these latest scandalous comments.

'They do not seem to appreciate that as an independent woman I can perfectly well afford to buy my own jewels,' I quite reasonably pointed out. 'I have never been in the business of accepting gifts from admirers, or selling my favours, for all I have frequently been propositioned. Once from an abbess, no less, who attempted to procure me for a lord with an offer of one hundred guineas.'

Tommy laughed out loud. 'That is quite a sum, you should have accepted.'

'I do not take my marriage vows as lightly as you, husband dear.'

He quickly changed the subject back to the gossip mongers. 'This piece in the *Town and Country Magazine* features a tête-à-tête subtitled "Memoirs of the Doating Lover and the Dramatic Enchantress". It gives an embarrassing history of poor Malden's recent amours.' Tommy handed it to me to read.

'How very sad. But if *I* am this so-called enchantress, they say that I am "not so easy a conquest as many imagined" which for once they have absolutely correct. The paper's views on my personal charms and talents are quite flattering, but who can be feeding them these details? Who is privy to the engagements in our diary?'

'Our servants?' Tommy suggested, as he flicked through another news sheet.

'No, I will not believe it. My servants are ever loyal as they know that I treat them well. The papers must have spies, determined to fabricate any facts they cannot ascertain for themselves.'

'I'm sure you are right.' Tommy chuckled. 'But it says here that Malden not only purchased the diamonds, but provided you with a crimson and silver carriage, which is "the admiration of all the charioteering circles of St James's". If that is so, where have you hidden it, dearest wife?'

We both burst out laughing. 'I have so many I forget. Such is the lot of fame!'

Tommy may have been sympathetic to the gossip in the press, but at that time he knew nothing of the letters from the prince, which were causing me so much heartache. Not that I felt any sense of guilt about this correspondence as my husband's behaviour continued as shameless as ever. He showed no respect for my position or my sensitivities. Tommy generally passed his leisure hours squandering my money at the gaming table, drinking himself into oblivion, or cavorting with loose women of ill repute, not least carrying on his affair with the pair lodged in Maiden Lane.

Even my own servants complained of his illicit advances.

One night I returned home from a rehearsal to find the door of my chamber locked. 'Tommy, are you in there?' I called, rapping on the door with a sharp knuckle. 'Let me in at once.'

It was no great surprise to find that my rapacious husband was not alone. But the woman in question was one of our kitchen maids, exceedingly plain even to ugliness, being short, squat and dirty. I dismissed her on the spot.

Such indifference to my feelings naturally destroyed any sense of duty or esteem on my part. And the increasing adoration of the prince, who must surely be the most enchanting of mortals, hourly occupied my mind on the possibility of a separation. In the scores of the most eloquent letters His Royal Highness sent, he constantly assured me of his lasting affection. By comparison with the contempt and embarrassment I experienced from my own husband, and the manner in which I laboured to earn our living while he frittered it away, I grew weary of the effort of trying to keep my marriage alive.

Yet without Tommy's protection where would that leave me? Therefore I still hesitated, reluctant to bring upon myself the reproaches of the world.

'His Highness has suggested that you adopt a disguise in order to meet him incognito.'

I frowned at Malden, perplexed. 'But you said the prince did not attend masquerades or adopt disguises. What is he asking of me?'

Malden continued with evident pain. 'He wishes you to don male attire, as you do in your cross-dressing roles, such as the character he saw you play in *The Irish Widow*. Then he would have you smuggled into the Queen's House.'

I was utterly shocked. 'I will do no such thing! What if I were to be seen?'

'He thinks it unlikely, as you would meet in the privacy of his apartments there, and were anyone to see you the disguise would offer protection.'

'Indeed it would not, since I am famous for such roles. You may tell His Royal Highness that the indelicacy of such a step, as well as the danger of detection, makes me shrink from his proposal. I have more respect for myself than to take the risk.'

My refusal apparently threw His Royal Highness into the most distressing agitation, as was expressed by the letter I received from him the very next day, which Malden reluctantly handed over.

'I apologise in advance for this missive, but His Highness does tend to react with some degree of hysteria whenever he cannot have what he most desires. I lament the day I ever engaged myself in this activity. I declare I am the most miserable and unfortunate of mortals,' he mourned.

Yet again I offered my heartfelt sympathy, for he was by now a dear friend. 'He should not make such requests of me, it is true. But to put an end to my correspondence with the prince seems too painful a remedy. I confess to being utterly fascinated by him: by the beauty of his letters, by his accomplishments, and any doubts I feel are more than soothed by his profession of inviolable attachment.'

Malden looked deeply concerned. 'Yet he is a royal prince with many demands upon him, so I cannot swear he would remain faithful. And think of the risk to your own reputation, Mary.'

I smiled gently, knowing that the poor man was playing devil's advocate, needing to obey the prince, who was his friend and master, and yet wishing to have me for himself. 'I am all too aware that, in the eyes of the world, the reputation of a wife must remain unsullied even though a husband may indulge his fancies as he chooses. Fashionable circles do allow for a wife to err so long as she is discreet, and her husband continues to offer her the sanction of his protection. More than one woman I know suffering matrimonial turpitude has indulged in such practices.'

'Perhaps they do not have as much to lose.'

'That is true, but could I reconcile myself to remaining under the same roof of a husband I no longer honour, and whose good will I would, in fact, be forfeiting? It is all most confusing and almost impossible to follow both my heart and my duty.'

It was also true that the attentions of my so illustrious admirer might actually add éclat to my popularity, rather than demean it.

'Tommy's worldly prospects would not necessarily suffer, so long as he was willing to turn a blind eye,' Malden pointed out, and I thought about this for some moments.

'But for all my husband's infidelities, I could not allow him to become the object of ridicule and contempt, to see him publicly cuckolded and scorned. Were I to abandon both career and husband, what protection would I have? Taking everything into account, you are right, I dare not take the risk.'

'I am vastly relieved to hear it.'

More gifts arrived, all of which I returned, but the managers of Drury Lane were not oblivious to the rumours circulating about my alleged affair with both prince and 'pander'. I had played Rosalind for the first time at the end of January, and repeated the role at my benefit on the 7 April. The first performance attracted some criticism, as I still possessed the fault of over-emphasis, but there was much improvement in the second. I had learned a great deal in the three years since I first trod the boards. Should I risk throwing all that away?

Perhaps suspecting that I might decide to retire at the close of the season, Sheridan offered me a considerable increase in salary. 'You are hourly rising in a profession which you have enthusiastically embraced, Mary. I trust you will not decide to quit after all you have invested in it.'

I returned no decisive answer.

It was certainly true that I did love working in the theatre, and valued the independence it gave me. The public plaudits I received at every performance never failed to excite me, and were far too gratifying to be relinquished without regret. Yet after all those months of correspondence, all those heartfelt declarations of love I had received daily, I felt as if Florizel, as the prince liked to call himself, had already won me by letter. It was a poetic seduction if you like, and my longing to meet with the prince in person, my growing desire for him, could no longer be denied.

Then one day Malden brought me another letter, albeit with some reluctance. It was signed by the prince and sealed with the royal arms, so marked by true affection that I could scarcely take it in. The contents came as such a complete surprise that I burst into tears. Never had I felt so moved, so humbled.

'Are you aware of its contents?' I asked Malden.

'I am. His Highness has offered you a bond for £20,000 as proof of his good will and protection for your future. A sum to be paid at the period of His Royal Highness's coming of age.'

Tears were rolling down my cheeks. Even so I was shocked by the indelicacy of entering into any pecuniary engagements with a prince. I had, after all, expected nothing more than to possess his heart. Yet without doubt the sum was both generous and much needed. 'Can this be true?'

'The prince appreciates the sacrifices you would make by quitting the stage, and wishes you to be assured of his long-term protection.'

How could I refuse such generosity? 'Then I will agree to a meeting, and if as a consequence I decide to accept the prince's offer, I shall brave the censure of the world and rely for protection and friendship on the one man for whom I will sacrifice everything.'

A meeting was arranged to take place at Lord Malden's residence in Mayfair. But yet again the restrictions imposed upon the prince prevented him from keeping our appointment. My disappointment this time was hard to bear.

'You must understand, Mary, that despite being almost eighteen the prince's life remains strictly controlled. His studies begin two hours before breakfast, and continue throughout the day. He is tutored in politics, history, the arts and commerce, agriculture and finance, more topics than you can imagine. There is nothing that he must not fully understand. He is an intelligent and bright young man with an important destiny.'

'I do appreciate that, Malden, yet constant disappointment seems to be the mark of our relationship.'

'He has again suggested you come to Buckingham Palace.'

'Absolutely not, such a visit would place us both in peril of discovery.'

'Then may I suggest you meet on the banks of the Thames at Kew, opposite the old palace which is the summer residence of the elder princes. I would accompany you, Mary, and we could go at dusk in suitably dark attire. The prince would slip out to meet you, with his brother Frederick to keep watch.'

This was the plan upon which we agreed.

On the night in question, Malden and I travelled to Kew and crossed to the wooded island known as Eel Pie Island. It was so named because the Three Swans Inn, where we dined, was famous for that dish. Fortunately there was the usual degree of music and revelry so we were not remarked upon, although I grew increasingly anxious and nervous as we waited for the signal.

Excitement was bubbling in me as I contemplated my first meeting with the prince. I admired him greatly, and felt grateful for his affection. He was the most engaging of created beings. We had corresponded for many months, and his eloquent letters, the exquisite sensibility which breathed through every line, his ardent professions of adoration, had combined to shake my feeble resolution.

In the dusk of evening we could barely make out the glimmer of a handkerchief being waved on the opposite shore, but Malden took my hand with an encouraging smile, and helped me to step into the boat. The slap of the waves, the rustle of the willow trees that hung over the water, all served to add to the magic of the moment.

Moments later we landed before the iron gates of old Kew Palace, and I saw the prince himself striding down the avenue, his brother beside him. My heart was racing as he hastened towards us, Prince Frederick and Malden tactfully staying some distance away as His Highness rushed forward to grasp my hands in his.

'At last! I cannot believe the difficulties we have endured in arranging this so longed-for meeting. Even so, it must be brief.'

I was quite lost for words, overwhelmed by the reality of being so close to a royal prince. Even the scent of sandalwood on his person was utterly intoxicating. His arms slipped about

me, and I swear I could feel the beat of his heart as he pressed me
to him.

'You cannot imagine how I have dreamed of this moment. I
thought we might never meet . . .' He started as we heard the
sound of people approaching from the palace, and the moon
chose that very moment to slip out from behind a dark cloud
and illuminate the scene. Fearful of being discovered, we instantly
sprang apart as Prince Frederick called across to us.

'Another time, my love,' he softly murmured, pressing his lips
to my brow before striding away with his brother. I stood bereft,
shaking with emotion, only vaguely aware of Malden taking my
arm to lead me back to the boat.

Sensing my disappointment he attempted to console me. 'Do
not fret, Mary, we can arrange another meeting.'

I could not think beyond what had just occurred, what I had
experienced when Florizel had at last taken me in his arms.

I returned home in some trepidation, fearing Tommy might
have discovered the truth of my absence, only to find my wastrel
husband laid out cold on the floor of the drawing room in a
drunken stupor. With a sigh I called a manservant to remove
him, then locked myself in my chamber where I snuggled between
the sheets and indulged myself with recalling the events of the
evening, and the protestations of love that had so moved me.

My heart had been captured. The prince's royal status no
longer filled me with a terrified awe. I saw him now as a lover
and a friend. No matter what happened in the future, the grace
of his person, the irresistible sweetness of his smile, the tenderness of his melodious yet manly voice would live forever in my
heart.

Our meetings took place regularly after that, and always in the
same place and at the same time, fortunately without interruption
on future occasions. We would walk along the shore arm in arm,
locked in our own private world by the enfolding darkness, the
gentle slap of the water the only sound as we talked of whatever
came into our heads. I always wore a darkly coloured cloak,
Malden a black greatcoat, and the prince often disguised himself
as a watchman. I would delight to see how eagerly he would
climb over the gate to come to me. Only Prince Frederick chose

to wear his favourite buff coat, a most conspicuous colour which alarmed us, although we said not a word on the subject.

'You are my very own Perdita, and I your Florizel,' the prince would say, pressing me to his heart. 'How I adore you and long to make you mine. If only we could be together always.'

'I too lament the distance which destiny has placed between us,' I confessed, knowing how my soul would have idolised such a husband! 'But you are a royal prince, and young still. Who knows what the future might bring. I cannot risk leaving the stage to rely entirely upon your protection.'

'Is my offer not generous enough for you?' he asked, his seductive gaze sparking fresh desire in me.

'It is not simply a matter of money, although I admit I need an income to live by which the theatre so ably provides because of the success I have achieved. Were I to quit, to break my marriage vows, then I would feel obliged to leave my husband, thereby losing my respectability.'

'I would see that you were well taken care of, my love, with your own establishment.'

I shuddered at this. 'You wish me to become a courtesan? I have no desire to prove the critics right in their assessment of women in the acting fraternity.'

'No one would dare to criticise the lover of a royal prince.' He looked so certain of his own ability to control the gossip mongers, I could almost believe it to be true. 'In any case, my brother Frederick is to go to Hanover in a few months' time, and when I turn eighteen in August I will be granted an establishment of my own.'

'Then an attachment to a married woman might injure Your Royal Highness in the opinion of the world. I beg you to consider most carefully. I could not bear to bring calumny upon you or the royal family. And the scandal could destroy the very love that is growing between us.'

'It would never do that!' Gathering me close in his arms, his kisses and caresses grew ever more passionate and daring. 'I only know that I must have you, dearest Perdita. The very touch of your lips sends me wild with desire.'

I felt very much the same, a passion awakened in me that I had not experienced before. Certainly my husband had never aroused such intensity of feeling in me. Yet I was fearful of allowing things to go too far, too quickly, so I would gently disengage myself and delicately change the subject, obliging him to again take my arm as we strolled beneath the hanging branches of the willows.

We would speak of world affairs, of manners and fashion, of people we knew, and the prince would tell me of his life growing up in the royal house, and of the strict regime to which he was subject. Nothing could be more delightful than these midnight promenades. Sometimes he would delight me with a song, the sound of his voice breaking the silence of the night, weakening my resistance still further.

'I am so torn,' I told my old friend, the Duchess of Devonshire. I had not yet plucked up the courage to discuss this subject further with my mother, but felt in dire need of female advice. 'The prince's attachment to me seems to increase with each meeting. I consider myself the most fortunate of creatures, but we cannot continue in this fashion. Should I relinquish my profession? And what of my husband?'

'Are either as important to you as the love of a prince?' she wryly asked. 'George is a dear soul, and a great favourite of mine. Does your husband treat you half so well?'

I shook my head. 'Not in the slightest. He wastes my money, beds our own maids and is no doubt even now in some bawdy house with one of his whores.'

'Discretion, dear Mary, is everything, I agree. My own husband can in no way claim to be faithful since I discovered he was engaged in a liaison with Lady Jersey. She was not the first, nor I doubt will she be the last, but he does try to be discreet. I shall consider it my right also to take a lover, should the mood take me, once I have fulfilled my duty on the question of an heir, that is.' Her expression for a moment was pained, and I squeezed her hand in sympathy.

'You will fall pregnant again soon, I am sure of it.'

She smiled over-brightly. 'Successful you most certainly are, Mary. You have gained much acclaim for which, as your friend, I am proud and pleased for you. Yet in all honesty I have to say that however you might wish otherwise, acting will never bring you respectability.'

It seemed that I had less to lose than I had first thought. And my love for the prince could no longer be denied.

Malden escorted me to a house on the corner of Kew Road, where I slipped quietly in through a private entrance at the back, out of sight of any passers-by, artfully disguised in my domino and mask. The prince was waiting for me with eager impatience, two glasses of ruby red wine already poured, glowing in the soft light of a silver candelabra that graced the supper table.

I never touch wine, and what we ate I cannot recall, as food was the last thing on my mind, and on the prince's too. He soon disposed of all pretence of eating and pulled me into his arms to devour me with kisses. Never had I felt such passion, such burning desire.

'You are utterly enchanting, I cannot wait to possess you, dearest Perdita.'

There was a slight moment of embarrassment as he struggled unsuccessfully with my laces and ribbons, but then we both fell on to the bed in hoots of laughter.

'Perhaps we should call your maid,' he teased, kissing my nose and mouth, smoothly moving down to suckle my breast. From that moment I was lost in paradise. I felt treasured, warm and safe in his arms. My gown slid easily from my shoulders, and if I helped him it was out of an eagerness of my own.

He took off my silk stockings with a tenderness that was deliciously erotic, slipping one garter on to his wrist as a keepsake. He unlaced my petticoat and stays with trembling hands, freed my breasts from the restrictions of my tight bodice with a wondrous awe. And I as eagerly helped him to remove his brocade coat, silk shirt and breeches, smoothing my exploring hands over his powerful chest and shoulders.

The prince proved to be an exciting and vigorous lover, and surprisingly skilled for one so young. So it was that in the solitude of a stranger's house, I finally gave myself to him, and tasted sensual love for the first time.

The house became our secret trysting place. We would meet as frequently as the prince, or Florizel as he liked me to call him, could escape his duties. After we had made love we would enjoy music, wine and song, dancing or card parties with specially invited friends. Here, in our own private sanctum, we felt safe to savour the delights each could give to the other, and enjoy a riotous social life. And always I wore the prince's miniature hung upon a ribbon around my neck.

Sheridan made one last effort to persuade me to stay on at Drury Lane with offers of a further rise in salary, but accepted my determination to retire with an air of sad resignation. 'I rather expected this, Mary, and can only hope you are making the right decision.'

'I sincerely believe that to be the case, but I hope we may remain friends?' I said, emotion choking my throat.

'Always! I too am growing somewhat tired of the theatre, and giving more attention to my political interests. Life changes and we must move with it.'

In those last two months of my career I believe I worked harder than ever, on one occasion in May playing eight roles in eleven nights. Perhaps in deciding to leave the stage, I threw off my inhibitions at last and produced my best performances. In the role of Widow Brady in *The Irish Widow*, one of my favourite parts, the *London Courant* wrote that I executed the role 'with truth and propriety'. It was not an easy one to play since I had to change from an Irish accent to a deep male voice when she disguises herself as her brother. Even the *Morning Post*, my sternest critic, wrote 'Mrs Robinson stands eminently distinguished from the other performers'.

I couldn't help but wonder how much more I might have achieved, had I chosen to remain in the theatre. I felt as if I had barely finished my apprenticeship and had so much more to give.

I played Perdita one more time, and other favourite roles including Juliet, Imogen, Viola, and Rosalind. Then in my last appearance I played Sir Harry Revel, in the comedy of *The Miniature Picture* by Lady Craven, and Widow Brady again.

My throat closed in a grip of misery as I felt quite unable to continue, very close to fainting. Fortunately, the person on the stage with me was the one to begin the scene, which allowed time for me to collect myself. How I stumbled through the play I shall never know, my performance felt mechanical and dull, yet

the applause from the audience at the end was warm and gratifying, a most moving accolade to the end of my career.

Doing my utmost to smile I sang the final song. 'Oh, joy to
you all in full measure. So wishes and prays Widow Brady!'

'And that,' I informed my colleagues as we entered the Green
Room together, 'was not only the last song in *The Irish Widow*,
but of my appearances at the Drury Lane. I shall appear no more
after this night.'

Mr Moody, who had played in the farce with me, looked
utterly stricken. 'You will be sorely missed, Mrs Robinson.'

The effort to conceal the emotion I felt on quitting a profession
I loved so much was suddenly too much, and I burst into tears.

Never had I imagined the day would come when I would no
longer tread the boards, the place where I had so often received
the most heart-warming testimonies of public approbation. I had
worked so hard and achieved such high acclaim. Now I was flying
into an uncertain and unknown future, one which might bring
only disappointment. I was overwhelmed by emotion, barely able
to speak as I bid farewell to my fellow actors and accepted their
warm felicitations and good wishes with a regret almost too hard
to bear.

When I suggested to my husband that it was time we parted,
it was with less regret, although Tommy didn't seem in the least
surprised, so must have been aware of the rumours after all. 'I'm
willing to continue to give you my protection, Mary, should you
need it,' he generously offered.

'I couldn't ask that of you, Tommy. It would only make you
into a laughing stock. Better we go our separate ways in a civilised
fashion.'

'We gave it our best shot, eh?' he sportingly remarked, as if
we'd been engaged in a form of clay pigeon shooting.

'I'm sure you'll manage to find comfort elsewhere,' I wryly
observed.

'As will you. And mayhap the prince will see fit to reward my
generosity in lending him my wife.'

I was irritated by this assumption on his part, guessing it was
the true motivation behind his generous offer not to leave. 'Is that
all that matters to you, whether the liaison might prove beneficial
to yourself?'

'Of course not, but I hope we will ever remain friends. I truly wish you to be happy,' he graciously added, tenderly kissing me on each cheek.

'I see no reason why I should not be.'

A day or two later, on Sunday afternoon at the beginning of June, I called upon my dear friend the duchess, feeling in need of her reassurance that I had done the right thing. I was shown into her parlour to find she already had a visitor, but she nevertheless made me most welcome, striding towards me with hands outstretched to kiss me on each cheek.

'Ah, Mary, come and meet Charles James Fox, my most open-hearted and liberal-minded friend and fellow Whig. I know you have heard me mention his brilliance as a member of parliament on numerous occasions, and are familiar with his efforts to reform the government. He is also, you will be glad to hear, a close friend of the prince.'

He grinned most amiably as he took my hand. 'I fear Georgiana greatly exaggerates my influence, but I am delighted to make your acquaintance, Mrs Robinson.'

I instantly warmed to the merry twinkle in his dark eyes beneath the shaggy brows, the bulbous nose and plump cheeks that wobbled as he laughed. He was even more corpulent than the public gossip sheets would have us believe, and not handsome in any degree, yet I liked him on sight.

Georgiana patted his unshaven chin as if he were a pet dog of which she was particularly fond. 'He is the most pleasure-loving dissolute, able to out-drink anyone, and has gambled at least one fortune away.'

'Where is the point of money if not to make it go round,' Fox cheerily remarked. 'And I am always willing to pause any game of hazard when the house is sitting and requires my presence in some important debate or other. I cannot say fairer than that.'

Georgiana laughed out loud. 'Fortunately, White's and Almack's stay open around the clock to accommodate you, and other incorrigible gamblers such as my own good self. But enough of this flippancy, we have been discussing the riots that took place yesterday, and are this morning in all the papers. Did you see them, Mary? Did you notice how red the skies were from the burning buildings?'

'Indeed, we quite feared for our lives.'

'I watched from my balcony here. Lord George Gordon must be a fanatic to incite such a catastrophe.'

'The fellow is unbalanced, opposed to the granting of perfectly reasonable rights to Catholics,' Fox said. 'The rabble took over Parliament while he lectured the House on the wrongs of popery, then dashed off to harangue the Lords in the same way. Members were in a complete panic, rushing in all directions, fighting off punches by the demonstrators, the less fleet of foot being kicked to the ground.' He met Georgiana's wide-eyed gaze with a sad shake of the head. 'The duke's carriage was detained by the crazed mob, who forced him to shout "No Popery" several times in a loud voice, before agreeing to release it.'

The duchess put her hands to her mouth in startled dismay. 'Oh, my poor William. How very unnerving for him. Is he safe?'

'He is fine, dear lady, but having done their worst at Westminster, the rioters went on to ransack the city, as you saw for yourself.'

'No doubt fuelled by drink and quite beside themselves with rage,' she agreed. 'They plundered shops and houses, and burned down the King's Bench Prison. I never saw such mayhem. They even stormed Newgate, I believe, to release four of their fellow rioters who had been arrested, and other inmates along with them.'

I picked up one of the news-sheets that lay scattered about the table. 'This says there are four hundred dead.'

'Oh, how terrible!'

'The duke asked me to instruct you to leave town,' Fox informed the duchess in urgent tones.

Georgiana nodded. 'I have already made arrangements to move at once to Chiswick. My servants are even now preparing my carriage. I cannot stay here another day.'

'Most wise. Then if you have no further need of me, I must return to ascertain if there have been any further catastrophes. Good day to you, my dear Georgiana, and Mrs Robinson. I feel certain you and I will become great friends.'

I smiled. 'My pleasure, sir.' Whereupon he gave a small head bow and hastily took his leave. The duchess clasped her hands together and heaved a great sigh.

'Sadly this means that I shall miss the king's birthday celebrations tomorrow. Oh, and I was so looking forward to wearing my beautiful new blue gown with the embroidered gauze drapery.'

'I am sorry you will not be present, Your Grace. I should have liked a friend to be present as this is my first royal function.'

Georgiana almost gaped at me. 'You have been invited to the king's ball at St James's Palace?'

'Not to the ball precisely, but, thanks to the prince, I am invited to watch from the spectator's box.'

There was the very slightest pause, then my dear friend issued a warning. 'Don't expect too much, Mary. It was most daring of the prince, or a sign of his current rebellion, to issue such an invitation, but it will not have been with the king's blessing. Do take care.'

I was to remember her words vividly when Monday evening arrived. Because of the riots, and an attempted attack upon St James's Palace earlier that day, there were fewer of the nobility attending the ball than expected. Malden and I were admitted into the Lord Chamberlain's box without question, but the prince did not approach to offer a welcome. I had sternly warned myself that this might be the case, but it was hard to accept in reality.

'Does my darling Florizel not look utterly magnificent?' The prince was wearing a sky blue silk coat, beautifully embroidered with silver, and I could not take my eyes from him.

'You do appreciate that His Highness cannot ask you to dance, Mary?'

Carefully swallowing my disappointment, I brightly remarked, 'That is only to be expected. I am content simply to be here.'

In truth I found it exceedingly painful to be forced to sit and silently watch the man I adored take the floor with other ladies. He opened the ball by dancing with the Lady Augusta Campbell, daughter of the Duke of Argyll, quite pretty and with the most adorable ringlets. I saw her hand him two rosebuds from her bouquet, and later the prince told me that she had said it was 'emblematical of herself and him'. Did she imagine a burgeoning intimacy between them?

As I watched, my heart yearning to take her place, I saw the prince call the Earl of Cholmondeley to his side and hand over the rosebuds. Slanting a glance in my direction he whispered some instruction in his ear. To my complete astonishment that gentleman crossed the floor and presented the flowers to me with a low bow, his face quite devoid of expression.

'From His Royal Highness with his compliments.'

I took the delicate blooms and tucked them into my décolletage, casting the prince a shy smile of gratitude, and more tellingly to his partner one of pure triumph. I felt empowered by the gesture, proud that His Highness would risk public censure in order to honour me, while publicly mortifying so exalted a rival.

We continued our clandestine meetings throughout that summer of 1780, nearly always accompanied by Malden and Prince Frederick. Meanwhile, the scandal of the rosebuds naturally excited comments in the press. The papers daily indulged the malice of my rivals and worst enemies, which are ever prolific on stage, by repeating the most scurrilous nonsense respecting the Prince of Wales and myself. I found it quite impossible to prevent the torrent of abuse that poured upon me from all quarters as lampoons and caricatures.

> A noted beauty, (Perdita her name,
> No matter where brought up, or whence she came,)
> Though bless'd with charms above her narrow soul,
> Was curs'd with pride not reason could controul.
> Wher'er she came contending suitors bow'd.
> (Enough to make the giddy strumpet proud.)

'Did I not warn you that this would happen?' my mother said, deeply distressed by what she considered to be a shocking state of affairs. 'They accuse you of seducing an innocent young prince, with the assistance of your pimp of a husband.'

'Pay no heed, Mama, as you well know the prince has pursued me for months, and the seduction is all on his side, with no help from Tommy.'

'I dare say you are enjoying your new role as a fashionable leader of the ton?'

'Crowds gather wherever I go. Whenever I appear in public I am overwhelmed by the press of the multitude, frequently obliged to quit Ranelagh owing to the crowd assembled round my box. They gaze upon me with open curiosity. Even in the streets I can scarcely enter a shop without experiencing the greatest inconvenience. Many times I have waited hours before quitting an establishment, until the crowd surrounding my carriage has dispersed. Such proceedings have become a national absurdity.'

'It is no laughing matter, Mary. You are a woman of notoriety now.'

I did not much care for this description, although I sympathised with my mother's viewpoint, knowing it was her anxiety for my future happiness which affected her judgment.

'Mama, I am not the first lady to become the mistress of a prince, nor the first this prince has enjoyed. We cannot choose who we love. Didn't Papa say as much years ago?'

'And we know why that was, do we not?'

Realising it was unwise to continue along those lines, I quickly changed tack. 'I cannot understand their interest. People know well enough who I am. Have I not been on stage for three seasons with ample opportunity to view me. It pains me that my fame is greater now, as mistress to a prince, than when I was an actress.'

Mama sniffed her disapproval. 'You seem to be the most talked about woman of the day. The papers are full of gossip and lampoons about Florizel and Perdita. And what of the royal household, what is their opinion of this scandal?'

I sighed, but could not resist admitting to my latest embarrassment. This was my mother, after all, and we were close. 'I recently attended the Oratorio, and as the prince and I cannot be seen together, I seated myself opposite to His Highness, as is my wont. Unfortunately, our fond glances were again noticed and remarked upon, and when I returned the next evening I was denied admittance.'

Mama put her hands to her cheeks in horror. 'Oh, how very mortifying.'

I gave a careless shrug, as if it was of no importance, even though I had been cut to the quick to be barred from the theatre. 'I have the prince's love so I am resolved to fear no one. I held on to my dignity and merely instructed Mr Robinson, who had generously escorted me, to pay his guinea, which he did, and we ascended to our box anyway, in complete defiance.

'What's more, at the end of the evening I made sure that I placed myself in a situation where I was in full view of the prince as he went to his chair. He gazed long and adoringly at me as he departed, making it very clear to everyone present that he wanted me there.'

'Oh, my dearest girl, I fear you may find life as a royal courtesan more trying than you ever anticipated.'

My mother, as ever, was much wiser in these matters than I. Knowing that I was truly the mistress of the prince's heart was a wondrous feeling, more thrilling than I could ever have dreamed possible, but sadly the position failed to gain me the respectable place in society for which I craved. In truth, I felt rather removed from it.

'I would so love to have you with me, dearest Perdita, whenever I attend the theatre or military reviews, but it is not possible. I would like to invite you to join one of the royal hunts at Windsor, but the king would never allow it. Matters may improve when I come of age at twenty-one, but even then I suspect His Majesty will continue to control me. Such is my lot in life. No masquerades, no gambling or drunkenness, and no lounging about Hyde Park.'

'And no affairs with actresses,' I added, kissing his adorable mouth.

My darling Florizel chuckled. 'As you see, I do not obey my father in every respect.'

In August, when he turned eighteen, he was considered old enough to rule for himself, in the sad event this were to become necessary. A private ball was held to celebrate his birthday at Windsor, to which I was not invited. How I longed to be at his side on this great day, but I was excluded from such celebrations. I watched the parade in Windsor Great Park at midday, heard the twenty-one gun salute, ached to be in the royal barge with

my Florizel as the regatta sailed forth. But I was merely a spectator, standing with Tommy on the banks of the Thames.

'Do you not resent how he neglects you?' my husband asked.

'If he does, it is but out of duty,' I tartly responded. 'Not as
you did, from selfishness.'

'Such is my flaw,' Tommy affably conceded. 'Yet I feel His
Highness could do more for you.'

If I privately agreed with this assessment, I did not express an
opinion on the subject. When I met with the prince the next
day, his mood was glum.

'I am to have no establishment of my own, no London house,
after all,' he complained, with no small degree of resentment. 'I
am to continue to share with my brothers.'

'Why has the king reneged on his promise?'

'Can you not guess, dearest Perdita? It is punishment for this
very improper attachment. Nor will I be granted the independent
income I was pledged, so cannot yet honour my bond to you
until I come fully of age.'

'That matters not,' I cried, wrapping my arms about him, and
meant it with all my heart. I could see how hurt and angry he
was by this rebuff, and felt mortified for my dear Florizel as well
as filled with guilt that I might be the cause. 'Did I not say this
could happen? Oh, Your Highness, what can we do?'

'I'm afraid there is nothing to be done. The king declares that
he hates having these scandalous stories "trumpeted in the papers",
as he describes it. He believes his enemies will use them to wound
him. I, of course, assured my father that it will be my principal
object through life to merit the parental attachment and kindness
he professes towards me.'

'Then we must part?' I asked, unable to still the tremor of fear
in my voice.

'Indeed not, Perdita my love,' he assured me, pulling me close
in his arms to kiss me most fervently. 'The king and I disagree
on most matters of any importance, certainly on politics. As you
know I increasingly favour Fox and the Whig party, all thanks
to my uncle the Duke of Cumberland, and our good friends
Sheridan and the Duchess of Devonshire. The more my father
castigates me, the more he drives me into the arms of the opposition. But at eighteen I will behave as I think fit. I intend to

be my own man and refuse to be constantly dictated to, ordered about like some recalcitrant child. I believe it is time that I publicly acknowledged you.'

The Prince wasted no time in setting me up with my own establishment in fashionable Cork Street, a house that had formerly belonged to the Countess of Derby who caused a scandal by deserting her husband and children for her lover the Duke of Dorset. The property was of modest proportions but lavishly furnished and appointed, and the prince granted me a modest sum to buy paintings, books and ornaments to my own taste. Living in the heart of Mayfair was a considerable step up from the previous home I'd shared with Tommy in Covent Garden.

'I have devoted hours shopping for the right accoutrements to dress the house,' I told the Duchess of Devonshire when next I visited. Her house in Piccadilly was now but an easy stroll from my own. 'Even longer scouring the advertisements on the front pages of the newspapers, seeking the best milliners or mantua-makers, portrait painters and booksellers. And I am quite taken by the notion of a new phaeton.'

'What of your dear child?' asked Georgiana, who was still hoping for the illusive heir. 'Why is she not with you today?'

'I do assure you I am not like the countess. Leaving a husband may be forgivable, but nothing would induce me to forsake my darling Maria. While I have agreed to leave her temporarily with my mother, for the sake of the prince's reputation, I have in no way abandoned her. I fully intend to spend many hours with her every single day.'

The duchess considered me with a thoughtful raising of her brow, her silence speaking volumes.

'How could I not agree to such a reasonable request? I believe that my exalted status as a royal mistress will allow me to improve my child's future too.'

She gave me a wry smile. 'I believe you are angling for a title, Mary, rather like Barbara Palmer, mistress to Charles II, who became the Duchess of Cleveland.'

I found myself blushing. 'I assure you the thought had not occurred to me, but we are very much in love, so is there any reason why not?'

'I can think of many reasons, not least the king's opinion on such a matter. George is only a prince, remember, not a monarch. But we shall see. Take care, dear friend, that you do not confuse a simple affair with love and ambition.'

'I have every confidence in his devotion to me,' I said, stubbornly refusing to listen to my friend's advice.

As if to prove his commitment, the prince held a ball for me, at Weltje's Club. Etiquette demanded that he open it with one of the aristocracy, and I was happy that he chose the duchess as partner. Later he did indeed dance with me, which was a complete delight. I felt proud to take my place at his side as the prince's acknowledged mistress, dressed in a new gown of rose silk. And I of course wore his miniature about my neck.

I soon set tongues wagging by entertaining lavishly in my new role, sending giddy female hearts beating with envy. Every new gown I wore, the very latest Paris had to offer, was imitated and emulated to the smallest degree. I drove about Hyde Park in my new blue and silver phaeton, drawn by milk white ponies, my post-boys in matching jackets. I had the panels ornamented with a pretty basket of flowers set above a wreath of roses, with my initials MR painted beneath. If it looked from a distance rather like the prince's five-pearled coronet, then so be it.

Oh, and how the inquisitive bystanders gathered to watch me pass by, blocking my passage with their curiosity, at great inconvenience to my progress. But ever the actress, I knew how to play to the crowds and not be alarmed by them. I might wear a straw hat, tied at the back of my head in the style of a *paysanne*, or a cravat and riding jacket. On other days I would be painted, powdered, patched and rouged to perfection as any fashionable leader of the ton should be.

'Am I living dangerously by inciting such envy?' I asked the prince.

He laughed, amused by my concerns. 'After so many years with only a dull and proper monarch, is it any wonder if they come to worship at the feet of your beauty?'

My cheeks pinked with pleasure at his words, and to my shame I relished every moment of my new-found fame. How could I not be delighted by the prince's acknowledgement of me? I was young still, headstrong, and bewitched by love for the first time in my life.

Being at the height of my beauty I was frequently sought by artists eager to paint my portrait, including Hoppner, Romney and Sherwin. I spent many hours in Sherwin's painting room, and we became such good friends that I would call upon him in his studios whenever the fancy took me. We'd talk for hours on all manner of subjects. On one occasion when I called Mama was with me, as I wished to show her a drawing of myself Sherwin had made in preparation for the portrait. His young apprentice let us in, saying his master was not at home.

'Then fetch the drawing for me, will you, as a favour?' I gave him my most winning smile.

'If you'll do a favour for me,' he cheekily remarked, and began humming a popular song: 'I'll reward you with a kiss.'

Laughing, I pecked a kiss on each cheek. 'There, you little rogue, now will you do as I ask?'

Mama chided me for flirting, and frowned even more when she viewed the sketch. 'He has certainly captured your likeness, but that is a most daring décolletage.'

'Do not my ringlets fall provocatively to my shoulder?'

She gave me a telling look, as only a mother can. 'If you say so, dear.'

'Sherwin is a most serious painter, and wishes to use me as a model for a biblical subject. I suggested I be Solomon's concubine and kneel at the feet of my master, the prince.' I gave a rueful smile. 'Unfortunately, he thought it would be inappropriate to ask His Highness to act as model.'

'I should think so,' my mother retorted, looking quite shocked.

'He suggested we ask Malden, but I declined. Kneel to him? I would die first. I would not encourage the gossip-mongers to think he is anything more than a friend.'

'I have long had reservations about your friendship with that man, dearest, but take care, all of this attention is rather going to your head, which I have to say was ever a flaw of yours.'

Taking the sketch I returned it to the goggle-eyed apprentice, and flounced out of the door, my mother scurrying after me. I was growing rather tired of these naysayers.

Taking no notice of my mother's warning, I recklessly took a

side box at the opera, unheard of for a woman in my situation.
I could hear the ladies chattering their disapproval behind their
fans whenever I took my seat. Such boxes were generally the
preserve of the nobility and persons of rank, so they clearly
considered it presumptuous and arrogant for a woman of my
humble status to occupy one.

'No doubt they will not dare to sit in a box close by, in case
my notoriety should sully them or their daughters,' I said to
Malden, who was always delighted to escort me when Tommy
or the prince were unavailable. 'The *Morning Post* obviously thinks
so, claiming I'm no better than an orange woman.' I laughed.
'They evidently see me as Nell Gwyn rather than the Duchess
of Cleveland.'

'Nell was of humble stock, and never received a title,' Malden
quietly reminded me.

I gave him a look meant to quell. 'I am no east-end prostitute,
Malden, and the equal of any woman in the land. You know me
to be a respectable, warm-hearted, affectionate mother and faithful
friend, do you not?'

He smiled. 'You know full well that you can do no wrong in
my eyes. Do I not adore you?'

'What a sweet man you are. How I wish it was you that I
loved,' and I kissed his cheek, causing him to flush with pleasure.

'Not half so much as do I.'

I laughed. 'But am I not also serious, sensitive, thoughtful and
well read?'

'And a talented poet.'

'Indeed,' I agreed, although I had not written a word in some
time.

The press, however, did not see me in quite that light, and
there were many more scurrilous paragraphs and cartoons
published in the weeks following, all of which I ignored. Let
them say what they liked. I felt secure in the prince's love.

One afternoon I called upon an old actress friend of mine, Sophia
Baddeley. She had once been revered at the Lane for her beautiful
singing voice, before establishing herself as a courtesan. Her lovers
included Viscount Melbourne, Lord Grosvenor, George Garrick
and Prince Frederick, amongst others of the nobility plus one or

two fellow actors. She once apparently refused an offer by Lord Northumberland before marrying a husband who treated her very badly. Some might call her vain, a spoilt spendthrift, but for all she was ten years or so older than myself I had always found her to be friendly and great fun.

Ever popular with the public, she was sadly now in ill health and a state of near destitution. Her companion, a Miss Elizabeth Steel, let me in, her interested gaze taking in the style and richness of my equipage before showing me into a small parlour where the poor lady sat huddled in a chair.

'Oh, the ingratitude of mankind!' I cried, shocked by the sight of my former friend, a vision far removed from the stunning beauty she had once been when she had used to call upon me with the Countess of Tyrconnel and the Marchioness Townshend.

The place was dingy and rather unkempt, and there was the sound of a baby crying somewhere in the background. Miss Steele hurried out of the room, presumably to quieten it.

'I come bearing the compliments of the Duke of Cumberland who humbly pays his respects and on learning of your pecuniary distress, asked me to give you this.' Taking a seat beside her, I handed over a purse containing a few coins, ten guineas in fact, no small sum. Mrs Baddeley made no move to take it from me, although there were tears in her eyes. I gently squeezed her hand.

'His Highness wished me to assure you that more would be forthcoming, if needed.'

'I need no charity, thank you, Mary!'

I glanced about at the sparse furnishings, feeling the cold dampness of the room on this autumn day, at the evidence of a half drunk bottle of gin beneath a small side table. No doubt she was in need of such comfort living here in Spitalfields, after the grandeur of Clarges Street, but to sink so low . . . The sight of it reminded me of Meribah Lorrington, and I shuddered. Was this what became of a royal mistress once she was discarded? Surely not! Sophia had been particularly profligate, notorious, and debt-ridden, not to mention suffering an addiction to laudanum.

'Will you allow the duke to offer you a little comfort?' I persisted.

'Why did you come?'

I was stunned by the coldness of her tone. 'Because you and I were once friends, were we not? Do you not remember the card games we used to play with Mrs Parry, and the actress, Mrs Abbington? Besides which, we are of the same profession.'

'You mean whores?'

I flushed, partly from embarrassment but also with annoyance. 'I meant the theatre. As well as a friend, you were ever an icon to a young new actress such as myself. I even named my second child after you, although she sadly perished within weeks of her birth.'

This seemed to startle her, and a tear slid down her pale cheek. 'Oh, Mary, I am so sorry. I too am a mother, so can appreciate the pain that must have caused.'

'Then will you not allow me to be of service? I wish only to help.'

'You would do better to help yourself, by not taking up with a prince. It will only lead to heartbreak. These royals will say anything to satisfy their own desires, but once sated, or they see a more desirable quarry on the horizon, they will turn away from you without a sigh of regret.'

I felt a clench of fear inside, which I strived to ignore. 'Far better a loving prince than a straying husband who draws on my purse strings too often.'

'I would also advise staying well clear of cheating husbands.'

I smiled. 'The prince too would have me stay away from Tommy but he continues to seek me out when he wishes to dip in my purse. How can I refuse when I am still his wife? And we remain on friendly terms. I am sorry things have turned out badly for you, Sophia, but I am most fortunate as the prince has made me the happiest of women.' I told her of our clandestine meetings at Kew, and how the prince would scale locked gates in his eagerness to reach me.

'I'm glad to see you so happy, but it will not last.'

I hastened to rebut this remark. 'I assure you his affection for me is of no short duration.'

She gave a sad shake of her head. 'Don't ever give up your writing, Mary. You may need that skill one day. Now take your charity and leave, if you please. My pride is all I have left that is of any value.'

I was on my feet in a second, stunned by this dismissal even as my heart went out to her, filled with admiration for the woman's resilience and independent spirit. But I dare not tell the duke that I had failed in my mission. 'I will not leave you in this state, dear friend. Take the money for the sake of your child. I shall call again when we will talk some more, perhaps of happier days.' And leaving the purse on the table I hurried out, back to my phaeton and my celebrity life. But the image of this dear lady disturbed my sleep for many nights to come.

It seems Mrs Baddeley's warnings about staying away from a straying husband at least proved to be wise. I certainly wished Tommy had stayed well away from me when on the seventh of October I caught him making love to a young girl in one of the boxes at Covent Garden Theatre. To say I was angry is to greatly understate the depth of my emotion. I was outraged, quite beside myself with fury.

'How could you humiliate me and be so careless of my reputation as to carry out such an act in the full public gaze?'

'What reputation?' he chortled.

'You could at least consider how His Highness might react to such behaviour.'

My husband simply put back his head and roared with laughter, which caused me to completely lose my temper. Grabbing him by the hair I dragged him from the box and marched him out of the theatre, screaming at him all the while, much to the amusement of the audience.

I took him home and berated him for hours, determined to teach foolish Tommy the meaning of penitence.

Predictably, I was attacked by the press, ruthlessly accused of being 'a ripe mine of diseases', as if I were some cheap harlot. Malden was again heralded as one of my lovers, together with all the usual artillery of slander.

Worse was to come in November when a caricature appeared of me under the title *Florizel and Perdita*. In this I was dressed in a most revealing gown, a Welsh hat perched upon my head, surrounded by boxes of cosmetics labelled carmine, perfume and pomatum. The figure of my husband wearing horns stood to one side, while the prince in Roman costume stood on the other. Below it was the most offensive poem I had ever read.

Sometimes she'd play the Tragic Queen,
Sometimes the Peasant poor,
Sometimes she'd step behind the Scenes
And there she'd play the W—

It continued in this fashion, finishing with:

Her husband too, a Puny Imp,
Will often guard the door,
And humbly play Sir Peter Pimp
While she performs the W—

I was mortified, feeling myself persecuted at every turn. I was no whore or prostitute, but a prince's mistress, an entirely different creature altogether. Determined not to reveal any weakness I appeared at a masquerade the very next day, choosing Malden again as escort, as I had no wish to be even seen in close proximity to my husband.

'At least I still have the love of my darling Florizel,' I insisted, head high as I faced the gossip-mongers.

Then just before Christmas I received a note from the prince. I stared at it in utter disbelief as it bore but a few words. 'We must meet no more.'

There was no explanation. No apology. Nothing! Our beautiful affair that had begun with an avalanche of letters declaring his undying love for me was apparently at an end.

Hurt beyond words, I wrote at once to His Royal Highness, asking for an explanation. How could I believe it when only days before I'd spent hours with the prince at Kew, his love for me undiminished, or so it had seemed. I received no reply. I wrote again, needing an answer to this cruel and extraordinary mystery. When still I heard nothing I was overcome by panic and resolved to speak to him in person, whatever the cost, and embarked upon a mad enterprise.

Knowing the prince to be at Windsor I set out in a small pony phaeton, accompanied by my postilion, a mere boy. It was a foolish escapade, a crazy act on my part as dusk was already falling when we quitted Hyde Park Corner, the winter night cold and damp. With some relief we stopped to take refreshment and rest the horses at Hounslow Heath, warming ourselves by a blazing log fire as we supped oxtail soup.

'Take care, good lady, every carriage which has crossed the heath this last ten nights has been attacked by footpads and robbed.'

Until that moment, the prospect of personal danger had not occurred to me, although I was aware that highwaymen, whether on foot or horseback, were not the romantic chivalrous beings of romance. They would violate or kill a lone woman even as they robbed her, without a moment's hesitation, yet I shrugged these concerns away.

'I have far greater worries on my mind,' I told him, resolved to continue no matter what the danger.

We had scarcely reached the middle of the heath when my pony was startled by the sudden appearance of a cloaked figure who, dashing out of the darkness, made a lunge for the reins. I cried out in alarm. To his credit the boy instantly spurred the animal to a gallop. Our light vehicle bounded forward, causing the ruffian to lose his grip. We drove at full tilt, the footpad running behind, doing his utmost to overtake us. Fortunately the pony easily outran him and by the time we reached the Magpie, a small inn on the edge of the heath, my heart was racing with fear. Although I felt strangely exhilarated at my own bravery.

Only then did I realise that I was still wearing the prince's miniature about my neck. I swear my would-be assailant could only have wrested it from me by strangling me first.

My sense of achievement was short-lived. As I sat by the fire warming my toes, a familiar figure appeared whom I recognised as none other than the bewitchingly beautiful Elizabeth Armistead. I recalled that I'd often heard the prince speak of his admiration for this woman when seeing her in plays, frequently expressing his wish to meet the lady.

She was a notorious demirep whose background was shady to say the least. She had been born into poverty, then became a hairdresser's model before installing herself in a brothel. It was admittedly an exclusive one where the Viscount Bolingbroke, reputedly captivated by her beauty, rescued her and established her in lodgings so that she could do a trial for Covent Garden.

She was without question a beauty, tall and elegant, if now somewhat past her prime, and had ever been skilful at attracting rich protectors such as Lord Cavendish and the Duke of Dorset to name but two. Now, it seemed, she had looked higher still, for I couldn't help but notice she was accompanied by Meynell, the prince's man. I realised with sinking heart that she must be returning from an assignation with His Highness. I well knew the prince's fondness for older ladies.

Here then was the reason for my Florizel's hitherto inexplicable conduct. Had he believed all the bad press insinuating an affair between myself and Malden? Was this the reason he had looked elsewhere? I intended to shortly discover the answer to these questions.

But to my great dismay, on my arrival at Windsor, His Royal Highness refused to see me. My agonies knew no bounds. My heart was broken.

I poured out my troubles to Malden, who was deeply sympathetic. 'My dear Mary, I am so sorry, although I have to admit that I too have lost the favour of the prince for some inexplicable reason.'

I looked at him in astonishment. This was not at all what I had wished to hear, and did little to ease my distress. 'I do not understand why he has turned against us, unless he believes all the foul rumours put about by the press that you and I have been intimate.'

He gave a wry smile. 'I would not mind being cast out, were that true, but I believe you must have a multitude of secret enemies, Mary. Those who are only too eager to part you from the prince, as so illustrious a lover could not fail to excite envy.'

A sickness washed over me as I recalled my own mother's warning not to let my new-found fame go to my head. How I had preened and flaunted myself, inciting jealousy at every turn. Why had I not listened to her wise advice, and that of my good friend the duchess?

'It is true that women of all descriptions are eager to attract His Highness's attention, but I have neither the rank nor the power to oppose such adversaries. Much as I might weep, it seems there is nothing to be done. The prince has abandoned me and taken a new mistress.'

I waited for Malden to point out that he had warned me this might happen, and greatly appreciated his silence when he refrained from doing so. He merely put his arms about me and held me close. I could feel the pounding of his heart, smell the pomade he always wore secreted about his person, dandy that he was.

'How am I to survive? I have quitted both husband and profession and my creditors are gathering like predatory wolves while the prince does not even answer my letters. My future prospects look dire!'

Malden, as always, came to my aid. 'Allow me to help, Mary.'

'I do not ask *you* for money, My Lord, knowing you are almost as poor as myself.'

He smiled kindly. 'But with better prospects. Fear not, I mean only to act as go-between and speak on your behalf. I will make every effort to gain you the allowance owed to you. Someone must tactfully remind His Highness of the bond he signed in your favour. I'm sure the matter can be satisfactorily resolved.'

It did my heart good to hear such confidence expressed. Neglected by the prince, Malden was the friend upon whom I most relied now for assistance.

The result of his intervention on my behalf was that the prince not only sent his respects, he requested that I meet him at the house of Lord Malden in Clarges Street. I could hardly believe my good fortune.

'Dear sweet man,' I cried, kissing Malden full upon the lips.

'I am a fool to myself,' he sighed.

I hurried to meet the prince in all eagerness, quite certain this marked a renewal of our former friendship and affection, and as my darling Florizel gathered me in his arms, it was as if we had never been estranged. 'You can be assured, sire, of my undying devotion and complete loyalty.' At which declaration he kissed me gently upon the mouth.

'Believe me, dear Perdita, I do not believe the calumnies perpetrated against you.'

'Nor those against Malden, I trust, who is your loyal servant and friend? I swear there has been no intimacy between us.'

'Yet he does admit to loving you.'

'That is no fault of mine, nor his either. Please believe me that we are innocent of all charges. He is not, and never shall be, my lover. I beg you to give us justice.'

He smoothed his hands over my shoulders which I'd left daringly bare, my milk-white breasts blossoming provocatively above the low neckline of my gown as I'd hoped to entice him in just such a manner. 'I accept there have been falsehoods printed against you,' he murmured, his greedy gaze devouring me. 'How silky your skin is, dear Perdita. I had forgotten how very beautiful you are.'

This time when he kissed me it was with a greater fervour, very like the passion we had enjoyed in those delightful months together. I encouraged him to slip a hand inside my bodice to caress my breasts, which he was more than eager to do.

My darling Florizel wasted no time in stripping off my gown, and within moments we were lying on the bed, my legs sprawled wide while he pounded inside me. What utter bliss, what triumph and joy to make him mine once more.

'Never for one moment have I ceased to love you,' he murmured when, sated, we afterwards lay breathless in each other's arms.

'Why then did you forsake me?

He let out a small sigh. 'The truth is that the king loathes the bad publicity, not least the embarrassing business with your husband and that harlot in the box. He was so anxious for me to end the affair that His Majesty offered me an apartment of my own in Buckingham Palace.'

'Oh, my darling, how wonderful!' What else could I say? My lover had abandoned me for the sake of his new-found independence. Who better than I to understand such an appeal?

'There were other conditions, of course,' he continued, settling my head upon his chest where he could stroke my soft auburn curls. 'I am allowed to invite friends to dine only twice a week. I may visit a playhouse provided I give due notice to the king and am accompanied by my regular attendants. I must attend church every Sunday, the Drawing Room at St James's Palace when the king is present, and that of the queen. Naturally there must be no attendance at masquerades, no gambling or drunken behaviour. Last, but by no means least, no private assemblies.'

I lifted my head to look at him in startled dismay. 'You mean no more visits to my house in Cork Street?'

'I'm afraid not, dear Perdita. I am to keep away from anything the least improper.' His smile was rueful.

I wondered in what way visiting Mrs Armistead might be considered proper, when visiting *me* was not. But even I dare not ask such a question. 'Then we must reinstate our clandestine meetings at Kew.'

'What a joy those were,' he chortled.

We passed a blissfully happy afternoon together, in the most friendly and delightful fashion, our love and passion for each other as strong as ever. I flattered myself that all our differences were behind us.

What words can express my chagrin when, on meeting His Royal Highness the very next day in Hyde Park, he quickly turned his head away to avoid seeing me, affecting not even to know me!

I felt as if I had been physically struck! Yet again I was totally ignorant of any just cause for so sudden a change. Overwhelmed at being so cruelly cut by the man I adored, my distress knew no bounds. Let heaven be my witness, I blamed not the prince. I did then, and ever shall, consider his mind to be both noble and honourable. Nor could I convince myself that his heart, the seat of so many virtues, could possibly be cold or unjust.

But in my heart I knew that I had lost him and felt utterly alone, cast adrift in a dark and vengeful world.

My estrangement from Florizel soon became the subject of public speculation, the news-sheets again hurling their brickbats upon my defenceless head. Tommy was at my side the moment he heard.

'How I regret ever having lost you, Mary. You know that I still hold you in deep affection. Could we not reunite and try again?'

'No, Tommy, we could not. Though I remain very fond of

you, your predilection for prostitutes is even worse than that
of the prince. You offended me most publicly, despite my
having shared my good fortune with you as best I may. Because
of your constant demands upon my purse, and my efforts to
present myself well for His Highness, my own debts now
amount to almost seven thousand pounds. What am I to do?
With no allowance or income from the theatre, my creditors
are circling with increasing impatience, pressing to be paid in
cash or kind.'

My husband, of course, had no solution, and melted away, no
doubt to build up yet more debts, and leaving me cooling my
heels in frustration.

Time hung heavy on my hands, the empty hours stretching
before me with nothing to fill my days, and little prospect of
improvement. I joylessly circled Ranelagh, Vauxhall and the
Pantheon, struggling to remember happier times but recalling
only the bad, such as Lyttelton's attempted abduction. And being
winter, even the gardens were too bare and frost-laden to cheer
me. My mind was even blank of the verses I once so artlessly
created.

So it was with some relief that a few short weeks after the
prince wrote ending our affair, I agreed to sit for a portrait for
George Romney. The artist's normal charge was twenty guineas
for a half-length portrait, less than Sir Joshua Reynolds or
Gainsborough but still expensive. However, he offered to paint
me for no charge at all, as he claimed my beauty would win him
new custom among aristocratic circles.

'I very much doubt it. I am no longer in favour with the
aristocratic ladies, Mr Romney. None wish to imitate me now.
They consider me to be a fallen woman.'

He smiled at that. 'They will ever admire and wish to emulate
your beauty, Mrs Robinson, albeit if it is tainted with envy. I
could make engravings and prints of such a portrait to advertise
my skills. It would be to our mutual benefit.'

'Then I thank you and accept, kind sir.' Privately, I hoped that
the prince would see the portrait and fall in love with me all
over again.

We agreed that for this picture I would wear a demure, Quaker-
like gown and cap, no daring décolletage, my hands tucked neatly

inside a fur muff. But as I patiently sat for hour upon hour, I
began to seriously consider my future. Much as I might castigate
poor Tommy for his failings, I couldn't help contemplating the
recklessness in disposing of both husband and career, losing both
reputation and income in one fell swoop.

'I dare say you have heard news of my new rival, the Armistead?'
I said to the duchess as we sipped coffee together one morning.
Maria Elizabeth, now quite the young miss of six was being
pandered to with a selection of dolls to keep her amused while
we quietly talked.

'Yes, Mary, I have. I learned of it through my brother-in-law,
George Cavendish, whose mistress she still was at the time. He
discovered her betrayal when he called upon her one night,
only to find the Prince of Wales skulking behind her bedroom
door.'

I saw the all too evident amusement in her eyes even as I
put a hand to my mouth in shock. 'What on earth did his lordship do?'

'He made a low bow and retreated. The prince clearly had
precedence.' Even I was laughing by this time, although I quickly
sobered. 'My situation grows ever more precarious, so I am
considering a return to my profession.'

Georgiana frowned as she handed me a macaroon. 'And what
do your former colleagues think of the idea?'

I sighed. 'Those whom I consulted warned me that the public
would never tolerate my return to the stage. But Sophia Baddeley
made a successful comeback, so why shouldn't I?'

'Sadly, dear Mary, I'm afraid I must agree with your friends'
assessment. You are a better woman than Mrs Baddeley, it is true,
but no matter how you might proclaim your innocence, it is
generally believed that you and Malden *were* engaged in an affair.
I even believed it myself at one time,' she added with a chuckle.
A response which hurt me deeply.

'How then am I to provide an ample and honourable income
for myself and my child, if I do not return to the stage?'

'Sadly, you must find some other way. The public would never
accept you back in such a prominent and public position. You
are, I'm afraid, a ruined woman.'

I winced at such a description, my throat closing, quite unable to swallow the dry crumbs of the biscuit. 'How so?'

'There is no doubt you would continue to be pilloried in the press, the subject of yet more ridicule,' she gently warned me. 'It is most inopportune that you lost the prince just as he has been formerly acknowledged as heir to the throne. In some respects that leaves him with less control over his life, at least until he turns twenty-one. Therefore, I would suggest a life of penitent retirement for some considerable time. I see no other option, Mary, if you are not to avoid complete notoriety.'

Much as I might object to the duchess's analysis of my situation, this time I vowed to listen to her advice.

I went into rural retreat, hiring a cottage not far from the palace at Kew, perhaps secretly hoping an opportunity might present itself for me to speak to the prince. If nothing else I could remind him that I still possessed his letters.

Sadly, in the few short weeks I quietly festered there, I saw no sign of him. Soon growing bored I returned to town, my future still unresolved. In a show of defiance, the very first day following my arrival I attended a masquerade dressed in a most becoming military costume in scarlet and apple green. Escorted by Malden and Lord Cholmondeley, I was immediately brought up to date with the latest news and scandals.

'Would you believe the prince has now stolen my mistress, Grace Dalrymple Eliot?' Cholmondeley informed me in injured tones. 'I once rescued her from a French convent when her brother ensconced her there, and she has been under my protection ever since. This is how she repays me.'

'You mean Dally the Tall?' I asked, using her more common name. 'Are you saying that Florizel has betrayed us both, My Lord?'

'He has indeed. I have lost a most pleasant companion, and you, Mary, now have two rivals.'

'Why would he sink so low?' I asked Malden, ever my source of information on the prince.

'Because His Highness is desperate for the return of his letters, but deeply fearful that retrieving them might cost him a deal of money. And the Armistead might well prove to be another such drain upon his purse. He imagines that spreading his favours wide is less dangerous. George is also embroiling himself more and more with his libertine uncle the Duke of Cumberland, as he misses his brother Frederick who's still in Germany.'

Filled with furious rebellion I treated myself to a new phaeton, together with four chestnut ponies. I would add it to the account being charged against my former lover. Dressed in a blue coat prettily trimmed with silver, a plumed feather atop a most dashing hat, I drove about Hyde Park at a reckless pace determined to make heads turn.

It was Malden now who issued a warning. 'Take care, Mary, the news-sheets are revelling in this rivalry between yourself and the Armistead.'

I laughed. 'It seems to me the papers are fighting a war against each other almost as fiercely as that between ourselves. The *Morning Post* continues with its hostility towards me, while the *Morning Herald*, whose owner is a friend of mine, is hostile to my rival.'

'They are describing it as a cat fight, claiming the pair of you are exchanging looks of "fiery indignation", and using "repeated broadsides of grinnings and spittings to the no small entertainment of the neighbourhood" as you drive about in your yellow equipages!'

'It is a most fashionable colour,' I quipped. 'But I have resolved to ignore their venom. Nevertheless, it hurts more than I can say to see the Armistead seated opposite the prince at the theatre while I must keep my distance.'

It all came to a head one night in February when the Armistead drew off a glove, seeming to flourish it at me before tossing it down as if it were a gauntlet.

I shuddered at my own humiliation, knowing I was beaten. My rival had triumphed. I would never win my Florizel back now. He was forever lost to me.

My prospects were becoming ever more dire with each passing hour, but I had no intention of going quietly. I still had the prince's letters, and the bond. If they were the only protection I possessed, then I would use them to my best advantage.

In March I learned the prince was unwell. 'Some say the illness is being put down to his debauched life with the Duke of Cumberland,' Malden informed me. 'Although he may simply be hiding away in fear from the possible publication of his letters.'

'I have as yet made no decision about them,' I demurred.

'Yet you are considering it? I should warn you, Mary, that such a ploy may not work. It might well have the opposite affect and scupper any chance you have of the prince settling your debts.'

I turned away, choosing not to answer.

I soon learned to my cost the power of such documents. A piece entitled 'Letters from Perdita to a Certain Israelite' suddenly appeared in the press, quite out of the blue, the author hiding behind anonymity. But I guessed these were the letters I had written to 'Jew' King, the implication being that we'd engaged in a flirtatious affair whereas my sole purpose had been to sweeten him for the sake of gaining further loans for my debt-ridden husband. My efforts to help Tommy had come back to haunt me.

Worse, the article was filled with lies and slander, claiming that Tommy was a swindler, that I had revelled in a string of affairs including one when barely a girl with a captain whom I had declined to marry, and with Lord Lyttelton. The proposal I received at thirteen had certainly been real enough, to my great amusement at the time, but talk of an affair between us was utterly ludicrous. As for Lyttelton, I would have slit my own throat rather than bed that man. Added to such fantasies came an account of our months in the Fleet. Only the latter was undeniably true, the rest being pure make-believe, or a twisted version of the truth. Was this King's revenge upon Tommy, for my husband not repaying all the money he owed? Or for my rejection of his advances?

Having besmirched my name the money lender then had the temerity to call at my house. The maid showed him into the drawing room where he sprawled in a chair, looking around as if he owned the place. I sat facing him, perched on the edge of mine, making no offer of refreshment.

'Let us come straight to the point, shall we, to spare further embarrassment. I am willing to return the letters to you, Mrs Robinson, as I'm sure you would wish me to do. The cost of such a transaction would be £400.'

I barely managed to stifle a gasp. 'If you imagine I can put my hands on such a sum you are even more of a fantasist than those letters imply.'

He laughed. 'There is no requirement for me to prove their veracity.'

An icy chill gripped me. This man could spread whatever lies he chose, and I could do nothing to prove my innocence. Nevertheless, I had no intention of allowing him to think he had beaten me. 'I will refute every word, sue for libel if needs be.'

'Those were but a few samples,' he continued. 'I am compiling the entire collection into a book, which my publisher expects will sell at least 10,000 copies. I shall ask him to send you a copy when it is out, shall I?'

I was on my feet in a second, tugging on the bell pull to summon the maid. 'I would be obliged, Mr King, if you would leave my house this instant.'

He did not move a muscle. 'Did I say £400? I fear I misled you. The sum, in fact, would be £2,000. Were you to refuse to pay I would find myself obliged to inform your lover, Lord Malden, of your infidelity and plant more vicious tales about you in the press.'

I almost laughed out loud at this mistaken assumption. Fortunately, even I was not so recklessly foolish. 'You may do your worst, blackmail will not move me.'

'That remains to be seen,' he chortled. 'It all depends upon what further scandals your letters reveal, does it not?'

Fortunately, a footman appeared at that moment in answer to my call, or I might well have done something I would afterwards regret. I had never felt more like punching the loathsome little man upon the chin.

His blackmail plan did not work. I still had some friends in the press, it seemed, and the letters were largely dismissed as forgeries, which is indeed what they were. King's book sold barely one hundred copies.

And yet I was seriously considering a form of blackmail of my own.

That spring I took a post as fashion correspondent for the *Lady's Magazine*, which I hoped would assist me in building a new career. My writing, I thought, could yet be my salvation, as Mrs Baddeley had suggested. But it would not be easy as my muse seemed to have deserted me. I hoped writing about fashion would be less taxing than creating a poem out of nothing, and I'd be paid well for it. I began by announcing 'The Perdita', a chip hat with a bow tied under the chin and pink ribbons puffed around the crown. It proved to be most popular. This gave a much needed boost to my fragile confidence as my situation grew ever more desperate.

I rarely saw Tommy, as he was by then living in Stafford Street in Saint Mary le Bow near Cheapside. At least my husband asked for no further favours, perhaps realizing he'd bled me dry.

I had sacrificed everything for the prince so naturally felt I deserved some recompense for having abandoned a profitable and independent career. I wrote yet another letter to him, requesting His Highness not only settle my debts but grant me an annuity. Surely all ladies living under a gentleman's protection were so entitled. I wished His Highness to appreciate that I was acting in good faith and had every wish to return his letters, if only for his own peace of mind.

The *Morning Post*, still my arch enemy, then accused me of having an affair with the Earl of Derby in order to seduce him away from my rival on stage, Elizabeth Farren, 'in a fit of envy and vexation'. As a consequence of this liaison, I was apparently pregnant, as also was my daughter. They clearly did not appreciate that Maria was only six.

'What will they accuse me of next?' I cried, to any friend who would listen. 'They have even added a decade to my age, which is unforgivable.'

I imagined His Majesty the king steaming with anger, furiously writing to his son about the latest scandals to blacken my name. When no response came in answer to my very reasonable request, and anticipating my creditors foreclosing at any moment with no hope of paying them off, a certain recklessness came upon me. I refurbished my wardrobe and began to hold wild parties at my home. Cork Street came alive with fashionable carriages constantly rolling up to my door.

In the end, I took the only option left to me and threatened to publish the letters, gladly handing the entire business over to Malden.

Lord Malden met the prince at his apartments at Buckingham Palace and negotiations began, rumbling on over many months as letters were exchanged between lawyers, meeting after meeting taking place as no agreement was reached. I was finally visited by Colonel Hotham, the prince's man of business, who offered me £5,000.

'What of the £20,000 promised by the bond?' I protested, believing I was entitled to better treatment. 'I will only return the letters in exchange for settling all my debts, which this sum will not do.'

The sum would not even cover my debts. I vented my wrath in a furious letter to His Highness. 'I shall quit England instantly but no earthly power shall make me ever receive the smallest support from you.' I accused the prince of insulting me, and swore I would never solicit the smallest favour from him ever again. It was as well that I calmed down before sending the letter, accepting Malden's advice to destroy it.

Lord Malden again met the prince where the dispute grew ever more bitter as he pressed for provision for my future. 'I pointed out that he was accountable for your debts, Mary, as you had incurred them on the repeated assurances that he would honour your expenses.'

'Indeed, and I forsook my career, my husband, and my independence on the strength of that promise.'

'His Highness refuses absolutely to commit himself without the king's consent, which appears to be quite impossible to achieve. The prince insists that you offer absolute security that the restitution of the letters will be complete, with no originals or copies retained.'

'Does he not trust me?'

'He fears you may publish copies if not satisfied with the settlement.'

'Then His Highness must settle the matter fairly, as agreed by the bond.'

In disgust I wrote one last letter to my erstwhile lover:

> I have ever acted with the strictest honour and candour
> . . . I do not know what answer may be thought sufficient,
> the only one I can, or ever will be induced to give, is that
> I am willing to return every letter I have ever received from
> his R.H. I have ever valued those letters as dearly as my
> existence, and nothing but my distressed situation ever should
> have tempted me to give them up at all.

Malden later informed me that the king had approached the prime minister, Lord North, on the matter, asking for his assistance.

'Is that a good sign?'

'We can but hope so.'

At length I felt bound to agree to the £5,000, with the proviso that more would come later when the prince came of age. At which point I readily handed over the letters in early September, 1781, to Colonel Hotham, the prince's treasurer.

'It feels little consolation for the difficulties I suffered, and when I so deeply feel the loss of the prince's love, as well as my own degradation.'

In a last act of rebellion I ordered another carriage, a *Boüe de Paris*. 'It bids fair to kick the yellow brimstone-coloured equipages quite out of doors,' I boasted to my friend, trying not to notice Malden's grimace of disapproval.

'You are still young,' he consoled me. 'Your charm and beauty have already gained you the friendship of some of the most enlightened and engaging people of our time.'

I could only agree with him, since my friends included such as Sherwin, Sheridan and Garrick, and the Duchess of Devonshire, of course. All persons of talent or distinction. Yet I recognised no such talent in myself as I remained sunk in my own private sorrow.

'I can no longer go on in this fashion,' I announced to my mother. 'I intend to make a tour to Paris.' Flight was humiliating and dreadful to contemplate, but I felt quite unable to remain in England.

'That is a splendid notion!' she agreed. 'Allow yourself a few months in the brilliant metropolis of France, dearest, and it will soon take your mind away from all your troubles.'

Dear Georgiana, the Duchess of Devonshire helped me to procure letters of introduction to some notable French families, and to Sir John Lambert, resident English banker at Paris.

So it was that I quitted London and left for France via Margate and Ostend, if with a heavy heart. I had given up every single one of the prince's letters, as instructed, but I still possessed his miniature. And the bond.

Seven

Queen of the Courtesans

TARLETON, thy mind, above the poet's praise
Asks not the labour'd task of flatt'ring lays!
As the rare gem with innate lustre glows,
As round the oak the gadding Ivy grows,
So shall thy worth, in native radiance live!

Mary Darby Robinson
'Ode to Valour'

The day after my darling Maria turned seven, on the 19 October 1781, the pair of us, with a handful of servants, crossed the English Channel. I recalled my mother's fears about going to sea but actually found the journey both pleasant and relaxing, and neither of us suffered the slightest discomfort. On our eventual arrival, Sir John Lambert went out of his way to procure a commodious and fashionable apartment for us, where we settled most comfortably. He also hired me a carriage, and a box at the opera, not that I had any great wish to face society.

I fear that for some days I hid in my chamber, thinking on circumstances, of how I came to be here all alone in a foreign land, leaving my lost love across the sea at home. How I ached for my Florizel, to feel his arms about me, his adoring gaze on mine. And how I regretted the loss of his letters which had ever comforted me. But wallowing in self-pity was doing no good at all for my oversensitive soul.

At length my valiant, if rather ancient, chevalier persuaded me to step out and see the sights of Paris. As amiable and stylish as one would expect a Frenchman to be, Sir John seemed determined to devote himself entirely to my needs, and I did begin to enjoy myself. We saw the Louvre, explored the Tuileries Gardens, and he readily escorted me to many Parisian establishments to allow me to take advantage of the new fashions. I marvelled at the Palace of Versailles with its gilt and mirrors, although I was appalled by the filth, with dog turds everywhere.

'Can no one think to clean them up?' I complained, but Sir John merely shrugged, in that delightfully Gallic way.

He held many literary gatherings, parties and entertainments on my behalf, which inspired further invitations, most of which I declined. At the few events I did attend, I met the most brilliant and celebrated of guests who overwhelmed me with their generosity and admiration.

The French seemed quite taken with me, declaring my beauty shone with bright perfection. They admired my sultry eyes, which I have always considered rather dark and unappealing, and my mesmerising voice. But they also remarked upon my cultivated manner, intelligence and firm, independent spirit. Comments which I greatly appreciated as it was all most flattering. It seemed everyone wished to meet *La Belle Anglaise*, which is how I came to be known.

It was at one of these affairs that Sir John introduced me to the Duc de Chartes, among other notables.

'Ah, Mrs Robinson, permit me to say that you are even more beautiful in person than legend has it. No wonder the prince took you to his bed.'

My reputation, it seemed, had preceded me.

The duke claimed to be descended from Louis XIII, no doubt from the wrong side of the blanket. He was undoubtedly a stylish and witty man, but as I came to know him better I considered him to be a compound of ambition and degradation, vanity and folly, courage and audacity. A libertine if ever I saw one.

He made a great fuss of inviting me to the races on the plaines des Sablons, to fetes and parties, all meant to capture the attention of *La Belle Anglaise*. But despite his elegance and undeniable wealth, I found no difficulty in declining his invitations as he did not attract me in the slightest.

But then on my birthday, the twenty-seventh of November, the duke staged a magnificent fete in my honour at his home at Monceaux, so that I could not, in all civility, refuse. I took with me a German lady as companion, with whom I had recently become acquainted, and Sir John kindly agreed to act as chaperone.

The Duc de Chartres had clearly set out to impress, creating the most extraordinary and magnificent scene. Serpentine paths wound their way through the gardens of his estate, with streams, fountains, cascades and artefacts representing all ages and cultures. There was a Chinese pagoda, Egyptian pyramid, Venetian bridge and Dutch windmill, among other follies. My initials were hung in every tree, the whole illuminated with strings of lamps interwoven with wreaths of artificial flowers.

I couldn't help but be reminded of those early visits to Vauxhall with Tommy, and sighed a little at the memory of those halcyon days of my youth.

But this was more gaudy, more outrageous, the most carefully staged seduction scene one could possibly imagine.

'I know I shall triumph over your heart, Mrs Robinson,' he arrogantly asserted.

Fortunately, the duke's very hauteur repelled me, and I managed to hold him off. Still nursing the pain of losing my beloved Florizel, I was not interested in an affair. Nevertheless, good manners demanded that I at least converse with the fellow, and I confess I took advantage of his good will by mentioning a secret ambition of mine.

'I believe the queen has recently provided France with an heir.'

'The dauphin was born last month, a fine, healthy child.'

'My compliments to Her Majesty. I had hoped, while staying in your beautiful metropolis, of witnessing the beauties of Marie Antoinette in person, if only that were possible.'

'Ah, there is no reason why you should not, dear Mrs Robinson. I would be more than happy to arrange it for you.'

I rewarded him with my most winning smile. 'Would you truly do that for me?'

Taking my hand, he kissed it, and I steeled myself not to snatch it away. 'The king and queen hold public dinners in their apartments at Versailles, which we call the *Grand Couvert*. The word *couvert* meaning place setting in French. I should be delighted to personally escort you.'

'You are most kind.' To see the queen in person, was an offer I could not refuse.

★   ★   ★

The first requirement was that I be suitably attired. Having secured the necessary permission from Her Majesty, the duke also provided me with the name of her dressmaker. Mademoiselle Rose Bertin, the royal milliner and modiste, occupied a shop in the rue de Saint-Honoré where she held court as if she herself were a queen upon a throne. I wasted no time in visiting her.

'I wish to be eye-catching. To be elegant and stylish in the latest French fashion, but suited to my own individual taste.'

'I can provide all of that and more, madame, assuming you can afford me.'

I stiffened, closing my mind to the fact that I had not quite managed to pay off all my debts with the sum Malden had won for me. Determined not to be intimidated by the lady, I smiled sweetly. 'But of course.'

She created for me the most beautiful pale green lustring gown with a tiffany petticoat, festooned with delicate lilacs. The head-dress was equally magnificent, composed entirely of white feathers. And although I considered myself to be a typical rosy-cheeked English maid, still aglow with good health and youth, I stained them with patches of rouge, suitably in keeping with the fashion of the French court.

As I entered the dining room, the *Grand Couvert* was, to my eyes, astonishing. My gaze was captured instantly by the glorious ceiling with its paintings and gilded stucco, by the crimson damask upon the walls, the fashionable tapestries and stylish furniture. I felt completely overawed by the scene. The moment he saw me the Duc de Chartes at once left the king's side and hurried over.

'Is it not magnificent?' he whispered, pride in his role very evident in his tone as he secured me a place from where I could easily view the queen.

The silver set upon the long table reminded me of the goblets brought by the prince for our romantic assignations. Perhaps the English royal family also had a passion for all things French. The table itself afforded a magnificent display of epicurean luxury. The king and queen sat on armchairs, facing the public who stood some distance away, together with a cluster of courtiers, separated from the royal diners by a crimson cord.

'Only specially invited guests and members of the royal

household are allowed to sit and dine with the king and queen at the table,' my escort explained.

'Who then are those ladies seated on that row of stools close by?' I asked.

'They are the duchesses and ladies in waiting. Only they are allowed the privilege of sitting so close to Their Majesties.'

The room was crowded, dogs wandering about searching for scraps as the king and queen ate. Or rather, King Louis ate, acquitting himself with more alacrity than grace. Marie Antoinette, I noticed, ate nothing.

'Why does she not eat? She does not even take off her gloves.'

'Her Majesty dislikes such formal occasions as these, forced upon her by etiquette, and has but a small appetite. She takes her coffee and croissants of a morning, but shows little interest in food thereafter.' He frowned slightly. 'Unfortunately, the fact she does not eat a morsel of this meal, makes her appear somewhat aloof in the eyes of the public.'

'Oh, but she is so elegant, and beautiful with her milk-pale skin, grey-blue eyes, rosebud lips and delicately slender frame. Her expression is sweetness itself.' I could hardly take my eyes from her.

'She is also quite vivacious and outgoing, a social butterfly who loves to party, play cards and wear extravagant fashions.' He laughed. 'As do we all.'

A verse began to form in my mind, which later developed into a full poem.

> Oh! I have seen her, like a sun, sublime,
> Diffusing glory on the wings of Time.
> And, as revolving seasons own his flight,
> Marking each brilliant minute with delight.

As I watched, I became aware of how she regarded me with equal curiosity, even overhearing one or two comments she made which were most flattering. Very slowly she drew off one of her gloves to lean for a few moments on her hand, allowing me to gaze in open admiration at her white, polished arms, before slowly pulling it on again.

The queen's gaze then seemed to focus upon the miniature of

the Prince of Wales I still wore pinned to my bosom, the diamonds glittering in the light from the thousands of candles that lit the room.

The next day the Duc de Chartres came to my apartment with a surprising request.

'The queen was quite taken with the miniature you wear, and asks if she may borrow it.'

I was stunned, and far from happy by this demand, but who could refuse a queen? 'It is most precious to me,' I hastened to point out.

'Her Majesty wishes me to assure you it will be safely returned.'

And so it was, a day or two later, brought by the Duc de Lauzun, a close friend of the Duc de Chartes, together with an exquisite netted purse by the queen's own hand, as a gift of thanks.

Lauzun called regularly after that. I thought him manly and quite prepossessing, a fine looking fellow in his flamboyant wig and brocade silk jacket. He seemed to me a man of exquisite sensitivity, an admirer of literature and fine arts, lively, well-informed, and irresistibly fascinating. He was the idol of women and the example for all men at the most polished court in Europe. Unfortunately, he was also every inch a libertine. This unfortunate prince, with all the volatility of the national character, disgraced human nature by his vices, while the elegance of his manners rendered him a model to his contemporaries. My feelings towards him were equally contradictory. And I could see at once that he was attracted to me, declaring that he liked my lively, open nature.

Perhaps I was growing bored with Paris, or allowed him to appeal to my vanity. Whatever the reason, I am ashamed to say that I did succumb to the gentleman's charms. We engaged in a brief affair, which had no meaning to me beyond the pleasures it brought. How could I love anyone but my darling Florizel. But Lauzun at least offered some balm to my wounded pride.

Like all men he loved to talk about himself. He had recently returned from America where he'd been engaged in the War of Independence, so had many tales to relate.

'I feel a great pride to have raised, equipped and trained a body of dragoons who became known as Lauzun's Legion, comprising soldiers not only from France but countries as diverse as Germany, Russia, Italy, Sweden, Poland and England.'

'How come you accept soldiers from England in your legion, when you fight on the side of the rebels?'

He winked. 'I am at heart an Anglophile, owning a residence in Pall Mall, and like your politician, Fox, I follow my conscience. He too has been against the war from the start, and would willingly grant the Americans independence, if only to break their ties with my own country. We are all complex creatures with our own views on what is right and wrong.'

He spoke at length of battles fought and lost, including the recent one at Yorktown which fell to the Americans. But sated by our love making, I barely listened to half what he had to say on the subject. My attention was, however, caught by the tale of a confrontation between himself and Lieutenant-Colonel Banistre Tarleton. 'He is known to the Americans as Butcher Tarleton, while you British regard him as a hero.'

'Indeed he is. I have often read of the colonel's exploits with great patriotic pride. He sounds to be a fine soldier.'

'His sabre-wielding force was fearsome to behold. I faced him with some trepidation. I heard my advance guard firing their pistols and advanced at a gallop to find a terrain upon which I could open battle. I saw as I approached that the English cavalry outnumbered mine by three to one; I charged them without drawing rein. Tarleton came towards me with raised pistol. We were about to fight a duel between our lines, when his horse was overthrown by one of his dragoons pursued by one of my lancers. I dashed upon him, to take him prisoner; a troop of English dragoons thrust themselves between us, and covered his retreat: his horse remained in my hands.'

Gripped by his tale, I asked in awe, 'Did you kill him?'

'Indeed not. He obtained another horse and charged me a second time without breaking my line. I charged him a third time, routed part of his cavalry, and pursued him as far as the earthworks of Gloucester.'

I sighed. 'A brave man. I'm glad he survived, and you too, Lauzun.'

'He was a worthy opponent, and will return home to great acclaim, I am sure. I arrived in France at the height of the celebrations surrounding the birth of the Dauphin to learn that the representative I had appointed to care for my estate in my absence has near bankrupted me.'

'I know how that feels,' I sympathised.

Fascinated as I was by these new acquaintances, I felt my time in France was drawing to a close. I was anxious to return to London, to see Mama and my dear friends. Lauzun escorted me to the boat where we made a fond farewell. Then Maria and I journeyed home, our luggage bulging with Paris fashions. And perhaps at the back of my mind was a desire to meet this hero in person.

It felt good to be back in London even if I was obliged to move in with Lord Malden in his house on the west side of Berkeley Square, since Maria and I had nowhere else to go. Having inherited his grandmother's money, he generously offered to act as my protector.

'I will stay only until I find a house of my own to rent,' I sternly warned him.

'Dearest Perdita, you are more than welcome to stay with me as long as you wish.' Capturing my face between his gentle palms he kissed me most tenderly. 'There is no need for you to leave when we can live together most contentedly here. You know that I have ever loved you, and to prove my sincerity I shall settle an annuity of £200 upon you to secure your independence. I do not ask you to love me in return, only grant me your affection and friendship. I adore you, and cannot imagine a life without you. It is as simple as that.'

I was not so naïve as to fail to understand that favours in the business of the bedroom would also be required. But it was true that I was fond of him, popinjay that he was, and dear Malden was the truest of men, more faithful than any other I had known. How could I refuse? Whenever a man declares his undying love for me, my generous heart simply melts with pity. I let out a little sigh. 'You are far too good to me, dear George. Perhaps I could stay for a little while, see how we go on.'

He beamed with delight. 'Excellent! Then the matter is settled.'

I cannot think what possessed me. A momentary weakness

perhaps. Admittedly, the £200 a year was tempting, even though it would not cover my expenses any more than the prince's £5,000 had settled my debts. But it was better than nothing, as was a rent-free house in Berkeley Square. Sometimes, I told myself firmly, one had to be mercenary to survive.

And bedding dear Malden was no great hardship. He surely deserved some reward for his devotion and labours on my behalf over the years. Oh, but there was little sensual joy or excitement in our relationship, at least so far as I was concerned. His love making was as tender and bland as dear Tommy's in the early days of our marriage, and I as indifferent. Would I never find another love to consume me?

The arrangement did, however, allow me to slip back into society as if I had never been away. I was able to attend the opera early in the new year where I wore the white satin gown with purple breast-bows. My headdress was naturally in the French style, a cap compounded of matching feathers entwined with flowers fastened with diamond pins. I vow the audience were more entranced by my appearance than whatever was happening on stage, and many lingered at the end of the performance to watch me select a box to rent. According to the *Herald*, I looked 'supremely beautiful'. Such comments were balm to my soul. At a second appearance I wore the Rose Bertin gown, which brought gasps of admiration.

The fashionable world seemed agog to view the gowns I had brought with me from Paris, and I stepped easily back into the role of fashion icon.

Perversely, one Friday evening at the King's Theatre where everyone attending was in fancy dress, I wore my black domino but did not unmask, thus maintaining an intriguing air of mystery. We danced for the entire evening illuminated by a myriad of coloured lamps, the upper tiers of boxes draped with garlands and bows. It was utterly magical. And it was good to be back among old friends.

Dear old Sheridan, Fox and Georgiana, and Malden of course, were fascinated to hear my tales of the Duc de Chartes and how he had pursued me to no avail. They loved the story of Queen Marie Antoinette at the *Grand Couvert*. I made a passing mention to Lauzun, repeating his tales of the battles he had fought in the

American War of Independence, and his encounter with 'Butcher' Tarleton.

'Ah yes, the fellow rode into London on horseback only last week, very much receiving the hero's welcome,' Fox put in. 'What more can a dashing young soldier ask than to be presented to the king and queen, fêted with parties and balls, and admired by young princes who envy him his adventures in America.'

'Did you see him? How did he look? What is he like?'

Fox pretended to consider. 'As if he had fought in a war, but then I am not a young woman, merely a politician, so cannot judge.'

'You are certainly no judge of fashion or style,' the duchess quipped, brushing crumbs from the plump politician's dusty waistcoat and adjusting his neck cloth which was ever askew.

Fox's own style was charmingly eccentric, a fabricated slovenliness that gave him an honest and simple appearance, which served only to increase his popularity with the general populace. He generally wore a frock-coat and breeches in buff and Washington blue, an outfit that had seen better days but clearly demonstrated his support for the colonists. More often than not he went without either hat or wig, his greying curls uncombed, his plump chin bearing several days growth, and a pair of downward sloping bushy eyebrows shielding kind and gentle eyes.

'I may be no dandy now, dear lady, preferring to be seen as an ordinary sort of fellow, but I'll have you know I did once appear in red heeled shoes and blue cascading curls.'

Laughing off this quip, the duchess turned to me. 'Ban Tarleton, as I believe he is called by his friends, seemed affable enough, Mary, and not unhandsome.'

'Oh my! Lauzun told me so much about him that I would love to meet such a hero in the flesh.'

Sheridan said, 'I believe he is to have his portrait painted.'

I leaned forward, eager to hear more. 'When? By whom?'

'Sir Joshua Reynolds. I fear I cannot give you details of the artist's diary, Mary, although I'm sure a few questions in the right quarters would tell you all you need to know,' he finished, a wry smile on my old friend's face.

I wasted no time in visiting Reynolds's studio in Leicester Fields, an octagonal room attached to his home which included an exhibition gallery and a spacious and elegant room for his sitters. Having sat for him on a previous occasion, I artlessly suggested he might like to repeat the experience.

'I do not have the money to pay you, Sir Joshua, but I feel sure you would profit from the prints and engravings you could sell of such a portrait.'

'Indeed I would, dear Mrs Robinson, since posters and prints of your beauteous person are ever in demand.'

He was more than willing to agree mutually beneficial terms, and as he consulted his diary to set dates for my sittings, I easily discovered details of the colonel's visits, and arranged that a couple of my sittings coincided, taking place just before his own. Sir Joshua was only too happy to oblige, proud to be the chosen artist to capture this great British hero on canvas.

I could hardly wait to meet him.

Reynolds began with numerous small sketches, swiftly drawing the shape of my face and figure, making separate sketches of individual features such as my nose and hands. Once the actual painting began he would peer into my face then rush to his easel to paint what he saw, constantly on the move back and forth, dashing his brush upon the canvas, painting furiously, almost in a frenzy. Occasionally he would stand back to consider the effect from a distance, eyes pensively narrowed. Often there were other people present to watch the artist at work.

My sittings always took place at two o'clock, so that the light was the same. I would be seated before a red velvet curtain upon a chair mounted with casters and raised on a dais in a room lit by a window set high in the wall.

On the day in question I was beset with a strange attack of nerves, knowing I was at last to meet the man I had heard so much about. Yet dressed for the portrait in a black gown with a white lacy fichu, black hat with a white plume, and my favourite black ribbon about my throat, I surely looked well enough. My auburn curls were not on view but powdered as fashion dictates, and my expression, as others would describe when the portrait was finished, was serious, even sultry.

When Colonel Tarleton walked into the room I felt as if I had encountered a god. Something stirred inside me that had never before been touched, as if cupid's arrow had indeed pierced my heart. My lungs seemed robbed of all breath, quite unable to draw in air while this deity held sway.

He was not particularly tall, being around five foot six or seven, but fit and tough, with strong muscular thighs. In uniform for the portrait he was wearing tan boots with turnover tops, tight-fitting white doeskin breeches, a short green jacket with black facings and gold lace, and upon his head a shako hat with black swan's feathers that largely covered his dark hair. His eyes, I could not help but notice, were brown and meltingly soft, and there was a boyish quality to his good looks despite the sabre he wore at his side. He was exceeding handsome with a classically aquiline nose, and a mouth that was enticingly kissable, or so I thought. He was twenty-eight years old, and at the peak of his manhood.

No words were spoken between us until my sitting ended, but as I rose to step down from the dais, he hurried to offer his assistance. 'Do not be afraid to take my hand, though I have lost two fingers I can use my pen and will draw my sword when I can be of service to my country.'

Smiling, I took the damaged hand without flinching.

'Mrs Robinson, may I say how honoured I am to meet you.'

'You know me?' I teased, casting him a sidelong glance that might have been flirtatious.

'The whole nation knows of the wondrous Perdita.'

I frowned slightly, not wishing to constantly be associated with that name as it reminded me of the prince. 'But you have been in the Americas, so how can that be possible? I doubt you ever set foot in Drury Lane while I was there.'

'Sadly, that is true,' he admitted as he led me out of the studio to the changing room where my maid waited. 'Nevertheless, your fame has crossed the ocean. A British army base in Charleston, formerly a bordello, was captured in 1780 and named Perdita's after you.'

I laughed even as I pretended to be shocked. 'A bordello?'

'*Formerly* a bordello. I assure you that no unseemly connotation was meant by naming the base after you, Mrs Robinson. The men simply adore you, have your posters and prints everywhere and are honest worshippers at the feet of your beauty. Now I can see why.'

I blushed a little, too flustered to find a witty response.

'Perhaps you could wait so that we might talk later, when Sir Joshua is finished with me?' he said.

I widened my eyes in disbelief, adopting my loftiest expression. 'I'm afraid not. I have better things to do with my time than wait upon soldiers who name bordellos after me,' and walked away, head high, knowing that I had deliberately misunderstood him. But I had certainly caught his attention.

Our paths crossed again on the second of February, and the mere sight of him set my heart racing. He was, as the press had dubbed him, a 'pocket Adonis', and certainly very much in vogue, his name on everyone's lips. But what I wanted, even then, was those enticing lips on mine.

'I believe we have much in common,' I said, unashamedly leading the conversation as we waited for his sitting to begin, although we had never formally been introduced.

He gave a wry smile. 'A former actress and a soldier, I find that hard to credit?'

'I mean as we were both born in sea ports, you in Liverpool and I in Bristol.' I'd made it my business to learn some facts about him, and his accent was undeniably Lancastrian. 'I believe that, like mine, your father was also a businessman, although much more successful.'

'You are well informed,' he quipped, a teasing light in those chocolate brown eyes. 'My mother came from the Chorley area of Lancashire but settled into a large house on Water Street in Liverpool on marriage where she produced six sons and a daughter. My father was a merchant and former mayor of the city, but many would say that making a fortune out of West Indian sugar plantations and the slave trade was exploitation rather than success.'

'Perhaps so, but I am in a poor position to judge when my own father exploited native Indians in unsuccessful projects in the Arctic. We cannot be blamed for our parents' actions.'

'That is very true. My family have had trade interests in the Chesapeake, New England, and Newfoundland as well as the Caribbean for a century or more. They dealt in many cargoes, only one of which was human slaves. And in cities such as Liverpool and Bristol it is hard to find a balanced view on the subject.'

'But you did not choose to follow in your father's footsteps?' I found this reassuring, assuming him to be as much against slavery as any right-minded individual.

'I was destined for the law, entered University College in November, 1771, but despite the best efforts of a brilliant professor I was not a diligent student. Nor did I improve when in the Middle Temple, so I persuaded my mother to buy me a commission in the army. She was willing to find £800 to make me a cornet.'

'And that is how your famous career began, as a cornet?'

'As inconsequential as it seems, yes. Fortunately, through hard work, daring deeds and the support of Lord Cornwallis and Sir Henry Clinton, I have enjoyed rapid promotion.'

'I heard about some of these daring deeds of yours from the Duke of Lauzun.'

'Ah, yes, he thought he had me, but only succeeded in capturing my horse.'

I chuckled. 'He didn't seem too concerned, is rather an admirer in fact. Is it true what they say, that you have killed more men and lain with more women than any other man?'

He put back his head and laughed out loud. 'Let's say I'm working on it. How about you, Mrs Robinson? Do you have a new conquest now your liaison with the prince is over, or is it not the done thing to ask?'

I was outraged by his presumption, and for the first time felt grateful for Malden's protection. I would not have him think me easy. 'I am with Lord Malden now, were it any business of yours.'

He was called in for the sitting at that precise moment, but as he got up to go, leaned close to whisper in my ear. 'Mayhap I should make it my business.' And he slipped away, leaving me gasping.

The rest of that month turned into a complete misery as I cracked my shin while out driving, and, fearing it might be broken, was laid up for a while. I didn't see the colonel for some weeks, learning later that he'd returned to his native city, and to a true hero's welcome. I read in the papers that as he approached the outskirts of Liverpool, church bells were rung and thousands gathered. They even unhitched the horses and pulled his carriage themselves into the heart of the city. Bonfires were lit, officials held special events to honour this famous son of Liverpool, while I ached for his return, so that I could spar with him again.

As Lord Malden's mistress I was now considered to be a leading member of the demi-monde, sometimes named the Cyprian Corps among other epithets, however reluctant I might be to accept that fact. I liked to consider myself above that rabble, being more intelligent than rivals such as Dally the Tall, The Armistead, and Gertrude Mahon, known as the Bird of Paradise for her love of bright colours. They were all jealous of the fame I had achieved in Paris, a triumph that had passed Dally the Tall by when she spent time there, even though she did succumb to an affair with the Duc de Chartes. Her revenge upon me came when she announced she was carrying the prince's child, which I found disturbingly difficult to grasp. 'How could Florizel love her more than me?'

'He doesn't,' Malden assured me. 'The prince denies the child is his, as it could just as easily be that of Cholmondeley.'

I tossed back my curls. 'It is of no concern to me whose child it is. I have a new life now.'

'Indeed, my love, and a good one,' Malden said, kissing me.

If my current lover did not excite me, I certainly enjoyed being the centre of attention where dress and fashion were concerned, and created something of a sensation by using a cataract muff. This had long fluffy hairs that hung down like a waterfall, and as a muff was considered to be a gift from Venus to keep Adonis warm, the *Lady's Magazine* made much of it.

A demi-rep is also required to own at least two carriages, as well as live in the most fashionable part of town, the expenses borne by her protector. I was able to do all of that with impeccable taste. Unfortunately, I had never succeeded in finding a man rich enough to afford me. Lord Malden certainly wasn't, and maintaining the look and requirements of the role was once more rapidly leading me into debt. Credit, of course, was easily achieved in anticipation of them all being settled when the prince came of age. Some people even believed that the gallant Florizel was already financing me, as well as Malden.

March came in as a cold month with several falls of snow, which found me ill in bed suffering from the influenza and feeling very sorry for myself. But then I heard that the colonel was back in town attending more rounds of parties and masquerades.

'Tarleton has rented a house in St. James's Place and picked up two race horses which he has named Adrastus and Antiquity,' my good friend Fox cheerfully informed me. 'He is often seen about town wearing his Legion uniform, particularly at his old haunt, The Cocoa Tree. He has also fallen in quite naturally with Whig friends who like to gather at Brooks's.'

I did not much care for the sound of this. Gambling had grown into a pet hate of mine ever since my experiences with Tommy, although Georgiana and Fox himself were notorious enthusiasts of the gaming tables, which so far as I could see did them no good at all. 'I'm sure what the colonel does with his spare time is of no concern of mine,' I loftily remarked, even as I itched to know more.

'I'll keep you informed,' he chortled, accurately guessing my thoughts.

However, by the end of March, Lord North, the Prime Minister, had resigned over the debacle of the American War of Independence. Desperately trying to hang on to the colony had cost the country dear, both in money and in lives. The king took ship to Hanover for a while, to escape the fallout.

'Shelburne may be the king's favourite but I'll make damn sure he can never form a government,' Fox railed. 'The fellow may count himself a Whig, but not one I would follow. Rockingham should take office, and bring into effect the reforms we badly need.'

Thereafter, my fat friend was too busy electioneering to concern himself over my trifling affairs.

I, of course, was the talk of the town as not only Reynold's portrait, but two others by Gainsborough and Romney were exhibited at the Royal Academy in April, resulting in much comment on which artist, if any, had best managed to capture my likeness. The Gainsborough, it was thought, did not succeed half so well. But none of my portraits were believed to do justice to my beauty. I was deeply flattered and, it would appear, more in demand than ever.

Tarleton's own portrait brought forth more mixed reviews. In the background Sir Joshua had painted the colonel's horse, plus a flag and smoke from the battle. Peter Pindar, the satirist, called it 'distinctly Trojan' implying it looked wooden. He was clearly unimpressed while I stood before it in dazed admiration.

'Do you approve?' The soft voice in my ear melted my insides to water.

I took a moment before turning to smile into those bewitching brown eyes. 'Sir Joshua is a superb artist and can make even the dullest subject look presentable,' I quipped.

He chortled with delight. 'You never disappoint with your wit, dear Mrs Robinson. May I say that I find your own portrait quite enchanting.'

'Only quite?'

His gaze moved slowly over my face, studying my pinked cheeks, the blue of my eyes, lingering longest over the curve of my mouth. 'I prefer the flesh and blood to the painted version.'

I was struggling to capture my breath. 'There seem to be many people here who would not agree with you.'

'But they are not standing where I am standing. Do you not find the crowds somewhat overwhelming? Would you care to take a walk in the park, and enjoy a little fresh air?'

Smiling into his eyes I rested my hand upon his arm. I would have followed him to the ends of the earth, had he asked.

The walk led to a drive in Hyde Park, and then to dinner, not only on that afternoon but on numerous occasions in the weeks following. Malden, who rather took my fidelity for granted, never queried where I spent the hours we were apart. Yet I was wary, knowing this double life could not continue for long. Ban Tarleton excited me as no other man ever had, so when he offered me supper in his rooms in Hill Street, I did not hesitate to accept. I wanted him.

If supper was served, we neither of us noticed it. The moment the servant withdrew I fell into his arms. There was a frantic quality about our coupling, a desperate need to tear off clothing, to dispose of whatever prevented the melding of our bodies. He had seduced me with his sardonic glances, by the touch of his fingers as they would brush lightly upon my cheek. Now he took me in very truth and for the first time in my life I knew what it was to burn with sensual desire, and to be filled by a man. I felt as if I were a part of him, that we were one flesh. We could not get enough of each other, and wrong as it was, I felt no shame. Maria Elizabeth was fortunately staying with Mama for a while, and Malden held no rights over me. Tarleton's bed was where I belonged, and somehow or other I meant to stay in it.

Our feelings for each other could not be denied. We were lovers, more than lovers judging by the depth of the emotion between us. Every moment that I could escape my official protector, I spent in Tarleton's bed. Oddly enough, Malden accepted the colonel's presence in our lives without question. Rather as he had once accompanied Tommy and me, or come on outings with the prince, now the threesome was a different equation. Malden, Tarleton and myself would often attend masquerades, balls, and the theatre together.

'I love the theatre,' Tarleton admitted. 'I used to tread the boards in an old playhouse with a company of officer friends. We formed our own theatrical group whose motto was "We act Monday, Wednesday, and Friday."'

I laughed, finding the idea of soldiers performing rather amusing, never sure when to take him seriously. 'What kind of plays did you put on?'

'Oh, major works such as *Duke or No Duke*,' he said, resolutely straight-faced as I laughed all the more. 'Together with a little Shakespeare, of course.'

'I do wish I'd seen you act. I'm sure it would have been hilarious.'

'Would that I had seen you at Drury Lane,' he softly murmured.

'Ah yes,' Malden agreed. 'Mrs Robinson was a veritable star shining in the firmament, most definitely worth seeing.'

The pair of them were firm friends by this time, often going off to The Cocoa Tree or Brooks's together, the latter having earned a notorious reputation as a gambling hell as well as a gossip shop for Whig politicians. They got along famously and loved nothing more than to play jokes upon their friends.

One day they brought me word that a rake by the name of Pugh had made offensive remarks about my reputation, and had offered twenty guineas for ten minutes' conversation with me.

'By "conversation", does that mean what I think it means?' I asked, instantly suspicious.

'That is what the poor fellow imagines,' Tarleton agreed, with a merry twinkle in his eye. 'We thought we should grant his wish, in view of his comments against you.'

'I heartily agree.'

Grinning broadly, the pair of them scurried off to shortly return with the scoundrel in question. The three of us settled ourselves in comfort, politely inviting him to join us. I set my watch upon the table by my chair, and ignoring my two comrades directed my conversation entirely to Mr Pugh. Looking bewildered, as well he might, he offered little by way of response beyond the odd strained comment.

Glancing at my watch again, I smiled. 'Ah, sadly our ten minutes is up. Thank you so much for calling, Mr Pugh. I so enjoyed our conversation.' I did not forget to relieve him of his twenty guineas.

But we could not go on in this fashion. It seemed to me that the only decent thing to do was to openly confess to Malden about this tumultuous event that had taken place in my life. Cheating was not in my nature. I had fully intended to do so, perhaps it was the fact I was worrying so much about how to approach the issue that I failed to notice a phaeton bearing down upon me while out driving in Hyde Park, always jammed with traffic. Before I realised what was happening, my small chariot had been overturned. I knew nothing more until I woke in my own bed in the house in Berkeley Square. But it was not Malden who sat by my side, holding my hand. It was Tarleton.

'I thought I had lost you,' he cried, the moment I opened my eyes.

'Never,' I said, managing a weak smile. It was at that moment I noticed my protector standing in the doorway. I quickly squeezed Tarleton's hand. 'Leave us, please,' and taking the hint he tactfully withdrew.

Perhaps I had underestimated the depth of my good friend's attachment, but I could see at once that he was deeply hurt at having discovered our attachment.

'How can you be so foolish? He's a good enough fellow, I'll admit, but he's a *soldier*. He will never be faithful to you, Perdita, never wait upon your every wish and need, as do I.'

'Malden – George – I never asked you to wait upon my every wish, but please forgive me for I cannot help myself. I believe I am falling in love with him. I have never felt this way before. I'm very fond of you, dear George, as you know, but I think I *love* Ban Tarleton. *He* is my life now.'

Anger sparked in him, an emotion I had rarely seen before in my patient lord. 'He will be the ruin of you. You know that he only seduced you on the strength of a bet?'

I felt the blood drain from my face. 'What are you saying?'

'He would ask about you as we tossed the dice for hazard, or played faro. I made our situation very clear, that you were my mistress, that we were a faithful, devoted, contented couple. He seemed to think that amusing and said no demi-rep was entirely faithful. He bet me a hundred guineas that he could seduce you. Not only that, but once having used you, he would then return you to me.'

I felt sick. 'You lie!'

'If you do not believe me, ask him. He seemed to imply that women of your sort, a courtesan, are happy to share their favours.'

My cheeks, my hands, my entire body burned as if with a fever, and yet I was shivering with cold. Every surface of my skin prickled and itched, my heart pounding with pain. 'I do not believe you!'

How could I? Such a claim, if true, would destroy me.

'Very well, you have made your feelings perfectly clear, Perdita. I will leave you to your war hero.'

Malden moved out that very day, having already generously signed the house over to me in a bid to offer me some security. However, he made no offer to pay the rent, not that I would expect him to, but a house of this size, in prestigious Berkeley Square, would be quite beyond my means to maintain alone.

My most pressing concern was to speak at once to Tarleton. He was not at his lodgings, so I sought him in the most likely spot, The Cocoa Tree, and there he was, deeply absorbed in some game or other. I strode right over.

'May we have a word in private?' I asked, not wishing our personal business to be overheard by the gawping onlookers gathered about the table.

He barely glanced at me. 'In a moment, Mary, I'm rather tied up at present.'

It was almost an hour later before he could tear himself away from the game and give me his undivided attention. As we strolled through Green Park I informed him that my relationship with Lord Malden was at an end. My outward calm masked a rage and fear that was building inside me with a terrifying force, and I finished my account by asking the question that was burning into my soul.

'He tells me that you seduced me for a bet. Is that true?'

He paused, swivelling about to laugh in that merry boyish way of his. I had already discovered his fun-loving nature, that he was outgoing and sociable, a true party animal who loved a good joke. These practical japes, his ease and self-confidence, might irritate at times, but he also possessed the most gentle manners and a charm that could inspire great loyalty, not only among his friends but with his men, who had saved his life more than once.

'It was but a prank, Mary,' he confessed.

'A prank! You took me to your bed for a prank?'

'No, I took you to my bed because I wanted you. The prank was upon your protector. Don't tell me you care for that over-dressed peacock?'

'That is not the issue, but you clearly won the bet, so I dare say that is the most important thing so far as you are concerned.' And turning on my polished heels, I stormed off. I could hear him calling after me, but I did not even look back. I was done with Ban Tarleton.

My pride, as ever, had led me to make such a stand, but however justified, I'd never felt more miserable. Looking back over my life I felt I had suffered more than I deserved from the betrayal of men who claimed to love me, from my father to Tommy, to the prince, and now the man I already thought of as the love of my life. Not that the colonel had spoken of his feelings towards me in quite those terms, but he had certainly implied them by the crackle of fire that had ignited between us from our very first meeting. Yet he was as bad as all the rest.

I knew in my heart that parting from him was the right thing to do. Gambling to excess could destroy lives, and taking up with another such as my beleaguered husband would not be a good idea, although who did not dabble in this day and age? It was a national passion, an obsession.

I felt utterly bereft. How could this man have become so important to me in such a short time?

Cast adrift without a protector of any sort I turned to my friend Charles James Fox for help. He too was a gambler, and a drinker, as were all my Whig friends. Fox claimed once to have gambled from Tuesday night until Friday with no sleep, taking time off only to debate in the House of Commons. He'd apparently won thousands in a game of hazard, only to lose it all again plus several thousands more in the process.

But he was a caring, open-hearted man, ever ready to give a friend a helping hand. He gladly leant me a sum to tide me over, even though I knew his own finances hovered on the brink of bankruptcy.

On the first of July when Rockingham died suddenly, Fox was up for consideration as a candidate for the premiership, which did not surprise me. First elected to Parliament for Midhurst in Sussex back in 1768 at only nineteen, he was a most able and popular member, and a skilled orator. He had that rare facility to see the good in people, making them feel important and wanted. People warmed to his charms because they saw him as modest and caring, simply because of the time and attention he gave to them. How much of this was genuine and how much political was hard to judge, but it was in complete contrast to the gambling, dissolute side to his character, ever his downfall.

The king, however, chose to appoint the Earl of Shelburne, whereupon Fox instantly resigned from his position as Foreign Secretary. I, and his other friends, attempted to console him, and calm his anger.

'It is not the first time, nor probably the last that I will be obliged to resign from government. I do not regret supporting Rockingham and shall now throw in my lot with North.'

Sheridan issued a mild warning. 'Have you considered that were you to set aside your quarrel with the king, and this political manoeuvring, the rewards that come with high office might prove beneficial to your high gambling debts?'

'You know that money, dear fellow, has never swayed me.' He

laughed. 'A man of honour must live by his principles, even if his wit, and skill at the cards, frequently fail him.'

Fox's dispute with the king had not been helped by his strong friendship with His Majesty's eldest son. He acted rather like a father-figure to the young prince, one he was more willing to accept in that role than his own. For this reason alone, Charles James Fox seemed the very person I needed to help me.

'Twelve months from now His Royal Highness will come of age, and I know how long these matters take to negotiate. More than ever I need His Highness to honour the bond he voluntarily gave me.' I handed the papers to Fox. 'The £5,000 staved off my creditors but did not cover all the debts I had accrued on the prince's behalf. I must think of my future security, and that of my daughter, having lost my career for his sake.'

'I'm sorry you have been treated so poorly by His Royal Highness. I would have you know that the problem is not of George's making.'

'Oh, I do realise that. He was ever kind to me, and only relinquished me under pressure from the king.'

'I fear the entire Hanoverian tribe is ruled by the Royal Marriages Bill. I was against it as my own mother's family disapproved of her marriage to my father. I believe a person has the right to marry whoever they choose, which sadly did not endear me with the king. I was obliged to resign from the government on that occasion too. I took my revenge, however, by befriending his son. But as I have no other pressing claims upon my time at present, you can safely leave this matter with me, Mrs R,' he said, kindly patting my hand. 'I'm quite sure something can be arranged.'

Since Fox was so willing to devote himself entirely to my campaign, I gladly agreed to put myself at his disposal to drive him about town in my pony phaeton. He had, in any case, been obliged to give up his own carriage, and indeed his house due to bankruptcy proceedings brought against him. But I had no hesitation in offering him accommodation, as he was a good friend to me, and was willing to pay for the lodgings.

He loved to stand at my window, railing at his rival Shelburne who lived in Landsdowne House opposite, easily visible from this vantage point. 'You don't mind my standing here, do you, Mrs R? Only I like to keep an eye on what the fellow is up to, his comings and goings, don't you know.'

The local press were likewise keeping an eye on Fox and myself, reporting on our own 'comings and goings' which were not at all complimentary.

The *Morning Post*, as ever, was most critical, claiming Fox was wasting his time and talents 'on the turf, in gaming houses, and sacrifices to the Cyprian Goddess'.

The suggestion being that we were engaged in an affair.

'Why they always make that assumption is wearying,' I sighed, as I wrote to the paper a strongly worded denial that our friendship was anything other than 'perfectly political'.

Nevertheless, gossip continued to be rife, claiming Fox was 'languishing at the feet of Mrs Robinson', or calling me the 'Harlot of the Day' and Fox a 'kept man', while lampoons and cartoons set about demolishing the pair of us. One, called *Perdito and Perdita – or – the man and woman of the people*, was a caricature showing me holding the reins as I drove him about town.

'At whose feet would you prefer to languish?' I teased him one morning as we waited in a queue of carriages on the Mall. 'Has no lady captured your heart?'

'Ah, now I must confess there is one.'

I was instantly intrigued. 'Do I know her?'

He gave me a wry smile. 'I fear you do, and you are not the best of friends.'

I gazed at him askance. 'Not the Armistead? I have seen you send her languishing looks. Goodness, you are blushing. It is she, is it not?'

'I fear I do feel a certain warmth for the lady.'

I could not help but laugh. 'A raging fever more like. What an incestuous lot we are. Well, the prince has done with her, so why not try your luck?'

'I believe I may, dear Mrs R. I believe I may do just that.'

The most offensive cartoon appeared in late August. Entitled *The Thunderer* by James Gillray, it depicted an unnaturally well-endowed Fox standing beside a figure with the Prince of Wales' feathers in place of a head. Impaled on a pike above a tavern sign bearing the inscription 'The Whirligig' was a female figure with exposed bosom, legs spread wide revealing naked thighs above her stocking tops, presumably meant to represent me.

'Since we are all aware that a whirligig is a large cage in which army prostitutes are hoisted for punishment, I find this cartoon both obscene and insulting.'

'Personally, I find it jolly flattering that anyone could imagine you would choose me, an overweight, ugly old drunkard as a lover.'

We both laughed at this description. 'Do not underrate yourself, dear friend. You are the kindest man I know, and most talented.'

Perhaps even the *Morning Post* thought that Gillray had overstepped the mark on this occasion, for the next day they issued a piece in my defence for once.

'Listen to this,' I said, as Fox and I took dinner with our usual group of friends. '"Formed by the hand of nature for almost every opposite pursuit to that in which the whirl of life has engaged her, Perdita but half enjoys her present situation; yet she gives to it every grace and embellishment of which it is susceptible . . . her soul turns unsatisfied away from whatever princes can bestow!" There is more, but what think you of that? Can they be on my side for once?'

'Not before time,' Sheridan grumbled.

Then the *Morning Chronicle* published an anonymous letter on its front pages, castigating Tarleton for his lack of generosity towards the soldier who saved his life during an encounter with Indians in New York. A few days later a second more poisonous letter appeared, also anonymous, but this time accusing him of the slaughter of unarmed men at Waxhaws and gross misjudgement at Cowpens which resulted in the destruction of almost his entire force. I at once hurried to his side, all our differences forgotten.

'I wish you to know that not for a moment do I believe you deliberately slaughtered a defeated enemy about to surrender.'

I stood on his doorstep on a damp summer's day and once again freely offered my heart. Ban appeared most moved by this declaration of faith and ushered me inside out of the rain, calling upon his servant to take my coat and bring refreshment. Once seated in the comfort of his drawing room, I upon the sofa, he in a chair opposite, he gave his explanation, hesitantly, and with much pain.

'The Battle of Cowpens was undoubtedly a disaster, mainly due to fine American tactics by General Morgan. British forces were ill-prepared and overconfident. Nevertheless, my men fought to the bitter end, giving their all. In the forty-eight hours before the battle we ran out of food, and they had less than four hours sleep after marching over difficult terrain. By the time they reached the battlefield they were exhausted and malnourished, yet we dared not delay.'

He paused here to speculate on this decision, knotting his fingers as if in an agony of reflection. 'Were I to have my time again, I would deploy them differently, but everything is always clearer in retrospect. We suffered devastating losses that day, and yes, it marked the beginning of the end of the war. I offered my resignation, which Cornwallis refused to accept.'

'But why this letter? What would anyone have to gain by destroying your military career? You are a hero.'

'Perhaps for that very reason. I suspect it came from Lieutenant Roderick MacKenzie, who was badly wounded that day, and blames me with a burning hatred. As for Waxhaws, Abraham Buford, the American commander, at first refused an offer to surrender, but when my men attacked his forces were only too eager to throw down their arms. I suspect many of them were raw recruits with little battle experience. Buford did ultimately realise that all was lost, but I was unhorsed when the white flag was raised, and never saw it. Unfortunately, believing me to be dead, my men engaged in a vindictive revenge not easily restrained. Slaughter happens in war.'

Again he paused, the agony of that day still etched upon his handsome face. 'After the battle ended, we took our quota of prisoners, but the wounded of both sides were treated with equal humanity and every possible convenience. I did not target civilians, nor conduct personal vendettas. As always I did a job that had to be done and took no pleasure in it. I deeply regretted the outcome which earned me a reputation for giving no quarter, and the epithet "Butcher Tarleton". One, presumably, I will never live down.'

On impulse I went to kneel before him, gathered his dear face in my hands and kissed him. 'Those who were there will know the truth, and anyone who has fought in battle will understand the way decisions are made under impossible conditions. Others will make their own judgement. So be it. Either way, you must remain strong in the knowledge that when called upon to do so, you were prepared to give your life for your men and your country. No one can ask more.'

Sliding his arms about my waist he pulled me close, holding me lovingly between his knees. 'Are we friends again, Mary? Am I forgiven for that other piece of misjudgement?'

Chuckling, I kissed that perfect nose of his. 'I dare say that can be arranged.'

Eight

A Colonel's Lady

Is it to love, to fix the tender gaze,
To hide the timid blush, and steal away;
To shun the busy world, and waste the day
In some rude mountain's solitary maze?

Mary Darby Robinson
'Sonnet VI: Is It to Love'

I took him to my old home at Egham, near Windsor where we spent some weeks together blissfully alone, celebrating my birthday with particular joy this year. Unfortunately, word leaked out of our reconciliation and a piece appeared in the *Morning Post* filled with obscene double entendre.

Yesterday, a messenger arrived in town, with the very interesting and pleasing intelligence of the Tarleton armed ship having, after a chase of some months, captured the Perdita frigate, and brought her safe into Egham port. The Perdita is a prodigious fine clean bottomed vessel, and has taken many prizes during her cruise, particularly the Florizel, a most valuable ship belonging to the Crown, but which was immediately released after taking out the cargo.

There was much more of this nature, but I had read enough. 'Why do the papers constantly attack me? When will they let me be?' I would complain as Ban and I rode in the forest, or took a walk as we were doing today. Christmas was approaching and there was a thick hoar frost crisping the dead leaves and cracking twigs beneath our booted feet.

'Because the press love to gossip. They believe it sells papers.'
'But they are so malicious.'

He slipped his arm about me, tucking me close to his side beneath the warmth of his cloak. 'You are a strong woman. Do not let this nonsense hurt you.'

'That is easy for you to say.'

'Not so. I know how it feels to be a pariah, and the subject of malice. Not everyone sees me as a hero. Following the Cowpens debacle I continued fighting for my country, losing two fingers at a costly British victory at Guilford Courthouse in March. By October, after yet more defeats, Cornwallis finally surrendered at Yorktown. But even then I was not forgiven. The enemy still hated me for the slaughter at Waxhaws. Even my fellow officers refused to eat or talk with me, partly blaming me for losing the colony. Someone even tried to kill me. I feared for my life when the bed I slept in was stabbed repeatedly. By a stroke of good fortune I was not in it at the time.'

'Goodness, that's terrible! Why would they be so vindictive?'

'Feelings run high in war.' He kissed my brow. 'Now that I have you it no longer matters, and nothing the *Morning Post* says could hurt me half as much.'

'You are right. We must keep things in proportion.'

The days passed in perfect accord, filled with our passion for each other, and the pleasure we found simply being together, riding, walking, talking, eating, and then making love all over again. It was a magical time, and such a joy to have him all to myself.

One morning we were returning from our usual ride, passing through the old town of Windsor when I noticed a small party of hunters approaching. I pulled up at once, and Ban did likewise.

'What is it?'

'I believe it is the prince. Ah yes, and he has seen us.'

Slowing his horse to a walk he came over, and to my great astonishment pulled off a glove, reached for my hand and shook it, grinning in a most friendly fashion. 'Mrs Robinson, what a pleasure to see you again after all this time.'

'Your Highness.' Quite unable to think of a sensible word to say by way of response, all I could do was put one hand to my blushing cheeks and venture a shy smile. Fortunately my good manners saved me as I remembered my companion. 'Allow me to introduce my good friend, Banistre Tarleton. I'm sure Your

Highness will have heard of the colonel's exploits in the War of Independence.'

'Ah, indeed I have. Well done, sir, and let us not fret too much about the outcome. America was bound to shrug off the mother country at some point. Do you like hunting? The royal hunt passes this way every morning and generally meets with good sport. I shall look for you to join us tomorrow, eh?'

'Thank you, sire, I should be honoured.'

'Perdita and I are old friends, are we not?'

'I trust so, Your Highness,' I said, my smile warmer this time. And as my erstwhile royal lover went on his way, I could not help but feel a wave of relief. It seemed that the feud between us had at last dissipated.

This was proved to be the case when Fox came to an agreement with the prince that in addition to the £5,000 already paid, on his coming of age I would be granted an annuity of five hundred pounds, the moiety of which was to pass to my daughter at my death. This settlement was to be considered as an equivalent for the bond of twenty thousand pounds given by the prince, paid in consideration for the sacrifice I made of a lucrative profession at his request.

It felt as if all my troubles were over at last, and happiness had been restored to me in the best possible way with Ban.

Come the new year we were back in town, making no secret of our attachment, strolling arm in arm everywhere together. Continuing with our morning rides in Hyde Park I would wear my favourite riding habit, a pale pearl colour with jonquil facings, or one in brown with a scarlet waistcoat.

'Did I ever tell you how divine you look in your riding habit?' he complimented me one morning.

'Then I shall wear it always, provided you will always be in a riding habit when you come to visit me,' I teased.

He laughed out loud. 'Ever the sharp wit, dear lady.'

'At least my wit, such as it is, does not bear malice.'

One blustery day the skirts of my gown became caught as I dismounted in Hyde Park, and despite Ban's best efforts to prevent it, I revealed rather more than was quite decent. A lampoon appeared in the paper the very next day in which two fat gentlemen were depicted looking up my skirts with a quizzing glass, declaring the perspective made their mouths water and how they would be happy to 'cover' me.

I resolutely ignored such ribald remarks as this was a happy time for me. I was deeply and passionately in love, blissfully content and adored in return.

We frequently attended the Pantheon, Vauxhall and Ranelagh, and also the theatre and opera. I took a box and decorated it most stylishly with pink satin chairs and wall-to-wall mirrors, which created quite a stir.

By then we had become a celebrity couple. Tarleton, with his famously cropped hair, looked most handsome in his hussar uniform of blue jacket, waistcoat and leather boots that fitted as tight as silk stockings, and I was very much the fashion icon. *Lady's Magazine* made much of my style by naming the Perdita Hood after me, made of Italian lawn and tied under the chin with a large bow. I also liked to wear a white chip hat, trimmed with roses or feathers, or one with a band of black velvet around the crown, fastened with a diamond buckle. This they named the Robinson Hat. Then there was the Robinson gown, simply styled in chocolate poplin with plain cuffs of scarlet silk, similar to the Quaker-like gown I wore at my wedding and my first visit to Ranelagh with Tommy, which had become a trademark style of mine ever since.

And then there were my gold-clocked stockings for which I was dubbed 'Lark-heeled Perdita'. It seemed that I still set the fashion that others followed with flattering avidity.

'However much the ladies might attempt to emulate you, they cannot match your natural beauty,' Ban would say, which made me love him all the more.

I next appeared at the opera in a completely new style of gown dubbed 'déshabillé' that I had copied from Marie-Antoinette. It was quickly named the Perdita chemise or the Chemise de la Reine. Being free of hoops, tight-lacing and panniers, it was as beguilingly simple as a nightgown, and very much suited my style. It soon became all the rage and even aristocratic ladies adopted it, at least in private, including the dear duchess, not simply the Cyprian Corps. Unfortunately this resulted in some comments and criticism in the press, as it made it much harder to judge a lady's status by her appearance.

All this fuss over the excesses of fashion set my muse working on a poem which, years later, when I was attempting to earn my living by my pen, I published under the pen-name of Tabitha Bramble.

> Long petticoats to hide the feet,
> Silk hose, with clocks of scarlet;
> A load of perfumes, sick'ning sweet,
> Made by Parisian Varlet.

I was also sporting yet another new carriage, as much a part of my extravagant style as my gowns and hats.

Tommy, my never-to-be-forgotten husband, was in Italy, working with my brother John. Fox had won his lady and at last taken up with his much-adored Elizabeth Armistead. Then Ban came to me one day with what he termed 'exciting news'.

'What is it, my love? You look alight with enthusiasm.'

'I am indeed. Lord Shelburne, Secretary of Colonial Affairs, has offered Cornwallis the post of governor and commander in chief in India. And Cornwallis has asked me to command his cavalry.'

I was horrified. 'India! Are you saying that you are to go to India?'

He drew me into his arms. 'I know you will be sad to see me go, Mary, and I accept that a voyage to that part of the world carries danger, but I am a military man and it is my duty. I had hoped to be involved in the defence of Gibraltar, but that didn't happen. This is exactly the opportunity I have longed for.'

Tears filled my eyes even as I kissed him and wished him well. 'I cannot say that I am happy about losing you, or that I do not fear for your safety, but I do understand.'

I watched in silent dismay as he made his preparations, sold off his horses and closed down his house. Then to my blessed relief, everything changed. Lord Shelburne resigned from the cabinet in February, which instantly put an end to the plan.

Ban was mortified at losing this chance. 'I shall not give up hope. Fox is already heavily engaged in electioneering, and if there is to be a new government, Cornwallis may still be offered the post.'

'We must wait and hope for the best,' I consoled him, secretly praying for the exact opposite.

But his disappointment cut deep, adding to the bitterness Ban already felt over his damaged career, and he threw himself into a mad social whirl by way of distraction. We partied, danced and dined, and he visited the gaming houses, Brooks's, Weltje's and other clubs with increasing regularity. He also became heavily involved with the prince, Fox, Sir John Lade and Sir Harry Featherstone who held race meetings at his home, Uppark in Sussex. But while Sir Harry, one of the wealthiest young men in England and sought after by all mothers with eligible young daughters, enjoyed an income of £10,000 a year, my darling Ban was on half pay with only a modest £350.

In addition he spent money on extravagant clothes, bought new horses and a carriage. Meanwhile his creditors, fearful that at any moment he might depart for India, not only demanded cash in hand, but settlement of all his debts. He was obliged to borrow money from Drummond's Bank and even from the owner of Weltje's Club. I grew fearful of where this mad recklessness might lead.

'I beg you to stop. Please give up the gaming table, Ban, and this mad way of living, or it will destroy you as it did my husband Tommy.'

'This is merely a temporary difficulty,' he assured me. 'I've suffered one or two unfortunate losses recently, but one good win would soon put matters right. It is but £1,000, and can easily be recovered.'

I could not prevent a small gasp of dismay. '*A thousand pounds!* That is a huge sum of money, my love. And if you go on losing, could easily double.'

'Then I would sell my commissions. I've already written to my mother and brothers for a loan or settlement, so far with no response. I may have to pay a visit as they probably feel somewhat neglected. Do not worry, my love. All will be well.'

Ban travelled to Liverpool at the end of May, but on his return in June he looked no happier. His plea for help had failed.

'She blames me, doesn't she?' I guessed, and even as he demurred, I could see by the way he avoided meeting my gaze that I was correct.

'Like all mothers she dislikes my profligate lifestyle and wishes me to settle down, marry and produce heirs.' He spoke in dismissive tones, as men do about their mothers. It made me recall the pressure my own had put upon me to marry at only fifteen, and how I had regretted that day ever since.

'Would that I were a free woman,' I said, unable to prevent my anguish spilling out.

'You have nothing to fear, Mary, I have no wish for marriage and will never give you up.'

'How can you resist when the pressure is so great? I know what it is to feel a responsibility to one's family.'

Capturing my face between his hands, he gently kissed me. 'All will be well, I promise you. Cornwallis has offered to put in a good word for me, and persuade my family to help. You won't ever lose me, Mary. You know full well how I am mad with love for you,' and to prove the truth of his words he took me to bed and made love to me there and then, awakening that passion between us that was never dormant for long.

Afterwards we slept contentedly entwined, only to wake and make love again. Later, gently kissing my brow, he rose from my bed and began pulling on his breeches, shirt and jacket. 'You stay where you are, my darling, all warm and cosy, while I go and discuss terms with my creditors, and perhaps touch one or two of my friends for a loan. I'm feeling lucky tonight so I might try one more throw of the dice.'

'No, please, no more gambling, I beg you.' But he was already striding away, oblivious to my pleas.

After he had gone, I sank my face into my pillows and wept. How could I have been so foolish as to find myself again in the very same situation I had been in with Tommy? But I knew the answer even as I berated my own stupidity. Unlike my husband, I was madly in love with Ban Tarleton. What I had felt for Thomas Robinson had been no more than a fond affection, the prince had turned my head with his flattery and persistence, and I had mistaken the passion he'd evoked in me for love. But now I was twenty-five years old, a mature woman not a silly young girl, and with Banistre Tarleton this was the real thing. This was the man I wished to spend the rest of my life with.

★   ★   ★

Nothing changed in the weeks following although Cornwallis was apparently in touch with the Tarleton family attempting to produce a plan to resolve the situation. I, however, had other concerns on my mind, as I'd discovered that I was again in a delicate condition. I chose not to tell Ban at this stage, not until I was a little further into the pregnancy, and hopefully his financial difficulties had been resolved.

One night, not feeling well enough to accompany him, I sat at home waiting and praying he would return soon from The Cocoa Tree, but could not resist glancing at his papers as I tidied them away. And there I found a most damning letter from his mother. They say that eavesdroppers hear no good of themselves, and prying eyes no doubt suffer the same fate.

The words seemed to leap off the page as his mother condemned my influence and my lifestyle, claiming that my personal failings were poison for her beloved son. She went on to demand that he leave me and go to the Continent. In return for this sacrifice the family would settle his debts. The letter ended:

> London can not, nor must not be your place of residence. It will give me real pleasure and satisfaction to hear that your connection with Mrs Robinson is at an end. Without that necessary step all my endeavours to save you from impending destruction will be ineffectual.'

Slipping the letter safely back where I had found it, I knew, in that moment, that whether or not I was carrying his child, I should give him up. I should encourage Ban to do as his mother asked, perhaps even find a young heiress to wed, one with the finances necessary to lift him forever out of his financial difficulties.

Yet I knew in my heart that I could never relinquish him. I would love him till I died, and I believed he loved me too. Some other solution must be found.

It was a sultry night in late July and I was at the opera, seated in my box, the Duc de Lauzun by my side as he was currently paying a short visit to his house on Pall Mall.

'Wasn't the colonel expected to join you?' he asked, as the curtain rose upon the second act and still Ban had not appeared.

I had barely stopped looking for him from the moment we'd arrived at the theatre, yet there was still no sign and I was growing concerned, even while doing my utmost not to show it. 'He must have been delayed for some reason. I'm sure he'll be here soon.'

But he still had not appeared by the time the performance ended.

'I insist upon seeing you safely home,' the duke said.

'That is most kind, and you must join us for supper. I dare say Ban will be there already, waiting for me at home.'

But he was not, and I instantly became alarmed. Despite his growing gambling addiction, it was not like him to break his word.

'Do not fret, dear lady. I shall go and make enquiries at his various clubs, The Cocoa Tree, and among his friends, and bring him home to you,' Lauzun generously offered.

'You are most kind, sir.'

But the duke quickly returned with grim news indeed. 'I am reliably informed that the colonel has departed for France.'

'*What?*' I was utterly devastated. 'I cannot believe that he would leave without even saying goodbye.'

'Perhaps it was a decision of the moment,' the duke suggested. 'Would he be in danger of arrest for debt, were he to remain in England?'

I bleakly conceded this to be true, thinking of Tommy's arrest and how I had dutifully followed him into the Fleet. I made an instant decision not to allow that to happen again, nor to let Ban go without a fight. I tactfully withdrew my offer of supper and saw the duke on his way, then sent my manservant to Fox begging for a loan of £1,000 to release Ban from the threat of prison.

I paced the floor in anguish, but less than an hour later my messenger returned with £300 cash and the promise of another £500 by morning. How generous and kind my old friend was.

'I must take this money to the colonel now. Can we catch him, John, before he reaches Dover?' I asked of my manservant.

'Possibly, if we were to leave at once, madam. But you cannot think to go now, it is too late.'

'But we must. If we delay, he could take ship for France by morning and we'd miss him altogether.'

'But madam, your horses are not up to such a journey.'

'Then run and hire me a coach if that will make changing the horses easier.' I refused to listen to any further argument, and with the duke gone and my mother visiting family in Bristol, there was no one to dissuade me. I ran upstairs to kiss my daughter, who would be safe in the care of her nursemaid while I was away. In any case, I fully expected to be home before she woke, with Ban beside me. Then without even pausing to change my gown and despite the lateness of the hour, I set out at once in a hired coach with my manservant, to follow Ban to Dover.

The night was not a cold one, it being late July, although there was a brisk breeze whenever I opened the window to look out, as I did constantly. I longed to see a sign of his vehicle ahead of me but the road remained stubbornly empty. We barely stopped long enough to do more than change the horses, refusing every offer of refreshment. But the further we travelled the rougher the road became, bouncing and tossing me about on the seat so that I was beginning to feel as sick as I'd been on that stormy crossing over the River Severn.

'This is madness. You should stop now, madam, and return home at once,' my loyal servant insisted.

'I am fine, John, do stop fussing.' I held on to the strap like grim death, but a strange ache had started in my back, and pains were shooting up and down my legs. Was he right? Was this indeed madness? Putting one hand to my stomach I thought of the precious child I carried, praying I could keep it safe. The journey seemed endless and I was relieved when next we stopped to put on fresh horses, as I felt sure I was about to throw up.

'You should stay here and rest for the night, madam,' my servant pleaded, seeing how drawn and pale I looked. But I would not hear of it.

'No, we must keep going. I cannot lose him now.'

The thought of spending my life, even a few months, without Ban, was more than I could contemplate. But the coach had barely lurched forward more than a few yards, the cooler night air now making me shiver, when my hand slipped from the strap and blackness overwhelmed me as I collapsed in a dead faint.

I woke in a strange bed, a woman I did not recognise in attendance. I felt hot and sticky, a burning pain in my back and legs, my limbs feeling oddly twitchy and restless. 'Where am I? Am I in Dover? Where is Ban?' I could barely croak out the words.

'Oh, madam, how glad I am to see you've come round at last. You've been that delirious I fair feared for your life.' Her face was old and pinched, and wore a pitying look of sadness that struck a cold wave of fear in me.

'What is it? What has happened? Did the coach overturn?'

'No, madam, not at all. You collapsed, is all, but fortunately your servant was able to quickly fetch help, the coach not having gone more'n a few yards from the inn door.'

'When was that? How long have I been here?' My thoughts were still focused on the purpose of my journey. If I was still at the inn, then I might be too late to catch Ban before he left for France. 'What time is it?' I started to tug at the bed clothes but found my hands were curled up and my fingers could not grasp the blankets.

'Ooh, don't you stir a muscle now, not until you're fully recovered.'

'Recovered from what? Tell me what has happened.'

She glanced about her as if seeking rescue but, sick as I was, I could see that she and I were alone in the dingy inn bedroom. Wringing her hands the old woman said, 'Sadly, ma'am, the jolting of the coach didn't do your poor wee babby any good at all.'

I stared at her in shock, and in a whisper asked the dreaded question. 'Are you saying that I've lost it?'

'I did me best, ma'am, but you was only what – three months gone, three and a half at most? Mebbe had you been further along it might have survived, but your little son was too fragile to . . .'

I turned my face away, unable to bear to listen to the details she was giving me. My reckless drive across country had indeed been madness, which had resulted in the loss of my precious child. A *son*! Ban's son. The pain of my grief was catastrophic and I began to sob.

'There, there, ma'am, don't take on. You need to rest. Don't you fret now, I'll take good care of you.'

And so she did, but her best efforts could not control my feverish sweats, or the pain that overwhelmed me as once again my temperature soared. I sank into a delirium where reality and dreams, or rather nightmares, merged into one.

How long it was before I recovered sufficiently to speak again, I cannot say. The passage of time was never explained to me. I knew only the misery of losing my child as well as Ban. And then I discovered my loss was greater even than that. When I made an attempt to sit up and rise from my sick bed, I found to my horror that my legs, having stopped their twitching, wouldn't move at all.

I screamed with pain whenever I attempted to move, and in deep distress, my self-appointed nurse at last went running for a doctor.

What he had to say was not good. 'I fear the fever you suffered following your miscarriage has left you partially paralysed.'

I stared at him in horror, quite unable to take in what he was saying.

'It is likely that the condition will only be temporary, but it is essential that you rest for some weeks, when you will then hopefully make a slow recovery.'

Even I could hear the doubt in his tone. *Paralysed!* Fear beat a slow pulse within as I considered the harsh reality of that terrifying word, one I refused to acknowledge and would never use again. I tried to flex my fingers, but they remained stubbornly curled inward to my palm, like those of a witch in a pantomime. He saw my efforts and put out a hand to stop me.

'There is much we can do to improve movement. We can try massage and hot baths, perhaps a stay in Brighton as cold sea water bathing is said to be excellent for the circulation. With your permission I will speak to your manservant and get him to make the necessary arrangements.'

So it was that by the end of August I was residing in Brighton with Maria Elizabeth and Mama.

'You realise we are not far from Steine, the prince's home,' my mother gently reminded me. 'Do you wish me to communicate to His Highness that you are here?'

'No! We have overcome our differences, but I have no wish to see him on this occasion. Nor anyone else for that matter, save for Ban.'

'And where is *he* when most needed?' she said with a sniff of disapproval.

Stifling a sigh I clung to my patience, generally at a low ebb these days because of the constant pain I suffered. It felt very like a dragon gnawing with giant teeth at my joints, which had me weeping with anguish into my pillow night after sleepless night. 'He is almost certainly in France, waiting for his family to relieve his financial difficulties. And don't say a word on that subject either, Mama.'

'Then I shall take dear Maria for a walk,' she announced and flounced off, leaving me to my morose thoughts.

I doubted Ban would even be aware of the disaster that had befallen me when I had executed my desperate plan to save him and keep him by my side. I grieved for my lost lover, and for our son. How different it could all have been if I had reached him in time. But I would not think of that. I must concentrate on getting well, as the doctor had instructed.

I took regular dips in the sea, and sea-water baths in a building called The Temple, set below the cliffs. I even drank sea water, which was most disagreeable.

We lodged on the sea front at the Old Ship Hotel, and at any other time, for any other reason, would have found it extremely pleasant. Brighton was a small, quaint, fishing village where society flocked to consult Dr Russell, famous for his cures. It was set amongst beautiful countryside of cornfields and rolling downs where John, my devoted manservant, would sometimes drive me to enliven my day.

Generally, when I wasn't undergoing treatment, I would sit on the veranda gazing upon the long shingle beach where Mama was now playing a jolly ball game with Maria to amuse her.

I closed my eyes, dozing gently in the warmth of the sun, when I heard a familiar step on the path below, then felt the touch of a soft kiss upon my lips. My eyes flew open in delighted astonishment.

'Ban! Can it truly be you, or am I dreaming?'

He laughed, that warm, so-familiar sound that I loved so much, put his arms about me and kissed me some more. 'Do I seem real now?'

'Oh, my darling. How did you know I was here?'

'For once you can thank the papers for their gossiping,' he said, dropping into a chair beside me. 'The *Herald* reported in late July "Mrs Robinson lies dangerously ill at her house at Berkeley Square". A second report a few days later stated that you were not quite as bad as expected, but still unwell. Unfortunately I did not see either report until one of my brothers cut out the pieces and posted them to me only last week, out of pity, knowing how I ached for you. It included a more recent one which said you had gone to Brighthelmstone to aid your recovery. I at once made arrangements to take the Dieppe to Brighton ferry and here I am. Under an assumed name, I might add, and my visit must be fleeting as I have no wish to run the risk of arrest, even for you, my darling.'

'Oh, no, you must take no risks on my behalf, but it is so wonderful to see you.' I wrapped my arms about his neck and held him tight, drinking in the beloved smell of him, the warmth of his cheek pressed to mine. I wept a little, with joy, and he laughingly wiped away my tears. Then we sat holding hands as lovers do, gazing into each other's eyes in rapturous contentment.

'I have to say that the *Herald* soon ceased to be sympathetic, claiming you were not ill at all but sulking over the loss of your lover, and the "declining influence of her charms". Looking at you now, my love, I wish that were indeed the case as you look far from well.'

'I am suffering from a form of rheumatic gout, born of a fever, but you must not worry. The doctors are optimistic of an eventual recovery.'

'But what caused it? How did such a fever come about?'

I told him then about my mad dash for Dover, and the child I had lost, and saw the sadness in his eyes deepen.

'I was not even on the Dover road as I sailed from Southampton. The fault is entirely mine for running off like that without a word. I knew if I even saw you one more time I would lose the will to leave at all.'

So that was the reason. Relief flooded through me, knowing that he did love me, after all. 'I quite understand, but it is no one's fault. It was an unfortunate accident. These things happen.'

'Much as I miss you, dearest, I must remain on the Continent until such time as my debts are settled.'

'Oh, I do so agree. I have no wish for you to suffer the rigours of the Fleet, as did I when but a girl. It is too terrible to contemplate. Fox leant me £300 for you, promising more, although I have been obliged to use some of it myself to pay doctors' bills and accommodation these last weeks. You can have whatever is left, and write to Fox yourself. He may still be willing to help.'

'I believe he has enough difficulties of his own. In any case, I truly hope and believe my family will come up with the money, given time.'

'On condition you stay away from *me*,' I drily added.

'Ah, you know about that, do you?'

'I accidentally came upon a letter from your mother,' I confessed.

'I have already informed her that I have no intention of giving you up, and that you are not the cause of my bankruptcy. She will have to accept it in the end.'

We spent the happiest two days together, our kisses as passionate as ever even if because of my poor state of health we didn't take our love making too far. He would gently massage my clawed hands, rub my sore stiff legs, and once carried me down to the gardens for a delightful picnic. Ban propped himself against a tree while I rested in his arms, listening to his plans for the future.

'While I await a new commission in India, Cornwallis has suggested I spend the winter studying military science in southern France.'

'But you will return to me soon, my love?'

'I will,' he agreed, lightly kissing my brow.

Not a single person was aware of his presence in Brighton beyond my own dear family and servants, who had dutifully promised not to breathe a word, so it was unfortunate that who should come along the path towards us at that very moment but the Earl of Pembroke.

'Ah, Mrs Robinson I do believe, the lady I once offered to save from the Fleet, if I recall correctly.'

I was startled, but could not help remembering how Angelina Albanesi had told me of His Lordship's generous offer, even as she made no apology for sleeping with my husband. I had dismissed it as yet another slur upon my virtue, but had become vaguely acquainted with Lord Pembroke since. He had often used to come to Drury Lane to watch me perform. Now I smiled politely as I struggled to sit up, helped by Ban. 'My Lord, I did not realise you were in Brighton.'

His face clouded with a pain I recognised, though his response was typically cool and brisk as he hastened to mask it. 'My nine-year-old daughter is dying of consumption, so we are here to take benefit from the sea air. And yourself, Mrs Robinson? You are as pretty as ever, but illness has left its mark. Clearly, visiting the opera on the day of a miscarriage was not a good idea.'

Quite at a loss as to how to respond to this, I squeezed Ban's hand, warning him to remain silent too. This poor man clearly had little sympathy to spare for the pain of others.

He exchanged a few more polite remarks upon the weather, the gardens, and the aftermath of the American war with Ban, then he hurried away, presumably back to his sick child. We looked at each other in dismay.

'Do you think he will tell anyone that he saw you?' I asked.

'We can but hope not. But I dare stay no longer, dearest. With luck I shall be home by the spring.'

'You promise?'

'Nothing would keep me from your side. Now I must leave with all speed.' Then he helped me back to the hotel, supporting me with tender care while I dragged my feet along with the help of my crutches. Once more ensconced in my chair on the veranda, he gave me a last farewell kiss that set my head spinning, then left. Maria held me while I wept.

I returned to Berkeley Square in November, having stayed with relatives in Bristol for a few weeks to continue my recuperation. By then I'd given up my box at the opera, and didn't feel ready to take it up again so attempted to concentrate upon my writing. This was not easy, my mind too clouded with pain and loss, and I struggled to find inspiration. The pity of it was that I badly needed the money, the agreed £500 annuity from the prince nowhere near enough to cover my debts and living costs.

Setting my quill pen aside in despair, I sat instead for another Sir Joshua Reynold's portrait, which helped pass the time without any effort on my part. I rather hoped a new set of prints and posters might restore me to society. It was, however, a far more serious, pensive portrait this time, in keeping with my mood. I took little joy in it.

By January 1784 my pain had lessened considerably and my health was beginning to improve. Thus encouraged I accepted the prince's kind offer to use his box, and went at last to the opera, feeling quite desperate to escape the confinement of the house, dress in a fine gown and go out into society. It meant a great fuss as my servants were obliged to convey me everywhere.

They would pull on long white cotton sleeves before lifting and carrying me to the box, much to the fascination of the audience, returning at the end of the performance to carry me back to my carriage. Tiresome but sadly necessary. I dreamed of a time when my legs would be strong enough to walk more than a few paces without crippling pain.

The *Herald* celebrated my reappearance by reporting that I was seen looking beautiful in a blue hat.

> Now winter surrounds us, and chills with frost those feelings which depend upon the blood; the Perdita comes forth to cheer us, and with the potent rays of beauty counteracts the severity of the season.

It felt good to be noticed and admired again. Sadly, the night out in the cold air had not been a wise decision, and I paid the price with three weeks of severe rheumatic pain. However, undaunted, I had my own box back by the end of the month, and once again became a regular at the theatre. I could also often be seen taking the air in Hyde Park, being lifted carefully from my carriage so that I might walk a few paces along the path, ably supported by the nobly patient John.

As promised, Ban returned to me in March. I was sitting by the window when I saw the carriage draw up, and thought I might explode with joy. He sprang out, glancing up to give me a jaunty wave. Had I been able to, I would have run into his arms. Instead, I pulled myself up from my chair so that when he entered the drawing room he would see how much I had improved.

He flung open the door, took one long look at me then in two strides swept me up into his arms. To be held in his embrace once again was the answer to all my hopes and dreams.

'My mother and brothers between them finally paid off my debts,' he told me later as we lay in bed together. 'Despite their disapproval, nothing would keep me from your side.'

We had made love unhindered by my lack of mobility, which didn't seem to trouble Ban in the slightest. I simply gave myself up to the pleasure of having him inside me. Even my clawed fingers obeyed as I sought to stroke his beloved face and neatly cropped head. He rocked against me, lifting my useless body to him, since I could not do that for myself. Oh, but the passion we enjoyed was undiminished, possibly even enhanced by our time apart. I wanted to savour every moment, glorying in the way I felt the power of him run through me like fire.

As we idled away the hours and days following with love-making, parts of a poem began to grow in my head, the first time in months.

> She trac'd the passions, at command,
> Each yielded to her potent hand!
> Inspir'd her glowing breast with new and fierce delight!

But if we had hoped to keep Ban's arrival a secret, it was a vain one. The *Morning Post* wrote:

> The gallant Tarleton is again on duty in Berkeley Square.
> He is no longer Perditus but Restoratus. His skill is as great
> as ever and he can go through all the evolutions from loading
> to firing, with the tattoo only.

I laughed it off, determined that no double entrendre would spoil my happiness. 'I may have some difficulty walking, but other parts of me are still in full working order.'

'I would give testament to that,' teased Ban, and proved the truth of my words all over again. 'However, my love, I fear that I must leave you for a short time yet again. In order to mollify my family I have agreed to stand for Parliament. I've always expressed an interest in politics, and I must do something since my military career seems to be languishing in the doldrums.'

I laughed. 'Fox would welcome you, I'm sure. He has been very irritable since his coalition with North collapsed in December over the India Bill, and the king appointed twenty-four-year-old William Pitt as the new First Minister. Poor Fox has gradually lost his majority.'

'Now Parliament has been dissolved.'

'But Fox is determined to fight back and the dear Duchess of Devonshire is canvassing for him, as usual, happily exchanging kisses for votes. He hopes to at least be re-elected as MP for Westminster.'

'I'm sure he will succeed, while I have some doubts over my own chances. My family are doing what they can, of course, buying favours in Liverpool if not with kisses then with whatever hard cash they can afford. So it is to my home town that I must now go, dearest. I hate to leave you the moment I have arrived home, but it is necessary if I am to get elected.'

'Ah, but this time you will be back in my arms within weeks, not months. Don't worry, I shall keep busy.' I was not half so unconcerned over his absence as I made out. Even a week apart from this man I adored was one too many.

While Ban was away I was delighted to find that my muse returned, and I happily occupied myself writing satirical verse in order to help Fox. When my fingers tired, as they soon did, I would drive about town in my carriage wearing his colours of buff and blue, sporting a jaunty red brush in my hat. I became known as the Cyprian divinity of Berkeley Square, which made me laugh.

But perhaps my efforts paid off as Fox did indeed retain his seat. Ban, sadly, was not elected.

'I fear my decision to stand for Parliament has also put paid to my military career. The East India Company have implied they may not now allow me to accompany Cornwallis, were he ever to go to India. They consider me too political.'

I felt a huge relief at this news while Ban buried his disappointment by spending even more time with the prince and his brothers, engaging in tennis and cricket, and less admirable activities. He was a man who excelled at sport, not just those two favourites, but boxing, riding, horse-racing and fox-hunting, more often than not with a bet or two attached.

The summer flew by in a whirl of fun and happiness, although worryingly, our creditors continued to gather like devilish birds of prey. To my very great delight, the Duc du Lauzun came on another visit and I was able to thank him personally for his efforts on my behalf on that terrible night of my ride to Dover. To my astonishment, he and Ban made a pair of merry pranksters about town.

'How is it that you have become such fast friends when you were once fighting to the death on the battlefield?' I asked, somewhat bewildered.

They both looked at me in surprise, and then at each other. 'That was a job, dearest,' Ban explained.

'Indeed, our patriotic duty which need not stand in the way of friendship,' Lauzun added.

'Not when that duty has been done,' Ban agreed.

'When it comes to war and comradeship, I find men impossible to understand.'

Ban laughed. 'Then do not worry your pretty head over it, my love, as thankfully the war is over. Sadly, peace is presenting even greater problems, now that my income is reduced.'

The duke was instantly sympathetic. 'Should your creditors become too pressing, then the pair of you are most welcome to come and stay with me at any time. The warmer climate would be good for your health, Mary.'

Such generosity of friendship brought tears of gratitude to my eyes.

Throughout the election campaign the papers had pilloried me mercilessly, accusing me of greed and vanity, the reason for it quite beyond my comprehension. The most hurtful caricature appeared in August 1784 in *Rambler's Magazine* entitled *Perdita Upon her Last Legs*, in which I was shown attempting to beg money from the Prince of Wales. I thought this a particularly cruel double entendre. Why would the press never leave me alone?

And yet . . .

My situation was becoming so dire that when I visited Brighton later that month, and discovered that the prince was also staying, I did, in my desperation, write him a begging letter. His response was to offer his sympathy and good wishes, but doubted it would be 'within the compass of my means to rescue you from the abyss you apprehend that is before you . . .'

I would watch his indulgences at Brighton and elsewhere, and feel a deep resentment over his refusal to help me beyond the agreed annuity, a pitifully small sum considering all I had sacrificed on his behalf.

By January of the following year, the inevitable could be put off no longer. 'I fear we must take up the duke's kind offer, as I am bankrupt,' I mourned to Ban, who held me close in a warm hug to offer what consolation he could. But then he was in no better state himself.

I agreed that all my effects must go to auction, save for the prince's miniature which I always keep about my person.

'Is that because you still feel a lingering love for His Highness?' teased Ban, knowing full well that was not the case. I playfully tapped that perfect nose of his.

'Not at all, but one can never be sure if and when my creditors might descend upon Berkeley Square.'

We did not linger to watch my precious belongings come under the hammer but set off for the Continent on the thirteenth of August 1784. How could I bear to stay and watch them be virtually given away? They included the Gainsborough half-portrait, which we later learned was knocked down for thirty-two guineas. Then there was a Wilton carpet, two large pier glasses in gilt frames, double-branched gilt Gerondoles, a pair of tables with marble tops, six cabriole elbow chairs in white and gold, curtains, cushions, fire screens and goodness knows what else. All the precious items that furnished my home, wherever that might be.

Naturally the press were crowing with delight, stating that a life of wanton dissipation had reduced me to penury and poverty. Apparently my constitution and the use of my limbs were also done for, and death stared me in the face. Not a happy thought.

Warmly wrapped in furs and my famous Perdita Hood on the Brighton to Dieppe ferry boat with the three people I loved most in all the world, my daughter Maria, Mama and Ban, I felt sad but very much alive. And as we were heading for warmer climes I fully expected that my health could only benefit. What more could I ask?

We settled most comfortably at the Hotel de Russie in the rue de Richelieu in Paris, living quite contentedly throughout a warm and sunny autumn, enjoying walks by the Seine and in the

Tuileries Gardens. But as October came in, so did the cold winds and my rheumatic gout flared up again.

'We need to make a decision on where we should spend the winter, and how to secure the extra funds we need. This hotel is deliciously luxurious, but hugely expensive. We must make more sensible provision for the months ahead.'

'I agree, but let us not worry too much about money until after the auction,' Ban said by way of comfort. 'I'm thinking of writing a history of the campaigns, and rather hoped you might help with the project?'

'Oh, that is an excellent idea. You know I will do all I can to assist. I'm sure it would sell well. And I shall write more poems, which might also bring in some much-needed cash.'

We were happily engrossed making our plans as we entered the hotel, deciding to head further south, perhaps to the Côte d'Azur, so did not notice the young man until he clapped a hand on Ban's shoulder.

'Brother, I have found you at last.'

Ban looked startled for a moment, then clasped the man in a rough embrace. 'John, goodness, what a surprise.' In stark contrast to this welcome, his tone, I noticed, was bristling with suppressed anger. We had not counted on being discovered, particularly by Ban's family. 'What on earth are you doing here?'

'Looking for you, what else?'

Ban scowled. 'Was that necessary? How did you find us?'

'It was not easy.' His gaze shifted to sweep over me. 'Mrs Robinson, I'm pleased to meet you at last.'

I saw by his eyes that he found no pleasure in our meeting at all. 'And I you,' I murmured, politely inclining my head.

Later, as we dined, the tension between the two brothers was palpable despite the excellent wine and food we consumed. It was quite clear by the way he pressed Ban to return home with him, that his purpose in coming here was to bring about a separation and steal his brother away from me. Ban listened to a lengthy lecture in silence then finally snapped.

'At one time Mother was anxious for me to remain on the Continent, so here I am again, and where I intend to remain. We plan to spend the winter in warmer climes for the sake of Mrs Robinson's health, and no, I will not abandon her.'

'Our mother is not well. She needs you home.'

I could see that Ban did not believe this tale, but feeling responsible for the disagreement between the brothers, I attempted to intervene. 'Please, there is really no need for you to stay in France all winter for my sake, Ban, if your mother needs you. I could take up my own brother John's offer and make a home with him in Leghorn, Italy. I should be perfectly fine there for the winter, only too glad to escape the calumny and persecution of life in England.' Living with my brother was the last thing I wanted as it would deprive me of my independence, and I certainly had no wish to spend an entire winter without the man I loved.

Ban clearly agreed for he cast me the kind of telling look which said that I had broken our secret pact, which I suppose in a way, I had. 'No, dearest, you would not be fine. Has not your physician urged you to try the spa waters of Aix-la-Chapelle? As a leading health resort he considered it far more suitable for you than Italy.'

'That is very true.' I gave his brother an apologetic little smile, feeling very far from sorry inside.

He left the following morning, although I very much doubted their mother would welcome the message he was taking to her.

A week later we began our progress south, staying for a time in Villefranche, near Nice. The *Morning Post* had reported I was wintering 'upon the scanty pittance gleaned from the remnant of her amorous treasures'. And in January my finances were such that I was indeed obliged to write first to Colonel Hotham, then to the prince to remind him to continue to send my allowance.

> I should not have made any application to Colonel Hotham, but being in want of money (on account of Lord Malden neglecting to pay his annuity these fifteen months past) – will I trust be deem'd a sufficient apology.

I pointed out that I dare not return to England due to the danger of arrest for debt. Nevertheless, my letter was worded with affection, as our feud was over. I received no response.

By February we had taken up Lauzun's kind offer and were staying at his chateau in the south of France. After a short stay we moved on to Aix-la-Chapelle in Germany, where we settled most comfortably.

Known as Aachen by the Germans it was quite a cosmopolitan little town, welcoming guests from every corner of Europe: aristocrats and princes, bishops and politicians, whoever could afford the exorbitant costs of such luxury for the sake of their health, and even those like ourselves who could not. It boasted a delightful promenade, theatre, beautiful park and many other amusements considered necessary for relaxation and mental stimulation.

More importantly, I could take advantage of the hot springs, pump room, steam baths and extensive bathing facilities. 'I shall like it here. It has everything we need.'

I loved having Ban all to myself without the distractions of gentlemen's clubs and gaming tables, or young ladies who could never resist flirting with such a handsome man. We would spend hours each day working contentedly together on his history of the campaigns, examining documents, letters, pamphlets and the like.

I had found a tutor for Maria, now ten, and she was happily learning languages. I supervised the rest of her education personally, setting her suitable books to read, and subjects to write about. She was a bright little girl and flourishing despite the difficulties of my circumstances, and my tendency at times to be a little short-tempered due to the pain I suffered. It was a perfect family time, and I wanted nothing to spoil it.

I made full use of the bathing facilities and drinking fountains as I sought a cure, or at least respite from my pain, making only one complaint. 'I do find the water singularly disagreeable to drink.'

'Why does it smell like bad eggs?' my daughter asked, holding her nose.

I laughed. 'The thermal springs contain sulphur, I believe.'

It was a most dreadful odour, despite the vapour baths being impregnated with aromatic herbs, and the waters scattered with rose leaves. I enjoyed regular massage and gentle, underwater exercise. The air was bracing and therefore healthy, but hot baths if continued for any length of time are considered enervating so these were followed by a cold one to stimulate circulation. I would gasp and cry out when plunged into one.

'Oh, prepare me a little first, I pray, by at least sponging me down with a cool cloth.'

'But then you would lose the benefit of the change in temperature, ma'am,' I was told. I suffered the treatment with stoic endurance, desperately wanting to be well again.

'I am far too young to spend the rest of my life as an invalid,' I wept one night, after a day that had been anything but relaxing. 'You will grow tired of me and my ailments.' It was my chief concern that Ban might find a new love without the problems I presented.

'Never,' he assured me, and pulling me into his arms set about proving his love in the best possible way.

Thankfully, there was also time for socialising, and we would attend balls and concerts, and rural breakfasts. We made new friends in the Duke and Duchess of Chatelet, who were most kind to me. If I was in the grip of a rheumatic spasm, the dragon biting its teeth into my joints particularly badly, they'd devise strategies to relieve my sufferings, or at least distract me from them. The couple greatly cheered my spirits, as did my darling Ban. Then one day he came to me wearing a most gloomy expression.

'I'm afraid I must leave you for a while, my love, and take a trip home,'

'Why must you?' I snapped. I readily admit that I was not in a particularly good mood when he made this announcement, due to the pain and the treatment I was forced to endure. But at the same time my heart trembled with fear. Was he saying that he'd had enough of waiting upon a cripple?

'I must attend to my parlous financial affairs.'

'Could you not do that by letter?'

'No, my love, I could not. I also need to make enquiries about a possible future posting. We cannot stay here for ever. We must make proper provision for when we return home.'

'I suspect you are simply bored.'

'Oh, Mary, how could I ever be bored with you, are you not my soul mate? I would much prefer to remain here with you.'

'Then it is this obsession with gambling that is in your blood. Swear to me you will never again roll a dice,' I cried, furious tears rolling down my cheeks.

'Dearest, I have no such desire.'

'Swear it!'

'Very well, I swear it. No more tossing of the dice. I will be gone but a short time, and back by your side before you have had time to miss me.'

That could never be the case, as well he knew, but no matter how much I railed and sobbed and sulked, he kept his word and returned to London, and no doubt to his family in Liverpool. Most of all I feared his family's influence might lure him away from me for good in the end.

That was the first of several visits over the coming months, none of which I welcomed as I never could accept the necessity for these frequent absences. I would be contentedly settling to having him back in my arms, then quite out of the blue he would come to tell me he was leaving.

'Why must you go so often? Are you gambling again? Can you not bear to be away from Brooks's or The Cocoa Tree?'

'Dearest Mary, please do not excite yourself. It does your health no good at all.'

'*Do not tell me what to do!*'

He had the temerity to laugh. 'I would not dream of doing so. It is your independent spirit that I most admire about you.'

'That and my money, which you have spent on your gaming. Are you seeing other women?'

He let out a heavy sigh. 'You know that I have no wish to hurt you, nor to quarrel with you.'

'That does not answer my question. What whore are you bedding now?'

'Dammit, Mary, you go too far. You offend my honour.'

'*You do not know the meaning of the word!*' I screamed, at which point we stared at each other in fury and horror, knowing there was no greater insult to a soldier. The next second he was upon me, ripping my nightgown from my naked body and we were making love with a passion that filled me with an exultant joy. Feeling his powerful thighs against my weakling limbs, the way he filled every part of me, making me his entirely, excited me more than words could describe.

Our relationship was ever volatile, but I consoled myself that he could not stay away from me too long, any more than I could tolerate his absences. We were as one, entirely besotted and dependent upon each other.

While Ban was away, Maria Elizabeth was a great support and comfort. When the pain kept me awake at nights she would sing to me, or ask a mandolin player to serenade me from beneath my window. I would lie awake long into the night listening to him, albeit with tears of pain in my eyes, and in my heart until my lover was back in my arms once again.

On his return Ban would be bursting with vitality and energy, and with news of the latest fashions, scandal and gossip, which was always welcome. Content as I was on the Continent and enjoyed the milder climate, a part of me still ached for the life I had left behind in London. He brought word of the prince's affair with Maria Fitzherbert, a lady not only much older than he, which was unsurprising, but of the Catholic faith.

'It has certainly set tongue's wagging,' Ban said. 'The ton is agog over the scandal. There is even talk they have taken part in a clandestine marriage.'

'Goodness gracious. Has the prince run mad?' Naturally the rumours resulted in yet more caricatures in which I was depicted as the jilted lover.

'But we parted years ago,' I raged, tearing up the cartoons Ban had brought to show me. 'Why will they persist in linking me with the prince?'

'Because a royal lover is far more exciting than a mere colonel.'

I smiled. 'Not in my eyes, my darling.' And tossing the papers aside, gave myself up to my true love.

In December 1785, I learned that my father had died. He was over 60 years old and had apparently distinguished himself at the siege of Gibraltar, and saved Spanish sailors from drowning or dying in the burning ships. I was delighted to learn that he'd been commended by the Admiralty, then obtained a commission in St Petersburg when Catherine of Russia had called for British officers. Now, after two years in the Russian Imperial Service, he was gone from my life forever, without even the opportunity for me to say goodbye. As always, I put my thoughts into a poem.

Oh! my lov'd sire, farewell!
Though we are doom'd on earth to meet no more,
Still mem'ry lives, and still I must adore!

More startling still, I read of my own death in the *Morning Post*
of the fourteenth of July 1786. Enraged by the description of
myself as 'the natural daughter of a gentleman', which implied I
was illegitimate, and my mother as an innkeeper of all things, I
at once wrote to object, demolishing these fantasies they had
devised about me.

> Sir, I have the satisfaction of informing you that so far from
> being dead, I am in the most perfect state of health, except
> a trifling lameness, of which, by the use of the baths at this
> place, I have every reason to hope I shall recover in a month
> or six weeks.

My timing was perhaps somewhat over-optimistic but the piece had
annoyed me. Speaking of me in the past tense, it said, 'She was
genteel in her manners, delicate in her person, and beautiful in her
features.' Then caustically went on to say that I would have been
an ornament to my sex had I not succumbed to flattery, folly and
vice. They also published a mocking rhyming couplet, 'Let coxcombs
flatter and let fools adore. Here learn the lesson to be vain no more!'

Three weeks later the paper published my letter, but without
any apology.

In the summer of 1787 we moved to St Amand des Eaux. The
spa was smaller and less fashionable than Aix-La-Chapelle but
known for specialising in the treatment of rheumatism. I decided
to try the hot mud baths there and rented a delightful little
cottage, long and low with five windows at the front and four
set in the roof, with two awnings to pull down over the main
windows to provide shade. The cottage boasted a small garden
surrounded by a wooden fence where I loved to sit in the sun and
write my poetry, located as it was in a most pretty spot on the
edge of a forest.

Maria loved the little house so much that she drew a picture of
it to pin up on my bedroom wall. What a gifted child she

was, although at twelve rapidly turning into a young woman. She was growing taller by the day and had a dignity about her which was quite charming. Auburn haired like myself, her eyes a bewitching dark blue, with a healthy glow to her rosy cheeks which I loved to see. Above all else, I meant to keep my daughter healthy.

Ban was in London, attending parties and promoting the publication of his book: *History of the Campaigns of 1780 and 1781 in the Southern Provinces of North America.* 'Most people seem to realise it was largely written by you, my love,' he wrote in one of his many letters. 'But it has been well received as it is being viewed as an historical record rather than a personal memoir. I doubt it will make my fortune, but my family has at least agreed to reinstate my allowance. Just as well since I remain on half-pay.'

I responded that I was pleased by this news, even though it always set my heart racing with fear whenever he appealed to his family for assistance. 'But what of a future posting?' I dared to ask.

'Cornwallis has finally been posted as Commander-in-Chief to India, but did not offer to take me with him,' came his reply, rippling with bitterness. 'My campaign to be elected as a Whig MP has greatly offended Prime Minister Pitt and he refused to appoint a Whig to any command in India. I very much doubt Cornwallis tried very hard to change his mind, so I have switched my support to Clinton.'

I felt great sympathy for Ban, if considerable relief on my own account. I wanted him here with me, in France, not in faraway India.

I tried not to worry about the future as I wallowed in the loathsome black mud for hour upon hour. I would then be cleansed of the vile substance by being immersed and scrubbed in a hot bath. The baths were situated in a building rather like a greenhouse, separated from each other by wooden frames. Here I would be given massage and kneading, and the Aix Douche, which involved reclining on a wooden board while the spine was sprayed. The temperature was at first warm, going gradually cooler till needle sharp and cold. This was apparently most beneficial to chronic gout and rheumatism.

St Amand was also famous for its ditches where patients were treated with leeches. I resisted this for some time but was finally persuaded to give it a try. 'It is the most distasteful experience imaginable to be sucked by those noisome reptiles,' I complained to my ever-patient mother.

'But the treatment must be working, dear, as you are so much better.'

'You are right, and I should not complain.'

It was true that I was beginning to feel some improvement but sadly, pleasant and beneficial though my stay in St Amand was, I found no miracle cure.

'Will we next return to Aix-la-Chapelle?' Maria asked, having become quite accustomed to our wandering lifestyle.

'No, dearest, we will stay here in our delightful cottage, and having finished Ban's book, I shall concentrate once more upon my own.'

'Oh, yes, Mama, and when your hands get tired, I shall write to your dictation.'

And that is what we did, a partnership that was to last to the end of my days. I wrote a comic opera set in Villefranche, and when my crabbed hands grew tired, my daughter would take the quill pen and continue at my dictation. In this fashion I also managed to complete several poems including 'A Sonnet to the Evening' into which I poured emotion I could not otherwise express.

> Oft do I seek thy shade dear with'ring tree,
> Sad emblem of my own disast'rous state;
> Doom'd in the spring of life, alas! Like thee
> To fade, and droop beneath the frowns of fate;

Writing is such a wonderful therapy for a troubled heart.

Ban again stood for Parliament in September but failed to win a seat and rejoined us in Paris later that autumn where we were staying at the Hôtel d'Angleterre. He was as lively and loving as ever, sweeping me into his arms to devour me with his kisses and love making.

Naturally I worried about what he had been doing all summer. Had he been dallying with any of my rivals in the Cyprian Corps, or found himself a rich heiress? I thought it highly unlikely that this gloriously handsome hero could remain faithful during such a long absence. What man ever was? When I had discovered Tommy's betrayal my pride and dignity had been sorely injured. With Ban I knew in my heart that it would destroy me, as I loved him more than life itself. I burned with jealousy at the very thought of him with another woman. Keeping my emotions very firmly under control, I managed not to express these suspicions out loud.

Infidelity was not the only issue which tested my faith in him. The chief one, of course, was money! 'I trust you have returned with the coffers refilled?' I challenged him, once we had sated our neglected passion.

'My love, did I not explain that well reviewed though it may be, the book has not sold sufficient copies to make any significant profit. Some even saw it as a sneak attack on Cornwallis's reputation at a time when he was not present in the country to defend himself. It created some dispute but generally it is considered to be accurate.'

'Of course it is accurate, since you at least are in possession of all the facts, which your detractors are not.'

'Quite so,' he snapped.

Since he was clearly sensitive on the book's lack of success, I held my tongue and resisted broaching the subject again. We enjoyed a pleasant few weeks together, savouring the delights of Paris, dining in the finest hotels, attending balls and levees, and driving about in hired carriages. But as my finances once more slipped dangerously into debt, my discretion sank with it. Where was the money coming from to fund this high living? I could put the matter off no longer. I chose a moment when we were contentedly breakfasting in bed together, I sipping my chocolate while Ban tucked into toast and marmalade. It was still early but already we could hear the rattle of carriage wheels in the street, the cries of pedlars selling their wares.

I put my enquiry as gently as I could. 'Dearest, forgive my curiosity, but if you are still on half pay, albeit with the addition of an allowance from your family, will that be sufficient for us to maintain the lifestyle we both enjoy so much? As you have already explained, the book will not make your fortune.'

'I did not write it for profit. More to make my case and express my pride in a job well done in difficult circumstances. The good news is that I won a substantial bet which will keep us in the financial black for some time.'

I felt my blood start to heat, as if I were in one of the hot springs again, and carefully setting down my cup of chocolate on the side table, asked him outright. 'Then you *have* been gambling, even though you promised – nay, *swore* on your honour that you would not roll another dice.'

'It was a card game,' he flippantly responded.

'It's still gambling!' I longed to leap from the bed and stride from the room in a rage, but my condition prevented me from any such dramatic gesture. Frustrated, I attacked him all the more. 'Can you not be serious for once instead of carelessly drifting through life without a moment's serious thought.' I knew this to be an unfair criticism even as I spoke the words, yet couldn't seem to prevent my jealous rage from bubbling over. How dare he carelessly use my money as stake for a bet, dally in London and revel in society life while I was stuck with mud baths and leeches?

'You should be proud of me,' he joked, happily spreading marmalade on a second slice of toast. 'I prevented a duel between two of my friends who seemed hell-bent on self-destruction. And the royal brothers seem to have adopted me as something of a favourite. We've enjoyed many a game of cricket together, attend races and prize fights.'

I listened bemused as he spoke of my erstwhile royal lover being often insensible with drink, and of bets on whether a goose could run faster than a turkey.

'You behave like naughty boys at school. They have duped you into living the same kind of debauched life as do they. What of your military career?'

'That seems to be very much in the doldrums, I'm afraid.' I watched in disbelief as he bit on his toast and began to chew, as if this matter were of no great importance.

'So you recklessly abandon yourself to hedonism and gambling?'

'While my luck holds, why would I not?'

'Then if you are in funds again, you can repay what you have borrowed from me in the past. You used *my* money, remember, to finance your bets.'

Dabbing that so kissable mouth with his napkin, he rewarded me with a sad look in his soft brown eyes. 'It is not *your* money, dearest, as I understand it, but the prince's.'

I thought steam must come from my ears, the fury in me was so hot. 'Drat you, Ban Tarleton, you have an answer for everything. Yet you break every promise you make. You always say you will not be away long then stay in London for weeks, if not months, *and* continue to visit the gaming tables every night.'

'My wins at the gaming table have kept us well enough in the past. I see no reason why they should not continue to do so in the future.'

'Then you can do so without me!' I screamed, and picking up my cup of chocolate I flung it at the wall opposite, where it smashed into pieces leaving a brown stain running down the silk wallpaper.

He regarded me with a quiet sadness in his gaze. 'If that is your wish, Mary.' And rising from my bed, he did what I had so longed to do, he walked away.

My anger continued to simmer all day and I remained in my room, carefully avoiding his company. I loathed gambling with a vengeance. Had it not destroyed my life once already? I certainly had no intention of allowing it to do so again, or any wish to reacquaint myself with the Fleet. Only at supper time when I joined Mama and Maria at table, did I learn that Ban had left for London. This time I was quite certain that I'd lost him for good.

Having decided that the state of my health was probably as good as it was ever going to get, the three of us returned to London in April 1788. We settled at number 45 Clarges Street, just opposite Green Park, not far from my old friend the duchess in Piccadilly. Ban was residing at number 30, but although we exchanged a few polite words on the rare occasions we met, we remained estranged.

It felt odd to be back in London after three years on the Continent, but resolving to get back into society I hired a carriage and had John drive me about Hyde Park. Few people paid any attention, not the slightest in fact. The *Morning Post*, however, did not disappoint and printed a piece which, as was their wont, saw only the worst in me.

'Mrs Robinson, though better than when she left England, has returned in a very weakly situation, and appears deeply affected and oppressed in spirits.'

I privately refuted this and, my core of rebellion reawakened, began to entertain, something I had sorely missed while in France. The duchess, Fox, and even the prince and the Duke of York were soon regulars at social functions held at my new home, welcoming me back into the fold with open hearts.

In June the king fell ill with a bilious fever, and was reported to be suffering violent spasms and confined to the palace at Kew. The talk was all about the possibility of a regency, and of another Westminster election in progress that summer. I willingly joined in the campaign for the Foxite candidate, Lord John Townshend, as I had once done for Fox. But nothing was quite the same. It felt good to be back among friends but it was nothing like the old days. Despite my best efforts I no longer felt a part of the social scene.

'Perhaps it is because I am unable to properly participate,' I said to the duchess, who was as sympathetic as ever, and as ready with her advice.

'I doubt that has anything to do with it, dear Mrs Robinson. You still maintain much of your beauty, and are as stylish and elegant as before, but the world has changed. The public seem to have quite lost their appetite for gossip, are less interested in the Cyprian Corps, and no longer attempt to copy their gowns and carriages. Nor are they as interested in the old-style scandal that regularly used to appear in the press.'

I laughed. 'Well, that is a great relief for I have no wish to recapture past glories, even were it physically possible for me to do so. I blush with embarrassment when I dwell upon my earlier adventures, how foolish and headstrong I was, and how impulsive, vain and naïve.'

'You were but a girl who married too young.'

'My years of exile have changed me. I believe myself to be more mature now, more circumspect, and I have become quite passionate about my writing.'

'You are fortunate that unlike most in the Cyprian Corps, Mary, you are blessed with intelligence.'

'Which I hope I have learned to use to advantage, although I confess I still have my flaws, which we will not go into right now.' My brow momentarily puckered as I thought how the love of luxury and a proclivity for overspending that Ban and I both shared, had caused the rift between us. I stiffened my spine and took a deep breath. 'I mean this to be a new beginning for me, the fresh start I have long needed. I have made a decision to devote myself entirely to the literary life. In future I shall no longer be a woman of the people, but one of letters.'

Nine

The English Sappho

THOU art no more my bosom's friend;
Here must the sweet delusion end,
That charm'd my senses many a year,
Thro' smiling summers, winters drear;
O, friendship! am I doom'd to find
Thou art a phantom of the mind?

Mary Darby Robinson
'Lines to Him Who Will
Understand Them'

From that moment on I devoted myself to my writing, even though it was hard to stop thinking about Ban. My lover, I learned, was back to his old gambling habits but much as I missed him, I was determined not to become involved. Then my beloved daughter fell ill with suspected consumption, and trembling with fear I took her to Brighton, under doctor's orders, where we spent the summer.

Ban apparently went north to Liverpool to do some political campaigning as he still hoped to be elected at some point in the near future. According to reports this involved mob rule, fisticuffs, smashed bottles and broken bones, which would in no way deter him, since there was nothing Ban liked better than a good fight.

I hired a cottage against the sea wall, and the weeks slid by in a haze of worry and anxiety. Quite unable to concentrate on anything but nursing my darling child, I spent hours in dull misery gazing out to sea as the waves pounded relentlessly on the beach below my window. Sleep was equally impossible and one night I noticed a small boat come ashore. Two fishermen alighted carrying a body which they casually dropped on to the beach. Had the poor man suffered an accident, or was it the result of a murder that I witnessed? My imagination ran wild, but the corpse lay abandoned in the silvery light of the moon all that night, and was largely ignored by passers-by the next day. Distressed, I offered to donate a sum to provide this lost soul with a decent funeral. Instead, the body was merely shunted to one side and buried beneath a pile of stones, without ceremony.

'Such treatment is symbolic of an uncaring society,' I raged to my daughter, who was fortunately slowly recovering from what had turned out to be nothing more than a bad chest infection.

But the images of moonlit sea, deserted beach, a wrecked ship with a phantom crew remained with me, for I too felt like a lost soul, abandoned to a solitary life. The incident stayed in my mind and years later inspired me to write 'The Haunted Beach', at a time when I was again in a melancholic state, the one Coleridge so admired.

Only occasionally did I step out to take the air, with the aid of my crutches and loyal servants to support me. But as Maria made a full recovery I returned to my writing with new heart and strength, and began to contemplate a different future.

'Should we perhaps go to Italy, after all?' I suggested to my mother.

'I think you should write your poetry,' she urged, and for once I took her advice. But the years on the Continent with my darling Ban, whom I missed more than my once robust health, played on my mind. My temper had eased, my anger quite gone, replaced with an aching loss. Perhaps, even now, it was not too late to win him back. I wrote an ode to him, which I titled 'Lines to Him Who Will Understand Them'.

The poem went on to say how I might leave the country and embrace my muse. 'Britain, Farewell! I quit thy shore, My native country charms no more.' I wanted him to worry that *he* might lose *me*. It was published in *The World* under the pen-name Laura. Even so, I felt quite certain that Ban would recognise my style, and understand its meaning. I prayed the poem would inspire him to return to my side.

But I received no response.

I did, however, become a regular contributor to *The World*

under this new name, writing in the style of the Della Cruscans, a group of British poets based in Tuscany who had adopted a flowery, romantic style. Their leader, Robert Merry, had returned to England and published his poetry using the pen-name Della Crusca in *The World*. These expressed his search for love and were often responded to by another poet under the name Anna Matilda.

When he wrote a response to my Laura verse the poetic flirtation provoked an unexpected jealousy in Anna Matilda, who dubbed him a 'False Lover'.

As the flirting and jealousy of the poems continued, Mama idly remarked one day, 'I believe Mr Bell, owner of *The World*, thinks that first poem referred to Robert Merry, not to Tarleton.'

I found this mildly amusing but largely ignored it as the paper continued to publish my poetry, which became increasingly popular with readers in the months following, gaining many admirers. But because of all the accolades the poems were receiving, I finally came to a decision.

'Publishing anonymously gave me the courage to test my work without prejudice, but now I think it is perhaps time I revealed my true identity. Besides, the fame heaped upon dear Laura would be of greater benefit to my new career if the truth were known.'

The next poem I sent in under my own name, adding a note to the editor explaining that I had previously written under the pen-name of Laura.

'Look at this.' I said to my mother and daughter, eager to read them his reply. 'He says the poem is "vastly pretty" and that he is a great admirer of the genius of Mrs Robinson, but that "he is well acquainted with the author of the productions alluded to". What think you of that?'

My mother looked faintly disapproving but Maria burst out laughing. 'I think he is a very clever man to know a woman who does not exist. What will you do, Mama?'

'I shall ask him to call.'

I confess my request was more in the nature of an order, and he duly arrived at the appointed hour. 'Dear Mr Bell, how good of you to spare the time in your busy schedule.'

'How could I resist an invitation from the famous Perdita?'

My mother poured the tea and we exchanged a few polite words about the paper and poetry in general as we sipped the fragrant brew. Finally I could hold back no longer. 'I was intrigued by your response to my letter, and am most anxious to hear how you came to be acquainted with Laura. When did you meet?'

'Ah, well, it was a long time ago, I quite forget the details,' he mumbled, coughing and spluttering a little over his tea. I half glanced at my daughter, and the pair of us burst into merry laughter.

'Have I said something amusing, Mrs Robinson?' I could see that the poor man was blushing.

'Allow me to show you something, Mr Bell,' and I passed him the early drafts of several of my Laura poems, including the one he'd believed to be addressed to himself. 'You are not the only one who can hide behind a pseudonym.'

When he left my mother sternly remarked, 'You made your point most effectively, dear, one you clearly found hugely entertaining, but may well have done yourself no favours so far as your career with *The World* is concerned.'

'You are no doubt right, Mother,' I ruefully agreed.

Fortunately, I was invited to become house poet for a new paper, the *Oracle*, where I could write in my own style, so all turned out well in the end. My fame burgeoned and I soon became known as the English Sappho.

My Laura poem 'Lines To Him Who Will Understand Them' did, to my great surprise and delight, succeed in its original purpose. Within days of my former lover returning from the north, he came calling. He looked more handsome than ever as he was shown into my drawing room, if decidedly uncomfortable.

'I do not deny that I let you down, Mary, and you were no doubt glad to be rid of me. But I wish you to know that my present life is but a poor shadow of its former glory without you.'

How could any woman resist such as an apology? I held out my arms to him and as he fell into them, cradled him lovingly to my breast, where he belonged.

We spent part of that summer of 1789 in Brighton, enjoying the sunshine and sea breezes, and society life to a small degree. I felt alive again, relaxed and happy and in surprisingly good health. In August we learned of the storming of the Bastille that had taken place in Paris the previous month, which brought a chill to our hearts when we thought of our friends still in France.

'Dear Lauzun, I do hope he will be safe.'

While we had no sign of such a rebellion in England, the Regency Bill had been passed in February, which considerably raised the status of my erstwhile lover, if only providing the limited power Pitt was prepared to allow him.

'Had you not taken up with me, you might well have been in line for a title, as the Prince Regent's mistress,' Ban teased me.

I laughed. 'Power does not interest me in the slightest. I have no desire now to be Duchess of Cleveland as my relationship with Florizel is long past. I am happy to regard the prince as a friend, but having you back in my life is far more important.'

His kisses proved how right I was.

As it turned out the king recovered and the Regency Bill fell into abeyance.

The following summer Ban again stood for Parliament and this time was successful, being duly elected as Member of Parliament for Liverpool in June. Sadly, John, my elder brother, died in Italy later in the year. George was still living out there, and again wrote offering me a home. I loved my younger brother dearly, remembering how we had shared some difficult childhood years together, and how he had been with me through the early days of my marriage. I replied to say that while I would welcome a visit from him at any time, I had no plans at present to again seek exile. Ban and I had rediscovered our earlier contentment, and although his gambling habit continued, so did his good luck. All was well between us.

But then in December we clashed again over our very different stand on slavery. I was naturally opposed to it, while Ban's family had made their fortune from it, his brothers still involved in the trade. William Wilberforce was holding a debate in Parliament that very month in an effort to have it abolished, and my lover was to oppose him! Worse, he asked me to write his speech.

'I certainly will not!'

'But you always write my speeches, Mary.'

'Not this one. You cannot seriously mean to launch a campaign against the Abolishionists? You know full well I believe keeping slaves to be an absolute outrage, an abuse of the rights of man. How can you even consider opposing their salvation?'

'As an MP, I must do what is in the best interests of my constituents. Liverpool prospers by transporting goods across the oceans of the world, even if some of these are human flesh.'

'How dare you promote slavery, which is a vile sin, an abhorrence against mankind? That is not what the Whigs stand for.'

'It is not for me to meekly follow a political line, or to make judgements, but to stand up for the rights of my town. I would have thought, since you were raised in Bristol, another slave-dealing port, that you would sympathise with such an argument.'

'Never! Slavery is a gross malpractice that must be stopped.' I gazed at him with tears of anger and bitter disappointment in my eyes. 'How can you be so blind? Do you not realise how these slaves suffer, how they are cruelly treated, beaten, raped and debased as human beings?'

'They are not all badly treated.'

'Too many are, I have read articles to that effect.'

He snorted with derision. 'When have you believed everything the newspapers tell you?'

'Do not twist the argument around to me. This is about what is *right*! These poor beleaguered souls should be set free and paid a decent wage like everyone else. I find it deeply disturbing to discover that you actually *approve* of slavery.'

He let out a heavy sigh. 'I neither approve nor disapprove. This is economics, commerce.'

'This is about *human lives*!' I took a breath, struggling to calm myself as stress of any kind only resulted in exacerbating my pain. 'Fortunately, I believe William Wilberforce will win. Right will prevail.'

We spoke on the subject no more, since we could never agree. But in the months following, Ban fought Wilberforce every step of the way, much to my dismay and disgust. Why did this man I adore so often disappoint? It seemed we were quite unable to live apart, or together.

In May 1791, I published my new book of poetry. It was such a proud moment to hold this beautifully bound volume with marbled end papers in my hands, knowing that I had created it. It was printed by my old colleague John Bell of *The World*, since many of the poems had first appeared in his paper under the name of Laura.

This precious publication had been made possible by an impressive list of subscribers who each contributed one guinea for a copy, including the dear duchess, Fox, the Prince of Wales, and several of his royal brothers. Altogether no less than sixteen dukes and duchesses, thirty-three earls and countesses, and scores of other notables, not to mention many old friends such as Sheridan, Dorothy Jordan, George Colman, and even Sir Joshua Reynolds all contributed towards its publication. I considered myself fortunate indeed to have such loyal supporters. Even Ban's family subscribed, including his mother. I was deeply touched.

'What will people think of it, I wonder?' I asked of my daughter, who was turning into my best critic.

'That it is a fine book of poetry, which it is, Mama.'

'Will they not feel bemused that a frivolous woman better known for fashion and scandal is attempting to present herself as a serious poet?'

'If they do, it would be because of their ignorance, Mama, and not yours. No one could consider "Ode to the Muse" or "Ode to Melancholy" frivolous.'

By the time the volume of poetry came out I was in Bath, suffering quite badly from another spasm of rheumatic gout. Ban was with me, having recently returned from a short trip to his home town. I strived to accept my fate of persistent ill health and concentrate on the joy of seeing my book published. If I could not move my legs very well, at least I could still use my brain, and my imagination.

Unfortunately, I was blessed, or cursed, with a very stern physician who banned me not simply from committing my thoughts to paper, but, were it even possible, from thinking at all. Naturally I became frustrated beyond distraction, disobeyed his commands and resumed my work.

Maria was concerned when she caught me with pen in hand. 'Mama, what are you doing? You are not supposed to be writing, or even devising a poem in your head.'

'No truant escaped from school could receive more pleasure in eluding a severe master than do I. I must write. It is what I do. It is who I am.'

She smiled at me with perfect understanding and a merry twinkle in her blue eyes. 'Then you recite the words and I will write them for you. I can always pretend that I did the thinking too.'

And taking the quill pen from my ink-stained fingers our teamwork continued as before.

We remained for some time in Bath while Ban returned to London. My mother was somewhat scathing about this decision. 'I do question Tarleton's priorities. Why must he constantly abandon you to dash back to his dissolute life in London?'

I winced, hating to hear her adopt the same criticisms she had used against my husband, even if I might secretly agree with them. 'Please don't say such things. Ban Tarleton is not like foolish Tommy. He is now a Member of Parliament, and as such has duties to perform.'

Without even lifting her head from the neat copying of the poem in which she was engaged, Maria said, 'Whether or not that is the case, in this instant Grandmama is right. You deserve better.'

'Goodness, are you both attacking me now?'

'We wish only to protect you, Mama.'

'No doubt he has returned to his gambling and his woman-ising?' my mother commented in waspish tones.

'I really couldn't say. I did not enquire.'

The scratching of her pen continued as my daughter again quietly chimed in. 'Then perhaps it is time that you did.'

Since she was now seventeen, having grown into a fine, articulate young lady with a sensible head upon her young shoulders,

I did not feel able to quarrel with these comments. In truth, the pair of them could well be right in their assessment. Despite Ban's claims of complete fidelity and knowing full well that he loved me, I was growing increasingly suspicious that there was some other attraction my lover hurried back to so regularly, besides the gaming tables.

I blamed Ban's family in part for this. They'd constantly put pressure upon him as a boy and as a young man, disapproving of every decision he'd made in life. They did finally seem to have accepted our relationship, but far too late. Had they supported him in his choices, and been more reasonable, he may well have turned his life around and dealt more effectively with the bitterness that had come to consume him in recent years.

What they now had to contend with, as a consequence, was a man constantly seeking a new purpose to absorb him, a man who needed to find a more fulfilling role beyond the next turn of the card or throw of the dice. I could only hope that the world of politics would make up for what he had lost as a soldier.

And that I would not lose him in this maelstrom of change.

Setting these worries aside as best I could, I concentrated upon my writing, most ably assisted by my daughter, and published my first novel *Vancenza or Dangers of Credulity* on the second of February 1792. The tale was a Gothic romance set in fifteenth-century Spain, albeit with eighteenth-century morals, hidden secrets, seductions, suspected incest and villainous plotting. I naturally drew upon my own emotions and experiences, not least my intimate knowledge of marrying young and loving a prince, as did my heroine Elvira, all artfully fictionalised.

The entire print run sold out in one day. It was a joyous moment.

'I suspect the gossip-mongers and the curious wished to know what you had to say about the prince,' my mother caustically remarked, once again setting us at loggerheads.

'Rather than for the quality of the writing or excitement of the story, you mean?'

'I am not putting you down, Mary, I simply state the truth.

You are a person of notoriety, even more than I feared when you first begged to go on stage.'

Not a comforting assessment of one's life, but my mother did tend to live in the past. 'A person can change, Mama, and mature, given the opportunity.'

The book quickly ran through five editions, and I became a literary sensation. Whatever the reason for my success, I couldn't have been more thrilled.

My pleasure was marred only by the death of my old friend, Sir Joshua Reynolds, later in the month, and I published a *Monody* to his memory. On the fourteenth of February I also sent a sweetly romantic poem to Ban, entitled: 'My Dear Valentine'. He had been absent from my life too long. Could I win him back with my pen yet again?

I received no valentine in exchange, and no reply.

By July 1792 my debts were such they could no longer be ignored. 'I fear we must again leave these shores and face exile, if we are to remain safe,' I confessed to my disapproving parent.

While my mother embarked upon yet another of her endless lectures, my ever-patient daughter began packing.

What I didn't tell them was that I didn't even possess the funds for the journey. I wrote to Sheridan from Dover, opening my heart to ask for a loan.

> Mr dear Sheridan,
>
> You will perhaps be surprised to hear that after an irreproachable connection of more than ten years, I am suffered to depart, an exile from my country and all my hopes, for a few paltry debts. I sail this evening for Calais. Alone, broken-hearted, and without twenty pounds on the face of the earth . . .

Of course I was not quite alone, but I begged him to make no mention of this request to Tarleton. 'He will triumph in my sorrows and delight in hearing me humbled. I am finishing an opera in three acts, which I mean to offer you. I think it will succeed. At least I hope so. Pray send me a line.'

My old friend took pity on me and sent me one hundred

guineas by express messenger, saying he had previously won the
sum from my lover in a bet, so it was only just and proper that
it should be returned to me.

I left for France the very next evening with my mother, Maria,
and my loyal servants who carried me on board. I wondered if
I would ever see Ban again.

It was a most pleasant day for a sail, the sea calm, the breeze
a warm caress on my pale cheeks as we settled on deck in the
summer sunshine. But my thoughts turned inward and, seated in
my chair, I reached for my pen. Pouring my emotion on to the
page I began to write: 'Bounding billow, cease thy motion, Bear
me not so swiftly o'er . . .' The poem ran to several stanzas but
was heartrending to write.

> I have lov'd thee, – dearly lov'd thee,
> Through an age of worldly woe;
> How ungrateful I have prov'd thee
> Let my mournful exile show!

And despite our differences how every day I'd loved him more.

By the time it was done we had landed in Calais, and Maria
had copied it out and arranged for the steward to post it to the
Oracle on the ship's return. I knew they would be certain to
publish it.

'My intention is for us to go to Brother George, Mama, in
Leghorn, but we can stop off at Spa first, so that I might benefit
from a short bout of treatment before we embark on such a long
journey.'

We soon discovered that our plans must be put on hold as
France was in turmoil. Having declared war on Austria the roads
were full of marching troops, the very air thick with tension. We
had no option but to remain in Calais, along with several dozen
other frustrated passengers, until we could safely return home. I
became unwell so was not fit to travel when the rest of our party
left, but obliged to stay on. More terrifying still, in early August
news reached us that the king's Swiss Guard had been massacred
in the Tuileries, and the royal family taken to the grim fortress
known as the Temple. A republic had been declared.

While we were struggling to get our heads around

this calamitous news, my husband arrived. I stared at him in astonishment. 'What is this? Did Sheridan tell you where I was? If so, that was very wrong of him, although your journey has been wasted, Tommy, as I have no money to give you. I have none even for myself.'

He gently kissed me on each cheek. 'I'm not here for money, but for my daughter.'

'What?' I stared at him in horror. 'She is eighteen years old, a young woman grown. Why would you come for her now, when you have paid her no heed these long years past?'

'I come on her behalf, not mine. I bring an offer from my brother, Commodore William Robinson, who is willing to sponsor her in society. Would you not like that, Mary, since you are unable to fund her coming-out yourself?'

I longed to refute this, but had to bite back the sharp words tumbling in my head as it was all too true. I could do little for my daughter, nothing in fact.

Seeing that I was in want of an argument, he turned to her with a smile. 'Your Uncle William is well-placed and can do much for you, Maria. He has insisted, however, that you agree to relinquish both your parents. Hard as it may be for you to leave your mother, I'm sure she will be happy to cope alone for your sake. Is that not true, Mary?'

'Of course, if that is what she wants.' I managed a smile, wishing as ever not to be a burden to my child.

But Maria was a young lady with a mind of her own and stepped forward to stand before her neglectful father. 'Mama and I have never been separated and I do not intend us ever to be so.'

'I would suggest you think on this matter a little more before you decide,' my husband gently chided. 'The offer is, after all, in your best interest.'

'Why is it?' Maria challenged him. 'I am quite happy with my life as it is.'

'But you surely wish to be brought out?' Tommy protested. 'How else will you find a suitable husband?'

'When – *if* – I should ever desire to marry, *I* will choose my own husband.'

I put my crooked hands together and applauded this sentiment.

'Well said, darling girl.' Even my mother, I noticed, made no protest.

'In any case, Mama is not well enough to sail at present, and I will not leave her in dire straits.'

The subject, it appeared, was closed. Over the next week or two Tommy did his utmost to persuade Maria to change her mind, but she remained adamant. And then who should arrive next but Tarleton. For once, I did not fall into his arms, much as I might long to, but regarded him with a somewhat jaundiced eye. He soon drew me to one side and opened his heart to me.

'I read your poem, Mary, and confess the sweet words of your undying love resonated in my heart. It would in any case have drawn me to your side, were I not already about to take ship for these shores.'

I looked at him, not sure what he was trying to say. 'I don't quite understand. Are you saying you came because of my poem, or not?'

'These are dangerous times in France, and once I realised where you were, and how you still felt about me, I was anxious to put things right between us. However, since I am fluent in French and have influential friends, I have been asked to carry out a mission and report on certain matters.'

'What matters? To whom?'

'I am not at liberty to say but am bound for Paris.'

'You are gathering information on the war, on the revolution? So you did not come for me at all.'

'I would tell you if I could, but you were, and always will be, my major concern, Mary. You must know in your heart that I have no wish to lose you.'

I melted into his arms and he kissed me, as only Ban knows how. 'Nor I you, my darling.'

'Before I depart, I mean to see you safely aboard a ship bound for Dover, and I swear I will be gone no more than ten days at most.'

Once more reassured of his love, it was astonishing how quickly my health recovered, and we parted friends and as lovers once more. He saw us safely settled on board ship, and not a moment too soon as only days after we sailed there was news of a further uprising in Paris with all British banned from leaving France.

We arrived safely in early September and settled in at 13 St James's Place, where I anxiously waited for Ban to come to me. But as the days slipped by with still no sign, my anxiety increased daily. Paris was not a safe place to be at this time. By the end of the month I was close to despair when the door suddenly burst open and in he strode, as if he could not get to me fast enough. Laughing and kissing me, he carried me to my room where we completed our reunion with a passion more fervent even than usual. He smelled of sea air and foreign parts, of male sweat and ship's dust. Oh, but how I loved him, how I delighted in having his arms about me again, to savour his burning trail of kisses over my naked flesh and revel in the joy of his loving. He was the most infuriating, impossible man, and completely irresistible.

'But why did your mission take so long? You promised me you would be away no more than ten days,' I pouted.

'I was delayed over a problem in obtaining a passport, but the moment my ship docked I rushed to your side, my love. Did you miss me very badly?' he teased, winding an auburn curl about one finger.

'Not at all,' I airily remarked. 'I am quite indifferent to your presence.'

'Yes, I can see that by your response.' We both laughed, then as he licked my nipple with his tongue, we were instantly making love all over again. Eventually, when we paused long enough for me to catch my breath, I asked him about his trip.

'How was Paris?'

His smile instantly faded. 'The day you sailed, Mary, I was listening to the mobs shouting "*A la Lanterne!*" in the streets of Paris. They'd broken into one of the jails, dragged out the prisoners and battered and hacked them to death on the assumption they were royalists. I seized my only chance to escape by pretending to be a part of the crowd and ran along with them, shouting "*A la Lanterne!*" as loudly as any.'

'Oh, Ban, that must have been utterly terrifying.'

'I tried not to dwell on what would have happened had they

discovered my nationality. To witness such a horror would bring tears of pity from the most iron heart that ever inhabited the breast of man. The next day while I was dining with your would-be lover the Duc de Chartes, now promoted to the Duke of Orleans, we heard further disturbance in the street. The guests all hurried to look out of the window, but wished we hadn't when we saw the mutilated head of the Princess Lamballe held on a pike.'

I put my crabbed hands to my face in dismay. 'Was she not companion to Marie Antoinette?'

'She was indeed,' he gravely agreed. 'But let us dwell no more on such horrors. Put on your finest gown, my love, as we are going out on the town, starting with the theatre.'

Giggling with delight I rang for my maid. 'But first I have a gift for you, Ban.' I slid a gold ring on to his finger. 'It is to celebrate our reunion.'

'My darling, how very generous you are to me.'

'Wait, there is more. I have written a poem especially for the occasion.'

He laughed. 'Of course you have.'

I spoke the words softly to him, filled with my love.

> Oh! Take these little easy chains,
> And may they hold you while you live;
> For know each magic link contains
> The richest treasure I can give!

He said nothing, but I swear there were tears in his eyes.

Later, when I was gowned and bejewelled, my hair dressed and powdered to perfection, he lifted me in his arms, placed me in a carriage, and we drove to the Haymarket Theatre. I was glowing with happiness.

Our domestic life was all tranquillity and happiness once more, but Ban found himself caught up in the midst of a controversy that pitted Tory against Whig. The newspapers were speculating on why he had gone to Paris, since the Whigs were against war with France. The Tories, on the other hand, were readying their weapons, so where, the press asked, did Tarleton stand?

'For peace,' he declared, making his opinions clear in Parliament. 'A war would destroy Liverpool's commercial livelihood, and I am a faithful Whig. Britain must avoid involving herself in another war.'

'I agree with you absolutely,' I told him, determined to offer my full support.

Whatever our opinion on the matter, the clouds of war continued to gather and on the twenty-first of January 1793 Louis XVI, or Citizen Capet as he was now called, was guillotined. It is difficult to describe how we felt, beyond being utterly horrified by such an outcome and fearful for the rest of the royal family and our friends.

'I hope to join the Duke of York's campaign in Flanders,' Ban declared. 'I have already offered to raise a regiment.'

Sadly, he fell ill and was compelled to sit back and watch his comrades depart without him.

'Fate seems to be saying that my fighting days are over,' he mourned.

In August 1793 my mother died, and although we had often been at odds, her loss was a great blow to me. She had been at my side for my entire life and I could not contemplate the reality of a future without her. I then suffered a fall while staying at Cobham in Surrey, when the steps down which my servant was carrying me gave way. I was badly cut about the head and it was a month before I felt well enough to return to London.

But Madame Fate was not done with us yet.

Having recovered sufficiently to be back in the saddle, Ban sprained his knee so violently that he was again confined to quarters, as he called it, this time until late October. By then we were contentedly living at Englefield Cottage in Windsor, but my poor darling had been reduced to life as an invalid for almost the entire year, I acting as his most devoted nurse. Who better to understand the meaning of his pain?

'What a pair of crotchety old cripples we are,' I would laughingly tease him. But the year of 1793 was turning out to be far more devastating for our friends in France. I was particularly concerned for the queen, as it seemed her head too could soon be on the block.

I had recently made a new friend in Mary Wollstonecraft, an Anglo-Irish intellectual and fellow writer. She was very much a feminist who had recently published a book, *Vindication on the Rights of Woman.*

'Women should not be regarded as helpless, charming adornments in the household,' she would fervently declare.

'I have said as much for many years now,' I concurred. 'Yet it seems that because of my looks I am expected to have no brain. It has come as a shock to many that I have the ability to write poetry and novels.'

'I believe education holds the key to achieving a sense of self-respect and an improved sense of worth that will enable women to reach their full potential.'

As one of Mary Wollstonecraft's greatest admirers, I agreed with her on most things, but not on her view of the Queen of France, as she was extremely disapproving of that lady's extravagant tastes.

'As a radical, I myself spent time in Paris in 1792, where I was witness to Robespierre's reign of terror when I was conducting research for my book: *An Historical and Moral View of the Origins and Progress of the French Revolution.* I saw how the royal family, including the queen, had little idea of the troubles and needs of the people.'

I partly agreed with her, yet felt the need to defend the pretty lady who had admired the prince's miniature and returned it with a gift. 'Having met Her Majesty, I do not believe she is half as bad as she is painted,' I insisted. 'She has been subjected to any number of malicious lampoons, cartoons and critics, as have I. But I consider she has borne her sufferings, her humiliations, her anxieties, with the magnanimity of a heroine.'

'I see a new age of reason and benevolence close at hand,' she insisted.

Whether that was true or not, poor Marie Antoinette was guillotined on the sixteenth of October, 1793, her once golden hair gone white, her beautiful face haggard. I read the details in the morning papers, appropriately bordered in black, feeling sick at the images that tortured my mind.

I paid tribute to her with 'Monody to the Memory of the Late Queen of France', which I published later in the year, accompanied with an engraving of the widowed queen dressed in black, with no sign of her former extravagant style.

In November the Duke of Orleans – formerly Chartres – was also guillotined. I grieved for him, even though when he had pursued me with such diligence I'd done everything in my power to avoid a liaison, debauched rake that he was. Yet no man deserved such a death.

Then in December Ban came to me grim-faced with more bad news. 'I am sorry to inform you, my love, that our old friend Lauzun, now the Duc de Biron, has met the same fate.'

'Oh no, that cannot be!' I cried, and burst into tears, deeply upset. Our affair had been brief, little more than a flirtation, but he had always been there for me in my darkest hour. Once when he helped me search for Ban before that dangerous carriage drive to Dover, and again when we were penurious in France. Now he was gone and I would never be able to return the favour. How fragile life was.

Our own volatile, on-off love affair continued very much as before, Ban and I enjoying visits to Gray's Tomb and the churchyard at Stoke Poges, as I still maintained my passion for monuments. We were also invited to hunts and picnics in the woods of Cliveden. It might have been considered an idyllic life were not Ban still heavily involved with gambling at every opportunity, which was proving to be a heavy drain upon my purse. As if I had not suffered enough in that respect from Tommy. I returned to London in the new year, for once with some reluctance, knowing that easy access to his favourite gambling clubs was too great a temptation for him to resist.

Back in the summer of 1792 when I'd been forced to leave the country yet again because of debt, I'd been on the point of finishing a comic opera. On completion I'd sent it to Sheridan. Unfortunately, my old friend was by then more interested in politics than theatre and his successor, John Kemble, claimed to be snowed under with new plays. So when a year later it still hadn't been produced, I had withdrawn it. Now, my new play, *Nobody*, was an attempt at something different, and expressed my loathing for the gaming tables.

Drury Lane had been rebuilt and opened in 1794, large

enough to hold an audience of over three thousand, including one hundred and twenty-three spacious boxes most splendidly decorated and lined with blue silk. The new auditorium was of an impressive height, richly ornamented in Gothic and Chinese style.

My play was accepted and cast, although not without some difficulty, and finally appeared thanks to the intervention of Dorothy Jordan who greatly supported me in the enterprise, even calling at my house to discuss it with me.

Nobody, however, was not well received. Gambling is such a popular national pastime that the play was condemned before ever it appeared. The aristocratic ladies who so loved to visit the gaming tables to squander their husband's fortune, expressed their disapproval by hissing behind their fans. I asked for that to be withdrawn. I could suffer no more humiliation.

In February I had produced my second novel *The Widow, or a Picture of Modern Times* which was entirely different from *Vancenza*, as it commented on social themes in a modern setting. And Maria, who clearly shared my talent as well as my beauty, also published a novel entitled *The Shrine of Bertha*. I was so proud of her. But then William Gifford, a rival poet, gave both novels poor reviews, which upset her greatly.

'Why would he be so unkind, Mama?'

'Jealousy, dearest. It was me he wished to injure, not you. He probably hasn't even read either novel. I would advise you never to read reviews.'

'Easier said than done, Mama. Besides, you read them all the time, and complain over the comments.'

'Oh, I do, and as you know only too well, dearest, am easily put down by lack of appreciation for my work, sometimes vowing I will never pick up my pen again. I swear every day to quit my muse for ever, and am every day as constantly foresworn.'

We laughed at that, knowing that despite the occasional bad review I could never stop writing. Before the year was out I had produced more poetry, this time of a satirical nature, proving I was not simply a romantic poet.

But money became tighter than ever and we moved into a less fashionable house, my wild spending very much a thing of the past. Even so, my income bled away faster than I could earn it. I needed to maintain an elegant home, provide reasonably fashionable gowns for myself and my daughter, pay for a box at the theatre and keep a carriage which alone cost £200 per year. In addition to these basic necessities I had considerable medical bills to pay. Yet my publishers were making more money out of my books than I was, despite my prodigious output. As was my lover, his luck at the tables having run dry.

During that summer of 1794, Ban and I again quarrelled over money and for once *I* left *him*. Maria and I moved back to our old home at Windsor, although it took only a few sonnets to bring him back to my side. More good news arrived in October as Ban was at last promoted to the rank of major general and our idyll continued.

But not for long.

Over the coming year we seemed to drift ever further apart, Ban being brought particularly low when his brother John stood against him as a Tory.

'This is all Pitt's doing, and will undoubtedly split the Liverpool vote,' Ban complained, bristling with fury.

It seemed the Tories were mocking Ban's military record. One newspaper called him a Jacobin because he'd visited France for some unknown purpose, spoke the language fluently and wore his hair – as did the Revolutionaries – in the 'French Crop'. Another went so far as to say that were he re-elected, the French would overrun the country and kill the womenfolk.

'This paper likens me to a dog with his tail cut off,' he roared.

I tried to make light of the comments. 'Apparently a fierce cur who wears a black collar around his neck, and has two claws missing from his right paw. Take no notice. I have suffered all my life from such slights upon my character.'

'And more often than not you would write a stern letter in response.'

'True, but this is a political campaign, so perhaps it is best to address your remarks to your constituents and win them over, rather than engage in ill-tempered argument with the press.'

'They urge anyone who finds me to return me to my keeper, Mrs R. You are most certainly *not* my *keeper*!'

I smiled rather sadly. 'Are you quite certain about that? You do not contribute a great deal to our finances. The paper also suggests returning you to any of the gaming houses in Covent Garden. Perhaps they are your true home.'

He cast me a sour look although did not deny the charge. 'I shall leave at once for Liverpool, to begin my campaign.'

I kissed him fondly and wished him a safe journey, but there was a coolness between us.

Ban remained in Liverpool for some weeks where he dutifully reminded his constituents of his loyalty to the city, and how he had supported their best interests. His efforts must have paid off as he was duly elected. Perhaps things would improve for us now, I thought.

My own year seemed to be a good one as I published two more novels: *Angelina*, in three volumes, and *Hubert de Sevrac*, a Gothic romance. The latter sold well, particularly on the Continent. I also brought out a selection of sonnets, *Sappho and Phaon*, my most ambitious poetic work to date. This had taken some time to write, but was worth the effort as reviewers said it illustrated my mastery of technique and ability to express emotion and passion. The volume was also beautifully presented at the cost of half a guinea.

'Why do they call you the English Sappho?' Ban asked.

'Because they associate my work with intense emotion and passion. The original Grecian Sappho fell hopelessly in love with the handsome Ovid, but when he deserted her, she committed suicide by throwing herself off a cliff. Ah! why is rapture so allied to pain?'

'What nonsense, a real woman would never act so foolishly,' he scoffed.

I was not in the best of moods, my head fuzzy and aching from the opium I had recently taken in a desperate bid to ease the crippling pain in my joints. 'That wasn't the point I was trying to make. Do you not have the wit to understand anything the least profound that does not come in the shape of a playing card or dice? My reviewers recognise that I have personal experience of pain, separation, betrayal and loss. Therefore I can completely empathise with an ancient Greek poetess who suffered similar trials. Poetry is about emotion and sensitivities, not reality.'

'We have all suffered trials in life. Perhaps I should try my hand at writing verse.'

At one time I might well have laughed at the very idea of Ban playing poet, but at that precise moment I found his flippancy irritating as I was in such a fragile state of health. 'Is the lyre of Apollo tuned by an ass? I think not.'

'You don't believe I have the intellect?' he snapped.

'The only emotion you understand is a competitive desire to beat your opponent, whether at the gaming table, in the boxing ring or on the cricket pitch.'

Perhaps to prove me wrong, he did pen a few lines, which I found deeply hurtful.

> The limbs may languish, but the mind can't faint,
> Genius like freedom bows not to restraint;
> Down with all tyrants strikes upon my ear!
> Alas! I've got a female Robespierre.

'Why did you write such cruel words?' I challenged him. They seemed symbolic somehow, of our fractured relationship. 'Robespierre was guillotined for his reign of terror. Do you equate me with that villain?'

'Do you equate me with a man with no brain, one who wishes to confine you to the domestic front?'

'I did not accuse you of such. But I am all too aware that you do not care for my association with Mary Wollstonecraft and her feminist beliefs.'

'I have never objected to your writing, but I think the woman is too much the radical who drives you to make wild accusations that are unfounded and illogical.'

'I am entirely logical.'

'Then why imply that being a soldier makes me into some kind of idiot, as if planning a campaign requires no intelligence? While you, as a writer, are apparently a person of supreme intellect. I could easily claim that the opposite was the case, that you do nothing more challenging than make up pretty rhymes.'

I flushed bright crimson, instantly wanting to slap his arrogant face. 'Pretty rhymes? You think my brain as paralysed as my legs?'

I cried in fury, at last using that word I'd sworn never to utter again.

'On the contrary, there are times when it is far too agile.'

My mood swings, admittedly affected by the opium that I took for the pain, were only a part of the reason that I was so touchy and easily offended. I was deeply jealous of his freedom and physical fitness, and fearful of rivals for his love. While he resented my feminist philosophy, and the little supper parties I held for literary acquaintances such as William Godwin, John Bell and others, since we were content to talk about literature and poetry all night long, and not of the war, gambling, violent sports or slavery.

How different we had become, Ban and I.

Throughout the summer of 1797 I gave myself up to my writing, publishing another novel, *Walsingham*, very much a feminist novel which brought me some financial relief, if at great cost as the effort involved greatly affected my health.

My dear friend, Mary Wollstonecraft, tragically contracted puerperal fever following the birth of her daughter, also named Mary, and died on the tenth of September. Her husband, William Godwin, was utterly devastated as they'd only recently married after living together quite happily for years. I personally resolved to honour her memory by following her feminist philosophy in my writing.

But the difficulties in my own relationship came to a head on the twenty-third of May 1798 when Ban's mother Jane, who had been ill for some time, finally died. Her greatest wish in life had been to separate us, despite my having supported her son both financially and emotionally for fifteen years.

'I take it she has left you a sizeable inheritance?' I asked, once the funeral was over and the will had been read.

'She left me only £1,500, together with a list of my debts she'd settled over the years. It was certainly not the fortune I expected.'

'My own current debts amount to twelve hundred pounds, much of which were run up on your behalf. I would not expect you to cover all of them, but you could help by repaying something of what I have loaned you over the years.'

He gave a snort of bitter laughter. 'You gave the money readily, lavished it upon me, in fact, so I feel no necessity to do so. Have I not repaid you in kind?'

I flushed with annoyance, hating the fact that some of his argument was undoubtedly true, if hard to swallow when I was in such dire difficulties. 'Repaid me how? With your loyalty? How can I be certain of that, since you are so often absent? Is it true that you are pursuing an heiress in possession of a substantial fortune?'

Ignoring my question, he said, 'I've made it abundantly plain that I am not a rich man. I am no prince of the realm but a poor soldier still only on half pay, and with no other reliable source of income.'

'Yet you have lived like a prince, very often at my expense when your wins turned into losses.' The sting of his ingratitude wounded me deeply, plagued as I was with an oversensitive heart, and overly suspicious of what secrets he was keeping from me. 'I read recently in the *Oracle* that during one evening you were down by £800.'

He laughed, as if the incident were amusing. 'Ah, but I later recovered £312 on one card alone. The change in my luck is but temporary.'

'Then find someone else to finance your losses!' I screamed, exasperated to the limits of my endurance.

'Perhaps I will,' came his sharp response, and turning on his heel he walked away.

I fled to Bath, fully expecting him to return when his luck changed, as he had done many times before. When he failed to appear, I stubbornly took his name out of every poem or manuscript in which it featured. 'To a dear friend' became 'To a once dear friend'. I even removed his name from 'Ode to Valour', and denied that the character, General Grey Crop in my new novel, was in any way based upon him.

'I only portray the follies not the vices of individuals,' I told the press, when asked.

Nevertheless, as ever, I poured my emotion into my poems, recalling how Ban had broken my heart, and how much I still loved him.

When ling'ring sickness wrung thy breast,
And bow'd thee to the earth, or nearly,
I strove to lull thy mind to rest –
For then I lov'd thee, Oh! How dearly.

He called upon me one more time, if briefly, later in the year, but we had little to say to one another. The visit was awkward, our conversation stilted and overly polite. Perhaps he could see how I trembled at the mere sight of him.

'Are you in good health, Mary?'

'Perfectly, thank you. And you?'

He chose not to answer, as if unwilling to bludgeon my pride with his own rude health, when it was perfectly plain I was anything but well. 'Napoleon is gathering his forces and preparing to attack Spain and Portugal. I wished you to know that I am to command His Majesty's forces in Portugal, and on the twelfth of December will be presented to the king at a levee.'

'Congratulations! I know this is what you have long wanted. I'm pleased for you.'

'It is kind of you to say so.'

We were talking like strangers, after over *fifteen* years together!

He hadn't even bothered to sit down, clearly anxious to have done with me. 'I will call another day, Mary, as I shall ever be your friend.'

It was not his friendship I craved, at least not that alone. I needed his heart, his love, but it seemed he had gifted that elsewhere. Only days later I read in the paper what his courage had failed to tell me. It was the announcement of an engagement between Miss Susan Priscilla Bertie and General Tarleton. The piece ended upon a caustic note as it wished him well. 'Forgetful of the general's peccadillos, we hope for him all the happiness afforded by youth and £20,000.'

So he had found his rich heiress after all.

The happy couple were married on the seventeenth of December, 1798. The love affair I had believed would last a lifetime, was finally over.

One parting sigh, one tender tear bestow,
And seem at least unwillingly to go!
So shall that sigh repay me for my fate,
That tear for all my sorrows compensate.

Epilogue

Feminist and Poet

SWEET Nymph, enchanting Poetry!
I dedicate my mind to Thee.
Oh! from thy bright Parnassian bow'rs
Descend, to bless my sombre hours;

Mary Darby Robinson
Ode to the Muse

1799

Maria and I were spending much of our time at Englefield Cottage where I became something of a recluse, although I did have many old friends who would come for dinner or to stay overnight as our guest, including Sheridan, William Godwin, and Samuel Taylor Coleridge, a new friend and fellow poet who invited me to stay with his family at Greta Hall in Keswick, Cumberland. My health did not allow me to face the hazardous journey or the inclement weather, but I wrote a poem to his new son, Derwent, on the child's birth. Later, I published my own *Lyrical Tales* in honour of his.

These last months since Ban's marriage had been the very worst of my life. I thought for a time that the grief would overwhelm me. Losing Ban had felt as if I were dealing with his death, and then I would remember that he was still alive and as handsome as ever, but no longer a part of my life. He would never again come bounding up the steps into my home to sweep me into his arms and carry me off to bed. We would never attend the theatre together, or drive about Hyde Park in the morning sunshine. Nor would he be around to massage my aching limbs, or tease me out of a depression.

He was gone from my life forever, had chosen another in my place, and for a time I was obsessed with a need for revenge.

In my next novel, *The False Friend*, I created a character by the name of Treville, an evil priest who perishes on his way to Lisbon. It was published in February 1799, in good time to provide a thought-provoking read for the new Mrs Tarleton before embarking on her own journey. I wondered if Ban would read it, or if he ever thought of me. I wanted him to be filled with regrets, to remember the long happy years we had spent together, the adventures we'd enjoyed, the passion. I wanted him to hurt as I was hurting.

> In vain you fly me! on the madd'ning main,
> Sappho shall haunt thee 'mid the whirlwind's roar;

I even considered taking out my bitterness on Susan Priscilla Bertie too, as she was exceedingly pretty and only twenty years old. I discovered she spoke several languages, was proficient at drawing, geometry, astronomy and music, and was the illegitimate daughter of Captain Robert Bertie, one of Ban's reprehensible friends of his youth. Before his untimely death in July 1779, Bertie had bequeathed his name and his fortune to the child, and Lord Cholmondeley, the girl's uncle by marriage, had brought her up together with Georgiana, the illegitimate daughter of my rival, Dally the Tall, and the Prince of Wales.

What a small world it was, and how astonishing that Ban should marry his old friend's daughter. But my research brought me to the conclusion that she was an innocent, more to be pitied than condemned for stealing my lover. *The Natural Daughter, with Portraits of the Leadenhead Family*, published later that year by Longman and Rees, whilst taking a swipe at the Tarleton family through the fictional Leadenheads, a vulgar family who had also made their fortune out of slavery, did not, as originally intended, malign her in any way.

Revenge had proved to be poor compensation for my loss.

But could I ever forget Ban? Not in a thousand lifetimes! Could I live without him? I must somehow learn to do so. I told myself that I had grown used to his absences over the years. And I still had my wonderful daughter, my faithful companion, who made her opinion of my lover's actions very clear.

'I have half-expected this moment for years, Mama. How can

you compete with £20,000 a year? Let him go. Think of him no more. Be your own woman, as Mary Wollstonecraft would expect you to be.'

It was true that my late friend's philosophy on the status of women still resonated in my soul. I turned away from writing fiction and wrote *Letter to Women of England*. For this I used the pseudonym Ann-Francis Randal, in order to protect the work from my Perdita image.

I would often look with pride at my beloved Maria, this fine young woman who had devoted every moment of her young life to me, the ink stains on her pretty fingers no small proof of her efforts on my behalf.

'What of you, dearest, do you hope to find a good man and marry one day?' I asked her one day.

But she shook her head most firmly. 'I have experienced enough of the trials of marriage and infidelities of men. I am content with living a life of independence and freedom, one in which I can control my own destiny.'

I smiled in open admiration. 'How wise you are, my child. There may come a time when women can choose their own partners and marry for love, when marriage is not ruled by money and family politics. Until that happy day, we still have our writing, do we not?'

'We do indeed, Mama, and all of life's experiences are grist to the writer's mill,' she added with a grin, which made us both laugh.

I had loved three men in my life: a profligate husband, a rapacious prince whose miniature I still wore about my neck, and last but by no means least, a national hero. All of them had loved me too in their way. Sadly, none had been without flaws or remained faithful.

But then I had flaws of my own. Despite my vanity and pride, my quick temper, my eccentricities and rapacious literary ambitions, I believe Banistre Tarleton had truly loved me, that I lost him only because of money and family duty. As for my feminist leanings, the remark he had once made that he'd never objected to my writing, nor ever attempted to confine me in any way, was perfectly true. He had been a fair man, kind and tolerant of my disabilities, and an exciting and wonderful lover. Ban

Tarleton was the love of my life, the one who would ever live in my heart, and I had managed, at last, to shelve my bitterness against him.

For now I had become what I had always longed to be, a woman of letters.

Author's Note

I was inspired to write about Mary Robinson because I thought her a woman of talent and great courage. She married far too young, suffering from family pressure as was often the case at a time when love was not considered essential in a marriage. She was the first to own up to her own flaws of vanity and pride, not least her predilection for spending. She lived in an age of extremes, one almost as celebrity driven as our own today. This novel is entirely based on fact, much of it based on her own memoirs, backed up by less emotional biographies. There were sometimes differences of opinion between these, and when in doubt I went to the primary source. So far as her alleged affair with Charles James Fox is concerned, the evidence seemed mainly to come from a piece in the *Morning Chronicle*, so of doubtful origin, and a letter to Tarleton which is open to interpretation. Unlike many courtesans, Mary was intelligent and gifted, who later achieved the promised potential of her youth despite many disappointments in life and suffering from a crippling disease from a very young age. It is impossible to accurately diagnose the exact nature of the illness which struck her down on that fateful night. Very likely it was an acute form of rheumatic fever that possibly affected the nerves, perhaps caused by an infection during her miscarriage. Quite common at that time. She was an early feminist, a writer of Gothic romance as well as poetry, who has largely been forgotten, and despite the considerable pain she must have suffered, she continued writing to her death. She died practically penniless in 1800, of dropsy, a retention of fluid on the chest which causes heart failure, again often linked with rheumatic fever. She asked for a lock of hair to be sent to the prince, and one to Tarleton. She was buried in a corner of the churchyard at Old Windsor, apparently still wearing the prince's miniature. Her daughter, Maria Elizabeth, never married, but continued to live on at Englefield Cottage with Elizabeth Weale, who had nursed her mother to the end. She died in 1818, was buried in the same tomb, and is said to haunt the Old Windsor churchyard.

Sources

For those interested in reading further on the subject of Mary Robinson, the following were invaluable:

Memoirs Of Mary Robinson, Perdita, from the edition edited by her daughter, with introduction and notes by J. Fitzgerald Molloy.

Perdita by Paula Byrne, 2004

The Prince's Mistress: A Life of Mary Robinson by Hester Davenport, 2004

Dr Johnson's London by Liza Picard, 2000

Aristocrats by Stella Tillyard, 1994

Georgiana, Duchess of Devonshire by Amanda Foreman, 1998

The Life and Times of George III by John Clarke, 1972

The Romance of the English Theatre by Donald Brooks, 1945

The Green Dragoon: The Lives of Banastre Tarleton and Mary Robinson, NY 1957

A Biographical Dictionary of Actors, Actress etc. by Philip H. Highfill Jn et al. 1660-1800. US 1991.

http://digital.library.upenn.edu/women/robinson/1791/1791.html

http://www.best-poems.net/mary_robinson/index.html

http://www.lauzunslegion.com/

http://home.golden.net/~marg/bansite/_entry.html